CHIMAMANDA NGOZI ADICHIE grew up in Nigeria. Her first novel, *Purple Hibiscus*, was published in 2003 and longlisted for the Booker Prize. Her second novel, *Half of a Yellow Sun*, won the 2007 Orange Prize for Fiction. Her short-story collection, *The Thing Around Your Neck*, was published to critical acclaim in 2009. She received a MacArthur Fellowship in 2009, and in 2010 appeared on the *New Yorker*'s list of the best 20 writers under 40. *Americanah*, her third novel, was published in 2013.

From the reviews of *Half of a Yellow Sun*:

'I look with awe and envy at this young woman from Africa who is recording the history of her country. She is fortunate – and we, her readers, are even luckier'   EDMUND WHITE

'A magnificent novel, packed with memorable characters'
Independent

'Vividly written, thrumming with life, *Half of a Yellow Sun* is a remarkable novel. In its compassionate intelligence, as in its capacity for intimate portraiture, this novel is a worthy successor to such twentieth century classics as Chinua Achebe's *Things fall Apart* and V.S. Naipaul's *A Bend in the River*'
JOYCE CAROL OATES

'The many-sided nature of conflict is graphically realised in this stunning second novel . . . it has a ramshackle freedom and exuberant ambition'   *Observer*

'We do not usually associate wisdom with beginners, but here is a new writer endowed with the gift of ancient storytellers. Chimamanda Ngozi Adichie knows what is at stake, and what to do about it . . . She is fearless, or she would not have taken on the intimidating horror of Nigeria's civil war. Adichie came almost fully made'   CHINUA ACHEBE

CHIMAMANDA NGOZI ADICHIE

Half of a Yellow Sun

FOURTH ESTATE • *London*

Fourth Estate
An imprint of HarperCollins*Publishers*
77–85 Fulham Palace Road
Hammersmith
London W6 8JB
www.4thestate.co.uk

This edition published by Fourth Estate in 2014

1

First published in Great Britain by Fourth Estate in 2006
Published in paperback by Harper Perennial in 2007, reprinted 28 times

A catalogue record for this book is available from the British Library

ISBN 978-0-00-794567-2

Set in Bell MT

Printed and bound in Great Britain by Clays Ltd, St Ives plc

MIX
Paper from
responsible sources
FSC™ C007454

My grandfathers, whom I never knew,
Nwoye David Adichie and Aro-Nweke Felix Odigwe,
did not survive the war.

My grandmothers, Nwabuodu Regina Odigwe and
Nwamgbafor Agnes Adichie, remarkable women
both, did.

This book is dedicated to their memories:
ka fa nodu na ndokwa.

And to Mellitus, wherever he may be.

Today I see it still –
Dry, wire-thin in sun and dust of the dry months –
Headstone on tiny debris of passionate courage.

– Chinua Achebe,
From 'Mango Seedling' in *Christmas in Biafra and Other Poems*

PART ONE

The Early Sixties

§ 1 §

Master was a little crazy; he had spent too many years reading books overseas, talked to himself in his office, did not always return greetings, and had too much hair. Ugwu's aunty said this in a low voice as they walked on the path. 'But he is a good man,' she added. 'And as long as you work well, you will eat well. You will even eat meat every day.' She stopped to spit; the saliva left her mouth with a sucking sound and landed on the grass.

Ugwu did not believe that anybody, not even this master he was going to live with, ate meat *every day*. He did not disagree with his aunty, though, because he was too choked with expectation, too busy imagining his new life away from the village. They had been walking for a while now, since they got off the lorry at the motor park, and the afternoon sun burned the back of his neck. But he did not mind. He was prepared to walk hours more in even hotter sun. He had never seen anything like the streets that appeared after they went past the university gates, streets so smooth and tarred that he itched to lay his cheek down on them. He would never be able to describe to his sister Anulika how the bungalows here were painted the colour of the sky and sat side by side like polite, well-dressed men, how the hedges separating them were trimmed so flat on top that they looked like tables wrapped with leaves.

His aunty walked faster, her slippers making *slap-slap* sounds that echoed in the silent street. Ugwu wondered if she, too, could feel the coal tar getting hotter underneath, through her thin soles. They went past a sign, ODIM STREET, and Ugwu mouthed *street*, as he did whenever he saw an English word that was not too long. He smelt something sweet, heady, as they walked into a compound, and was sure it came from the white flowers clustered on the bushes at the entrance. The bushes were shaped like slender hills. The lawn glistened. Butterflies hovered above.

'I told Master you will learn everything fast, *osiso-osiso*,' his aunty said. Ugwu nodded attentively although she had already told him this many times, as often as she told him the story of how his good fortune came about: While she was sweeping the corridor in the Mathematics Department a week ago, she heard Master say that he needed a houseboy to do his cleaning, and she immediately said she could help, speaking before his typist or office messenger could offer to bring someone.

'I will learn fast, Aunty,' Ugwu said. He was staring at the car in the garage; a strip of metal ran around its blue body like a necklace.

'Remember, what you will answer whenever he calls you is *Yes, sah!*'

'Yes, sah!' Ugwu repeated.

They were standing before the glass door. Ugwu held back from reaching out to touch the cement wall, to see how different it would feel from the mud walls of his mother's hut that still bore the faint patterns of moulding fingers. For a brief moment, he wished he were back there now, in his mother's hut, under the dim coolness of the thatch roof; or in his aunty's hut, the only one in the village with a corrugated-iron roof.

His aunty tapped on the glass. Ugwu could see the white curtains behind the door. A voice said, in English, 'Yes? Come in.'

They took off their slippers before walking in. Ugwu had never seen a room so wide. Despite the brown sofas arranged in a semicircle, the side tables between them, the shelves crammed with books, and the centre table with a vase of red and white plastic flowers, the room still seemed to have too much space. Master sat in an armchair, wearing a singlet and a pair of shorts. He was not sitting upright but slanted, a book covering his face, as though oblivious that he had just asked people in.

'Good afternoon, sah! This is the child,' Ugwu's aunty said.

Master looked up. His complexion was very dark, like old bark, and the hair that covered his chest and legs was a lustrous, darker shade. He pulled off his glasses. 'The child?'

'The houseboy, sah.'

'Oh, yes, you have brought the houseboy. *I kpotago ya.*' Master's Igbo felt feathery in Ugwu's ears. It was Igbo coloured by the sliding sounds of English, the Igbo of one who spoke English often.

'He will work hard,' his aunty said. 'He is a very good boy. Just tell him what he should do. Thank, sah!'

Master grunted in response, watching Ugwu and his aunty with a faintly distracted expression, as if their presence made it difficult for him to remember something important. Ugwu's aunty patted Ugwu's shoulder, whispered that he should do well, and turned to the door. After she left, Master put his glasses back on and faced his book, relaxing further into a slanting position, legs stretched out. Even when he turned the pages he did so with his eyes on the book.

Ugwu stood by the door, waiting. Sunlight streamed in through the windows, and from time to time, a gentle breeze lifted the curtains. The room was silent except for the rustle of Master's page turning. Ugwu stood for a while before he began to edge closer and closer to the bookshelf, as though to hide in it, and then, after a while, he sank down to the floor, cradling his raffia bag between his knees. He looked up at the ceiling, so high up, so piercingly white. He closed his eyes and tried to reimagine this spacious room with the alien furniture, but he couldn't. He opened his eyes, overcome by a new wonder, and looked around to make sure it was all real. To think that he would sit on these sofas, polish this slippery-smooth floor, wash these gauzy curtains.

'*Kedu afa gi?* What's your name?' Master asked, startling him.

Ugwu stood up.

'What's your name?' Master asked again and sat up straight. He filled the armchair, his thick hair that stood high on his head, his muscled arms, his broad shoulders; Ugwu had imagined an older man, somebody frail, and now he felt a sudden fear that he might not please this master who looked so youthfully capable, who looked as if he needed nothing.

'Ugwu, sah.'

'Ugwu. And you've come from Obukpa?'

'From Opi, sah.'

'You could be anything from twelve to thirty.' Master narrowed his eyes. 'Probably thirteen.' He said *thirteen* in English.

'Yes, sah.'

Master turned back to his book. Ugwu stood there. Master flipped past some pages and looked up. '*Ngwa*, go to the kitchen; there should be something you can eat in the fridge.'

'Yes, sah.'

Ugwu entered the kitchen cautiously, placing one foot slowly after the other. When he saw the white thing, almost as tall as he was, he knew it was the fridge. His aunty had told him about it. A cold barn, she had said, that kept food from going off. He opened it and gasped as the cool air rushed into his face. Oranges, bread, beer, soft drinks: many things in packets and cans were arranged on different levels and, at the top, a roasted, shimmering chicken, whole but for a leg. Ugwu reached out and touched the chicken. The fridge breathed heavily in his ears. He touched the chicken again and licked his finger before he yanked the other leg off, eating it until he had only the cracked, sucked pieces of bones left in his hand. Next, he broke off some bread, a chunk that he would have been excited to share with his siblings if a relative had visited and brought it as a gift. He ate quickly, before Master could come in and change his mind. He had finished eating and was standing by the sink, trying to remember what his aunty had told him about opening it to have water gush out like a spring, when Master walked in. He had put on a print shirt and a pair of trousers. His toes, which peeked through leather slippers, seemed feminine, perhaps because they were so clean; they belonged to feet that always wore shoes.

'What is it?' Master asked.

'Sah?' Ugwu gestured to the sink.

Master came over and turned the metal tap. 'You should look around the house and put your bag in the first room on the corridor. I'm going for a walk, to clear my head, *i nugo?*'

'Yes, sah.' Ugwu watched him leave through the back door. He was not tall. His walk was brisk, energetic, and he looked like Ezeagu, the man who held the wrestling record in Ugwu's village.

Ugwu turned off the tap, turned it on again, then off. On and off and on and off until he was laughing at the magic of the running water and the chicken and bread that lay balmy in his stomach. He went past the living room and into the corridor. There were books piled on the shelves and tables in the three bedrooms, on the sink and cabinets in the bathroom, stacked from floor to ceiling in the study, and in the storeroom, old journals were stacked next to crates of Coke and cartons of Premier beer. Some of the books were placed face down, open, as though Master had not yet finished reading them but had hastily gone on to another. Ugwu tried to read the titles, but most were too long, too difficult. *Non-Parametric Methods. An African Survey. The Great Chain of Being. The Norman Impact Upon England.*

He walked on tiptoe from room to room, because his feet felt dirty, and as he did so he grew increasingly determined to please Master, to stay in this house of meat and cool floors. He was examining the toilet, running his hand over the black plastic seat, when he heard Master's voice.

'Where are you, my good man?' He said *my good man* in English.

Ugwu dashed out to the living room. 'Yes, sah!'

'What's your name again?'

'Ugwu, sah.'

'Yes, Ugwu. Look here, *nee anya*, do you know what that is?' Master pointed, and Ugwu looked at the metal box studded with dangerous-looking knobs.

'No, sah,' Ugwu said.

'It's a radiogram. It's new and very good. It's not like those old gramophones that you have to wind and wind. You have to be very careful around it, very careful. You must never let water touch it.'

'Yes, sah.'

'I'm off to play tennis, and then I'll go on to the staff club.' Master picked up a few books from the table. 'I may be back late. So get settled and have a rest.'

'Yes, sah.'

After Ugwu watched Master drive out of the compound, he went and stood beside the radiogram and looked at it carefully, without touching it. Then he walked around the house, up and down, touching books and curtains and furniture and plates, and when it got dark, he turned the light on and marvelled at how bright the bulb that dangled from the ceiling was, how it did not cast long shadows on the wall like the palm oil lamps back home. His mother would be preparing the evening meal now, pounding *akpu* in the mortar, the pestle grasped tightly with both hands. Chioke, the junior wife, would be tending the pot of watery soup balanced on three stones over the fire. The children would have come back from the stream and would be taunting and chasing one another under the breadfruit tree. Perhaps Anulika would be watching them. She was the oldest child in the household now, and as they all sat around the fire to eat, she would break up the fights when the younger ones struggled over the strips of dried fish in the soup. She would wait until all the *akpu* was eaten and then divide the fish so that each child had a piece, and she would keep the biggest for herself, as he had always done.

Ugwu opened the fridge and ate some more bread and chicken, quickly stuffing the food in his mouth while his heart beat as if he were running; then he dug out extra chunks of meat and pulled out the wings. He slipped the pieces into his shorts' pockets before going to the bedroom. He would keep them until his aunty visited and he would ask her to give them to Anulika. Perhaps he could ask her to give some to Nnesinachi too. That might make Nnesinachi finally notice him. He had never been sure exactly how he and Nnesinachi were related, but he knew they were from the same *umunna* and therefore could never marry. Yet he wished that his mother would not keep referring to Nnesinachi as his sister, saying things like, 'Please take this palm oil down to Mama Nnesinachi, and if she is not in, leave it with your sister.'

Nnesinachi always spoke to him in a vague voice, her eyes unfocused, as if his presence made no difference to her either way. Sometimes she called him Chiejina, the name of his cousin who looked nothing at all like him, and when he said, 'It's me', she would say, 'Forgive me, Ugwu my brother,' with a distant formality that meant she had no wish to make further conversation. But he liked going on errands to her house. They were opportunities to find her bent over, fanning the firewood or chopping *ugu* leaves for her mother's soup pot, or just sitting outside looking after her younger siblings, her wrapper hanging low enough for him to see the tops of her breasts. Ever since they started to push out, those pointy breasts, he had wondered if they would feel mushy-soft or hard like the unripe fruit from the *ube* tree. He often wished that Anulika wasn't so flat-chested – he wondered what was taking her so long anyway, since she and Nnesinachi were about the same age – so that he could feel her breasts. Anulika would slap his hand away, of course, and perhaps even slap his face as well, but he would do it quickly – squeeze and run – and that way he would at least have an idea and know what to expect when he finally touched Nnesinachi's.

But he was worried that he might never get to touch them, now that her uncle had asked her to come and learn a trade in Kano. She would be leaving for the North by the end of the year, when her mother's last child, whom she was carrying, began to walk. Ugwu wanted to be as pleased and grateful as the rest of the family. There was, after all, a fortune to be made in the North; he knew of people who had gone up there to trade and came home to tear down huts and build houses with corrugated-iron roofs. He feared, though, that one of those pot-bellied traders in the North would take one look at her, and the next thing he knew somebody would bring palm wine to her father and he would never get to touch those breasts. They – her breasts – were the images saved for last on the many nights when he touched himself, slowly at first and then vigorously, until a muffled moan escaped him. He always started with her face, the fullness of her cheeks and the ivory tone of her teeth, and then he imagined her arms around him, her body moulded to his. Finally, he let her breasts form; sometimes they felt hard, tempting him to bite into them, and other times they were so soft he was afraid his imaginary squeezing caused her pain.

For a moment, he considered thinking of her tonight. He decided not to. Not on his first night in Master's house, on this bed that was nothing like his hand-woven raffia mat. First, he pressed his hands into the springy softness of the mattress. Then, he examined the layers of cloth on top of it, unsure whether to sleep on them or to remove them and put them away before sleeping. Finally, he climbed up and lay on top of the layers of cloth, his body curled in a tight knot.

He dreamed that Master was calling him – *Ugwu, my good man!* – and when he woke up Master was standing at the door, watching him. Perhaps it had not been a dream. He scrambled out of bed and glanced at the windows with the drawn curtains, in confusion. Was it late? Had that soft bed deceived him and made him oversleep? He usually woke with the first cockcrows.

'Good morning, sah!'

'There is a strong roasted-chicken smell here.'

'Sorry, sah.'

'Where is the chicken?'

Ugwu fumbled in his shorts' pockets and brought out the chicken pieces.

'Do your people eat while they sleep?' Master asked. He was wearing something that looked like a woman's coat and was absently twirling the rope tied round his waist.

'Sah?'

'Did you want to eat the chicken while in bed?'

'No, sah.'

'Food will stay in the dining room and the kitchen.'

'Yes, sah.'

'The kitchen and bathroom will have to be cleaned today.'

'Yes, sah.'

Master turned and left. Ugwu stood trembling in the middle of the room, still holding the chicken pieces with his hand outstretched. He wished he did not have to walk past the dining room to get to the kitchen. Finally, he put the chicken back in his pockets, took a deep breath, and left the room. Master was at the dining table, the teacup in front of him placed on a pile of books.

'You know who really killed Lumumba?' Master said, looking up from a magazine. 'It was the Americans and the Belgians. It had nothing to do with Katanga.'

'Yes, sah,' Ugwu said. He wanted Master to keep talking, so he could listen to the sonorous voice, the musical blend of English words in his Igbo sentences.

'You are my houseboy,' Master said. 'If I order you to go outside and beat a woman walking on the street with a stick, and you then give her a bloody wound on her leg, who is responsible for the wound, you or me?'

Ugwu stared at Master, shaking his head, wondering if Master was referring to the chicken pieces in some roundabout way.

'Lumumba was prime minister of Congo. Do you know where Congo is?' Master asked.

'No, sah.'

Master got up quickly and went into the study. Ugwu's confused fear made his eyelids quiver. Would Master send him home because he did not speak English well, kept chicken in his pocket overnight, did not know the strange places Master named? Master came back with a wide piece of paper that he unfolded and laid out on the dining table, pushing aside books and magazines. He pointed with his pen. 'This is our world, although the people who drew this map decided to put their own land on top of ours. There is no top or bottom, you see.' Master picked up the paper and folded it, so that one edge touched the other, leaving a hollow between. 'Our world is round, it never ends. *Nee anya*, this is all water, the seas and oceans, and here's Europe and here's our own continent, Africa, and the Congo is in the middle. Farther up here is Nigeria, and Nsukka is here, in the southeast; this is where we are.' He tapped with his pen.

'Yes, sah.'

'Did you go to school?'

'Standard two, sah. But I learn everything fast.'

'Standard two? How long ago?'

'Many years now, sah. But I learn everything very fast!'

'Why did you stop school?'

'My father's crops failed, sah.'

Master nodded slowly. 'Why didn't your father find somebody to lend him your school fees?'

'Sah?'

'Your father should have borrowed!' Master snapped, and then, in English, 'Education is a priority! How can we resist exploitation if we don't have the tools to understand exploitation?'

'Yes, sah!' Ugwu nodded vigorously. He was determined to appear as alert as he could, because of the wild shine that had appeared in Master's eyes.

'I will enrol you in the staff primary school,' Master said, still tapping on the piece of paper with his pen.

Ugwu's aunty had told him that if he served well for a few years, Master would send him to commercial school where he would learn typing and shorthand. She had mentioned the staff primary school, but only to tell him that it was for the children of the lecturers, who wore blue uniforms and white socks so intricately trimmed with wisps of lace that you wondered why anybody had wasted so much time on mere socks.

'Yes, sah,' he said. 'Thank, sah.'

'I suppose you will be the oldest in class, starting in standard three at your age,' Master said. 'And the only way you can get their respect is to be the best. Do you understand?'

'Yes, sah!'

'Sit down, my good man.'

Ugwu chose the chair farthest from Master, awkwardly placing his feet close together. He preferred to stand.

'There are two answers to the things they will teach you about our land: the real answer and the answer you give in school to pass. You must read books and learn both answers. I will give you books, excellent books.' Master stopped to sip his tea. 'They will teach you that a white man called Mungo Park discovered River Niger. That is rubbish. Our people fished in the Niger long before Mungo Park's grandfather was born. But in your exam, write that it was Mungo Park.'

'Yes, sah.' Ugwu wished that this person called Mungo Park had not offended Master so much.

'Can't you say anything else?'

'Sah?'

'Sing me a song.'

'Sah?'

'Sing me a song. What songs do you know? Sing!' Master pulled his glasses off. His eyebrows were furrowed, serious. Ugwu began to sing an old song he had learned on his father's farm. His heart hit his chest painfully. '*Nzogbo nzogbu enyimba, enyi . . .*'

He sang in a low voice at first, but Master tapped his pen on the table and said 'Louder!' so he raised his voice, and Master kept saying 'Louder!' until he was screaming. After singing over and over a few times, Master asked him to stop. 'Good, good,' he said. 'Can you make tea?'

'No, sah. But I learn fast,' Ugwu said. The singing had loosened something inside him, he was breathing easily and his heart no longer pounded. And he was convinced that Master was mad.

'I eat mostly at the staff club. I suppose I shall have to bring more food home now that you are here.'

'Sah, I can cook.'

'You cook?'

Ugwu nodded. He had spent many evenings watching his mother cook. He had started the fire for her, or fanned the embers when it started to die out. He had peeled and pounded yams and cassava, blown out the husks in rice, picked out the weevils from beans, peeled onions, and ground peppers. Often, when his mother was sick with the coughing, he wished that he, and not Anulika, would cook. He had never told anyone this, not even Anulika; she had already told him he spent too much time around women cooking, and he might never grow a beard if he kept doing that.

'Well, you can cook your own food then,' Master said. 'Write a list of what you'll need.'

'Yes, sah.'

'You wouldn't know how to get to the market, would you? I'll ask Jomo to show you.'

'Jomo, sah?'

'Jomo takes care of the compound. He comes in three times a week. Funny man, I've seen him talking to the croton plant.' Master paused. 'Anyway, he'll be here tomorrow.'

Later, Ugwu wrote a list of food items and gave it to Master.

Master stared at the list for a while. 'Remarkable blend,' he said in English. 'I suppose they'll teach you to use more vowels in school.'

Ugwu disliked the amusement in Master's face. 'We need wood, sah,' he said.

'Wood?'

'For your books, sah. So that I can arrange them.'

'Oh, yes, *shelves*. I suppose we could fit more shelves somewhere, perhaps in the corridor. I will speak to somebody at the Works Department.'

'Yes, sah.'

'Odenigbo. Call me Odenigbo.'

Ugwu stared at him doubtfully. 'Sah?'

'My name is not Sah. Call me Odenigbo.'

'Yes, sah.'

'Odenigbo will always be my name. *Sir* is arbitrary. You could be the *sir* tomorrow.'

'Yes, sah – Odenigbo.'

Ugwu really preferred *sah*, the crisp power behind the word, and when two men from the Works Department came a few days later to install shelves in the corridor, he told them that they would have to wait for Sah to come home; he himself could not sign the white paper with typewritten words. He said *Sah* proudly.

'He's one of these village houseboys,' one of the men said dismissively, and Ugwu looked at the man's face and murmured a curse about acute diarrhoea following him and all of his offspring for life. As he arranged Master's books, he promised himself, stopping short of speaking aloud, that he would learn how to sign forms.

In the following weeks, the weeks when he examined every corner of the bungalow, when he discovered that a beehive was lodged in the cashew tree and that the butterflies converged in the front yard when the sun was brightest, he was just as careful in learning the rhythms of Master's life. Every morning, he picked up the *Daily Times* and *Renaissance* that the vendor dropped off at the door and folded them on the table next to Master's tea and bread. He had the Opel washed before Master finished breakfast, and when Master came back from work and was taking a siesta, he dusted the car over again, before Master left for the tennis courts. He moved around silently on the days that Master retired to the study for hours. When Master paced the corridor talking in a loud voice, he made sure that there was hot water ready for tea. He scrubbed the floors daily. He wiped the louvres until they sparkled in the afternoon sunlight, paid attention to the tiny cracks in the bathtub, polished the saucers that he used to serve kola nut to Master's friends. There were at least two visitors in the living room each day, the radiogram turned on low to strange flutelike music, low enough for the talking and laughing and glass clinking to come clearly to Ugwu in the kitchen or in the corridor as he ironed Master's clothes.

He wanted to do more, wanted to give Master every reason to keep him, and so one morning, he ironed Master's socks. They didn't look rumpled, the black ribbed socks, but he thought they would look even better straightened. The hot iron hissed and when he raised it, he saw that half of the sock was glued to it. He froze. Master was at the dining table, finishing up breakfast, and would come in any minute now to pull on his socks and shoes and take the files on the shelf and leave for work. Ugwu wanted to hide the sock under the chair and dash to the drawer for a new pair but his legs would not move. He stood there with the burnt sock, knowing Master would find him that way.

'You've ironed my socks, haven't you?' Master asked. 'You stupid ignoramus.' *Stupid ignoramus* slid out of his mouth like music.

'Sorry, sah! Sorry, sah!'

'I told you not to call me sir.' Master picked up a file from the shelf. 'I'm late.'

'Sah? Should I bring another pair?' Ugwu asked. But Master had already slipped on his shoes, without socks, and hurried out. Ugwu heard him bang the car door and drive away. His chest felt weighty; he did not know why he had ironed the socks, why he had not simply done the safari suit. Evil spirits, that was it. The evil spirits had made him do it. They lurked everywhere, after all. Whenever he was ill with the fever, or once when he fell from a tree, his mother would rub his body with *okwuma*, all the while muttering, 'We shall defeat them, they will not win.'

He went out to the front yard, past stones placed side by side around the manicured lawn. The evil spirits would not win. He would not let them defeat him. There was a round, grassless patch in the middle of the lawn, like an island in a green sea, where a thin palm tree stood. Ugwu had never seen any palm tree that short, or one with leaves that flared out so perfectly. It did not look strong enough to bear fruit, did not look useful at all, like most of the plants here. He picked up a stone and threw it into the distance. So much wasted space. In his village, people farmed the tiniest plots outside their homes and planted useful vegetables and herbs. His grand-mother had not needed to grow her favourite herb, *arigbe*, because it grew wild everywhere. She used to say that *arigbe* softened a man's heart. She was the second of three wives and did not have the special position that came with being the first or the last, so before she asked her husband for anything, she told Ugwu, she cooked him spicy yam porridge with *arigbe*. It had worked, always. Perhaps it would work with Master.

Ugwu walked around in search of *arigbe*. He looked among the pink flowers, under the cashew tree with the spongy beehive lodged on a branch, the lemon tree that had black soldier ants crawling up and down the trunk, and the pawpaw trees whose ripening fruits were dotted with fat, bird-burrowed holes. But the ground was clean, no herbs; Jomo's weeding was thorough and careful, and nothing that was not wanted was allowed to be.

The first time they met, Ugwu had greeted Jomo and Jomo nodded and continued to work, saying nothing. He was a small man with a tough, shrivelled body that Ugwu felt needed a watering more than the plants that he targeted with his metal can. Finally, Jomo looked up at Ugwu. '*Afa m bu Jomo*,' he announced, as if Ugwu did not know his name. 'Some people call me Kenyatta, after the great man in Kenya. I am a hunter.'

Ugwu did not know what to say in return because Jomo was star-ing right into his eyes, as though expecting to hear something remarkable that Ugwu did.

'What kind of animals do you kill?' Ugwu asked. Jomo beamed, as if this was exactly the question he had wanted, and began to talk about his hunting. Ugwu sat on the steps that led to the backyard and listened. From the first day, he did not believe Jomo's stories – of fighting off a leopard barehanded, of killing two baboons with a single shot – but he liked listening to them and he put off washing Master's clothes to the days Jomo came so he could sit outside while Jomo worked. Jomo moved with a slow deliberateness. His raking, watering, and planting all somehow seemed filled with solemn wis-dom. He would look up in the middle of trimming a hedge and say, 'That is good meat,' and then walk to the goatskin bag tied behind his bicycle to rummage for his catapult. Once, he shot a bush pigeon down from the cashew tree with a small stone, wrapped it in leaves, and put it into his bag.

'Don't go to that bag unless I am around,' he told Ugwu. 'You might find a human head there.'

Ugwu laughed but had not entirely doubted Jomo. He wished so much that Jomo had come to work today. Jomo would have been the best person to ask about *arigbe* – indeed, to ask for advice on how best to placate Master.

He walked out of the compound, to the street, and looked through the plants on the roadside until he saw the rumpled leaves close to the root of a whistling pine. He had never smelt anything like the spicy sharpness of *arigbe* in the bland food Master brought back from the staff club; he would cook a stew with it, and offer Master some with rice, and afterwards plead with him. *Please don't send me back home, sah. I will work extra for the burnt sock. I will earn the money to replace it.* He did not know exactly what he could do to earn money for the sock, but he planned to tell Master that anyway.

If the *arigbe* softened Master's heart, perhaps he could grow it and some other herbs in the backyard. He would tell Master that the garden was something to do until he started school, since the head-mistress at the staff school had told Master that he could not start midterm. He might be hoping for too much, though. What was the point of thinking about a herb garden if Master asked him to leave, if Master would not forgive the burnt sock? He walked quickly into the kitchen, laid the *arigbe* down on the counter, and measured out some rice.

Hours later, he felt a tautness in his stomach when he heard Master's car: the crunch of gravel and the hum of the engine before it stopped in the garage. He stood by the pot of stew, stirring, holding the ladle as tightly as the cramps in his stomach felt. Would Master ask him to leave before he had a chance to offer him the food? What would he tell his people?

'Good afternoon, sah – Odenigbo,' he said, even before Master had come into the kitchen.

'Yes, yes,' Master said. He was holding books to his chest with one hand and his briefcase with the other. Ugwu rushed over to help with the books. 'Sah? You will eat?' he asked in English.

'Eat what?'

Ugwu's stomach got tighter. He feared it might snap as he bent to place the books on the dining table. 'Stew, sah.'

'Stew?'

'Yes, sah. Very good stew, sah.'

'I'll try some, then.'

'Yes, sah!'

'Call me Odenigbo!' Master snapped before going in to take an afternoon bath.

After Ugwu served the food, he stood by the kitchen door, watching as Master took a first forkful of rice and stew, took another, and then called out, 'Excellent, my good man.'

Ugwu appeared from behind the door. 'Sah? I can plant the herbs in a small garden. To cook more stews like this.'

'A garden?' Master stopped to sip some water and turn a journal page. 'No, no, no. Outside is Jomo's territory, and inside is yours. Division of labour, my good man. If we need herbs, we'll ask Jomo to take care of it.' Ugwu loved the sound of *Division of labour, my good man*, spoken in English.

'Yes, sah,' he said, although he was already thinking of what spot would be best for the herb garden: near the Boys' Quarters where Master never went. He could not trust Jomo with the herb garden and would tend it himself when Master was out, and this way, his *arigbe*, his herb of forgiveness, would never run out. It was only later in the evening that he realized Master must have forgotten about the burnt sock long before coming home.

Ugwu came to realize other things. He was not a normal houseboy; Dr Okeke's houseboy next door did not sleep on a bed in a room, he slept on the kitchen floor. The houseboy at the end of the street with whom Ugwu went to the market did not decide what would be cooked, he cooked whatever he was ordered to. And they did not have masters or madams who gave them books, saying, 'This one is excellent, just excellent.'

Ugwu did not understand most of the sentences in the books, but he made a show of reading them. Nor did he entirely understand the conversations of Master and his friends but listened anyway and heard that the world had to do more about the black people killed in Sharpeville, that the spy plane shot down in Russia served the Americans right, that De Gaulle was being clumsy in Algeria, that the United Nations would never get rid of Tshombe in Katanga. Once in a while, Master would stand up and raise his glass and his voice – 'To that brave black American led into the University of Mississippi!' 'To Ceylon and to the world's first woman prime minister!' 'To Cuba for beating the Americans at their own game!' – and Ugwu would enjoy the clink of beer bottles against glasses, glasses against glasses, bottles against bottles.

More friends visited on weekends, and when Ugwu came out to serve their drinks, Master would sometimes introduce him – in English, of course. 'Ugwu helps me around the house. Very clever boy.' Ugwu would continue to uncork bottles of beer and Coke silently, while feeling the warm glow of pride spread up from the tips of his toes. He especially liked it when Master introduced him to foreigners, like Mr Johnson, who was from the Caribbean and stammered when he spoke, or Professor Lehman, the nasal white man from America who had eyes that were the piercing green of a fresh leaf. Ugwu was vaguely frightened the first time he saw him because he had always imagined that only evil spirits had grass-coloured eyes.

He soon knew the regular guests and brought out their drinks before Master asked him to. There was Dr Patel, the Indian man who drank Golden Guinea beer mixed with Coke. Master called him *Doc*. Whenever Ugwu brought out the kola nut, Master would say, 'Doc, you know the kola nut does not understand English,' before going on to bless the kola nut in Igbo. Dr Patel laughed each time, with great pleasure, leaning back on the sofa and throwing his short legs up as if it were a joke he had never heard before. After Master broke the kola nut and passed the saucer around, Dr Patel always took a lobe and put it into his shirt pocket; Ugwu had never seen him eat one.

There was tall, skinny Professor Ezeka, with a voice so hoarse he sounded as if he spoke in whispers. He always picked up his glass and held it up against the light, to make sure Ugwu had washed it well. Sometimes, he brought his own bottle of gin. Other times, he asked for tea and then went on to examine the sugar bowl and the tin of milk, muttering, 'The capabilities of bacteria are quite extraordinary.'

There was Okeoma, who came most often and stayed the longest. He looked younger than the other guests, always wore a pair of shorts, and had bushy hair with a parting at the side that stood higher than Master's. It looked rough and tangled, unlike Master's, as if Okeoma did not like to comb it. Okeoma drank Fanta. He read his poetry aloud on some evenings, holding a sheaf of papers, and

Ugwu would look through the kitchen door to see all the guests watching him, their faces half frozen, as if they did not dare breathe. Afterwards, Master would clap and say, in his loud voice, 'The voice of our generation!' and the clapping would go on until Okeoma said sharply, 'That's enough!'

And there was Miss Adebayo, who drank brandy like Master and was nothing like Ugwu had expected a university woman to be. His aunty had told him a little about university women. She would know, because she worked as a cleaner at the Faculty of Sciences during the day and as a waitress at the staff club in the evenings; sometimes, too, the lecturers paid her to come in and clean their homes. She said university women kept framed photos of their student days in Ibadan and Britain and America on their shelves. For breakfast, they had eggs that were not cooked well, so that the yolk danced around, and they wore bouncy, straight-hair wigs and maxi-dresses that grazed their ankles. She told a story once about a couple at a cocktail party in the staff club who climbed out of a nice Peugeot 404, the man in an elegant cream suit, the woman in a green dress. Everybody turned to watch them, walking hand in hand, and then the wind blew the woman's wig off her head. She was bald. They used hot combs to straighten their hair, his aunty had said, because they wanted to look like white people, although the combs ended up burning their hair off.

Ugwu had imagined the bald woman: beautiful, with a nose that stood up, not the sitting-down, flattened noses that he was used to. He imagined quietness, delicacy, the kind of woman whose sneeze, whose laugh and talk, would be soft as the under feathers closest to a chicken's skin. But the women who visited Master, the ones he saw at the supermarket and on the streets, were different. Most of them did wear wigs (a few had their hair plaited or braided with thread), but they were not delicate stalks of grass. They were loud. The loudest was Miss Adebayo. She was not an Igbo woman; Ugwu could tell from her name, even if he had not once run into her and her housegirl at the market and heard them both speaking rapid, incomprehensible Yoruba. She had asked him to wait so that she could give him a ride back to the campus, but he thanked her and said he still had many things left to buy and would take a taxi, although he had finished shopping. He did not want to ride in her car, did not like how her voice rose above Master's in the living room, challenging and arguing. He often fought the urge to raise his own voice from behind the kitchen door and tell her to shut up, especially when she called

Master a sophist. He did not know what *sophist* meant, but he did not like that she called Master that. Nor did he like the way she looked at Master. Even when somebody else was speaking and she was supposed to be focused on that person, her eyes would be on Master. One Saturday night, Okeoma dropped a glass and Ugwu came in to clean up the shards that lay on the floor. He took his time cleaning. The conversation was clearer from here and it was easier to make out what Professor Ezeka said. It was almost impossible to hear the man from the kitchen.

'We should have a bigger pan-African response to what is happening in the American South really – ' Professor Ezeka said.

Master cut him short. 'You know, pan-Africanism is fundamentally a European notion.'

'You are digressing,' Professor Ezeka said, and shook his head in his usual superior manner.

'Maybe it *is* a European notion,' Miss Adebayo said, 'but in the bigger picture, we are all one race.'

'What bigger picture?' Master asked. 'The bigger picture of the white man! Can't you see that we are not all alike except to white eyes?' Master's voice rose easily, Ugwu had noticed, and by his third glass of brandy, he would start to gesture with his glass, leaning forwards until he was seated on the very edge of his armchair. Late at night, after Master was in bed, Ugwu would sit on the same chair and imagine himself speaking swift English, talking to rapt imaginary guests, using words like *decolonize* and *pan-African*, moulding his voice after Master's, and he would shift and shift until he too was on the edge of the chair.

'Of course we are all alike, we all have white oppression in common,' Miss Adebayo said dryly. 'Pan-Africanism is simply the most sensible response.'

'Of course, of course, but my point is that the only authentic identity for the African is the tribe,' Master said. 'I am Nigerian because a white man created Nigeria and gave me that identity. I am black because the white man constructed *black* to be as different as possible from his *white*. But I was Igbo before the white man came.'

Professor Ezeka snorted and shook his head, thin legs crossed. 'But you became aware that you were Igbo because of the white man. The pan-Igbo idea itself came only in the face of white domination. You must see that tribe as it is today is as colonial a product as nation and race.' Professor Ezeka recrossed his legs.

'The pan-Igbo idea existed long before the white man!' Master shouted. 'Go and ask the elders in your village about your history.'

'The problem is that Odenigbo is a hopeless tribalist, we need to keep him quiet,' Miss Adebayo said.

Then she did what startled Ugwu: she got up laughing and went over to Master and pressed his lips close together. She stood there for what seemed a long time, her hand to his mouth. Ugwu imagined Master's brandy-diluted saliva touching her fingers. He stiffened as he picked up the shattered glass. He wished that Master would not sit there shaking his head as if the whole thing were very funny.

Miss Adebayo became a threat after that. She began to look more and more like a fruit bat, with her pinched face and cloudy complexion and print dresses that billowed around her body like wings. Ugwu served her drink last and wasted long minutes drying his hands on a dishcloth before he opened the door to let her in. He worried that she would marry Master and bring her Yoruba-speaking housegirl into the house and destroy his herb garden and tell him what he could and could not cook. Until he heard Master and Okeoma talking.

'She did not look as if she wanted to go home today,' Okeoma said. '*Nwoke m*, are you sure you are not planning to do something with her?'

'Don't talk rubbish.'

'If you did, nobody in London would know.'

'Look, look – '

'I know you're not interested in her like that, but what still puzzles me is what these women see in you.'

Okeoma laughed and Ugwu was relieved. He did not want Miss Adebayo – or any woman – coming in to intrude and disrupt their lives. Some evenings, when the visitors left early, he would sit on the floor of the living room and listen to Master talk. Master mostly talked about things Ugwu did not understand, as if the brandy made him forget that Ugwu was not one of his visitors. But it didn't matter. All Ugwu needed was the deep voice, the melody of the English-inflected Igbo, the glint of the thick eyeglasses.

He had been with Master for four months when Master told him, 'A special woman is coming for the weekend. Very special. You make sure the house is clean. I'll order the food from the staff club.'

'But, sah, I can cook,' Ugwu said, with a sad premonition.

'She's just come back from London, my good man, and she likes her rice a certain way. Fried rice, I think. I'm not sure you could make something suitable.' Master turned to walk away.

'I can make that, sah,' Ugwu said quickly, although he had no idea what fried rice was. 'Let me make the rice, and you get the chicken from the staff club.'

'Artful negotiation,' Master said in English. 'All right, then. You make the rice.'

'Yes, sah,' Ugwu said. Later, he cleaned the rooms and scrubbed the toilet carefully, as he always did, but Master looked at them and said they were not clean enough and went out and bought another jar of Vim powder and asked, sharply, why Ugwu didn't clean the spaces between the tiles. Ugwu cleaned them again. He scrubbed until sweat crawled down the sides of his face, until his arm ached. And on Saturday, he bristled as he cooked. Master had never complained about his work before. It was this woman's fault, this woman that Master considered too special even for him to cook for. Just come back from London, indeed.

When the doorbell rang, he muttered a curse under his breath about her stomach swelling from eating faeces. He heard Master's raised voice, excited and childlike, followed by a long silence and he imagined their hug, and her ugly body pressed to Master's. Then he heard her voice. He stood still. He had always thought that Master's English could not be compared to anybody's, not Professor Ezeka, whose English one could hardly hear, or Okeoma, who spoke English as if he were speaking Igbo, with the same cadences and pauses, or Patel, whose English was a faded lilt. Not even the white man Professor Lehman, with his words forced out through his nose, sounded as dignified as Master. Master's English was music, but what Ugwu was hearing now, from this woman, was magic. Here was a superior tongue, a luminous language, the kind of English he heard on Master's radio, rolling out with clipped precision. It reminded him of slicing a yam with a newly sharpened knife, the easy perfection in every slice.

'Ugwu!' Master called. 'Bring Coke!'

Ugwu walked out to the living room. She smelt of coconuts. He greeted her, his 'Good afternoon' a mumble, his eyes on the floor.

'*Kedu?*' she asked.

'I'm well, mah.' He still did not look at her. As he uncorked the bottle, she laughed at something Master said. Ugwu was about to pour the cold Coke into her glass when she touched his hand and said, '*Rapuba*, don't worry about that.'

Her hand was lightly moist. 'Yes, mah.'

'Your master has told me how well you take care of him, Ugwu,' she said. Her Igbo words were softer than her English, and he was disappointed at how easily they came out. He wished she would stumble in her Igbo; he had not expected English that perfect to sit beside equally perfect Igbo.

'Yes, mah,' he mumbled. His eyes were still focused on the floor.

'What have you cooked us, my good man?' Master asked, as if he did not know. He sounded annoyingly jaunty.

'I serve now, sah,' Ugwu said, in English, and then wished he had said *I am serving now*, because it sounded better, because it would impress her more. As he set the table, he kept from glancing at the living room, although he could hear her laughter and Master's voice, with its irritating new timbre.

He finally looked at her as she and Master sat down at the table. Her oval face was smooth like an egg, the lush colour of rain-drenched earth, and her eyes were large and slanted and she looked like she was not supposed to be walking and talking like everyone else; she should be in a glass case like the one in Master's study, where people could admire her curvy, fleshy body, where she would be preserved untainted. Her hair was long; each of the plaits that hung down to her neck ended in a soft fuzz. She smiled easily; her teeth were the same bright white of her eyes. He did not know how long he stood staring at her until Master said, 'Ugwu usually does a lot better than this. He makes a fantastic stew.'

'It's quite tasteless, which is better than bad-tasting, of course,' she said, and smiled at Master before turning to Ugwu. 'I'll show you how to cook rice properly, Ugwu, without using so much oil.'

'Yes, mah,' Ugwu said. He had invented what he imagined was fried rice, frying the rice in groundnut oil, and had half-hoped it would send them both to the toilet in a hurry. Now, though, he wanted to cook a perfect meal, a savoury *jollof* rice or his special stew with *arigbe*, to show her how well he could cook. He delayed washing up so that the running water would not drown out her voice. When he served them tea, he took his time rearranging the biscuits on the saucer so that he could linger and listen to her, until Master said, 'That's quite all right, my good man.' Her name was Olanna. But Master said it only once; he mostly called her *nkem*, my own. They talked about the quarrel between the Sardauna and the premier of the Western Region, and then Master said something about waiting until she moved to Nsukka and how it was only a few weeks away after all. Ugwu held his breath to make sure he had heard clearly. Master was laughing now, saying, 'But we will live here together, *nkem*, and you can keep the Elias Avenue flat as well.'

She would move to Nsukka. She would live in this house. Ugwu walked away from the door and stared at the pot on the stove. His life would change. He would learn to cook fried rice and he would have to use less oil and he would take orders from her. He felt sad, and yet his sadness was incomplete; he felt expectant, too, an excitement he did not entirely understand.

That evening, he was washing Master's linen in the backyard, near the lemon tree, when he looked up from the basin of soapy water and saw her standing by the back door, watching him. At first, he was sure it was his imagination, because the people he thought the most about often appeared to him in visions. He had imaginary conversations with Anulika all the time, and, right after he touched himself at night, Nnesinachi would appear briefly with a mysterious smile on her face. But Olanna was really at the door. She was walking across the yard towards him. She had only a wrapper tied around her chest, and as she walked, he imagined that she was a yellow cashew, shapely and ripe.

'Mah? You want anything?' he asked. He knew that if he reached out and touched her face, it would feel like butter, the kind Master unwrapped from a paper packet and spread on his bread.

'Let me help you with that.' She pointed at the bedsheet he was rinsing, and slowly he took the dripping sheet out. She held one end and moved back. 'Turn yours that way,' she said.

He twisted his end of the sheet to his right while she twisted to her right, and they watched as the water was squeezed out. The sheet was slippery.

'Thank, mah,' he said.

She smiled. Her smile made him feel taller. 'Oh, look, those paw-paws are almost ripe. *Lotekwa*, don't forget to pluck them.'

There was something polished about her voice, about her; she was like the stone that lay right below a gushing spring, rubbed smooth by years and years of sparkling water, and looking at her was similar to finding that stone, knowing that there were so few like it. He watched her walk back indoors.

He did not want to share the job of caring for Master with anyone, did not want to disrupt the balance of his life with Master, and yet it was suddenly unbearable to think of not seeing her again. Later, after dinner, he tiptoed to Master's bedroom and rested his ear on the door. She was moaning loudly, sounds that seemed so unlike her, so uncontrolled and stirring and throaty. He stood there for a long time, until the moans stopped, and then he went back to his room.

2

Olanna nodded to the High Life music from the car radio. Her hand was on Odenigbo's thigh; she raised it whenever he wanted to change gears, placed it back, and laughed when he teased her about being a distracting Aphrodite. It was exhilarating to sit beside him, with the car windows down and the air filled with dust and Rex Lawson's dreamy rhythms. He had a lecture in two hours but had insisted on taking her to Enugu airport, and although she had pretended to protest, she wanted him to. When they drove across the narrow roads that ran through Milliken Hill, with a deep gully on one side and a steep hill on the other, she didn't tell him that he was driving a little fast. She didn't look, either, at the handwritten sign by the road that said, in rough letters, BETTER BE LATE THAN THE LATE.

She was disappointed to see the sleek, white forms of aeroplanes gliding up as they approached the airport. He parked beneath the colonnaded entrance. Porters surrounded the car and called out, 'Sah? Madam? You get luggage?' but Olanna hardly heard them because he had pulled her to him.

'I can't wait, *nkem*,' he said, his lips pressed to hers. He tasted of marmalade. She wanted to tell him that she couldn't wait to move to Nsukka either, but he knew anyway, and his tongue was in her mouth, and she felt a new warmth between her legs.

A car horn blew. A porter called out, 'Ha, this place is for loading, oh! Loading only!'

Finally, Odenigbo let her go and jumped out of the car to get her bag from the boot. He carried it to the ticket counter. 'Safe journey, *ije oma*,' he said.

'Drive carefully,' she said.

She watched him walk away, a thickly built man in khaki trousers and a short-sleeved shirt that looked crisp from ironing. He threw his legs out with an aggressive confidence: the gait of a person who would not ask for directions but remained sure that he would somehow get there. After he drove off, she lowered her head and sniffed herself. She had dabbed on his Old Spice that morning, impulsively, and didn't tell him because he would laugh. He would not understand the superstition of taking a whiff of him with her. It was as if the scent could, at least for a while, stifle her questions and make her a little more like him, a little more certain, a little less questioning.

She turned to the ticket seller and wrote her name on a slip of paper. 'Good afternoon. One way to Lagos, please.'

'Ozobia?' The ticket seller's pockmarked face brightened in a wide smile. 'Chief Ozobia's daughter?'

'Yes.'

'Oh! Well done, madam. I will ask the porter to take you to the VIP lounge.' The ticket seller turned around. 'Ikenna! Where is that foolish boy? Ikenna!'

Olanna shook her head and smiled. 'No, no need for that.' She smiled again, reassuringly, to make it clear it was not his fault that she did not want to be in the VIP lounge.

The general lounge was crowded. Olanna sat opposite three little children in threadbare clothes and slippers who giggled intermittently while their father gave them severe looks. An old woman with a sour, wrinkled face, their grandmother, sat closest to Olanna, clutching a handbag and murmuring to herself. Olanna could smell the mustiness on her wrapper; it must have been dug out from an ancient trunk for this occasion. When a clear voice announced the arrival of a Nigeria Airways flight, the father sprang up and then sat down again.

'You must be waiting for somebody,' Olanna said to him in Igbo.

'Yes, *nwanne m*, my brother is coming back from overseas after four years reading there.' His Owerri dialect had a strong rural accent.

'Eh!' Olanna said. She wanted to ask him where exactly his brother was coming back from and what he had studied, but she didn't. He might not know.

The grandmother turned to Olanna. 'He is the first in our village to go overseas, and our people have prepared a dance for him. The dance troupe will meet us in Ikeduru.' She smiled proudly to show brown teeth. Her accent was even thicker; it was difficult to make out everything she said. 'My fellow women are jealous, but is it my fault that their sons have empty brains and my own son won the white people's scholarship?'

Another flight arrival was announced and the father said, *'Chere!* It's him? It's him!'

The children stood up and the father asked them to sit down and then stood up himself. The grandmother clutched her handbag to her belly. Olanna watched the plane descend. It touched down, and just as it began to taxi on the tarmac, the grandmother screamed and dropped her handbag.

Olanna was startled. 'What is it? What is it?'

'Mama!' the father said.

'Why does it not stop?' The grandmother asked, both hands placed on her head in despair. *'Chi m!* My God! I am in trouble! Where is it taking my son now? Have you people deceived me?'

'Mama, it will stop,' Olanna said. 'This is what it does when it lands.' She picked up the handbag and then took the older, callused hand in hers. 'It will stop,' she said again.

She didn't let go until the plane stopped and the grandmother slipped her hand away and muttered something about foolish people who could not build planes well. Olanna watched the family hurry to the arrivals gate. As she walked towards her own gate minutes later, she looked back often, hoping to catch a glimpse of the son from overseas. But she didn't.

Her flight was bumpy. The man seated next to her was eating bitter kola, crunching loudly, and when he turned to make conversation, she slowly shifted away until she was pressed against the aeroplane wall.

'I just have to tell you, you are so beautiful,' he said.

She smiled and said thank you and kept her eyes on her newspaper. Odenigbo would be amused when she told him about this man, the way he always laughed at her admirers, with his unquestioning confidence. It was what had first attracted her to him that June day two years ago in Ibadan, the kind of rainy day that wore the indigo colour of dusk although it was only noon. She was home on holiday from England. She was in a serious relationship with Mohammed. She did not notice Odenigbo at first, standing ahead of her in a queue to buy a ticket outside the university theatre. She might never have noticed him if a white man with silver hair had not stood behind her and if the ticket seller had not signalled to the white man to come forwards. 'Let me help you here, sir,' the ticket seller said, in that comically contrived 'white' accent that uneducated people liked to put on.

Olanna was annoyed, but only mildly, because she knew the queue moved fast anyway. So she was surprised at the outburst that followed, from a man wearing a brown safari suit and clutching a book: Odenigbo. He walked up to the front, escorted the white man back into the queue and then shouted at the ticket seller. 'You miserable ignoramus! You see a white person and he looks better than your own people? You must apologize to everybody in this queue! Right now!'

Olanna had stared at him, at the arch of his eyebrows behind the glasses, the thickness of his body, already thinking of the least hurtful way to untangle herself from Mohammed. Perhaps she would have known that Odenigbo was different, even if he had not spoken; his haircut alone said it, standing up in a high halo. But there was an unmistakable grooming about him, too; he was not one of those who used untidiness to substantiate their radicalism. She smiled and said 'Well done!' as he walked past her, and it was the boldest thing she had ever done, the first time she had demanded attention from a man. He stopped and introduced himself, 'My name is Odenigbo.'

'I'm Olanna,' she said and later, she would tell him that there had been a crackling magic in the air and he would tell her that his desire at that moment was so intense that his groin ached.

When she finally felt that desire, she was surprised above everything else. She did not know that a man's thrusts could suspend memory, that it was possible to be poised in a place where she could not think or remember, but only feel. The intensity had not abated after two years, nor had her awe at his self-assured eccentricities and his fierce moralities. But she feared that this was because theirs was a relationship consumed in sips: She saw him when she came home on holiday; they wrote to one another; they talked on the phone. Now that she was back in Nigeria they would live together, and she did not understand how he could not show some uncertainty. He was too sure.

She looked out at the clouds outside her window, smoky thickets drifting by, and thought how fragile they were.

*   *   *

Olanna had not wanted to have dinner with her parents, especially since they had invited Chief Okonji. But her mother came into her room to ask her to please join them; it was not every day that they hosted the finance minister, and this dinner was even more important because of the building contract her father wanted. '*Biko*, wear something nice. Kainene will be dressing up, too,' her mother had added, as if mentioning her twin sister somehow legitimized everything.

Now, Olanna smoothed the napkin on her lap and smiled at the steward placing a plate of halved avocado next to her. His white uniform was starched so stiff his trousers looked as if they had been made out of cardboard.

'Thank you, Maxwell,' she said.

'Yes, aunty,' Maxwell mumbled, and moved on with his tray.

Olanna looked around the table. Her parents were focused on Chief Okonji, nodding eagerly as he told a story about a recent meeting with Prime Minister Balewa. Kainene was inspecting her plate with that arch expression of hers, as if she were mocking the avocado. None of them thanked Maxwell. Olanna wished they would; it was such a simple thing to do, to acknowledge the humanity of the people who served them. She had suggested it once; her father said he paid them good salaries, and her mother said thanking them would give them room to be insulting, while Kainene, as usual, said nothing, a bored expression on her face.

'This is the best avocado I have tasted in a long time,' Chief Okonji said.

'It is from one of our farms,' her mother said. 'The one near Asaba.'

'I'll have the steward put some in a bag for you,' her father said.

'Excellent,' Chief Okonji said. 'Olanna, I hope you are enjoying yours, eh? You've been staring at it as if it is something that bites.' He laughed, an overly hearty guffaw, and her parents promptly laughed as well.

'It's very good.' Olanna looked up. There was something wet about Chief Okonji's smile. Last week, when he thrust his card into her hand at the Ikoyi Club, she had worried about that smile because it looked as if the movement of his lips made saliva fill his mouth and threaten to trickle down his chin.

'I hope you've thought about coming to join us at the ministry, Olanna. We need first-class brains like yours,' Chief Okonji said.

'How many people get offered jobs personally from the finance minister,' her mother said, to nobody in particular, and her smile lit up the oval, dark-skinned face that was so nearly perfect, so symmetrical, that friends called her Art.

Olanna placed her spoon down. 'I've decided to go to Nsukka. I'll be leaving in two weeks.'

She saw the way her father tightened his lips. Her mother left her hand suspended in the air for a moment, as if the news were too tragic to continue sprinkling salt. 'I thought you had not made up your mind,' her mother said.

'I can't waste too much time or they will offer it to somebody else,' Olanna said.

'Nsukka? Is that right? You've decided to move to Nsukka?' Chief Okonji asked.

'Yes. I applied for a job as instructor in the Department of Sociology and I just got it,' Olanna said. She usually liked her avocado without salt, but it was bland now, almost nauseating.

'Oh. So you're leaving us in Lagos,' Chief Okonji said. His face seemed to melt, folding in on itself. Then he turned and asked, too brightly, 'And what about you, Kainene?'

Kainene looked Chief Okonji right in the eyes, with that stare that was so expressionless, so blank, that it was almost hostile. 'What about me, indeed?' She raised her eyebrows. 'I, too, will be putting my newly acquired degree to good use. I'm moving to Port Harcourt to manage Daddy's businesses there.'

Olanna wished she still had those flashes, moments when she could tell what Kainene was thinking. When they were in primary school, they sometimes looked at each other and laughed, without speaking, because they were thinking the same joke. She doubted that Kainene ever had those flashes now, since they never talked about such things any more. They never talked about anything any more.

'So Kainene will manage the cement factory?' Chief Okonji asked, turning to her father.

'She'll oversee everything in the east, the factories and our new oil interests. She has always had an excellent eye for business.'

'Whoever said you lost out by having twin daughters is a liar,' Chief Okonji said.

'Kainene is not just like a son, she is like two,' her father said. He glanced at Kainene and Kainene looked away, as if the pride on his face did not matter, and Olanna quickly focused on her plate so that neither would know she had been watching them. The plate was elegant, light green, the same colour as the avocado.

'Why don't you all come to my house this weekend, eh?' Chief Okonji asked. 'If only to sample my cook's fish pepper soup. The chap is from Nembe; he knows what to do with fresh fish.'

Her parents cackled loudly. Olanna was not sure how that was funny, but then it was the minister's joke.

'That sounds wonderful,' Olanna's father said.

'It will be nice for all of us to go before Olanna leaves for Nsukka,' her mother said.

Olanna felt a slight irritation, a prickly feeling on her skin. 'I would love to come, but I won't be here this weekend.'

'You won't be here?' her father asked. She wondered if the expression in his eyes was a desperate plea. She wondered, too, how her parents had promised Chief Okonji an affair with her in exchange for the contract. Had they stated it verbally, plainly, or had it been implied?

'I have made plans to go to Kano, to see Uncle Mbaezi and the family, and Mohammed as well,' she said.

Her father stabbed at his avocado. 'I see.'

Olanna sipped her water and said nothing.

After dinner, they moved to the balcony for liqueurs. Olanna liked this after-dinner ritual and often would move away from her parents and the guests to stand by the railing, looking at the tall lamps that lit up the paths below, so bright that the swimming pool looked silver and the hibiscus and bougainvillea took on an incandescent patina over their reds and pinks. The first and only time Odenigbo visited her in Lagos, they had stood looking down at the swimming pool and Odenigbo threw a bottle cork down and watched it plunk into the water. He drank a lot of brandy, and when her father said that the idea of Nsukka University was silly, that Nigeria was not ready for an indigenous university, and that receiving support from an American university – rather than a proper university in Britain – was plain daft, he raised his voice in response. Olanna had thought he would realize that her father only wanted to gall him and show how unimpressed he was by a senior lecturer from Nsukka. She thought he would let her father's words go. But his voice rose higher and higher as he argued about Nsukka being free of colonial influence, and she had blinked often to signal him to stop, although he may not have noticed since the veranda was dim. Finally the phone rang and the conversation had to end. The look in her parents' eyes was grudging respect, Olanna could tell, but it did not stop them from telling her that Odenigbo was crazy and wrong for her, one of those hot-headed university people who talked and talked until everybody had a headache and nobody understood what had been said.

'Such a cool night,' Chief Okonji said behind her. Olanna turned around. She did not know when her parents and Kainene had gone inside.

'Yes,' she said.

Chief Okonji stood in front of her. His *agbada* was embroidered with gold thread around the collar. She looked at his neck, settled into rolls of fat, and imagined him prying the folds apart as he bathed.

'What about tomorrow? There's a cocktail party at Ikoyi Hotel,' he said. 'I want all of you to meet some expatriates. They are looking for land and I can arrange for them to buy from your father at five or six times the price.'

'I will be doing a St Vincent de Paul charity drive tomorrow.'

Chief Okonji moved closer. 'I can't keep you out of my mind,' he said, and a mist of alcohol settled on her face.

'I am not interested, Chief.'

'I just can't keep you out of my mind,' Chief Okonji said again. 'Look, you don't have to work at the ministry. I can appoint you to a board, any board you want, and I will furnish a flat for you wherever you want.' He pulled her to him, and for a while Olanna did nothing, her body limp against his. She was used to this, being grabbed by men who walked around in a cloud of cologne-drenched entitlement, with the presumption that, because they were powerful and found her beautiful, they belonged together. She pushed him back, finally, and felt vaguely sickened at how her hands sank into his soft chest. 'Stop it, Chief.'

His eyes were closed. 'I love you, believe me. I really love you.'

She slipped out of his embrace and went indoors. Her parents' voices were faint from the living room. She stopped to sniff the wilting flowers in a vase on the side table near the staircase, even though she knew their scent would be gone, before walking upstairs. Her room felt alien, the warm wood tones, the tan furniture, the wall-to-wall burgundy carpeting that cushioned her feet, the reams of space that made Kainene call their rooms *flats*. The copy of *Lagos Life* was still on her bed; she picked it up, and looked at the photo of her and her mother, on page five, their faces contented and complacent, at a cocktail party hosted by the British high commissioner. Her mother had pulled her close as a photographer approached; later, after the flashbulb went off, Olanna had called the photographer over and asked him please not to publish the photo. He had looked at her oddly. Now, she realized how silly it had been to ask him; of course he would never understand the discomfort that came with being a part of the gloss that was her parents' life.

She was in bed reading when her mother knocked and came in.

'Oh, you're reading,' her mother said. She was holding rolls of fabric in her hand. 'Chief just left. He said I should greet you.'

Olanna wanted to ask if they had promised him an affair with her, and yet she knew she never would. 'What are those materials?'

'Chief just sent his driver to the car for them before he left. It's the latest lace from Europe. See? Very nice, *i fukwa?*'

Olanna felt the fabric between her fingers. 'Yes, very nice.'

'Did you see the one he wore today? Original! *Ezigbo!*' Her mother sat down beside her. 'And do you know, they say he never wears any outfit twice? He gives them to his houseboys once he has worn them.'

Olanna visualized his poor houseboys' wood boxes incongruously full of lace, houseboys she was sure did not get paid much every month, owning cast-off kaftans and *agbadas* they could never wear. She was tired. Having conversations with her mother tired her.

'Which one do you want, *nne*? I will make a long skirt and blouse for you and Kainene.'

'No, don't worry, Mum. Make something for yourself. I won't wear rich lace in Nsukka too often.'

Her mother ran a finger over the bedside cabinet. 'This silly housegirl does not clean furniture properly. Does she think I pay her to play around?'

Olanna placed her book down. Her mother wanted to say something, she could tell, and the set smile, the punctilious gestures, were a beginning.

'So how is Odenigbo?' her mother asked finally.

'He's fine.'

Her mother sighed, in the overdone way that meant she wished

Olanna would see reason. 'Have you thought about this Nsukka move well? Very well?'

'I have never been surer of anything.'

'But will you be comfortable there?' Her mother said *comfortable* with a faint shudder, and Olanna almost smiled because her mother had Odenigbo's *basic* university house in mind, with its sturdy rooms and plain furniture and uncarpeted floors.

'I'll be fine,' she said.

'You can find work here in Lagos and travel down to see him during weekends.'

'I don't want to work in Lagos. I want to work in the university, and I want to live with him.'

Her mother looked at her for a little while longer before she stood up and said, 'Good night, my daughter,' in a voice that was small and wounded.

Olanna stared at the door. She was used to her mother's disapproval; it had coloured most of her major decisions, after all: when she chose two weeks' suspension rather than apologize to her Heathgrove form mistress for insisting that the lessons on Pax Britannica were contradictory; when she joined the Students' Movement for Independence at Ibadan; when she refused to marry Igwe Okagbue's son, and later, Chief Okaro's son. Still, each time, the disapproval made her want to apologize, to make up for it in some way.

She was almost asleep when Kainene knocked. 'So will you be spreading your legs for that elephant in exchange for Daddy's contract?' Kainene asked.

Olanna sat up, surprised. She did not remember the last time that Kainene had come into her room.

'Daddy literally pulled me away from the veranda, so we could leave you alone with the good cabinet minister,' Kainene said. 'Will he give Daddy the contract then?'

'He didn't say. But it's not as if he will get nothing. Daddy will still give him ten per cent, after all.'

'The ten per cent is standard, so extras always help. The other bidders probably don't have a *beautiful* daughter.' Kainene dragged the word out until it sounded cloying, sticky: *beau-ti-ful*. She was flipping through the copy of *Lagos Life*, her silk robe tied tightly around her skinny waist. 'The benefit of being the ugly daughter is that nobody uses you as sex bait.'

'They're not using me as sex bait.'

Kainene did not respond for a while; she seemed focused on an article in the paper. Then she looked up. 'Richard is going to Nsukka too. He's received the grant, and he's going to write his book there.'

'Oh, good. So that means you will be spending time in Nsukka?'

Kainene ignored the question. 'Richard doesn't know anybody in Nsukka, so maybe you could introduce him to your revolutionary lover.'

Olanna smiled. *Revolutionary lover.* The things Kainene could say with a straight face! 'I'll introduce them,' she said. She had never liked any of Kainene's boyfriends and never liked that Kainene dated so many white men in England. Their thinly veiled condescension, their false validations irritated her. Yet she had not reacted in the same way to Richard Churchill when Kainene brought him to dinner. Perhaps it was because he did not have that familiar superiority of English people who thought they understood Africans better than Africans understood themselves and, instead, had an endearing uncertainty about him – almost a shyness. Or perhaps because her parents had ignored him, unimpressed because he didn't know anyone who was worth knowing.

'I think Richard will like Odenigbo's house,' Olanna said. 'It's like a political club in the evenings. He only invited Africans at first because the university is so full of foreigners, and he wanted Africans to have a chance to socialize with one another. At first it was BYOB, but now he asks them all to contribute some money, and every week he buys drinks and they meet in his house –' Olanna stopped. Kainene was looking at her woodenly, as if she had broken their unspoken rule and tried to start idle chatter.

Kainene turned towards the door. 'When do you leave for Kano?'

'Tomorrow.' Olanna wanted Kainene to stay, to sit on the bed and hold a pillow on her lap and gossip and laugh into the night.

'Go well, *jee ofuma*. Greet Aunty and Uncle and Arize.'

'I will,' Olanna said, although Kainene had already left and shut the door. She listened for Kainene's footsteps on the carpeted hallway. It was now that they were back from England, living in the same house again, that Olanna realized just how distant they had become. Kainene had always been the withdrawn child, the sullen and often acerbic teenager, the one who, because she did not try to please their parents, left Olanna with that duty. But they had been close, despite that. They used to be friends. She wondered when it all changed. Before they went to England, for sure, since they didn't even have the same friends in London. Perhaps it was during their secondary-school years at Heathgrove. Perhaps even before. Nothing had happened – no momentous quarrel, no significant incident – rather, they had simply drifted apart, but it was Kainene who now anchored herself firmly in a distant place so that they could not drift back together.

Olanna chose not to fly up to Kano. She liked to sit by the train window and watch the thick woods sliding past, the grassy plains unfurling, the cattle swinging their tails as they were herded by barechested nomads. When she got to Kano, it struck her once again how different it was from Lagos, from Nsukka, from her hometown Umunnachi, how different the North as a whole was from the South. Here, the sand was fine, grey, and sun-seared, nothing like the clumpy, red earth back home; the trees were tame, unlike the bursting greenness that sprang up and cast shadows on the road to Umunnachi. Here, miles of flatland went on and on, tempting the eyes to stretch just a little farther, until they seemed to meet with the silver-and-white sky.

She took a taxi from the train station and asked the driver to stop first at the market, so that she could greet Uncle Mbaezi.

On the narrow market paths, she manoeuvred between small boys carrying large loads on their heads, women haggling, traders shouting. A record shop was playing loud High Life music, and she slowed a little to hum along to Bobby Benson's 'Taxi Driver' before hurrying on to her uncle's stall. His shelves were lined with pails and other housewares.

'*Omalicha!*' he said, when he saw her. It was what he called her mother, too – Beautiful. 'You have been on my mind. I knew you would come to see us soon.'

'Uncle, good afternoon.'

They hugged. Olanna rested her head on his shoulder; he smelt of sweat, of the open-air market, of wares arranged on dusty wood shelves.

It was hard to imagine Uncle Mbaezi and her mother growing up together, brother and sister. Not only because her uncle's light-complexioned face had none of her mother's beauty, but also because there was an earthiness about him. Sometimes Olanna wondered if she would admire him as she did if he were not so different from her mother.

Whenever she visited, Uncle Mbaezi would sit with her in the yard after supper and tell her the latest family news – a cousin's unmarried daughter was pregnant, and he wanted her to come and stay with them to avoid the malice of the village; a nephew had died here in Kano and he was looking into the cheapest way to take the body back home. Or he would tell her about politics: What the Igbo Union was organizing, protesting, discussing. They held meetings in his yard. She had sat in a few times, and she still remembered the meeting where irritated men and women talked about the northern schools not admitting Igbo children. Uncle Mbaezi had stood up and stamped his foot. '*Ndi be anyi!* My people! We will build our own school! We will raise money and build our own school!' After he spoke, Olanna had joined in clapping her approval, in chanting, 'Well spoken! That is how it shall be!' But she had worried that it would be difficult to build a school. Perhaps it was more practical to try and persuade the Northerners to admit Igbo children.

Yet, now, only a few years later, her taxi was on Airport Road, driving past the Igbo Union Grammar School. It was break time and the schoolyard was full of children. Boys were playing football in different teams on the same field, so that multiple balls flew in the air; Olanna wondered how they could tell which ball was which. Clusters of girls were closer to the road, playing *oga* and *swell*, clapping rhythmically as they hopped first on one leg and then the other. Before the taxi parked outside the communal compound in Sabon Gari, Olanna saw Aunty Ifeka sitting by her kiosk on the roadside. Aunty Ifeka wiped her hands on her faded wrapper and hugged Olanna, pulled back to look at her, and hugged her again. 'Our Olanna!'

'My aunty! *Kedu?*'

'I am even better now that I see you.'

'Arize is not back from her sewing class?'

'She will be back anytime now.'

'How is she doing? *O na-agakwa?* Is her sewing going well?'

'The house is full of patterns that she has cut.'

'What of Odinchezo and Ekene?'

'They are there. They visited last week and asked after you.'

'How is Maiduguri treating them? Is their trading picking up?'

'They have not said they are dying of hunger,' Aunty Ifeka said, with a slight shrug. Olanna examined the plain face and wished, for a brief guilty moment, that Aunty Ifeka were her mother. Aunty Ifeka was as good as her mother, anyway, since it was Aunty Ifeka's breasts that she and Kainene had sucked when their mother's dried up soon after they were born. Kainene used to say their mother's breasts did not dry up at all, that their mother had given them to a nursing aunt only to save her own breasts from drooping.

'Come, *ada anyi*,' Aunty Ifeka said. 'Let's go inside.' She pulled down the wooden shutters of the kiosk, covering the neatly arranged cases of matches, chewing gum, sweets, cigarettes, and detergent, and then picked up Olanna's bag and led the way into the yard. The narrow bungalow was unpainted. The clothes hung out to dry were still, stiff, as if desiccated by the hot afternoon sun. Old car tyres, the ones the children played with, were piled under the *kuka* tree. Olanna knew the tranquil flatness of the yard would change soon, when the children came back from school. The families would leave doors open and the veranda and kitchen would fill with chatter. Uncle Mbaezi's family lived in two rooms. In the first, where worn sofas were pushed aside at night to make room for mats, Olanna unpacked the things she had brought – bread, shoes, bottles of cream – while Aunty Ifeka stood back watching, her hands behind her back. 'May another person do for you. May another person do for you,' Aunty Ifeka said.

Arize came home moments later and Olanna braced herself to stand firmly, so Arize's excited hug would not knock her down.

'Sister! You should have warned us that you were coming! At least we would have swept the yard better! Ah! Sister! *Aru amaka gi!* You look well! There are stories to tell, oh!'

Arize was laughing. Her plump body, her rounded arms, shook as she laughed. Olanna held her close. She felt a sense that things were in order, the way they were meant to be, and that even if they tumbled down once in a while, in the end they would come back together again. This was why she came to Kano: this lucid peace. When Aunty Ifeka's eyes began to dart around the yard, she knew it was in search of a suitable chicken. Aunty Ifeka always killed one when she visited, even if it was the last she owned, sauntering around the yard, its feathers marked with a splash or two of red paint to distinguish it from the neighbours' chickens, which had bits of cloth tied to their wings or paint of a different colour. Olanna no longer protested about the chicken, just as she no longer protested when Uncle Mbaezi and Aunty Ifeka slept on mats, next to the many relatives who always seemed to be staying with them, so that she could have their bed.

Aunty Ifeka walked casually towards a brown hen, grasped it quickly, and handed it to Arize to kill in the backyard. They sat outside the kitchen while Arize plucked it and Aunty Ifeka blew the chaff from the rice. A neighbour was boiling corn, and once in a while, when the water frothed over, the stove fire hissed. Children were playing in the yard now, raising white dust, shouting. A fight broke out under the *kuka* tree, and Olanna heard a child scream at another in Igbo, 'Your mother's pussy!'

The sun had turned red in the sky before it began its descent, when Uncle Mbaezi came home. He called out to Olanna to come and greet his friend Abdulmalik. Olanna had met the Hausa man once before; he sold leather slippers close to Uncle Mbaezi's stall in the market, and she had bought a few pairs that she took back to England but never wore because it was then the middle of winter.

'Our Olanna has just finished her master's degree. Master's degree at London University! It is not easy!' Uncle Mbaezi said proudly.

'Well done,' Abdulmalik said. He opened his bag and brought out a pair of slippers and held them out to her, his narrow face creased in a smile, his teeth stained with kola nut and tobacco and whatever else Olanna did not know, stains of varying shades of yellow and brown. He looked as if it were he who was receiving a gift; he had that expression of people who marvelled at education with the calm certainty that it would never be theirs.

She took the slippers with both hands. 'Thank you, Abdulmalik. Thank you.'

Abdulmalik pointed at the ripe gourdlike pods on the *kuka* tree and said, 'You come my house. My wife cook very sweet *kuka* soup.'

'Oh, I will come, next time,' Olanna said.

He muttered more congratulations before he sat with Uncle Mbaezi on the veranda, with a bucket of sugar cane in front of them. They gnawed off the hard, green peels and chewed the juicy, white pulp, speaking Hausa and laughing. They spit the chewed cane out on the dust. Olanna sat with them for a while, but their Hausa was too swift, too difficult to follow. She wished she were fluent in Hausa and Yoruba, like her uncle and aunt and cousin were, something she would gladly exchange her French and Latin for.

In the kitchen, Arize was cutting open the chicken and Aunty Ifeka was washing the rice. She showed them the slippers from Abdulmalik and put them on; the pleated red straps made her feet look slender, more feminine.

'Very nice,' Aunty Ifeka said. 'I shall thank him.'

Olanna sat on a stool and carefully avoided looking at the cockroach eggs, smooth black capsules, lodged in all corners of the table. A neighbour was building a wood fire in one corner and despite the slanting openings in the roof, the smoke choked the kitchen.

'*I makwa*, all her family eats every day is stockfish,' Arize said, gesturing towards the neighbour with pursed lips. 'I don't know if her poor children even know what meat tastes like.' Arize threw her head back and laughed.

Olanna glanced at the woman. She was an Ijaw and could not understand Arize's Igbo. 'Maybe they like stockfish,' she said.

'*O di egwu!* Like it indeed! Do you know how cheap the thing is?' Arize was still laughing as she turned to the woman. 'Ibiba, I am telling my big sister that your soup always smells so delicious.'

The woman stopped blowing at the firewood and smiled, a knowing smile, and Olanna wondered if perhaps the woman understood Igbo but chose to humour Arize's fun poking. There was something about Arize's effervescent mischief that made people forgiving.

'So you are moving to Nsukka to marry Odenigbo, Sister?' Arize asked.

'I don't know about marriage yet. I just want to be closer to him, and I want to teach.'

Arize's round eyes were admiring and bewildered. 'It is only women that know too much Book like you who can say that, Sister. If people like me who don't know Book wait too long, we will expire.' Arize paused as she removed a translucently pale egg from inside the chicken. 'I want a husband today and tomorrow, oh! My mates have all left me and gone to husbands' houses.'

'You are young,' Olanna said. 'You should focus on your sewing for now.'

'Is it sewing that will give me a child? Even if I had managed to pass to go to school, I would still want a child now.'

'There is no rush, Ari.' Olanna wished she could shift her stool closer to the door, to fresh air. But she didn't want Aunty Ifeka, or Arize, or even the neighbour to know that the smoke irritated her eyes and throat or that the sight of the cockroach eggs nauseated her. She wanted to seem used to it all, to this life.

'I know you will marry Odenigbo, Sister, but honestly I am not sure I want you to marry a man from Abba. Men from Abba are so ugly, *kai*! If only Mohammed was an Igbo man, I would eat my hair if you did not marry him. I have never seen a more handsome man.'

'Odenigbo is not ugly. Good looks come in different ways,' Olanna said.

'That is what the relatives of the ugly monkey, *enwe*, told him to make him feel better, that good looks come in different ways.'

'Men from Abba are not ugly,' Aunty Ifeka said. 'My people came from there, after all.'

'And do your people not resemble the monkey?' Arize said.

'Your full name is Arizendikwunnem, isn't it? You come from your mother's people. So perhaps you look like a monkey as well,' Aunty Ifeka murmured.

Olanna laughed. 'So why are you talking marriage-marriage like this, Ari? Have you seen anybody you like? Or should I find you one of Mohammed's brothers?'

'No, *no!*' Arize waved her hands in the air in mock horror. 'Papa would kill me first of all if he knew I was even looking at a Hausa man like that.'

'Unless your father will kill a corpse, because I will start with you first,' Aunty Ifeka said, and rose with the bowl of clean rice.

'There is someone, Sister.' Arize moved closer to Olanna. 'But I am not sure he is looking at me, oh.'

'Why are you whispering?' Aunty Ifeka asked.

'Am I talking to you? Is it not my big sister I am talking to?' Arize asked her mother. But she raised her voice as she continued. 'His name is Nnakwanze and he is from close to us, from Ogidi. He works at the railway. But he has not told me anything. I don't know if he is looking at me hard enough.'

'If he is not looking at you hard enough, there is something wrong with his eyes,' Aunty Ifeka said.

'Have you people seen this woman? Why can't I talk to my big sister in peace?' Arize rolled her eyes, but it was clear she was pleased and perhaps had used this opportunity to tell her mother about Nnakwanze.

That night, as Olanna lay on her uncle and aunt's bed, she watched Arize through the thin curtain that hung on a rope attached to nails on the wall. The rope was not taut, and the curtain sagged in the middle. She followed the up-down movement of Arize's breathing and imagined what growing up had been like for Arize and her brothers, Odinchezo and Ekene, seeing their parents through the curtain, hearing the sounds that might suggest an eerie pain to a child as their father's hips moved and their mother's arms clutched him. She had never heard her own parents making love, never even seen any indication that they did. But she had always been separated from them by hallways that got longer and more thickly carpeted as they moved from house to house. When they moved to their present home, with its ten rooms, her parents chose different bedrooms for the first time. 'I need the whole wardrobe, and it will be nice to have your father visit!' her mother had said. But the girlish laugh had not rung true for Olanna. The artificiality of her parents' relationship always seemed harder, more shaming, when she was here in Kano.

The window above her was open, the still night air thick with the odours from the gutters behind the house, where people emptied their toilet buckets. Soon, she heard the muted chatter of the night-soil men as they collected the sewage; she fell asleep listening to the scraping sounds of their shovels as they worked, shielded by the dark.

The beggars outside the gates of Mohammed's family home did not move when they saw Olanna. They remained seated on the ground, leaning against the mud compound walls. Flies perched on them in dense clusters, so that for a moment it seemed as if their frayed, white kaftans had been splashed with dark-coloured paint. Olanna wanted to put some money in their bowls but decided not to. If she were a man, they would have called out to her and extended their begging bowls, and the flies would rise in buzzing clouds.

One of the gatemen recognized her and opened the gates. 'Welcome, madam.'

'Thank you, Sule. How are you?'

'You remember my name, madam!' He beamed. 'Thank you, madam. I am well, madam.'

'And your family?'

'Well, madam, by the will of Allah.'

'Is your master back from America?'

'Yes, madam. Please come in. I will send to call Master.'

Mohammed's red sports car was parked in front of the sprawling sandy yard but what held Olanna's attention was the house: the graceful simplicity of its flat roof. She sat down on the veranda.

'The best surprise!'

She looked up and Mohammed was there, in a white kaftan, smiling down at her. His lips were a sensual curve, lips she had once kissed often during those days when she spent most of her weekends in Kano, eating rice with her fingers in his house, watching him play polo at the Flying Club, reading the bad poetry he wrote her.

'You're looking so well,' she told him, as they hugged. 'I wasn't sure you'd be back from America.'

'I was planning to come up to Lagos to see you.' Mohammed moved back to look at her. There was a tilt to his head, a narrowing of his eyes, that meant he still harboured hope.

'I'm moving to Nsukka,' she said.

'So you are finally going to become an intellectual and marry your lecturer.'

'Nobody said anything about marriage. And how is Janet? Or is it Jane? I mix up your American women.'

Mohammed raised one eyebrow. She could not help admiring his caramel complexion. She used to tease him about being prettier than she was.

'What did you do to your hair?' he asked. 'It doesn't suit you at all. Is this how your lecturer wants you to look, like a bush woman?'

Olanna touched her hair, newly plaited with black thread. 'My aunty did it. I quite like it.'

'I don't. I prefer your wigs.' Mohammed moved closer and hugged her again. When she felt his arms tighten around her, she pushed him away.

'You won't let me kiss you.'

'No,' she said, although it had not been a question. 'You're not telling me about Janet-Jane.'

'Jane. So this means I won't see you any more when you go to Nsukka.'

'Of course I'll see you.'

'I know that lecturer of yours is crazy, so I won't come to Nsukka.' Mohammed laughed. His tall, slim body and tapering fingers spoke of fragility, gentleness. 'Would you like a soft drink? Or some wine?'

'You have alcohol in this house? Someone must inform your uncle,' Olanna teased.

Mohammed rang a bell and asked a steward to bring some drinks. Afterwards, he sat thoughtfully rubbing his thumb and forefinger together. 'Sometimes, I feel my life is going nowhere. I travel and drive imported cars, and women follow me. But something isn't there, something isn't right. You know?' She watched him; she knew where he was going with this. Yet when he said, 'I wish things didn't change,' she was touched and flattered.

'You'll find a good woman,' she said limply.

'Rubbish,' he said, and as they sat side by side drinking Coke, she recalled the disbelieving pain on his face that had only deepened when she told him she had to end it right away because she did not want to be unfaithful to him. She expected that he would resist, she knew very well how much he loved her, but she had been shocked when he told her to go ahead and sleep with Odenigbo as long as she did not leave him: Mohammed, who often half-joked about coming from a lineage of holy warriors, the very avatars of pious masculinity. Perhaps it was why her affection for him would always be mingled with gratitude, a selfish gratitude. He could have made their break-up more difficult for her; he could have left her with much more guilt.

She placed her glass down. 'Let's go for a drive. I hate it when I visit Kano and only get to see the ugly cement and zinc of Sabon Gari. I want to see that ancient mud statue and go around the lovely city walls again.'

'Sometimes you are just like the white people, the way they gawk at everyday things.'

'Do I?'

'It's a joke. How are you going to learn not to take everything so seriously if you live with that crazy lecturer?' Mohammed stood up. 'Come, we should stop by first so you can greet my mother.'

As they walked past a small gate at the back and into the courtyard that led to his mother's chambers, Olanna remembered the trepidation she used to feel coming here. The reception area was the same, with gold-dyed walls and thick Persian rugs and grooved patterns on the exposed ceilings. Mohammed's mother looked unchanged, too, with the ring in her nose and the silk scarves around her head. She was fine-spun in the way that used to make Olanna wonder if she wasn't uncomfortable, dressing up every day and simply sitting at home. But the older woman did not have that old standoffish expression, did not speak stiffly with her eyes focused somewhere between Olanna's face and the hand-carved panelling. Instead she got up and hugged Olanna.

'You look so lovely, my dear. Don't let the sun spoil that skin of yours.'

'*Na gode.* Thank you, Hajia,' Olanna said, wondering how it was possible for people to switch affection off and on, to tie and untie emotions.

'I am no longer the Igbo woman you wanted to marry who would taint the lineage with infidel blood,' Olanna said, as they climbed into Mohammed's red Porsche. 'So I am a friend now.'

'I would have married you anyhow, and she knew it. Her preference did not matter.'

'Maybe not at first, but what about later? What about when we had been married for ten years?'

'Your parents felt the same way as she did.' Mohammed turned to look at her. 'Why are we talking about this now?' There was something inexpressibly sad in his eyes. Or maybe she was imagining it. Maybe she wanted him to seem sad at the thought that they would never marry. She did not wish to marry him, and yet she enjoyed dwelling on the things they did not do and would never do.

'Sorry,' she said.

'There's nothing to apologize for.' Mohammed reached out and took her hand. The car made rasping sounds as they drove past the gates. 'There's too much dust in the exhaust. These cars weren't made for our parts.'

'You should buy a hardy Peugeot.'

'Yes, I should.'

Olanna stared at the beggars clumped around the walls of the palace, their bodies and begging bowls covered in flies. The air smelt of the spicy-sour leaves from the neem tree.

'I am not like white people,' she said quietly.

Mohammed glanced at her. 'Of course you're not. You're a nationalist and a patriot, and soon you will marry your lecturer the freedom fighter.'

Olanna wondered if Mohammed's lightness hid a more serious mockery. Her hand was still in his and she wondered, too, if he was having difficulty manoeuvring the car with one hand.

* * *

Olanna moved to Nsukka on a windy Saturday, and the next day Odenigbo left for a mathematics conference at the University of Ibadan. He would not have gone if the conference was not focused on the work of his mentor, the black American mathematician David Blackwell.

'He is the greatest living mathematician, the greatest,' he said. 'Why don't you come with me, *nkem*? It's only for a week.'

Olanna said no; she wanted the chance to settle down when he was not there, to make peace with her fears in his absence. The first thing she did after he left was to throw away the red and white plastic flowers on the centre table.

Ugwu looked horrified. 'But mah, it is still good.'

She led the way outside to the African lilies and pink roses, freshly watered by Jomo, and asked Ugwu to cut some. She showed him how much water to put in the vase. Ugwu looked at the flowers and shook his head, as if he could not believe her foolishness. 'But it die, mah. The other one don't die.'

'Yes, but these are better, *fa makali*,' Olanna said.

'How better, mah?' He always responded in English to her Igbo, as if he saw her speaking Igbo to him as an insult that he had to defend himself against by insistently speaking English.

'They are just nicer,' she said, and realized that she did not know how to explain why fresh flowers were better than plastic ones. Later, when she saw the plastic flowers in a kitchen cupboard, she was not surprised. Ugwu had saved them, the same way he saved old sugar cartons, bottle corks, even yam peels. It came with never having had much, she knew, the inability to let go of things, even things that were useless. So when she was in the kitchen with him, she talked about the need to keep only things that were useful, and she hoped he would not ask her how the fresh flowers, then, were useful. She asked him to clean out the store and line the shelves with old newspapers, and as he worked she stood by and asked him about his family. It was difficult to picture them because, with his limited vocabulary, he described everyone as 'very good'. She went to the market with him, and after they bought the household items, she bought him a comb and a shirt. She taught him to cook fried rice with green peppers and diced carrots, asked him not to cook beans until they became pudding, not to douse things in oil, not to be too sparing with salt. Although she had noticed his body odour the first time she saw him, she let a few days pass before she gave him some scented powder for his armpits and asked him to use two capfuls of Dettol in his bath water. He looked pleased when he sniffed the powder, and she wondered if he could tell that it was a feminine scent. She wondered, too, what he really thought of her. There was clearly affection, but there was also a quiet speculation in his eyes, as if he was holding her up to something. And she worried that she came out lacking.

He finally started to speak Igbo to her on the day she rearranged the photos on the wall. A wall gecko had scuttled out from behind the wood-framed photo of Odenigbo in a graduating gown, and Ugwu shouted, '*Egbukwala!* Don't kill it!'

'What?' She turned to glance down at him from the chair she was standing on.

'If you kill it you will get a stomachache,' he said. She found his Opi dialect funny, the way he seemed to spit the words out.

'Of course we won't kill it. Let's hang the photo on that wall.'

'Yes, mah,' he said, and then began to tell her, in Igbo, how his sister Anulika had suffered a terrible stomachache after killing a gecko.

Olanna felt less of a visitor in the house when Odenigbo came back; he pulled her forcefully, kissed her, pressed her to him.

'You should eat first,' she said.

'I know what I want to eat.'

She laughed. She felt ridiculously happy.

'What's happened here?' Odenigbo asked, looking around the room. 'All the books on that shelf?'

'Your older books are in the second bedroom. I need the space for *my* books.'

'*Ezi okwu?* You've really moved in, haven't you?' Odenigbo was laughing.

'Go and have a bath,' she said.

'And what was that flowery scent on my good man?'

'I gave him a scented talcum powder. Didn't you notice his body odour?'

'That's the smell of villagers. I used to smell like that until I left Abba to go to secondary school. But you wouldn't know about things like that.' His tone was gently teasing. But his hands were not gentle. They were unbuttoning her blouse, freeing her breast from a bra cup. She was not sure how much time had passed, but she was tangled in bed with Odenigbo, warm and naked, when Ugwu knocked to say they had visitors.

'Can't they leave?' she murmured.

'Come, *nkem*,' Odenigbo said. 'I can't wait for them to meet you.'

'Let's stay here just a little longer.' She ran her hand over the curly hair on his chest, but he kissed her and got up to look for his underwear.

Olanna dressed reluctantly and went out to the living room.

'My friends, my friends,' Odenigbo announced, with an exaggerated flourish, 'this, finally, is Olanna.'

The woman, who was tuning the radiogram, turned and took Olanna's hand. 'How are you?' she asked. Her head was wrapped in a bright-orange turban.

'I'm well,' Olanna said. 'You must be Lara Adebayo.'

'Yes,' Miss Adebayo said. 'He did not tell us that you were illogically pretty.'

Olanna stepped back, flustered for a moment. 'I will take that as a compliment.'

'And what a proper English accent,' Miss Adebayo murmured, with a pitying smile, before turning back to the radiogram. She had a compact body, a straight back that looked straighter in her stiff orange-print dress, the body of a questioner whom one dared not question back.

'I'm Okeoma,' the man with the tangled mop of uncombed hair said. 'I thought Odenigbo's girlfriend was a human being; he didn't say you were a water mermaid.'

Olanna laughed, grateful for the warmth in Okeoma's expression and the way he held her hand a little too long. Dr Patel looked shy as he said, 'Very nice to see you finally,' and Professor Ezeka shook her hand and then nodded disdainfully when she said her degree was in sociology and not one of the proper sciences.

After Ugwu served drinks, Olanna watched Odenigbo raise his glass to his lips and all she could think of was how those lips had fastened around her nipple only minutes ago. She surreptitiously moved so that her inner arm brushed against her breast and closed her eyes at the needles of delicious pain. Sometimes Odenigbo bit too hard. She wanted the guests to leave.

'Did not that great thinker Hegel call Africa a land of childhood?' Professor Ezeka asked, in an affected tone.

'Maybe the people who put up those NO CHILDREN AND AFRICANS signs in the cinemas in Mombasa had read Hegel, then,' Dr Patel said, and chuckled.

'Nobody can take Hegel seriously. Have you read him closely? He's funny, very funny. But Hume and Voltaire and Locke felt the same way about Africa,' Odenigbo said. 'Greatness depends on where you are coming from. It's just like the Israelis who were asked what they thought of Eichmann's trial the other day, and one of them said he did not understand how the Nazis could have been thought great by anyone at any time. But they were, weren't they? They still are!' Odenigbo gestured with his hand, palm upward, and Olanna remembered that hand grasping her waist.

'What people fail to see is this: If Europe had cared more about Africa, the Jewish Holocaust would not have happened,' Odenigbo said. 'In short, the World War would not have happened!'

'What do you mean?' Miss Adebayo asked. She held her glass to her lips.

'How can you ask what I mean? It's self-evident, starting with the Herero people.' Odenigbo was shifting on his seat, his voice raised, and Olanna wondered if he remembered how loud they had been, how afterwards he had said, laughing, 'If we go on like this at night, we'll probably wake Ugwu up, poor chap.'

'You've come again, Odenigbo,' Miss Adebayo said. 'You're saying that if white people had not murdered the Herero, the Jewish Holocaust would not have happened? I don't see a connection at all!'

'Don't you see?' Odenigbo asked. 'They started their race studies with the Herero and concluded with the Jews. Of course there's a connection!'

'Your argument doesn't hold water at all, you sophist,' Miss Adebayo said, and dismissively downed what was in her glass.

'But the World War was a bad thing that was also good, as our people say,' Okeoma said. 'My father's brother fought in Burma and came back filled with one burning question: How come nobody told him before that the white man was not immortal?'

They all laughed. There was something habitual about it, as if they had had different variations of this conversation so many times that they knew just when to laugh. Olanna laughed too and felt for a moment that her laughter sounded different, more shrill, than theirs.

* * *

The following weeks, when she started teaching a course in intro-ductory sociology, when she joined the staff club and played tennis with other lecturers, when she drove Ugwu to the market and took walks with Odenigbo and joined the St Vincent de Paul Society at St Peter's Church, she slowly began to get used to Odenigbo's friends. Odenigbo teased her that more people came to visit now that she was here, that both Okeoma and Patel were falling in love with her, because Okeoma was so eager to read poems in which descriptions of goddesses sounded suspiciously like her and Dr Patel told too many stories of his days at Makerere, where he cast himself as the perfectly chivalrous intellectual.

Olanna liked Dr Patel, but it was Okeoma whose visits she most looked forward to. His untidy hair and rumpled clothes and dramatic poetry put her at ease. And she noticed, early on, that it was Okeoma's opinions that Odenigbo most respected, saying 'The voice of our generation!' as though he truly believed it. She was still not sure what to make of Professor Ezeka's hoarse superciliousness, his certainty that he knew better than everyone else but chose to say lit-tle. Neither was she sure of Miss Adebayo. It would have been easier if Miss Adebayo showed jealousy, but it was as if Miss Adebayo thought her to be unworthy of competition, with her *unintellectual* ways and her too-pretty face and her mimicking-the-oppressor Eng-lish accent. She found herself talking more when Miss Adebayo was there, desperately giving opinions with a need to impress – Nkrumah really wanted to lord it over all of Africa, it was arrogant of America to insist that the Soviets take their missiles out of Cuba while theirs remained in Turkey, Sharpeville was only a dramatic example of the hundreds of blacks killed by the South African state every day – but she suspected that there was a glaze of unoriginality to all her ideas. And she suspected that Miss Adebayo knew this; it was always when she spoke that Miss Adebayo would pick up a journal or pour another drink or get up to go to the toilet. Finally, she gave up. She would never like Miss Adebayo and Miss Adebayo would never even think about liking her. Perhaps Miss Adebayo could tell, from her face, that she was afraid of things, that she was unsure, that she was not one of those people with no patience for self-doubt. People like Odenigbo. People like Miss Adebayo herself, who could look a person in the eye and calmly tell her that she was illogically pretty, who could even use that phrase, *illogically pretty*.

Still, when Olanna lay in bed with Odenigbo, legs intertwined, it would strike her how her life in Nsukka felt like being immersed in a mesh of soft feathers, even on the days when Odenigbo locked himself in the study for hours. Each time he suggested they get married, she said no. They were too happy, precariously so, and she wanted to guard that bond; she feared that marriage would flatten it to a prosaic partnership.

§ 3 §

Richard said little at the parties Susan took him to. When she introduced him, she always added that he was a writer, and he hoped the other guests assumed he was distant in the way writers were, although he feared they saw through him and knew he simply felt out of place. But they were pleasant to him; they would be to anyone who was Susan's companion, as long as Susan continued to engage them with her wit, her laughter, her green eyes that sparkled in a face flushed from glasses of wine.

Richard didn't mind standing by and waiting until she was ready to leave, didn't mind that none of her friends made an effort to draw him in, didn't even mind when a pasty-faced drunk woman referred to him as Susan's *pretty boy*. But he minded the all-expatriate parties where Susan would nudge him to 'join the men' while she went over to the circle of women to compare notes on living in Nigeria. He felt awkward with the men. They were mostly English, ex-colonial administrators and business people from John Holt and Kingsway and GB Ollivant and Shell-BP and United Africa Company. They were reddened from sun and alcohol. They chuckled about how tribal Nigerian politics was, and perhaps these chaps were not quite so ready to rule themselves after all. They discussed cricket, plantations they owned or planned to own, the perfect weather in Jos, business opportunities in Kaduna. When Richard mentioned his interest in Igbo-Ukwu art, they said it didn't have much of a market yet, so he did not bother to explain that he wasn't at all interested in the money, it was the aesthetics that drew him. And when he said he had just arrived in Lagos and wanted to write a book about Nigeria, they gave him brief smiles and advice: The people were bloody beggars, be prepared for their body odours and the way they will stand and stare at you on the roads, never believe a hard-luck story, never show weakness to domestic staff. There were jokes to illustrate each African trait. The uppity African stood out in Richard's mind: An African was walking a dog and an Englishman asked, 'What are you doing with that monkey?' and the African answered, 'It's a dog, not a monkey' – as if the Englishman had been talking to him!

Richard laughed at the jokes. He tried, too, not to drift throughout the conversations, not to show how awkward he felt. He preferred talking to the women, although he had learned not to spend too long with a particular woman, or Susan would throw a glass at the wall when they got home. He was baffled the first time it happened. He had spent a short time talking to Clovis Bancroft about her brother's life as a district commissioner in Enugu years ago, and afterwards Susan was silent during the drive back in her chauffeur-driven car. He thought perhaps she was dozing off; it had to be why she was not talking about somebody's ghastly dress or the unimaginative hors d'oeuvres that had been served. But when they got back to her house, she picked up a glass from the cabinet and threw it against the wall. 'That horrible little woman, Richard, and right in my face, too. It's so awful!' She sat on the sofa and buried her face in her hands until he said he was very sorry, although he was not quite sure what he was apologizing for.

Another glass crashed some weeks later. He had talked to Julia March, mostly about her research on the *Asantehene* in Ghana, and stood absorbed, listening, until Susan came over and pulled him by the arm. Later, after the brittle splinter of shattering glass, Susan said she knew he didn't mean to flirt but he must understand that people were horribly presumptuous and the gossip here was vicious, just vicious. He had apologized again and wondered what the stewards who cleaned up the glass thought.

Then there was the dinner at which he talked about Nok art with a university lecturer, a timid Yoruba woman who seemed to feel just as out of place as he did. He had expected Susan's reaction and prepared to apologize before she got to the living room, so that he could save a glass. But Susan was chatty as they were driven home; she asked if his conversation with the woman had been interesting and hoped he had learned something that would be useful for his book. He stared at her in the dim interior of the car. She would not have said that if he had been talking to one of the British women, even though some of them had helped write the Nigerian constitution. It was, he realized, simply that black women were not threatening to her, were not equal rivals.

Aunt Elizabeth had said that Susan was vivacious and charming, never mind that she was a little older than he was, and had been in Nigeria for a while and could show him round. Richard did not want to be shown round; he had managed well on his past trips abroad. But Aunt Elizabeth insisted. *Africa* was nothing like Argentina or India. She said *Africa* in the tone of one repressing a shudder, or perhaps it was because she did not want him to leave at all, she wanted him to stay in London and keep writing for the *News Chronicle*. He still did not think that anybody read his tiny column, although Aunt Elizabeth said all her friends did. But she would: The job was a bit of a sinecure after all; he would not have been offered it in the first place if the editor were not an old friend of hers.

Richard did not try to explain his desire to see Nigeria to Aunt Elizabeth, but he did accept Susan's offer to show him around. The first thing he noticed when he arrived in Lagos was Susan's sparkle, her posh prettiness, the way she focused entirely on him, touched his arm as she laughed. She spoke with authority about Nigeria and Nigerians. When they drove past the noisy markets with music blaring from shops, the haphazard stalls of the streetside hawkers, the gutters thick with mouldy water, she said, 'They have a marvellous energy, really, but very little sense of hygiene, I'm afraid.' She told him the Hausa in the North were a dignified lot, the Igbo were surly and money-loving, and the Yoruba were rather jolly, even if they were first-rate lickspittles. On Saturday evenings, when she pointed at the crowds of brightly dressed people dancing in front of lit-up canopies on the streets, she said, 'There you go. The Yoruba get into huge debt just to throw these parties.'

She helped him find a small flat, buy a small car, get a driving licence, go to the Lagos and Ibadan museums. 'You must meet all my friends,' she said. At first, when she introduced him as a writer, he wanted to correct her: journalist, not writer. But he *was* a writer, at least he was certain he was meant to be a writer, an artist, a creator. His journalism was temporary, something he would do until he wrote that brilliant novel.

So he let Susan introduce him as a writer. It seemed to make her friends tolerate him, anyway. It made Professor Nicholas Green suggest he apply for the foreign research grant at Nsukka, where he could write in a university environment. Richard did, not only because of the prospect of writing in a university, but also because he would be in the southeast, in the land of Igbo-Ukwu art, the land of the magnificent roped pot. That, after all, was why he had come to Nigeria.

He had been in Nigeria for a few months when Susan asked if he would like to move in with her, since her house in Ikoyi was large, the gardens were lovely, and she thought he would work much better there than in his rented flat with the uneven cement floors where his landlord moaned about his leaving his lights on for too long. Richard didn't want to say yes. He didn't want to stay much longer in Lagos. He wanted to do more travelling through the country while waiting to hear back from Nsukka. But Susan had already redecorated her airy study for him, so he moved in. Day after day, he sat on her leather chair and pored over books and bits of research material, looked out the window at the gardeners watering the lawn, and pounded at the typewriter, although he was aware that he was typing and not writing. Susan was careful to give him the silences he needed, except for when she would look in and whisper, 'Would you like some tea?' or 'Some water?' or 'An early lunch?' He answered in a whisper, too, as if his writing had become something hallowed and had made the room itself sacrosanct. He did not tell her that he had written nothing good so far, that the ideas in his head had not yet coalesced into character and setting and theme. He imagined that she would be hurt; his writing had become the best of her hobbies, and she came home every day with books and journals from the British Council Library. She saw his book as an entity that already existed and could therefore be finished. He, however, was not even sure what his subject was. But he was grateful for her faith. It was as if her believing in his writing made it real, and he showed his gratitude by attending the parties he disliked. After a few parties, he decided that attending was not enough; he would try to be funny. If he could say one witty thing when he was introduced, it might make up for his silence and, more importantly, it would please Susan. He practised a droll, self-deprecating expression and a halting delivery in front of the bathroom mirror for a while. 'This is Richard Churchill,' Susan would say and he would shake hands and quip, 'No relation of Sir Winston's, I'm afraid, or I might have turned out a little cleverer.'

Susan's friends laughed at this, although he wondered if it was from pity at his fumbling attempt at humour more than from amusement. But nobody had ever said, 'How funny,' in a mocking tone, as Kainene did that first day in the cocktail room of the Federal Palace Hotel. She was smoking. She could blow perfect smoke rings. She stood in the same circle as he and Susan, and he glanced at her and thought she was the mistress of one of the politicians. He did that with the people he met, tried to guess a reason for their being there, to determine who had been brought by someone. Perhaps it was because he would not have been at any of the parties if it wasn't for Susan. He didn't think Kainene was some wealthy Nigerian's daughter because she had none of the cultivated demureness. She seemed more like a mistress: her brazenly red lipstick, her tight dress, her smoking. But then she didn't smile in that plastic way the mistresses did. She didn't even have the generic prettiness that made him inclined to believe the rumour that Nigerian politicians swapped mistresses. In fact, she was not pretty at all. He did not really notice this until he looked at her again as a friend of Susan's did the introductions. 'This is Kainene Ozobia, Chief Ozobia's daughter. Kainene's just got her master's from London. Kainene, this is Susan Grenville-Pitts, from the British Council, and this is Richard Churchill.'

'How do you do,' Susan said to Kainene, and then turned around to speak to another guest.

'Hello,' Richard said. Kainene was silent for too long, with her cigarette between her lips as she looked at him levelly, and so he ran his hand through his hair and mumbled, 'I'm no relation of Sir Winston's, I'm afraid, or I might have turned out a little cleverer.'

She exhaled before she said, 'How funny.' She was very thin and very tall, almost as tall as he was, and she was staring right into his eyes, with a steely blank expression. Her skin was the colour of Belgian chocolate. He spread his legs a little wider and pressed his feet down firmly, because he feared that if he didn't he might find himself reeling, colliding with her.

Susan came back and tugged at him but he didn't want to leave and when he opened his mouth, he wasn't sure what he was going to say. 'It turns out Kainene and I have a mutual friend in London. Did I tell you about Wilfred at the *Spectator*?'

'Oh,' Susan said, smiling. 'How lovely. I'll let you two catch up then. Be back in a bit.'

She exchanged kisses with an elderly couple before moving to a group at the other end of the room.

'You just lied to your wife,' Kainene said.

'She's not my wife.' He was surprised at how giddy he felt to be left standing with her. She raised her glass to her lips and sipped. She inhaled and exhaled. Silver ashes swirled down to the floor. Everything seemed to be in slow motion: The hotel ballroom enlarged and deflated and the air was sucked in and out of a space that seemed to be, for a moment, occupied only by himself and Kainene.

'Would you move away, please?' she asked.

He was startled. 'What?'

'There is a photographer behind you who is keen to take a photo of me, and particularly of my necklace.'

He moved aside and watched as she stared at the camera. She did not pose but she looked comfortable; she was used to having her photograph taken at parties.

'The necklace will be featured in tomorrow's *Lagos Life*. I suppose that would be my way of contributing to our newly independent country. I am giving fellow Nigerians something to covet, an incentive to work hard,' she said, coming back to stand beside him.

'It's a lovely necklace,' he said, although it looked gaudy. He wanted to reach out and touch it, though, to lift it off her neck and then let it settle back against the hollow of her throat. Her collarbones jutted out sharply.

'Of course it's not lovely. My father has obscene taste in jewellery,' she said. 'But it's his money. I see my sister and my parents looking for me, by the way. I should go.'

'Your sister is here?' Richard asked, quickly, before she could turn and leave.

'Yes. We're twins,' she said and paused, as if that were a momentous disclosure. 'Kainene and Olanna. Her name is the lyrical *God's Gold*, and mine is the more practical *Let's watch and see what next God will bring*.'

Richard watched the smile that pulled her mouth up at one end, a sardonic smile that he imagined hid something else, perhaps dissatisfaction. He didn't know what to say. He felt as if time was slipping away from him.

'Who is older?' he asked.

'Who is older? What a question.' She arched her eyebrows. 'I'm told I came out first.'

Richard cradled his wine glass and wondered if tightening his grasp any further would crush it.

'There she is, my sister,' Kainene said. 'Shall I introduce you? Everybody wants to meet her.'

Richard didn't turn to look. 'I'd rather talk to you,' he said. 'If you don't mind, that is.' He ran his hand through his hair. She was watching him; he felt adolescent with her gaze on him.

'You're shy,' she said.

'I've been called worse.'

She smiled, in the way that meant she had found *that* funny, and he felt accomplished to have made her smile.

'Have you ever been to the market in Balogun?' she asked. 'They display slabs of meat on tables, and you are supposed to grope and feel and then decide which you want. My sister and I are meat. We are here so that suitable bachelors will make the kill.'

'Oh,' he said. It seemed a strangely intimate thing to tell him, although it was said in the same dry, sarcastic tone that seemed natural to her. He wanted to tell her something about himself, too, wanted to exchange small kernels of intimacies with her.

'Here comes the wife you denied,' Kainene murmured.

Susan came back and pushed a glass into his hand. 'Here, darling,' she said, and then turned to Kainene. 'How lovely to meet you.'

'How lovely to meet *you*,' Kainene said and half-raised her glass towards Susan.

Susan steered him away. 'She's Chief Ozobia's daughter, is she? Whatever happened to her? Quite extraordinary; her mother is stunning, absolutely stunning. Chief Ozobia owns half of Lagos but there is something terribly *nouveau riche* about him. He doesn't have much of a formal education, you see, and neither has his wife. I suppose that's what makes him so *obvious*.'

Richard was usually amused by Susan's mini-biographies, but now the whispering irritated him. He did not want the champagne; her nails were digging into his arm. She led him to a group of expatriates and stopped to chat, laughing loudly, a little drunk. He searched the room for Kainene. At first, he could not find the red dress and then he saw her standing near her father; Chief Ozobia looked expansive, with the arching hand gestures he made as he spoke, the intricately embroidered *agbada*, whose folds and folds of blue cloth made him even wider than he was. Mrs Ozobia was half his size and wore a wrapper and headgear made out of the same blue fabric. Richard was momentarily startled by how perfectly almond-shaped her eyes were, wide-set in a dark face that was intimidating to look at. He would never have guessed that she was Kainene's mother, nor would he have guessed that Kainene and Olanna were twins. Olanna took after their mother, although hers was a more approachable beauty with the softer face and the smiling graciousness and the fleshy, curvy body that filled out her black dress. A body Susan would call *African*. Kainene looked even thinner next to Olanna, almost androgynous, her tight maxi outlining the boyishness of her hips. Richard stared at her for a long time, willing her to search for him. She seemed aloof, watching the people in their group with a now indifferent, now mocking expression. Finally, she looked up and her eyes met his and she tilted her head and raised her eyebrows, as if she knew very well that he had been watching her. He averted his eyes. Then he looked back quickly, determined to smile this time, to make some useful gesture, but she had turned her back to him. He watched her until she left with her parents and Olanna.

Richard read the next issue of *Lagos Life*, and when he saw her photo, he searched her expression, looking for what he did not know. He wrote a few pages in a burst of manic productivity, fictional portraits of a tall, ebony-coloured woman with a near-flat chest. He went to the British Council Library and looked up her father in the business journals. He copied down all four of the numbers next to OZOBIA in the phone book. He picked up the phone many times and put it back when he heard the operator's voice. He practised what he would say in front of the mirror, the gestures he would make, although he was aware that she would not see him if they spoke over the phone. He considered sending her a card or perhaps a basket of fruit. Finally, he called. She didn't sound surprised to hear from him. Or perhaps it was just that she sounded too calm, while his heart hammered in his chest.

'Would you like to meet for a drink?' he asked.

'Yes. Shall we say Zobis Hotel at noon? It's my father's, and I can get us a private suite.'

'Yes, yes, that would be lovely.'

He hung up, shaken. He was not sure if he should be excited, if *private suite* was suggestive. When they met in the hotel lounge, she moved close so that he could kiss her cheek and then led the way upstairs, to the terrace, where they sat looking down at the palm trees by the swimming pool. It was a sunny, luminous day. Once in a while, a breeze swayed the palms, and he hoped it would not tousle his hair too much and that the umbrella above would keep away those unflattering ripe-tomato spots that appeared on his cheeks whenever he was out in the sun.

'You can see Heathgrove from here,' she said, pointing. 'The iniquitously expensive and secretive British secondary school my sister and I attended. My father thought we were too young to be sent abroad, but he was determined that we be as European as possible.'

'Is it the building with the tower?'

'Yes. The entire school is just two buildings, really. There were very few of us there. It is so exclusive, many Nigerians don't even know it exists.' She looked into her glass for a while. 'Do you have siblings?'

'No. I was an only child. My parents died when I was nine.'

'Nine. You were young.'

He was pleased that she didn't look too sympathetic, in the false way some people did, as if they had known his parents even though they hadn't.

'They were very often away. It was Molly, my nanny, who really raised me. After they died, it was decided I would live with my aunt in London.' Richard paused, pleased to feel the strangely inchoate intimacy that came with talking about himself, something he rarely did. 'My cousins Martin and Virginia were about my age but terribly sophisticated; Aunt Elizabeth was quite grand, you see, and I was the cousin from the tiny village in Shropshire. I started thinking about running away the first day I arrived there.'

'Did you?'

'Many times. They always found me. Sometimes just down the street.'

'What were you running to?'

'What?'

'What were you running to?'

Richard thought about it for a while. He knew he was running away from a house that had pictures of long-dead people on the walls breathing down on him. But he didn't know what he was running towards. Did children ever think about that?

'Maybe I was running to Molly. I don't know.'

'I knew what I wanted to run to. But it didn't exist, so I didn't leave,' Kainene said, leaning back on her seat.

'How so?'

She lit a cigarette, as if she had not heard his question. Her silences left him feeling helpless and eager to win back her attention. He wanted to tell her about the roped pot. He was not sure where he first read about Igbo-Ukwu art, about the native man who was digging a well and discovered the bronze castings that may well be the first in Africa, dating back to the ninth century. But it was in *Colonies Magazine* that he saw the photos. The roped pot stood out immediately; he ran a finger over the picture and ached to touch the delicately cast metal itself. He wanted to try explaining how deeply stirred he had been by the pot but decided not to. He would give it time. He felt strangely comforted by this thought because he realized that what he wanted most of all, with her, was time.

'Did you come to Nigeria to run away from something?' she asked finally.

'No,' he said. 'I've always been a loner and I've always wanted to see Africa, so I took leave from my humble newspaper job and a generous loan from my aunt and here I am.'

'I wouldn't have thought you to be a loner.'

'Why?'

'Because you're handsome. Beautiful people are not usually loners.' She said it flatly, as if it were not a compliment, and so he hoped she did not notice that he blushed.

'Well, I am,' he said; he could think of nothing else to say. 'I've always been.'

'A loner and a modern-day explorer of the Dark Continent,' she said dryly.

He laughed. The sound spilt out of him, uncontrolled, and he looked down at the clear, blue pool and thought, blithely, that perhaps that shade of blue was also the colour of hope.

They met the next day for lunch, and the day after. Each time, she led the way to the suite and they sat on the terrace and ate rice and drank cold beer. She touched her glass rim with the tip of her tongue before she sipped. It aroused him, that brief glimpse of pink tongue, more so because she didn't seem conscious of it. Her silences were brooding, insular, and yet he felt a connection to her. Perhaps it was *because* she was distant and withdrawn. He found himself talking in a way he usually didn't, and when their time ended and she got up, often to join her father at a meeting, he felt his feet thicken with curdled blood. He did not want to leave, could not bear the thought of going back to sit in Susan's study and type and wait for Susan's subdued knocks. He did not understand why Susan suspected nothing, why she could not simply look at him and tell how different he felt, why she did not even notice that he splashed on more aftershave now. He had not been unfaithful to her, of course, but fidelity could not just be about sex. His laughing with Kainene, telling Kainene about Aunt Elizabeth, watching Kainene smoke, surely had to be infidelities; they felt so. His quickened heartbeat when Kainene kissed him goodbye was an infidelity. Her hand clasped in his on the table was an infidelity. And so the day Kainene did not give him the usual goodbye kiss and instead pressed her mouth to his, lips parted, he was surprised. He had not permitted himself to hope for too much. Perhaps it was why an erection eluded him: the gelding mix of surprise and desire. They undressed quickly. His naked body was pressed to hers and yet he was limp. He explored the angles of her collarbones and her hips, all the time willing his body and his mind to work better together, willing his desire to bypass his anxiety. But he did not become hard. He could feel the flaccid weight between his legs.

She sat up in bed and lit a cigarette.

'I'm sorry,' he said, and when she shrugged and said nothing, he wished he had not apologized. There was something dismal in the luxurious overfurnished suite, as he pulled on trousers that might just as well have stayed on and she hooked her bra. He wished she would say something.

'Shall we meet tomorrow?' he asked.

She blew the smoke through her nose and, watching it disappear in the air, asked, 'This is crude, isn't it?'

'Shall we meet tomorrow?' he asked again.

'I'm going to Port Harcourt with my father to meet some oil people,' she said. 'But I'll be back after noon on Wednesday. We could have a late lunch.'

'Yes, let's,' Richard said, and until she met him in the hotel lobby, days later, he worried that she would not come. They had lunch and watched the swimmers below.

She was a little more animated, smoked more, spoke more. She told him about the people she had met since she began to work with her father, how they were all the same. 'The new Nigerian upper class is a collection of illiterates who read nothing and eat food they dislike at overpriced Lebanese restaurants and have social conversations around one subject: 'How's the new car behaving?'' Once, she laughed. Once, she held his hand. But she did not ask him into the suite and he wondered if she wanted to give it time or if she had decided that it was not the sort of relationship she wanted with him after all.

He could not bring himself to act. Days passed before she finally asked if he wanted to go inside, and he felt like an understudy who hoped the actor would not show up and then, when the actor finally did fail to come, became crippled by awkwardness, not quite as ready as he had thought he was for the stage lights. She led the way inside. When he began to pull her dress up above her thighs, she pushed him away calmly, as if she knew his frenzy was simply armour for his fear. She hung her dress over the chair. He was so terrified of failing her again that seeing himself erect made him deliriously grateful, so grateful that he was only just inside her before he felt that involuntary tremble that he could not stop. They lay there, he on top of her, for a while, and then he rolled off. He wanted to tell her that this had never happened to him before. His sex life with Susan was satisfactory, though perfunctory.

'I'm so sorry,' he said.

She lit a cigarette, watching him. 'Would you like to come to dinner tonight? My parents have invited a few people.'

For a moment, he was taken aback. Then he said, 'Yes, I'd love to.' He hoped the invitation meant something, reflected a change in her perception of the relationship. But when he arrived at her parents' house in Ikoyi, she introduced him by saying, 'This is Richard Churchill,' and then stopped with a pause that felt like a deliberate dare to her parents and the other guests to think what they would. Her father looked him over and asked what he did.

'I'm a writer,' he said.

'A writer? I see,' Chief Ozobia said.

Richard wished he hadn't said he was a writer and so he added, as if to make up for saying he was a writer, 'I'm fascinated by the discoveries at Igbo-Ukwu. The bronze castings.'

'Hmm,' Chief Ozobia murmured. 'Do you have any family doing business in Nigeria?'

'No, I'm afraid not.'

Chief Ozobia smiled and looked away. He didn't say very much else to Richard for the rest of the evening. Neither did Mrs Ozobia, who followed her husband around, her manner regal, her beauty more intimidating close up. Olanna was different. Her smile was guarded when Kainene introduced them, but as they talked, she became warmer and he wondered if the flicker in her eyes was pity, if she could tell how keen he was to say the right things and yet didn't know what those right things were. Her warmth flattered him.

He felt strangely bereft when she sat far from him at the table. The salad had just been served when she began to discuss politics with a guest. Richard knew it was about the need for Nigeria to become a republic and stop claiming Queen Elizabeth as head of state, but he did not pay close attention until she turned to him and asked, 'Don't you agree, Richard?' as if his opinion mattered.

He cleared his throat. 'Oh, absolutely,' he said, even though he wasn't sure what it was he was agreeing with. He felt grateful that she had pulled him into the conversation, included him, and he was charmed by that quality of hers that seemed both sophisticated and naive, an idealism that refused to be suffocated by gritty reality. Her skin glowed. Her cheekbones rose as she smiled. But she lacked Kainene's melancholy mystique, which exhilarated and confused him. Kainene sat next to him and said little throughout dinner, once sharply asking a steward to change a glass that looked cloudy, once leaning over to ask, 'The sauce is nauseating, isn't it?' She was mostly inscrutable, watching, drinking, smoking. He ached to know what she was thinking. He felt a similar physical pain when he desired her, and he would dream about being inside her, thrusting as deep as he could, to try and discover something that he knew he never would. It was like drinking glass after glass of water and still emerging thirsty, and with the stirring fear that he would never quench the thirst.

Richard worried about Susan. He would watch her, the firm chin and green eyes, and tell himself that it was unfair to deceive her, to skulk in the study until she fell asleep, to lie to her about being at the library or museum or polo club. She deserved better. But there was a reassuring stability to being with her, a certain safety in her whispering and her study room with the pencil sketches of Shakespeare on the walls. Kainene was different. He left Kainene full of a giddy happiness and an equally dizzying sense of insecurity. He wanted to ask her what she thought of the things they never discussed – their relationship, a future, Susan – but his uncertainties muted him each time; he was afraid of what her answers would be.

He pushed any decisions away until the morning he woke up and thought about that day in Wentnor, when he was out playing and heard Molly calling him. 'Richard! Supper!' Instead of answering 'Coming!' and running to her, he dodged under a hedge, scraping his knees. 'Richard! Richard!' Molly sounded frantic this time, but he remained silent, crouched. 'Richard! Where are you, Dicky?' A rabbit stopped and watched him, and he locked eyes with the rabbit and, for those short moments, only he and the rabbit knew where he was. Then the rabbit leapt out and Molly peered under the bushes and saw him. She smacked him. She told him to stay in his room for the rest of the day. She said she was very upset and would tell Mr and Mrs Churchill. But those short moments had made it all worthwhile, those moments of pure plenary abandon, when he felt as if he, and he alone, were in control of the universe of his childhood. Recalling them, he decided he would end it with Susan. His relationship with Kainene might well not last long, but the moments of being with her, knowing he was not weighed down by lies and pretense, would make the brevity worthwhile.

His resolve buoyed him. Still, he put off telling Susan for another week, until the evening they returned from a party where she had drunk too many glasses of wine.

'Would you like a nightcap, darling?' she asked.

'Susan, I care very much about you,' he said in a rush. 'But I'm not quite sure that things are going very well – that is, things between us.'

'What are you saying?' Susan asked, although her hushed tone and blenched face told him that she knew very well what he was saying.

He ran his hand through his hair.

'Who is it?' Susan asked.

'It's not another woman. I just think our needs are different.' He hoped he did not sound insincere, but it was true; they had always wanted different things, always valued different things. He should never have moved in with her.

'It's not Clovis Bancroft, is it?' Her ears were red. They always turned red after she drank, but he was only noticing the strangeness of it now, the angry-red ears jutting out by her pale face.

'No, of course not.'

Susan poured herself a drink and sat on the arm of the sofa. They were silent for a while. 'I fancied you the minute I saw you and I didn't think I would, really. I thought how handsome and gentle he is, and I must have resolved there that I would never let you go.' She laughed quietly, and he noticed the tiny lines around her eyes.

'Susan – ' he said, and stopped, because there was nothing else to say. He hadn't known she thought these things of him. He realized how little they had talked, how their relationship had been like an artless flow with little input from them, or at least from him. The relationship had *happened* to him.

'It was all too rushed for you, wasn't it?' Susan said. She came and stood by him. She had regained her composure; her chin no longer quivered. 'You didn't get a chance to explore, really, to see more of the country like you wanted to; you moved in here and I've made you go to these ghastly parties with people who don't much care about writing and African art and that sort of thing. It must have been so awful for you. I'm terribly sorry, Richard, and I do understand. Of course, you must see a bit of the country. Can I help? I have friends in Enugu and Kaduna.'

Richard took the glass from her, put it down, and took her in his arms. He felt a faint nostalgia at the familiar apple scent of her shampoo. 'No, I'll be all right,' he said.

She didn't think it was really over, it was clear; she thought he would come back and he said nothing to make her think differently. When the steward in the white apron opened the front door to let him out, Richard was light with relief.

'Bye, sah,' the steward said.

'Goodbye, Okon.' Richard wondered if the inscrutable Okon ever pressed his ear to the door when he and Susan had their glass-breaking rows. He once asked Okon to teach him some simple sentences in Efik, but Susan had stopped it after she found them both in the study, Okon fidgeting as Richard pronounced the words. Okon had looked at Susan with gratitude, as if she had just saved him from a mad white man, and later, Susan's tone was mild when she said she understood that Richard didn't know how things were done. One couldn't cross certain lines. It was a tone that reminded him of Aunt Elizabeth, of views endorsed with an unapologetic, self-indulgent English decency. Perhaps if he had told Susan about Kainene, she would have used that tone to tell him that she quite understood his need to experiment with a black woman.

Richard saw Okon waving as he drove away. He had the overwhelming urge to sing, except that he was not a singing man. All the other houses on Glover Street were like Susan's, expansive, hugged by palm trees and beds of languid grass.

The next afternoon, Richard sat up in bed naked, looking down at Kainene. He had just failed her again. 'I'm sorry. I think I get overexcited,' he said.

'May I have a cigarette?' she asked. The silky sheet outlined the angular thinness of her naked body.

He lit it for her. She sat up from under the cover, her dark-brown nipples tightening in the cold, air-conditioned room, and looked away as she exhaled. 'We'll give it time,' she said. 'And there are other ways.'

Richard felt a swift surge of irritation, towards himself for being uselessly limp, towards her for that half-mocking smile and for saying there were other ways, as if he was permanently incapable of doing things the traditional way. He knew what he could do. He knew he could satisfy her. He just needed time. He had begun, though, to think about some herbs, potent manhood herbs he remembered reading about somewhere, which African men took.

'Nsukka is a little patch of dust in the middle of the bush, the cheapest land they could get to build the university on,' Kainene said. It was startling, how easily she slipped into mundane conversation. 'But it should be perfect for your writing, shouldn't it?'

'Yes,' he said.

'You might like it and want to stay on.'

'I might.' Richard slid under the covers. 'But I'm so pleased you'll be in Port Harcourt and I won't have to come all the way to Lagos to see you.'

Kainene said nothing, smoking with steady intakes, and for one terrified moment, he wondered if she was going to tell him that it was over when they both left Lagos and that, in Port Harcourt, she would find herself a man capable of *performing*.

'My house will be perfect for our weekends,' she said finally.

'It's monstrous. My father gave it to me last year as a bit of dowry, I think, an enticement for the right sort of man to marry his unattractive daughter. Terribly European when you think of it, since we don't have dowries, we have bride prices.' She put the cigarette out. She had not finished it. 'Olanna said she didn't want a house. Not that she needs one. Save the houses for the ugly daughter.'

'Don't say that, Kainene.'

'Don't say that, Kainene,' Kainene mimicked him. She got up and he wanted to pull her back. But he didn't; he could not trust his body and could not bear to disappoint her yet again. Sometimes he felt as if he knew nothing about her, as if he would never quite reach her. And yet, other times, lying next to her, he would feel a wholeness, a certainty that he would never need anything else.

'By the way, I've asked Olanna to introduce you to her revolutionary lecturer lover,' Kainene said. She pulled her wig off and, with her short hair worn in cornrows, her face looked younger, smaller. 'She used to date a Hausa prince, a pleasant, bland sort of fellow, but he did not have any of the crazed delusions she has. This Odenigbo imagines himself to be quite the freedom fighter. He's a mathematician but he spends all his time writing newspaper articles about his own brand of mishmash African socialism. Olanna adores that. They don't seem to realize how much of a joke socialism really is.' She put the wig back on and began to brush it; the wavy hair, parted in the middle, fell to her chin. Richard liked the clean lines of her thin body, the sleekness of her raised arm.

'Socialism could very well work in Nigeria if done right, I think,' he said. 'It's really about economic justice, isn't it?'

Kainene snorted. 'Socialism would never work for the Igbo.' She held the brush suspended in mid-air. 'Ogbenyealu is a common name for girls and you know what it means? "Not to Be Married by a Poor Man." To stamp that on a child at birth is capitalism at its best.'

Richard laughed, and he was even more amused because she did not laugh; she simply went back to brushing her hair. He thought about the next time he would laugh with her and then the next. He found himself often thinking about the future, even before the present was over.

He got up and felt shy when she glanced at his naked body. Perhaps she was expressionless only to hide her disgust. He pulled on his underwear and buttoned his shirt hurriedly.

'I've left Susan,' he blurted out. 'I'm staying at the Princewill

Guesthouse in Ikeja. I'll pick up the rest of my things from her house before I leave for Nsukka.'

Kainene stared at him, and he saw surprise on her face and then something else he was not sure of. Was it puzzlement?

'It's never been a proper relationship, really,' he said. He did not want her to think he had done it because of her, did not want her asking herself questions about their relationship. Not yet.

'You'll need a houseboy,' she said.

'What?'

'A houseboy in Nsukka. You'll need somebody to wash your clothes and clean your house.'

He was momentarily confused by the non sequitur. 'A houseboy? I can manage quite well. I've lived alone for too long.'

'I'll ask Olanna to find somebody,' Kainene said. She pulled a cigarette from the case, but she didn't light it. She put it down on the bedside table and came over and hugged him, a tremulous tightening of her arms around him. He was so surprised he did not hug her back. She had never embraced him that closely unless they were in bed. She did not seem to know what to make of the hug either, because she backed away from him quickly and lit the cigarette. He thought about that hug often, and each time he did he had the sensation of a wall crumbling.

Richard left for Nsukka a week later. He drove at moderate speed, pulling off the road once in a while to look at the hand-drawn map Kainene had given him. After he crossed the River Niger, he decided to stop at Igbo-Ukwu. Now that he was finally in Igbo land, he wanted to see the home of the roped pot before anything else. A few cement houses dotted the village; they marred the picturesque quality of the mud huts that were crowded on either side of dirt paths, paths so narrow he parked his car a long way away and followed a young man in khaki shorts who seemed used to showing visitors around. His name was Emeka Anozie. He had been one of the labourers who worked at the dig. He showed Richard the wide, rectangular ditches where the excavations had taken place, the shovels and pans that had been used to brush the dust off the bronzes.

'You want to talk to our big father? I will interpret for you,' Emeka offered.

'Thank you.' Richard felt slightly overwhelmed by the warm reception, by the neighbours who trailed in and said, 'Good afternoon, *nno*, welcome,' as if they did not even think about minding that he had come uninvited.

Pa Anozie had a dirty-looking cloth wound round his body and tied behind his neck. He led the way into his dim *obi*, which smelt of mushrooms. Although Richard had read about how the bronzes were found, he asked the question anyway. Pa Anozie nudged a pinch of snuff up his nostrils before he began telling the story. About twenty years ago, his brother was digging a well when he hit something metallic that turned out to be a gourd. He soon found a few others and brought them out, washed them, and called the neighbours to come in and see them. They looked well crafted and vaguely familiar, but nobody knew of anyone making anything like them. Soon, word got to the district commissioner in Enugu, who sent somebody to take them to the Department of Antiquities in Lagos. After that, nobody came or asked anything else about the bronzes for a while, and his brother built his well and life went on. Then, a few years ago, the white man from Ibadan came to excavate. There were long talks before the work began, because of a goat house and compound wall that would have to be removed, but the work went well. It was harmattan, but because they feared the thunderstorms, they covered the ditches with tarpaulins spread across bamboo sticks. They found such lovely things: calabashes, shells, many ornaments that women used to decorate themselves, snake images, pots.

'They also found a burial chamber, didn't they?' Richard asked.

'Yes.'

'Do you think it was used by the king?'

Pa Anozie gave Richard a long, pained look and mumbled something for a while, looking grieved. Emeka laughed before he translated. 'Papa said he thought you were among the white people who know something. He said the people of Igboland do not know what a king is. We have priests and elders. The burial place was maybe for a priest. But the priest does not suffer people like king. It is because the white man gave us warrant chiefs that foolish men are calling themselves kings today.'

Richard apologized. He did know that the Igbo were said to have been a republican tribe for thousands of years, but one of the articles about the Igbo-Ukwu findings had suggested that perhaps they once had kings and later deposed them. The Igbo were, after all, a people who deposed gods that had outlived their usefulness. Richard sat there for a while, imagining the lives of people who were capable of such beauty, such complexity, in the time of Alfred the Great. He wanted to write about this, to create something from this, but he did not know what. Perhaps a speculative novel where the main character is an archaeologist digging for bronzes who is then transported to an idyllic past?

He thanked Pa Anozie and got up to leave. Pa Anozie said something and Emeka asked, 'Papa is asking will you not take photo of him? All the white people that have come take photo.'

Richard shook his head. 'No, sorry. I haven't brought a camera.'

Emeka laughed. 'Papa is asking what kind of white man is this? Why did he come here and what is he doing?'

As he drove towards Nsukka, Richard, too, wondered just what he was doing and, more worrying, what he was going to write.

The university house on Imoke Street was reserved for visiting researchers and artists; it was sparse, near ascetic, and Richard looked over the two armchairs in the living room, the single bed, the bare kitchen cupboards, and felt instantly at home. The house was filled with a suitable silence. When he visited Olanna and Odenigbo, though, she said, 'I'm sure you must want to make the place a little more habitable,' so he said, 'Yes,' although he liked the soulless furnishing. He agreed only because Olanna's smile was like a prize, because her attention flattered him. She insisted that he hire their gardener, Jomo, to come in twice a week and plant some flowers in the yard. She introduced him to their friends; she showed him the market; she said she had found him the perfect houseboy.

Richard envisaged somebody young and alert like their houseboy, Ugwu, but Harrison turned out to be a small, stooped stick of a man, middle-aged, wearing an oversized white shirt that stopped below his knees. He bowed extravagantly at the beginning of each conversation. He told Richard with unconcealed pride that he had formerly worked for the Irish priest Father Bernard and the American professor Land. 'I am making very good beet salad,' he said that first day, and later Richard realized that he was proud not only of his salad but also of cooking with beets, which he had to buy in the 'specialty vegetable' stall because most Nigerians did not eat them. The first dinner Harrison cooked was a savoury fish, with the beet salad as a starter. A crimson beet stew appeared next to his rice the following evening. 'It is from an American recipe for potato stew that I am making this one,' Harrison said, as he watched Richard eat. The next day, there was a beet salad, and the next another beet stew, now frighteningly red, next to the chicken.

'No more, please, Harrison,' Richard said, raising his hand. 'No more beets.'

Harrison looked disappointed, and then his face brightened. 'But, sah, I am cooking the food of your country; all the food you are eating as children I cook. In fact, I'm not cooking Nigerian foods, only foreign recipe.'

'Nigerian food is quite all right, Harrison,' Richard said. If only Harrison knew how much he had disliked the food of his childhood, the sharp-tasting kippers full of bones, the porridge with the appalling thick skin on top like a waterproof lining, the overcooked roast beef with fat around the edges drenched in gravy.

'Okay, sah.' Harrison looked morose.

'By the way, Harrison, do you happen to know of any herbs for men?' Richard asked, hoping he sounded casual.

'Sah?'

'Herbs.' Richard gestured vaguely.

'Vegetables, sah? Oh, I make any of the salad of your country very good, sah. For Professor Land, I am making many different-different salad.'

'Yes, but I mean vegetables for sickness.'

'Sickness? You see doctor in Medical Centre.'

'I am interested in African herbs, Harrison.'

'But sah, they are bad, from the witch doctor. They are devilish.'

'Of course.' Richard gave up. He should have known that Harrison, with his excessive love for all things non-Nigerian, was not the right person to ask. He would ask Jomo instead.

Richard waited until Jomo arrived and then stood at the window watching him water the newly planted lilies. Jomo placed the watering can aside and began to pick the umbrella tree fruit; they had fallen during the previous night and lay, oval and pale yellow, on the lawn. Richard often smelt the over-sweetness of their rotting, a scent he knew he would always associate with living in Nsukka. Jomo held a raffia bag full of fruit when Richard came up to him.

'Oh. Good morning, Mr Richard, sah,' he said, in his solemn

manner. 'I want take the fruit to Harrison in case you want, sah. I no take them for myself.' Jomo placed the bag down and picked up his watering can.

'It's all right, Jomo. I don't want any of the fruit,' Richard said. 'By the way, would you know of any herbs for men? For men who have problems with . . . with being with a woman?'

'Yes, sah.' Jomo kept watering as if this was a question he heard every day.

'You know of some herbs for men?'

'Yes, sah.'

Richard felt a triumphant leap in his stomach. 'I should like to see them, Jomo.'

'My brother get problem before because the first wife is not pregnant and the second wife is not pregnant. There is one leaf that the *dibia* give him and he begin to chew. Now he has pregnant the wives.'

'Oh. Very good. Could you get me this herb, Jomo?'

Jomo stopped and looked at him, his wise, wizened face full of fond pity. 'It no work for white man, sah.'

'Oh, no. I want to write about it.'

Jomo shook his head. 'You go to *dibia* and you chew it there in front of him. Not for writing, sah.' Jomo turned back to his watering, humming tunelessly.

'I see,' Richard said, and as he went back indoors he made sure not to let his dejection show; he walked straight and reminded himself that he was, after all, the master.

Harrison was standing outside the front door, pretending to polish the glass. 'Is there something that Jomo is not doing well, sah?' he asked hopefully.

'I was just asking Jomo some questions.'

Harrison looked disappointed. It was clear from the beginning that he and Jomo would not get along, the cook and the gardener, each thinking himself better than the other. Once, Richard heard Harrison tell Jomo not to water the plants outside the study window because 'the sound of water is disturbing Sah writing.' Harrison wanted Richard to hear it, too, the way he spoke loudly, standing just outside the study window. Harrison's obsequiousness amused Richard, as did Harrison's reverence for his writing; Harrison had taken to dusting the typewriter every day, even though it was never dusty, and was reluctant to throw away manuscript pages he saw in the dustbin. 'You are not using this again, sah? You are sure?' Harrison would ask, holding the crumpled pages, and Richard would say that, yes, he was sure. Sometimes he wondered what Harrison would say if he told him that he wasn't even sure what he was writing about, that he had written a sketch about an archaeologist and then discarded it, written a love story between an Englishman and an African woman and discarded it, and had started writing about life in a small Nigerian town. Most of his material for his latest effort came from the evenings he spent with Odenigbo and Olanna and their friends. They were casually accepting of him, did not pay him any particular attention, and perhaps because of that, he felt comfortable sitting on a sofa in the living room and listening.

When Olanna first introduced him to Odenigbo, saying, 'This is Kainene's friend that I told you about, Richard Churchill,' Odenigbo shook his hand warmly and said, "'I have not become the king's first minister in order to preside over the liquidation of the British Empire.'"

It took Richard a moment to understand before he laughed at the poor imitation of Sir Winston Churchill. Later, he watched Odenigbo wave around a copy of the *Daily Times*, shouting, 'It is *now* that we have to begin to decolonize our education! Not tomorrow, now! Teach them our history!' and thought to himself that here was a man who trusted the eccentricity that was his personality, a man who was not particularly attractive but who would draw the most attention in a room full of attractive men. Richard watched Olanna as well, and each time he glanced at her he felt renewed, as if she had become more beautiful in the preceding minutes. He felt an unpleasant emotion, though, seeing Odenigbo's hand placed on her shoulder and, later, imagining them together in bed. He and Olanna said little to each other, outside of the general conversation, but a day before he left to visit Kainene in Port Harcourt, Olanna said, 'Richard, please greet Kainene.'

'I will,' he said; it was the first time she had mentioned Kainene.

Kainene picked him up at the train station in her Peugeot 404 and drove away from the centre of Port Harcourt towards the ocean, to an isolated three-storey house with verandas wreathed in creeping bougainvillea of the palest shade of violet. Richard smelt the saltiness of the air as Kainene led him through wide rooms with taste-fully mismatched furniture, wood carvings, muted paintings of land-scapes, rounded sculptures. The polished floors had a woody scent.

'I did wish it was closer to the sea, so we could have a better view. But I changed Daddy's décor and it's not too *nouveau riche*, I pray?' Kainene asked.

Richard laughed. Not just because she was mocking Susan – he had told her what Susan had said about Chief Ozobia – but because she had said *we*. *We* meant both of them; she had included him. When she introduced him to her stewards, three men in ill-fitting khaki uniforms, she told them, with that wry smile of hers, 'You will be seeing Mr Richard often.'

'Welcome, sah,' they said in unison, and they stood almost at atten-tion as Kainene pointed to each and said his name: Ikejide, Nnanna, and Sebastian.

'Ikejide is the only one with half a brain in his head,' Kainene said.

The three men smiled, as though they each thought differently but would of course say nothing.

'Now, Richard, I'll give you a tour of the grounds.' Kainene gave a mocking bow and led the way out through the back door to the orange orchard.

'Olanna asked me to say hello to you,' Richard said, taking her hand.

'So her revolutionary lover has admitted you into the fold. We should be grateful. It used to be that he allowed only black lecturers in his house.'

'Yes, he told me. He said that Nsukka was full of people from USAID and the Peace Corps and Michigan State University, and he wanted a forum for the few Nigerian lecturers.'

'And their nationalist passion.'

'I suppose so. He *is* refreshingly different.'

'Refreshingly different,' Kainene repeated. She stopped to flatten something on the ground with the sole of her sandals. 'You like them, don't you? Olanna and Odenigbo.'

He wanted to look into her eyes, to try and discern what she wanted him to say. He wanted to say what she wanted to hear. 'Yes, I like them,' he said. Her hand was lax in his and he worried that she would slip it away. 'They've made it much easier for me to get used to Nsukka,' he added, as if to justify his liking them. 'I've settled in quite quickly. And of course there's Harrison.'

'Of course, Harrison. And how is the Beet Man doing?'

Richard pulled her to him, relieved that she was not annoyed. 'He's well. He is a good man, really, very amusing.'

They were in the orchard now, in the dense interweaving of orange trees, and Richard felt a strangeness overcome him. Kainene was speaking, something about one of her employees, but he felt himself receding, his mind unfurling, rolling back on its own. The orange trees, the presence of so many trees around him, the hum of flies overhead, the abundance of green, brought back memories of his parents' house in Wentnor. It was incongruous that this tropical, humid place, with the sun turning the skin of his arms a mild scarlet and the bees sunning themselves, should remind him of the crumbling house in England, which was draughty even in summer. He saw the tall poplars and willows behind the house, in the fields where he stalked badgers, the rumpled hills covered in heather and bracken that spread for miles and miles, dotted with grazing sheep. *Blue remembered hills.* He saw his father and his mother sitting with him up in his bedroom, which smelt of damp, while his father read them poetry.

> *Into my heart on air that kills*
> *From yon far country blows:*
> *What are those blue remembered hills,*
> *What spires, what farms are those?*
>
> *That is the land of lost content*
> *I see it shining plain,*
> *The happy highways where I went*
> *And cannot come again.*

His father's voice would always deepen at the phrase *blue remembered hills*, and when they left his room, and for the weeks afterwards when they would be away, he would look out of his window and watch the far-off hills take on a blue tinge.

Richard was bewildered by Kainene's busy life. Seeing her in Lagos, in brief meetings at the hotel, he had not realized that hers was a life that ran fully and would run fully even if he was not in it. It was strangely disturbing to think that he was not the only occupant of her world, but stranger still was how her routines were already in place, after only a few weeks in Port Harcourt. Her work came first; she was determined to make her father's factories grow, to do better than he had done. In the evenings, visitors – company people negotiating deals, government people negotiating bribes, factory people negotiating jobs – dropped by, parking their cars near the entrance to the orchard. Kainene always made sure they didn't stay long, and she didn't ask him to meet them because she said they would bore him, so he stayed upstairs reading or scribbling until they left. Often, he would try to keep his mind from worrying about failing Kainene that night; his body was still so unreliable and he had discovered that thinking about failure made it more likely to happen.

It was during his third visit to Port Harcourt that the steward knocked on the bedroom door to announce, 'Major Madu came, madam,' and Kainene asked if Richard would please come down with her.

'Madu is an old friend and I'd like you to meet him. He's just come back from an army training course in Pakistan,' she said.

Richard smelt the guest's cologne from the hallway, a cloying, brawny scent. The man wearing it was striking in a way that Richard immediately thought was primordial: a wide, mahogany-coloured face, wide lips, a wide nose. When he stood to shake hands, Richard nearly stepped back. The man was huge. Richard was used to being the tallest man in a room, the one who was looked up to, but here was a man who was at least three inches taller than he was, and with a width to his shoulders and a firm bulk to his body that made him seem taller, *hulking*.

'Richard, this is Major Madu Madu,' Kainene said.

'Hello,' Major Madu said. 'Kainene has told me about you.'

'Hello,' Richard said. It was too intimate, to hear this mammoth man with the slightly condescending smile on his face say Kainene's name like that, as if he knew Kainene very well, as if he knew something that Richard did not know, as if whatever Kainene had told him about Richard had been whispered in his ear, amid the silly giggles born of physical intimacy. And what sort of name was Madu Madu anyway? Richard sat on a sofa and refused Kainene's offer of a drink. He felt pale. He wished Kainene had said, *This is my lover, Richard.*

'So you and Kainene met in Lagos?' Major Madu asked.

'Yes,' Richard said.

'She first told me about you when I called her from Pakistan about a month ago.'

Richard could not think of what to say. He did not know Kainene had talked to him from Pakistan and did not remember her ever mentioning a friendship with an army officer whose first name and surname were the same. 'And how long have you known each other?' Richard asked, and immediately wondered if he sounded suspicious.

'My family's compound in Umunnachi is right next to the Ozobias'.' Major Madu turned to Kainene. 'Aren't our forefathers said to be related? Only that your people stole our land and we cast you out?'

'It was your people who stole the land,' Kainene said, and laughed. Richard was surprised to hear the husky tone of her laughter. He was even more surprised at how familiarly Major Madu behaved, the way he sank into the sofa, got up to flip the album in the stereo, joked with the stewards serving dinner. Richard felt left out of things. He wished Kainene had told him that Major Madu would be staying for dinner. He wished she would drink gin and tonic like him rather than whisky with water like Major Madu. He wished the man would not keep asking him questions, as if to engage him, as if the man were the host and Richard the visitor. How are you enjoying Nigeria? Isn't the rice delicious? How is your book going? Do you like Nsukka?

Richard resented the questions and the man's perfect table manners.

'I trained at Sandhurst', Major Madu said, 'and what I hated most was the cold. Not least because they made us run every morning in the bloody cold with only a thin shirt and shorts on.'

'I can see why you'd find it cold,' Richard said.

'Oh, yes. To each his own. I'm sure you'll soon get very homesick here,' he said.

'I don't think so at all,' Richard said.

'Well, the British have just decided to control immigration from the Commonwealth, haven't they? They want people to stay in their own countries. The irony, of course, is that we in the Commonwealth can't control the British moving to *our* countries.'

He chewed his rice slowly and examined the bottle of water for a moment, as if it were wine whose vintage he wanted to know.

'Right after I came back from England, I was part of the Fourth Battalion that went to the Congo, under the United Nations. Our battalion wasn't well run at all, but despite that, I preferred Congo to the relative safety of England. Just because of the weather.' Major Madu paused. 'We weren't run well at all in the Congo. We were under the command of a British colonel.' He glanced at Richard and continued to chew.

Richard bristled; his fingers felt stiff and he feared his fork would slip from his grasp and this insufferable man would know how he felt.

The doorbell rang just after dinner while they sat on the moonlit veranda, drinking, listening to High Life music.

'That must be Udodi, I told him to meet me here,' Major Madu said.

Richard slapped at an irritating mosquito near his ear. Kainene's house seemed to have become a meeting place for the man and his friends.

Udodi was a smallish, ordinary-looking man with nothing of the knowing charm or subtle arrogance of Major Madu. He seemed drunk, almost manic, in the way he shook Richard's hand, pumping up and down. 'Are you Kainene's business associate? Are you in oil?' he asked.

'I didn't do the introductions, did I?' Kainene said. 'Richard, Major Udodi Ekechi is a friend of Madu's. Udodi, this is Richard Churchill.'

'Oh,' Major Udodi said, his eyes narrowing. He poured some whisky into a glass, drank it in one gulp, and said something in Igbo to which Kainene replied, in cold, clear English, 'My choice of lovers is none of your business, Udodi.'

Richard wished he could open his mouth and fluidly tell the man off, but he said nothing. He felt helplessly weak, the kind of weakness that came with illness, with grief. The music had stopped and he could hear the far-off whooshing of the sea's waves.

'Sorry, oh! I did not say it was my business!' Major Udodi laughed and reached again for the bottle of whisky.

'Easy now,' Major Madu said. 'You must have started early at the mess.'

'Life is short, my brother!' Major Udodi said, pouring another drink. He turned to Kainene. '*I magonu*, you know, what I am saying is that our women who follow white men are a certain type, a poor family and the kind of bodies that white men like.' He stopped and continued, in a mocking mimicry of an English accent, 'Fantastically desirable bottoms.' He laughed. 'The white men will poke and poke and poke the women in the dark but they will never marry them. How can! They will never even take them out to a good place in public. But the women will continue to disgrace themselves and struggle for the men so they will get chicken-feed money and nonsense tea in a fancy tin. It's a new slavery, I'm telling you, a new slavery. But you are a Big Man's daughter, so what you are doing with him?'

Major Madu stood up. 'Sorry about this, Kainene. The man isn't himself.' He pulled Major Udodi up and said something in swift Igbo.

Major Udodi was laughing again. 'Okay, okay, but let me take the whisky. The bottle is almost empty. Let me take the whisky.'

Kainene said nothing as Major Udodi took the bottle from the table. After they left, Richard sat next to her and took her hand. He felt as if he had disappeared, as if that was the reason Major Madu did not include him in the apology. 'He was dreadful. I'm sorry he did that.'

'He was hopelessly drunk. Madu must feel terrible right now,' Kainene said. She gestured to the file on the table and added, 'I've just got the contract to supply army boots for the battalion in Kaduna.'

'That's nice.' Richard drank the last drop from his glass and watched as Kainene looked through the file.

'The man in charge was Igbo, and Madu said he was keen to give the contract to a fellow Igbo. So I was lucky. And he's asking only for a five per cent cut.'

'A bribe?'

'Oh, aren't we innocent.'

Her mockery irritated him, as did the speed with which she had absolved Major Madu of any responsibility for Major Udodi's boorish behaviour. He stood up and began to pace the veranda. Insects were humming around the fluorescent bulb.

'You've known Madu for very long then,' he said finally. He hated calling the man by his first name; it assumed a cordiality he did not feel. But then he had no choice. He would certainly not call him Major; using a title would be too elevating.

Kainene looked up. 'Forever. His family and ours are very close. I remember once, years ago, when we went to Umunnachi to spend Christmas, he gave me a tortoise. The strangest and best present I ever got from anybody. Olanna thought it was wrong of Madu to take the poor thing out of its natural habitat and whatnot, but she didn't much get along with Madu anyway. I put it in a bowl, and of course it died soon afterwards.' She went back to looking through the file.

'He's married, isn't he?'

'Yes. Adaobi is doing her bachelor's in London.'

'Is that why you're seeing him so often?' His question came out in a near-croak, as though he needed to clear his throat.

She did not respond. Perhaps she had not heard him. It was clear that the file, the new contract, occupied her mind. She got up. 'I'll just make some notes for a minute in the study and join you.'

He wondered why he could simply not ask if she found Madu attractive and if she had ever been involved with him or, worse yet, was still involved with him. He was afraid. He moved towards her and put his arms around her and held her tightly, wanting to feel the beat of her heart. It was the first time in his life he felt as if he could belong somewhere.

1. The Book: The World Was Silent When We Died

For the prologue, he recounts the story of the woman with the calabash. She sat on the floor of a train squashed between crying people, shouting people, praying people. She was silent, caressing the covered calabash on her lap in a gentle rhythm until they crossed the Niger, and then she lifted the lid and asked Olanna and others close by to look inside.

Olanna tells him this story and he notes the details. She tells him how the bloodstains on the woman's wrapper blended into the fabric to form a rusty mauve. She describes the carved designs on the woman's calabash, slanting lines crisscrossing each other, and she describes the child's head inside: scruffy plaits falling across the dark-brown face, eyes completely white, eerily open, a mouth in a small surprised O.

After he writes this, he mentions the German women who fled Hamburg with the charred bodies of their children stuffed in suitcases, the Rwandan women who pocketed tiny parts of their mauled babies. But he is careful not to draw parallels. For the book cover, though, he draws a map of Nigeria and traces in the Y shape of the rivers Niger and Benue in bright red. He uses the same shade of red to circle the boundaries of where, in the Southeast, Biafra existed for three years.

4

Ugwu cleared the dining table slowly. He removed the glasses first, then the stew-smeared bowls and the cutlery, and finally he stacked plate on top of plate. Even if he hadn't peeked through the kitchen door as they ate, he would still know who had sat where. Master's plate was always the most rice-strewn, as if he ate distractedly so that the grains eluded his fork. Olanna's glass had crescent-shaped lipstick marks. Okeoma ate everything with a spoon, his fork and knife pushed aside. Professor Ezeka had brought his own beer, and the foreign-looking brown bottle was beside his plate. Miss Adebayo left onion slices in her bowl. And Mr Richard never chewed his chicken bones.

In the kitchen, Ugwu kept Olanna's plate aside on the Formica counter and emptied the rest, watching rice, stew, greens, and bones slide into the dustbin. Some of the bones were so well cracked they looked like wood shavings. Olanna's did not, though, because she had only lightly chewed the ends and all three still had their shape. Ugwu sat down and selected one and closed his eyes as he sucked it, imagining Olanna's mouth enclosing the same bone.

He sucked languidly, one bone after another, and did not bother to tone down the slurpy sounds his mouth made. He was alone. Master had just left for the staff club with Olanna and their friends. The house was always quietest now, when he could linger over nothing, with the lunch dishes in the sink and dinner far off and the kitchen bathed in incandescent sunlight. Olanna called this his Schoolwork Time, and when she was home, she would ask him to take his homework into the bedroom. She didn't know that his homework never took long, that he would sit by the window afterwards and struggle through difficult sentences in one of Master's books, looking up often to watch the butterflies dipping and rising above the white flowers in the front yard.

He picked up his exercise book while sucking the second bone. The cold marrow was tart on his tongue. He read the verse, which he had copied so carefully from the blackboard that it looked like Mrs Oguike's handwriting, and then closed his eyes and recited it.

> *I can't forget that I'm bereft*
> *Of all the pleasant sights they see,*
> *Which the Piper also promised me.*
> *For he led us, he said, to a joyous land,*
> *Joining the town and just at hand,*
> *Where waters gushed and fruit trees grew,*
> *And flowers put forth a fairer hue,*
> *And everything was strange and new.*

He opened his eyes and scanned the verse to make sure he had missed nothing. He hoped Master would not remember to ask him to recite it because, although he had memorized the verse correctly, he would have no answer when Master asked, What does it *mean*? Or, What do you *think* it is really saying? The pictures in the book Mrs Oguike gave out, of the long-haired man with happy rats following him, were incomprehensible, and the more Ugwu looked at them, the more certain he became that it was all some sort of senseless joke. Even Mrs Oguike did not seem to know what it meant. Ugwu had come to like her – Mrs Oguike – because she did not treat him with special concern, did not seem to notice that he sat alone in the classroom at break time. But she had noticed how fast he learnt the very first day when she gave him oral and written tests while Master waited outside the airless room. 'The boy will surely skip a class at some point, he has such an innate intelligence,' she had told Master afterwards, as if Ugwu were not standing right beside them, and *innate intelligence* instantly became Ugwu's favourite expression.

He closed the exercise book. He had sucked all the bones, and he imagined that the taste of Olanna's mouth was in his as he started to wash the dishes. The first time he sucked her bones, weeks ago, it was after he saw her and Master kissing in the living room on a Saturday morning, their open mouths pressed together. The thought of her saliva in Master's mouth had both repelled and excited him. It still did. It was the same way he felt about her moaning at night; he did not like to hear her and yet he often went to their door to press his ear against the cold wood and listen. Just as he examined the underwear she hung in the bathroom – black slips, slippery bras, white pants.

She had blended so easily into the house. In the evenings, when guests filled the living room, her voice stood out in its clear perfection, and he fantasized about sticking out his tongue at Miss Adebayo and saying, 'You cannot speak English like my madam, so shut your dirty mouth.' It seemed as if her clothes had always been in the wardrobe, her High Life music always come from the radiogram, her coconut scent always wafted over every room, and her Impala always parked in the driveway. Still, he missed the old days with Master. He missed the evenings when he would sit on the floor of the living room while Master talked in his deep voice and the mornings when he served Master's breakfast, knowing that the only voices that could be heard were theirs.

Master had changed; he looked at Olanna too often, touched her too much, and when Ugwu opened the front door for him, his eyes expectantly darted past into the living room to see if Olanna was there. Only yesterday, Master told Ugwu, 'My mother will be visiting this weekend, so clean the guest room.' Before Ugwu could say Yes, sah, Olanna said, 'I think Ugwu should move to the Boys' Quarters. That way we'll have a free guest room. Mama may stay a while.'

'Yes, of course,' Master said, so promptly that it annoyed Ugwu; it was as if Master would stick his head in a raging fire if Olanna asked him to. It was as if she had become the master. But Ugwu didn't mind moving to the room in the Boys' Quarters, which was empty except for some cobwebs and cartons. He could hide things he had saved there; he could make it fully his. He had never heard Master speak about his mother, and, as he cleaned the guest room later, he imagined what she would be like, this woman who had bathed Master as a baby, fed him, wiped his running nose. Ugwu was in awe of her already, for having produced Master.

He finished the lunch dishes quickly. If he was as quick in preparing the greens for the dinner pottage, he could go down to Mr Richard's house and talk to Harrison for a little while before Master and Olanna came back. These days, he shredded the greens with his hands instead of slicing them. Olanna liked them that way; she said they retained more of their vitamins. He, too, had started to like them, just as he liked the way she taught him to fry eggs with a little milk, to cut fried plantains in dainty circles rather than ungainly ovals, to steam *moi-moi* in aluminium cups rather than banana leaves. Now that she left most of the cooking to him, he liked to look through the kitchen door from time to time, to see who murmured the most compliments, who liked what, who took second helpings. Dr Patel liked the chicken boiled with *uziza*. So did Mr Richard, although he never ate the chicken skin. Perhaps the pale chicken skin reminded Mr Richard of his own skin. There was no other reason Ugwu could think of; the skin was, after all, the tastiest part. Mr Richard always said, 'Fantastic chicken, Ugwu, thank you,' when Ugwu came out to bring more water or to clear something away. Sometimes, while the other guests retired to the living room, Mr Richard would come into the kitchen to ask Ugwu questions. They were laughable questions. Did his people have carvings or sculptures of gods? Had he ever been inside the shrine by the river? Ugwu was even more amused that Mr Richard wrote his answers down in a small book with a leather cover. Some days ago, when Ugwu offhand-edly mentioned the *ori-okpa* festival, Mr Richard's eyes turned a brighter blue and he said he wanted to see the festival; he would ask Master if he and Ugwu could drive to his hometown.

Ugwu laughed as he brought the greens out of the refrigerator. He could not imagine Mr Richard during the *ori-okpa* festival, where the *mmuo* (Mr Richard said they were masquerades, weren't they, and Ugwu agreed, as long as masquerades meant spirits) paraded the village, flogged young men, and chased after young women. The *mmuo* themselves might even laugh at the sight of a pale stranger scribbling in a notebook. But he was pleased that he had mentioned the festival to Mr Richard, because it meant an opportunity to see Nnesinachi before she left for the North. To think how impressed she would be when he arrived in a white man's car, driven by the white man himself! She would certainly notice him this time, he was sure, and he could not wait to impress Anulika and his cousins and relatives with his English, his new shirt, his knowledge of sandwiches and running tap water, his scented powder.

Ugwu had just washed the shredded greens when he heard the doorbell. It was too early for Master's friends. He went to the door, wiping his hands on his apron. For a moment, he wondered if his aunty was really standing there or if he was seeing an image of her only because he had been thinking about home.

'Aunty?'

'Ugwuanyi', she said, 'you have to come home. *Oga gi kwanu?* Where is your master?'

'Come home?'

'Your mother is very sick.'

Ugwu examined the scarf tied round his aunty's head. He could see where it was threadbare, the fabric stretched thin. He remembered that when his cousin's father died, the family had sent word to her in Lagos, telling her to come home because her father was very sick. If you were far from home, they told you the dead person was very sick.

'Your mother is sick,' his aunty repeated. 'She is asking for you. I will tell Master that you will be back tomorrow, so he will not think we are asking for too much. Many houseboys do not even get to go home in years, you know that.'

Ugwu did not move, rolling the edge of the apron around his finger. He wanted to ask his aunt to tell him the truth, to say so if his mother was dead. But his mouth would not form the words. Remembering his mother's last illness, when she had coughed and coughed until his father left before dawn to get the *dibia* while the junior wife, Chioke, rubbed her back, frightened him.

'Master is not in,' he said finally. 'But he will be back soon.'

'I will wait and plead with him to let you come home.'

He led the way to the kitchen, where his aunty sat down and watched him slice a yam and then cut the slices into cubes. He worked fast, feverishly. The sunlight that came in through the window seemed too bright for late afternoon, too full of an ominous radiance.

'Is my father well?' Ugwu asked.

'He is well.' His aunty's face was opaque, her tone flat: the demeanour of a person who carried more bad news than she had delivered. She must be hiding something. Perhaps his mother really was dead; perhaps both his parents had fallen down dead that morning. Ugwu continued to slice, in a turgid silence, until Master came home, tennis whites plastered to his back with sweat. He was alone. Ugwu wished that Olanna had come home as well so that he could look at her face as he spoke.

'Welcome, sah.'

'Yes, my good man.' Master placed his racket down on the kitchen table. 'Some water, please. I lost all my games today.'

Ugwu had the water ready, ice cold in a glass placed on a saucer.

'Good evening, sah,' his aunty greeted.

'Good evening,' Master said, looking slightly perplexed, as if he was not certain who she was. 'Oh, yes. How are you?'

Before she could say more, Ugwu said, 'My mother is sick, sah. Please, sah, if I go to see her I will return tomorrow.'

'What?'

Ugwu repeated himself. Master stared at him and then at the pot on the stove. 'Have you finished cooking?'

'No, sah. I will finish fast-fast, before I go. I will set the table and arrange everything.'

Master turned to Ugwu's aunty. '*Gini me?* What is wrong with his mother?'

'Sah?'

'Are you deaf?' Master jabbed at his ear as if Ugwu's aunty did not know what it meant to be deaf. 'What is wrong with his mother?'

'Sah, her chest is on fire.'

'Chest on fire?' Master snorted. He drank all his water and then turned to Ugwu and spoke English. 'Put on a shirt and get in the car. Your village isn't far away, really. We should be back in good time.'

'Sah?'

'Put on a shirt and get in the car!' Master scribbled a note on the back of a flyer and left it on the table. 'We'll bring your mother here and have Patel take a look at her.'

'Yes, sah.' Ugwu felt breakable as he walked to the car, beside his aunty and Master. He felt as though his bones were broomsticks, the kind that snapped easily during the harmattan. The ride to his village was mostly silent. As they drove past some farms with rows and rows of corn and cassava like a neatly plaited hairstyle, Master said, 'See? This is what our government should focus on. If we learn irrigation technology, we can feed this country easily. We can overcome this colonial dependence on imports.'

'Yes, sah.'

'But instead, all the ignoramuses in government do is lie and steal. A number of my students joined the group that went to Lagos this morning to demonstrate, you know.'

'Yes, sah,' Ugwu said. 'Why are they demonstrating, sah?'

'The census,' Master said. 'The census was a mess, everybody forged figures. Not that Balewa will do anything about it, because he is as complicit as they all are. But we must speak out!'

'Yes, sah,' Ugwu replied, and in the midst of his worry about his mother, he felt a twinge of pride because he knew his aunty would have her eyes wide in wonder at the deep conversations he had with Master. And in English, too. They stopped a little way before the family hut.

'Get your mother's things, quickly,' Master said. 'I have friends visiting from Ibadan tonight.'

'Yes, sah!' Ugwu and his aunty spoke at the same time.

Ugwu climbed out of the car and stood there. His aunty dashed into the hut, and soon his father came out, eyes red-rimmed, looking more stooped than Ugwu remembered. He knelt in the dirt and clutched Master's legs. 'Thank, sah. Thank, sah. May another person do for you.'

Master stepped back and Ugwu watched his father sway, almost falling over backwards. 'Get up, *kunie*,' Master said.

Chioke came out of the hut. 'This is my other wife, sah,' his father said, standing up.

Chioke shook Master's hands with both of hers. 'Thank you, master. *Deje!*' She ran back inside and emerged with a small pineapple that she pressed into Master's hand.

'No, no,' Master said, pushing the pineapple back. 'Local pineapples are too acidic, they burn my mouth.'

The village children were gathering around the car to peer inside and run awed fingers over the blue body. Ugwu shooed them away. He wished Anulika were home, so she would go with him into their mother's hut. He wished Nnesinachi would drop by now and take his hand in hers and tell him soothingly that his mother's illness was not serious at all, and then lead him to the grove by the stream and untie her wrapper and offer him her breasts, lifting them up and forward towards him. The children were chattering loudly. Some women stood by and spoke in lower tones, their arms folded. His father kept asking Master to have some kola nut, palm wine, a stool to sit down, some water, and Master kept saying no, no, no. Ugwu wanted his father to shut up. He moved closer to the hut and looked in. His eyes met his mother's in the dim light. She looked shrivelled.

'Ugwu,' she said. '*Nno*, welcome.'

'*Deje*,' he greeted, and then remained silent, watching, while his aunty helped her tie her wrapper around her waist and led her out.

Ugwu was about to help his mother into the car when Master said, 'Step aside, my good man.' Master helped her into the car, asked her to lie down on the backseat, to stretch out as much as she could.

Ugwu suddenly wished that Master would not touch his mother because her clothes smelled of age and must, and because Master did not know that her back ached and her cocoyam patch always yielded a poor harvest and her chest was indeed on fire when she coughed. What did Master know about anything anyway, since all he did was shout with his friends and drink brandy at night?

'Stay well, we will send you word after a doctor has looked at her,' Master said to Ugwu's father and aunty before they drove off.

Ugwu kept himself from glancing back at his mother; he rolled his window down so the air would rush loudly past his ears and distract him. When he finally turned to look at her, just before they got to the campus, his heart stopped at the sight of her shut eyes, her lax lips. But her chest was rising and falling. She was breathing. He exhaled slowly and thought about those cold evenings when she would cough and cough, and he would stand pressed to the flinty walls of her hut, listening to his father and Chioke ask her to drink the mixture.

Olanna opened the door, wearing the apron that had an oil stain in front. His apron. She kissed Master. 'I've asked Patel to come,' she said and then turned to Ugwu's mother. 'Mama. *Kedu?*'

'I am well,' his mother whispered. She glanced around the room and seemed to shrink even more at the sight of the sofas, the radiogram, the curtains.

'I'll take her inside,' Olanna said. 'Ugwu, please finish in the kitchen and set the table.'

'Yes, mah.'

In the kitchen, Ugwu stirred the pot of pepper soup. The oily broth swirled, the hot spices wafted up and tickled his nose, and the pieces of meat and tripe floated from side to side. But he did not really notice. He was straining to hear something. It was long, too long, since Olanna had taken his mother in and Dr Patel went in to join them. The peppers made his eyes water. He remembered that last time when she was sick from the coughing, how she cried out that she could no longer feel her legs and the *dibia* asked her to tell the evil spirits to leave her alone. 'Tell them it is not yet your time! *Gwa ha kita!* Tell them now!' the *dibia* had urged her.

'Ugwu!' Master called. The guests had arrived. Ugwu went into the living room and his hands worked mechanically, serving kola nuts and alligator pepper, uncorking bottles, shovelling ice, laying out steaming bowls of pepper soup. Afterwards, he sat down in the kitchen and pulled at his toenails and imagined what was going on in the bedroom. He could hear Master's raised voice from the living room. 'Nobody is saying that burning government property is a good thing, but to send the army in to kill in the name of order? There are Tiv people lying dead for nothing. For nothing! Balewa has lost his mind!'

Ugwu did not know who the Tiv people were, but hearing the word *dead* made him shiver. 'It is not yet your time,' he whispered. 'Not yet your time.'

'Ugwu?' Olanna was at the kitchen door.

He flew off the stool. 'Mah? Mah?'

'You mustn't worry about her. Dr Patel says it's an infection and she will be fine.'

'Oh!' Ugwu was so relieved he feared he would float away if he raised one leg. 'Thank, mah!'

'Put the rest of the pottage in the fridge.'

'Yes, mah.' Ugwu watched her go back to the living room. The embroidery on her close-fitting dress gleamed and she looked, for a moment, like a shapely spirit who had emerged from the sea.

The guests were laughing now. Ugwu peeked into the living room. Many of them were no longer sitting upright but sloped on their seats, mellowed by alcohol, languorous with ideas. The evening was ending. The conversation would soften into tennis and music; then they would get up and giggle loudly at things that were not funny, such as the front door being difficult to open and the night bats flying too low. He waited for Olanna to go to the bathroom and Master to his study before he went in to see his mother, asleep, curled childlike on the bed.

She was bright-eyed the next morning. 'I am well,' she said. 'The medicine that doctor gave me is very powerful. But what will kill me is that smell.'

'What smell?'

'In their mouth. I smelt it when your madam and master came in to see me this morning and also when I went to ease myself.'

'Oh. That is toothpaste. We use it to clean our teeth.' Ugwu felt proud saying *we*, so that his mother would know that he too used it.

But she did not look impressed. She snapped her fingers and picked up her chewing stick. 'What is wrong with using a good *atu*? That smell has made me want to vomit. If I stay here much longer I will not be able to keep food in my stomach because of that smell.'

She looked impressed, though, when Ugwu told her that he would be living in the Boys' Quarters. It was like being given his own house, separate, all to himself. She asked him to show her the Boys' Quarters, marvelled that it was bigger than her hut, and, later, insisted that she was well enough to help in the kitchen. He watched her, bent over to sweep the floor, and remembered how she used to smack Anulika's bottom for not bending properly to sweep. 'Did you eat mushrooms? Sweep like a woman!' she would say, and Anulika would grumble that the broom was too short and it was not her fault that people were too stingy to buy longer brooms. Ugwu suddenly wished that Anulika were here, as well as the little children and the gossiping wives of his *umunna*. He wished his whole village were here, so he could join in the moonlight conversations and quarrels and yet live in Master's house with its running taps and refrigerator and stove.

'I will go home tomorrow,' his mother said.

'You should stay a few more days and rest.'

'I will go tomorrow. I shall thank your master and mistress when they return and tell them I am well enough to go home. May another person do for them what they have done for me.'

Ugwu walked with her to the end of Odim Street in the morning. He had never seen her walk so fast, even with the twined bundle balanced on her head, never seen her face so free of lines.

'Stay well, my son,' she said, and thrust a chewing stick into his hand.

On the day Master's mother arrived from the village, Ugwu cooked a peppery *jollof* rice. He mixed white rice into tomato sauce, tasted it, and then covered it and reduced the heat. He went back outside. Jomo had leaned his rake against the wall and was sitting on the steps eating a mango.

'That thing you are cooking smells very good,' Jomo said.

'It is for my master's mother, *jollof* rice with fried chicken.'

'I should have given you some of my meat. It will be better than the chicken.' Jomo gestured to the bag tied behind his bicycle. He had shown Ugwu the small furry animal wrapped in fresh leaves.

'I cannot cook bush meat here!' Ugwu said in English, laughing.

Jomo turned to look at him. '*Dianyi*, you now speak English just like the children of the lecturers.'

Ugwu nodded, happy to hear the compliment, happier because Jomo would never guess that those children with their cream-pampered skin and their effortless English sniggered whenever Mrs Oguike asked him a question because of how he pronounced his words, how thick his bush accent was.

'Harrison should come and hear good English from somebody who does not brag about it,' Jomo said. 'He thinks he knows everything just because he lives with a white man. *Onye nzuzu!* Stupid man!'

'Very stupid man!' Ugwu said. He had been just as vigorous last weekend when he agreed with Harrison that Jomo was foolish.

'Yesterday the he-goat locked the tank and refused to give me the key,' Jomo said. 'He said I am wasting water. Is it his water? Now if the plants die, what do I tell Mr Richard?'

'That is bad.' Ugwu snapped his fingers to show just how bad. The last quarrel between the two men was when Harrison hid the lawn mower and refused to tell Jomo where it was until Jomo rewashed Mr Richard's shirt, which had been splattered with bird droppings. It was Jomo's useless flowers, after all, that attracted the birds. Ugwu had supported both men. He told Jomo that Harrison was wrong to have hidden the lawn mower, and later he told Harrison that Jomo was wrong to have planted the flowers there in the first place, knowing they attracted birds. Ugwu preferred Jomo's solemn ways and false stories, but Harrison, with his insistent bad English, was mysteriously full of knowledge of things that were foreign and different. Ugwu wanted to learn these things, so he nurtured his friendship with both men; he had become their sponge, absorbing much and giving little away.

'One day I will wound Harrison seriously, *maka Chukwu*,' Jomo said. He threw away the mango seed, sucked so clean of the orange pulp that it was white. 'Somebody is knocking on the front door.'

'Oh. She has come! It must be my master's mother.' Ugwu dashed inside; he barely heard Jomo say goodbye.

Master's mother had the same stocky build, dark skin, and vibrant energy as her son; it was as if she would never need help with carrying her water pot or lowering a stack of firewood from her head. Ugwu was surprised to see the young woman with downcast eyes standing beside her, holding bags. He had expected that she would come alone. He had hoped she would come a little later, too, when the rice was done.

'Welcome, Mama, *nno*,' he said. He took the bags from the young woman. 'Welcome, Aunty, *nno*.'

'You are the one that is Ugwu? How are you?' Master's mother said, patting his shoulder.

'Fine, Mama. Did your journey go well?'

'Yes. *Chukwu du anyi*. God led us.' She was looking at the radiogram. Her green george wrapper hung stiff on her waist and made her hips look square-shaped. She did not wear it with the air of the women on campus, the women who were used to owning coral beads and gold earrings. She wore it in the way that Ugwu imagined his mother would if she had the same wrapper: uncertainly, as if she did not believe that she was no longer poor.

'How are you, Ugwu?' she asked again.

'I am well, Mama.'

'My son has told me how well you are doing.' She reached out to adjust her green headgear, worn low on her head, almost covering her eyebrows.

'Yes, Mama.' Ugwu looked down modestly.

'God bless you, your *chi* will break away the rocks on your path. Do you hear me?' She sounded like Master, that sonorous and authoritative tone.

'Yes, Mama.'

'When will my son be back?'

'They will return in the evening. They said you should rest, Mama, when you come. I am cooking rice and chicken.'

'Rest?' She smiled and walked into the kitchen. Ugwu watched her unpack foodstuffs from a bag: dried fish and cocoyams and spices and bitter leaf. 'Have I not come from the farm?' she asked. 'This is my rest. I have brought ingredients to make a proper soup for my son. I know you try, but you are only a boy. What does a boy know about real cooking?' She smirked and turned to the younger woman, who was standing by the door, arms folded and eyes still downcast, as if waiting for orders. 'Is that not so, Amala? Does a boy belong in the kitchen?'

'*Kpa*, Mama, no,' Amala said. She had a high-pitched voice.

'You see, Ugwu? A boy does not belong in the kitchen.' Master's mother sounded triumphant. She was standing by the counter, already breaking up some dried fish, extracting the needlelike bones.

'Yes, Mama.' Ugwu was surprised that she had not asked for a glass of water or gone inside to change first. He sat on the stool and waited for her to tell him what to do. It was what she wanted; he could sense that. She was looking over the kitchen now. She peered suspiciously at the stove, knocked on the pressure cooker, tapped the pots with her fingers.

'Eh! My son wastes money on these expensive things,' she said. 'Do you not see, Amala?'

'Yes, Mama,' Amala said.

'Those belong to my madam, Mama. She brought many things from Lagos,' Ugwu said. It irritated him: her assuming that everything belonged to Master, her taking command of his kitchen, her ignoring his perfect *jollof* rice and chicken.

Master's mother did not respond. 'Amala, come and prepare the cocoyams,' she said.

'Yes, Mama.' Amala put the cocoyams in a pot and then looked helplessly at the stove.

'Ugwu, light the fire for her. We are village people who only know firewood!' Master's mother said, with a short laugh.

Neither Ugwu nor Amala laughed. Ugwu turned the stove on. Master's mother threw a piece of dried fish into her mouth. 'Put some water to boil for me, Ugwu, and then cut these *ugu* leaves for the soup.'

'Yes, Mama.'

'Is there a sharp knife in this house?'

'Yes, Mama.'

'Use it and slice the *ugu* well.'

'Yes, Mama.'

Ugwu settled down with a cutting board. He knew she was watching him. When he started to slice the fibrous pumpkin leaves, she yelped, 'Oh! Oh! Is this how you cut *ugu*? *Alu melu!* Make them smaller! The way you are doing it, we might as well cook the soup with the whole leaves.'

'Yes, Mama.' Ugwu began slicing the leaves in strips so thin they would break up in the soup.

'That's better,' Master's mother said. 'You see why boys have no business in the kitchen? You cannot even slice *ugu* well.'

Ugwu wanted to say, Of course I slice *ugu* well. I do many things in the kitchen better than you do, but instead he said, 'My madam and I don't slice vegetables, we shred them with our hands because the nutrients come out better that way.'

'Your madam?' Master's mother paused. It was as if she wanted to say something but held herself back. The steam from boiling hung in the air. 'Show Amala the mortar so she can pound the cocoyams,' she said finally.

'Yes, Mama.' Ugwu rolled out the wood mortar from under the table and was rinsing it when Olanna came home. She appeared at the kitchen door; her dress was smart-fitting, her smiling face was full of light.

'Mama!' she said. 'Welcome, *nno*. I am Olanna. Did you go well?' She reached out to hug Master's mother. Her arms went round to enclose the older woman but Master's mother kept her hands to her sides and did not hug Olanna back.

'Yes, our journey went well,' she said.

'Good afternoon,' Amala said.

'Welcome.' Olanna hugged Amala briefly before turning to Master's mother. 'Is this Odenigbo's relative from home, Mama?'

'Amala helps me in the house,' Master's mother said. She had turned her back to Olanna and was stirring the soup.

'Mama, come, let's sit down. *Bia nodu ana*. You should not bother in the kitchen. You should rest. Let Ugwu do it.'

'I want to cook a proper soup for my son.'

There was a light pause before Olanna said, 'Of course, Mama.' Her Igbo had slipped into the dialect that Ugwu heard in Master's speech when his cousins visited. She walked around the kitchen, as if eager to do something to please Master's mother but uncertain what to do. She opened the pot of rice and closed it. 'At least let me help you, Mama. I'll go and change.'

'I hear you did not suck your mother's breasts,' Master's mother said.

Olanna stopped. 'What?'

'They say you did not suck your mother's breasts.' Master's mother turned to look at Olanna. 'Please go back and tell those who sent you that you did not find my son. Tell your fellow witches that you did not see him.'

Olanna stared at her. Master's mother's voice rose, as if Olanna's continued silence had driven her to shouting. 'Did you hear me? Tell them that nobody's medicine will work on my son. He will not marry an abnormal woman, unless you kill me first. Only over my dead body!' Master's mother clapped her hands, then hooted and slapped her palm across her mouth so that the sound echoed.

'Mama – ' Olanna said.

'Don't mama me,' Master's mother said. 'I said, Do not mama me. Just leave my son alone. Tell your fellow witches that you did not find him!' She opened the back door and went outside and shouted. 'Neighbours! There is a witch in my son's house! Neighbours!' Her voice was shrill. Ugwu wanted to gag her, to stuff sliced vegetables into her mouth. The soup was burning.

'Mah? Will you stay in the room?' he asked, moving towards Olanna.

Olanna seemed to get hold of herself. She tucked a plait behind her ear, picked up her bag from the table, and headed for the front door. 'Tell your master I have gone to my flat,' she said.

Ugwu followed her and watched as she got into her car and drove out. She did not wave. The yard was still; there were no butterflies flitting among the white flowers. Back in the kitchen, Ugwu was surprised to hear Master's mother singing a gently melodious church song: *Nya nya oya mu ga-ana. Na m metu onu uwe ya aka. . . .*

She stopped singing and cleared her throat. 'Where has that woman gone?'

'I don't know, Mama,' Ugwu said. He walked over to the sink and began to put away the clean plates in the cupboard. He hated the too-strong aroma of her soup that filled the kitchen; the first thing he would do after she left was wash all the curtains because that smell would soak into them.

'This is why I came. They said she is controlling my son,' Master's mother said, stirring the soup. 'No wonder my son has not married while his mates are counting how many children they have. She has used her witchcraft to hold him. I heard her father came from a family of lazy beggars in Umunnachi until he got a job as a tax collector and stole from hard-working people. Now he has opened many businesses and is walking around in Lagos and answering a Big Man. Her mother is no better. What woman brings another person to breastfeed her own children when she herself is alive and well? Is that normal, *gbo*, Amala?'

'No, Mama.' Amala's eyes focused on the floor as if she were tracing patterns on it.

'I heard that all the time she was growing up, it was servants who wiped her *ike* when she finished shitting. And on top of it, her parents sent her to university. Why? Too much schooling ruins a woman; everyone knows that. It gives a woman a big head and she will start to insult her husband. What kind of wife will that be?' Master's mother raised one edge of her wrapper to wipe the sweat from her brow. 'These girls that go to university follow men around until their bodies are useless. Nobody knows if she can have children. Do you know? Does anyone know?'

'No, Mama,' Amala said.

'Does anyone know, Ugwu?'

Ugwu placed a plate down noisily and pretended as if he had not heard her. She came over and patted his shoulder.

'Don't worry, my son will find a good woman and he will not send you away after he marries.'

Perhaps agreeing with the woman would make her exhaust herself quicker and shut her mouth. 'Yes, Mama,' he said.

'I know how hard my son worked to get where he is. All that is not to be wasted on a loose woman.'

'No, Mama.'

'I do not mind where the woman my son will marry comes from. I am not like those mothers who want to find wives for their sons only from their own hamlet. But I do not want a *Wawa* woman, and none of those Imo or Aro women, of course; their dialects are so strange I wonder who told them that we are all the same Igbo people.'

'Yes, Mama.'

'I will not let this witch control him. She will not succeed. I will consult the *dibia* Nwafor Agbada when I return home; the man's medicine is famous in our parts.'

Ugwu stopped. He knew many stories of people who had used medicine from the *dibia:* the childless first wife who tied up the second wife's womb, the woman who made a neighbour's prosperous son go mad, the man who killed his brother because of a land quarrel. Perhaps Master's mother would tie up Olanna's womb or cripple her or, most frightening of all, kill her.

'I am coming, Mama. My master sent me to the kiosk,' Ugwu said, and hurried out through the back door before she said anything. He had to tell Master. He had been to Master's office only once, driven in Olanna's car when she stopped by to pick up something, but he was sure he could find it. It was near the zoo and his class had visited the zoo recently, walking in a single file led by Mrs Oguike, and he had brought up the rear because he was the tallest.

At the corner of Mbanefo Street, he saw Master's car coming towards him. It stopped.

'This isn't the way to the market, is it, my good man?' Master asked.

'No, sah. I was coming to your office.'

'Has my mother arrived?'

'Yes, sah. Sah, something happened.'

'What?'

Ugwu told Master about the afternoon, quickly recounting the words of both women, and finished with what was the most horrible of all: 'Mama said she will go to the *dibia*, sah.'

'What rubbish,' Master said. '*Ngwa*, get into the car. You might as well drive back home with me.'

Ugwu was shocked that Master was not shocked, did not understand the gravity of the situation, and so he added, 'It was very bad, sah. Very bad. Mama nearly slapped my madam.'

'What? She slapped Olanna?' Master asked.

'No, sah.' Ugwu paused; perhaps he had gone too far with the suggestion. 'But it looked as if she wanted to slap my madam.'

Master's face relaxed. 'The woman has never been very reasonable, at any rate,' he said, in English, shaking his head. 'Get in, let's go.'

But Ugwu did not want to get into the car. He wanted Master to turn around and go to Olanna's flat right away. His life was organized, secure, and Master's mother would have to be stopped from disrupting things; the first step was for Master to go and placate Olanna.

'Get into the car,' Master said again, reaching across the front seat to make sure the door was unlocked.

'But, sah. I thought you are going to see my madam.'

'Get in, you ignoramus!'

Ugwu opened the door and climbed in, and Master drove back to Odim Street.

5

Olanna looked at Odenigbo through the glass for a while before she opened the door. She closed her eyes as he walked in, as if doing so would deny her the pleasure that the scent of his Old Spice always brought. He was dressed for tennis in the white shorts she had often teased him were too tight around his buttocks.

'I was talking to my mother or I would have come earlier,' he said. He pressed his lips to hers and gestured to the old boubou she was wearing. 'Aren't you coming to the club?'

'I was cooking.'

'Ugwu told me what happened. I'm so sorry my mother acted that way.'

'I just had to leave . . . your house.' Olanna faltered. She had wanted to say *our house*.

'You didn't have to, *nkem*. You should have ignored her, really.' He placed a copy of *Drum* magazine down on the table and began pacing the room. 'I've decided to talk to Dr Okoro about the Labour Strike. It's unacceptable that Balewa and his cronies should completely reject their demands. Just unacceptable. We have to show support. We can't allow ourselves to become disconnected.'

'Your mother made a scene.'

'You're angry.' Odenigbo looked puzzled. He sat down in the armchair, and for the first time she noticed how much space there was between the furniture, how sparse her flat was, how unlived in. Her things were in his house; her favourite books were in the shelves in his study. '*Nkem*, I didn't know you'd take this so seriously. You can see that my mother doesn't know what she's doing. She's just a village woman. She's trying to make her way in a new world with skills that are better suited for the old one.' Odenigbo got up and moved closer to take her in his arms, but Olanna turned and walked into the kitchen.

'You never talk about your mother,' she said. 'You've never asked me to come to Abba with you to visit her.'

'Oh, stop it, *nkem*. It's not as if I go that often to see her, and I did ask you the last time but you were going to Lagos.'

She walked over to the stove and ran a sponge on the warm surface, over and over, her back to Odenigbo. She felt as if she had somehow failed him and herself by allowing his mother's behaviour to upset her. She should be above it; she should shrug it off as the ranting of a village woman; she should not keep thinking of all the retorts she could have made instead of just standing mutely in that kitchen. But she was upset, and made even more so by Odenigbo's expression, as if he could not believe she was not quite as high-minded as he had thought. He was making her feel small and absurdly petulant and, worse yet, she suspected he was right. She always suspected he was right. For a brief irrational moment, she wished she could walk away from him. Then she wished, more rationally, that she could love him without needing him. Need gave him power without his trying; need was the choicelessness she often felt around him.

'What did you cook?' Odenigbo asked.

'Rice.' She rinsed the sponge and put it away. 'Aren't you going to play tennis?'

'I thought you would come.'

'I don't feel up to it.' Olanna turned around. 'Why is your mother's behaviour acceptable because she's a village woman? I know village women who do not behave this way.'

'*Nkem*, my mother's entire life is in Abba. Do you know what a small bush village that is? Of course she will feel threatened by an educated woman living with her son. Of course you have to be a witch. That is the only way she can understand it. The real tragedy of our postcolonial world is not that the majority of people had no say in whether or not they wanted this new world; rather, it is that the majority have not been given the tools to *negotiate* this new world.'

'Did you talk to her about this?'

'I didn't see the point. Look, I want to catch Dr Okoro at the club. Let's discuss this when I get back. I'll stay here tonight.'

She paused as she washed her hands. She wanted him to ask her to come back with him to the house, wanted him to say he would tell his mother off in front of her, for her. But here he was deciding to stay at her flat, like a frightened little boy hiding from his mother.

'No,' she said.

'What?'

'I said no.' She walked into the living room without drying her hands. The flat seemed too small.

'What is wrong with you, Olanna?'

She shook her head. She would not let him make her feel that there was something wrong with *her*. It was her right to be upset, her right to choose not to brush her humiliation aside in the name of an overexalted intellectualism, and she would claim that right. 'Go.' She gestured towards the door. 'Go and play your tennis and don't come back here.'

She watched him get up and leave. He banged the door. They had never had a quarrel; he had never been impatient with dissent from her as he was with others. Or it may simply be that he humoured her and did not think much of her opinions in the first place. She felt dizzy. She sat alone at her bare dining table – even her table mats were in his house – and ate the rice. It tasted bland, nothing like Ugwu's. She turned the radio on. She thought she heard rustles in the ceiling. She got up to go visit her neighbour Edna Whaler; she had always wanted to get to know the pretty black American woman who sometimes brought her cloth-covered plates of American biscuits. But she changed her mind at the door and didn't step out. After she left the half-eaten rice in the kitchen, she walked around the flat, picking up old newspapers and then putting them down. Finally, she went to the phone and waited for the operator.

'Give me the number quick, I have other things to do,' the lazy, nasal voice said.

Olanna was used to unprofessional and inept operators, but this was the rudest she had experienced.

'*Haba*, I will cut this line if you keep wasting my time,' the operator said.

Olanna sighed and slowly recited Kainene's number.

Kainene sounded sleepy when she picked up the phone. 'Olanna? Did something happen?'

Olanna felt a rush of melancholy; her twin sister thought something had to have happened for her to call. 'Nothing happened. I just wanted to say *kedu*, to find out how you are.'

'How shocking.' Kainene yawned. 'How's Nsukka? How's your revolutionary lover?'

'Odenigbo is fine. Nsukka is fine.'

'Richard seems taken by it. He even seems taken by your revolutionary.'

'You should come and visit.'

'Richard and I prefer to meet here in Port Harcourt. That tiny box they gave him for a house is not exactly suitable.'

Olanna wanted to tell Kainene that she meant visit *her*, her and Odenigbo. But of course Kainene understood what she meant and had simply chosen to misunderstand.

'I'm going to London next month,' she said instead. 'Maybe we could go together.'

'I have too much to do here. No holiday for me yet.'

'Why don't we talk any more, Kainene?'

'What a question.' Kainene sounded amused and Olanna imagined that mocking smile pulling up one side of her mouth.

'I just want to know why we don't talk any more,' Olanna said. Kainene did not respond. A static whining came over the telephone line. They were silent for so long that Olanna felt she had to apologize. 'I shouldn't keep you,' she said.

'Are you coming to Daddy's dinner party next week?' Kainene asked.

'No.'

'I should have guessed. Too opulent for your abstemious revolutionary and yourself, I take it?'

'I shouldn't keep you,' Olanna repeated, and placed the phone down. She picked it up again, and was about to give the operator her mother's number before she dropped it back. She wished there was somebody she could lean against; then she wished she was different, the sort of person who did not need to lean on others, like Kainene. She pulled at the phone wire to untangle it. Her parents had insisted on installing a phone in her flat, as if they did not hear her say that she would practically be living with Odenigbo. She had protested, but only mildly, the same limp *no* with which she greeted the frequent deposits to her bank account and the new Impala with the soft upholstery.

Although she knew Mohammed was abroad, she gave the operator his number in Kano; the nasal voice said, 'You are phoning too much today!' before connecting her. She held on to the receiver long after there was no response. Rustling sounds came from the ceiling again. She sat on the cold floor and leaned her head against the wall to see if it would feel less light, less unmoored. Odenigbo's mother's visit had ripped a hole in her safe mesh of feathers, startled her, snatched something away from her. She felt one step away from where she should be. She felt as if she had left her pearls lying loose for too long and it was time to gather them and guard them more carefully. The thought came to her slowly: She wanted to have Odenigbo's child. They had never really discussed children. She once told him that she did not have that fabled female longing to give birth, and her mother had called her *abnormal* until Kainene said she didn't have it either. He laughed and said that to bring a child into this unjust world was an act of a blasé bourgeoisie anyway. She had never forgotten that expression: childbirth as an act of blasé bourgeoisie – how funny, how untrue it was. Just as she had never seriously thought of having a child until now; the longing in the lower part of her belly was sudden and searing and new. She wanted the solid weight of a child, his child, in her body.

When the doorbell rang that evening as she climbed out of the bathtub, she went to the door wrapped in a towel. Odenigbo was holding a newspaper-wrapped package of *suya;* she could smell the smoky spiciness from where she stood.

'Are you still angry?' he asked.

'Yes.'

'Get dressed and we'll go back together. I will talk to my mother.'

He smelt of brandy. He came inside and placed the *suya* on the table, and in his bloodshot eyes she glimpsed the vulnerability that hid itself so well underneath his voluble confidence. He could be afraid, after all. She rested her face against his neck as he hugged her and said to him, quietly, 'No, you don't have to do that. Stay here.'

After his mother left, Olanna went back to Odenigbo's house. Ugwu said, 'Sorry, mah,' as if he were somehow responsible for Mama's behaviour. Then he fiddled with his apron pocket and said, 'I saw a black cat yesterday night, after Mama and Amala left.'

'A black cat?'

'Yes, mah. Near the garage.' He paused. 'A black cat means evil.'

'I see.'

'Mama said she would go to the *dibia* in the village.'

'You think the *dibia* has sent the black cat to bite us?' Olanna was laughing.

'No, mah.' Ugwu folded his arms forlornly. 'It happened in my village, mah. A junior wife went to the *dibia* and got medicine to kill the senior wife, and the night before the senior wife died a black cat came to the front of her hut.'

'So Mama will use the *dibia*'s medicine and kill me?' Olanna asked.

'She wants to divide you and Master, mah.'

His solemnness touched her. 'I'm sure it was just the neighbour's cat, Ugwu,' she said. 'Your master's mother can't use any medicine to divide us. Nothing can divide us.'

She watched him go back to the kitchen, thinking of what she had said. *Nothing can divide us.* Of course Odenigbo's mother's medicine from the *dibia* – indeed, all supernatural fetishes – meant nothing to her, but she worried again about her future with Odenigbo. She wanted certainty. She longed for a sign, a rainbow, to signify security. Still she was relieved to ease back into her life, their life, of teaching and tennis and friends that filled the living room. Because they came in the late evenings, she was surprised to hear the doorbell ring one afternoon, a week later, when Odenigbo was still at a lecture. It was Richard.

'Hello,' she said, letting him in. He was very tall; she had to tilt her head to look at his face, to see his eyes that were the blue colour of a still sea and his hair that fell across his forehead.

'I just wanted to leave this for Odenigbo,' he said, handing Olanna a book. She loved the way he pronounced Odenigbo's name, stressing it so earnestly. He was avoiding her eyes.

'Won't you sit down?' she asked.

'I'm in a bit of a hurry, unfortunately. I have to catch the train.'

'Are you going to Port Harcourt to see Kainene?' Olanna wondered why she had asked. It was obvious enough.

'Yes. I go every weekend.'

'Say hello to her for me.'

'I will.'

'I talked to her last week.'

'Yes. She mentioned it.' Richard still stood there. He glanced at her and quickly looked away, and she saw the redness creep up his face.

She had seen that look too many times not to know that he found her beautiful.

'How is the book coming along?' she asked.

'Quite well. It's incredible, really, how well-crafted some of the ornaments are, and they were clearly intended to be art; it wasn't an accident at all. . . . I mustn't bore you.'

'No, you're not.' Olanna smiled. She liked his shyness. She didn't want him to leave just yet. 'Would you like Ugwu to bring you some *chin-chin*? They're fantastic; he made them this morning.'

'No, thank you. I should be on my way.' But he did not turn to leave. He pushed his hair away from his face only to have it fall back again.

'Okay. Well, have a safe trip.'

'Thank you.' He still stood there.

'Are you driving? No, you're not, I remember. You'll take the train.' She laughed an awkward laugh.

'Yes, I'm taking the train.'

'Have a safe trip.'

'Yes. All right then.'

Olanna watched him leave, and long after his car had reversed out of the compound, she stood at the door, watching a bird with a blood-red breast, perched on the lawn.

In the morning, Odenigbo woke her up by taking her finger in his mouth. She opened her eyes; she could see the smoky light of dawn through the curtains.

'If you won't marry me, *nkem*, then let's have a child,' he said.

Her finger muffled his voice, so she pulled her hand away and sat up to stare at him, his wide chest, his sleep-swollen eyes, to make sure she had heard him properly.

'Let's have a child,' he said again. 'A little girl just like you, and we will call her Obianuju because she will complete us.'

Olanna had wanted to give the scent of his mother's visit some time to diffuse before telling him she wanted to have a child, and yet here he was, voicing her own desire before she could. She looked at him in wonder. This was love: a string of coincidences that gathered significance and became miracles. 'Or a little boy,' she said finally.

Odenigbo pulled her down and they lay side by side, not touching.

She could hear the raspy *caw-caw-caw* of the blackbirds that ate the pawpaws in the garden.

'Let's have Ugwu bring us breakfast in bed,' he said. 'Or is this one of your Sundays of faith?' He was smiling his gently indulgent smile, and she reached out and traced his lower lip with the slight fuzz underneath. He liked to tease her about religion's not being a social service, because she went to church only for St Vincent de Paul meetings, when she took Ugwu with her for the drive through dirt paths in nearby villages to give away yams and rice and old clothes.

'I won't go today,' she said.

'Good. Because we have work to do.'

She closed her eyes because he was straddling her now and as he moved, languorously at first and then forcefully, he whispered, 'We will have a brilliant child, *nkem*, a brilliant child,' and she said, 'Yes, yes'. Afterwards, she felt happy knowing that some of the sweat on her body was his and some of the sweat on his body was hers. Each time, after he slipped out of her, she pressed her legs together, crossed them at her ankles, and took deep breaths, as if the movement of her lungs would urge conception on. But they did not conceive a child, she knew. The sudden thought that something might be wrong with her body wrapped itself around her, dampened her.

6

Richard ate the pepper soup slowly. After he had spooned up the pieces of tripe, he raised the glass bowl to his lips and drank the broth. His nose was running, there was a delicious burning on his tongue, and he knew his face was red.

'Richard eats this so easily,' Okeoma said, seated next to him, watching him.

'Ha! I didn't think our pepper was made for your type, Richard!' Odenigbo said, from the other end of the dining table.

'Even I can't take the pepper,' another guest said, a Ghanaian lecturer in economics whose name Richard always forgot.

'This is proof that Richard was an African in his past life,' Miss Adebayo said, before blowing her nose into a napkin.

The guests laughed. Richard laughed too, but not loudly, because there was still too much pepper in his mouth. He leaned back on his seat. 'It's fantastic,' he said. 'It clears one up.'

'The finger chops are lovely too, Richard,' Olanna said. 'Thank you so much for bringing them.' She was sitting next to Odenigbo, and she leaned forwards to smile at him.

'I know those are sausage rolls, but what are these things?' Odenigbo was poking at the tray Richard brought; Harrison had daintily wrapped everything in silver foil.

'Stuffed garden eggs, yes?' Olanna glanced at Richard.

'Yes. Harrison has all sorts of ideas. He took out the insides and filled them with cheese, I think, and spices.'

'You know the Europeans took out the insides of an African woman and then stuffed and exhibited her all over Europe?' Odenigbo asked.

'Odenigbo, we are eating!' Miss Adebayo said, although she was stifling laughter.

The other guests laughed. Odenigbo did not. 'It's the same principle at play,' he said. 'You stuff food, you stuff people. If you don't like
what is inside a particular food, then leave it alone, don't stuff it with
something else. A waste of garden eggs, in my opinion.'

Even Ugwu looked amused as he came into the dining room to
clear up. 'Mr Richard, sah? I put the food in container for you?'

'No, keep it or throw it away,' Richard said. He never took any leftover food back; what he took back to Harrison were the compliments
from the guests about how pretty everything was, but he did not add
that the guests then bypassed his canapés to eat Ugwu's pepper soup
and *moi-moi* and chicken boiled in bitter herbs.

Everyone was moving to the living room. Soon, Olanna would
turn off the light because the fluorescent glare was too bright, and
Ugwu would bring more drinks, and they would talk and laugh and
listen to music, and the light that spilt in from the corridor would fill
the room with shadows. It was his favourite part of their evenings,
although he sometimes wondered if Olanna and Odenigbo touched
each other in the dimness. He shouldn't think about them, he knew; it
was no business of his. But he did. He noticed the way Odenigbo
looked at her in the middle of an argument, not as if he needed her to
be on his side, because he didn't seem ever to need anybody, but simply to know that she was there. He saw, too, how Olanna sometimes
blinked at Odenigbo, communicating things he would never know.

Richard placed his glass of beer on a side table and sat next to Miss
Adebayo and Okeoma. His peppery tongue still tingled. Olanna got
up to change the music. 'My favourite Rex Lawson first, before some
Osadebe,' she said.

'He's a little derivative, isn't he, Rex Lawson?' Professor Ezeka
asked. 'Uwaifo and Dairo are better musicians.'

'All music is derivative, Prof,' Olanna said, her tone teasing.

'Rex Lawson is a true Nigerian. He does not cleave to his Kalabari
tribe; he sings in all our major languages. That's original – and
certainly reason enough to like him,' Miss Adebayo said.

'That's reason *not* to like him,' Odenigbo said. 'This nationalism
that means we should aspire to indifference about our own individual
cultures is stupid.'

'Don't waste your time asking Odenigbo about High Life. He's
never understood it,' Olanna said, laughing. 'He's a classical music
person but loath to admit it in public because it's such a Western
taste.'

'Music has no borders,' Professor Ezeka said.

'But surely it is grounded in culture, and cultures are specific?' Okeoma asked. 'Couldn't Odenigbo then be said to adore the Western culture that produced classical music?'

They all laughed, and Odenigbo looked at Olanna in that way that softened his eyes. Miss Adebayo launched into the French ambassador issue again. She did not think the French should have tested atomic weapons in Algeria, of course, but she did not understand why it mattered enough for Balewa to break off diplomatic relations with France. She sounded puzzled, which was unusual.

'It's quite clear Balewa did it because he wants to take away attention from his defence pact with the British,' Odenigbo said. 'And he knows that slighting the French will always please his masters the British. He's their stooge. They put him there, and they tell him what to do, and he does it, Westminster parliament model indeed.'

'No Westminster model today,' Dr Patel said. 'Okeoma promised to read us a poem.'

'I have told you that Balewa simply did it because he wants the North Africans to like him,' Professor Ezeka said.

'North Africans to like him? You think he cares much for other Africans? The white man is the only master Balewa knows,' Odenigbo said. 'Didn't he say that Africans are not ready to rule themselves in Rhodesia? If the British tell him to call himself a castrated monkey, he will.'

'Oh, rubbish,' Professor Ezeka said. 'You are digressing.'

'You refuse to see things as they truly are!' Odenigbo shifted on his seat. 'We are living in a time of great white evil. They are dehumanizing blacks in South Africa and Rhodesia, they fermented what happened in the Congo, they won't let American blacks vote, they won't let the Australian Aborigines vote, but the worst of all is what they are doing here. This defence pact is worse than apartheid and segregation, but we don't realize it. They are controlling us from behind drawn curtains. It is very dangerous!'

Okeoma leaned closer to Richard. 'These two won't let me read my poem today.'

'They're in fine fighting form,' Richard said.

'As usual.' Okeoma laughed. 'How is your book coming along, by the way?'

'I'm ploughing on.'

'Is it a novel about expatriates?'

'Well, no, not quite.'

'But it's a novel, isn't it?'

Richard sipped his beer and wondered what Okeoma would think if he knew the truth – that even he did not know whether it was a novel or not because the pages he had written did not make any coherent whole.

'I'm very interested in Igbo-Ukwu art, and I want to make that a central part of the book,' he said.

'How so?'

'I've been utterly fascinated by the bronzes since I first read about them. The details are stunning. It's quite incredible that these people had perfected the complicated art of lost-wax casting during the time of the Viking raids. There is such marvellous complexity in the bronzes, just marvellous.'

'You sound surprised,' Okeoma said.

'What?'

'You sound surprised, as if you never imagined *these people* capable of such things.'

Richard stared at Okeoma; there was a new and quiet disdain in the way Okeoma stared back, a slight furrow to his eyebrows before he said, 'Enough, Odenigbo and Prof! I have a poem calling to you all.'

Richard sucked his tongue. The peppery burning was unbearable now, and he hardly waited for Okeoma to finish reading a strange poem – about Africans getting buttocks rashes from defecating in imported metal buckets – before he got up to leave.

'It's still all right to drive Ugwu to his hometown next week, Odenigbo?' he asked.

Odenigbo glanced at Olanna.

'Yes, of course,' Olanna said. 'I hope you enjoy watching the *ori-okpa* festival.'

'Have another beer, Richard,' Odenigbo said.

'I'm off to Port Harcourt early in the morning, so I must get to sleep,' Richard said, but Odenigbo had already turned back to Professor Ezeka.

'What about the stupid politicians in the Western House of Assembly that the police had to use tear gas on? Tear gas! And their orderlies carried their limp bodies to their cars! Imagine that!'

The thought that Odenigbo would not miss him after he was gone left Richard dispirited. When he got home, Harrison opened the door and bowed. 'Good evening, sah. The food is going well, sah?'

'Yes, yes, now let me get to sleep,' Richard snapped. He was not in the mood for what he was certain would follow: Harrison would offer to teach any of his friends' houseboys who wanted to learn the majestic recipes for sherry trifle or stuffed garden eggs. He went to his study and spread his manuscript pages out on the floor and looked at them: a few pages of a small-town novel, one chapter of the archaeologist novel, a few pages of rapturous descriptions of the bronzes. He started to crumple them, page by page, until he had a jagged pile next to his dustbin, and then he got up and went to bed with the sensation of warm blood in his ears.

He didn't sleep well; he felt as if he had just laid his head on the pillow before the blinding sunlight streamed in through his curtains and he heard Harrison's clatter in the kitchen and Jomo's digging in the garden. He felt brittle. He could not wait to sleep properly, with Kainene's thin arm pressed against his body.

Harrison served fried eggs and toast for breakfast.

'Sah? There are papers I am seeing on the ground in the study?' He looked alarmed.

'Leave them there.'

'Yes, sah.' Harrison folded and refolded his arms. 'You are taking your manscrit? I pack other papers for you?'

'No, I won't be working this weekend,' Richard said. The disappointment on Harrison's face did not amuse him as it usually did. He wondered, as he boarded the train, what it was Harrison did during the weekends. Perhaps he cooked himself tiny exquisite meals. He shouldn't have been so ill-tempered with the poor man; it wasn't Harrison's fault that Okeoma felt he was condescending. It was the look in Okeoma's eyes that worried him the most: a disdainful distrust that made him think of reading somewhere that the African and the European would always be irreconcilable. It was wrong of Okeoma to assume that he was one of those Englishmen who did not give the African the benefit of an equal intelligence. Perhaps he had sounded surprised, now that he thought of it, but it was the same surprise he would express if a similar discovery were made in England or anywhere else in the world.

Hawkers were milling about. 'Buy groundnuts!' 'Buy oranges!' 'Buy plantains!'

Richard beckoned to a young woman carrying a tray of boiled

groundnuts that he didn't really want. She lowered her tray and he took one, cracked it between his fingers, and chewed the nuts inside before he asked for two cups. She looked surprised that he knew about tasting first, and he thought sourly that Okeoma, too, would have been surprised. Before he ate each nut, he examined it – soft-boiled, light purple, shrivelled – and tried not to think of the crumpled pages in his study, until the train arrived in Port Harcourt.

'Madu's invited us to dinner tomorrow,' Kainene said, as she drove him from the train station in her long American car. 'His wife has just come back from overseas.'

'Has she?' Richard said little else, and instead looked at the hawkers on the road, shouting, gesturing, running after cars to collect their money.

The sound of the rain slapping against the window woke him up the next morning. Kainene lay beside him, her eyes half open in that eerie way that meant she was deeply asleep. He looked at her dark chocolate skin, which shone with oil, and lowered his head to her face. He didn't kiss her, didn't let his face touch hers, but placed it close enough so that he could feel the moistness of her breath and smell its faint curdled scent. He stretched and went to the window. It rained in slants here in Port Harcourt so that the water hit the windows and walls rather than the roof. Perhaps it was because the ocean was so close, because the air was so heavy with water that it let it fall too soon. For a moment, the rain became intense and the sound against the window grew loud, like pebbles being flung against the glass. He stretched again. The rain had stopped and the windowpanes were cloudy. Behind him, Kainene stirred and mumbled something.

'Kainene?' he said.

Her eyes were still half open, her breathing still regular.

'I'm going for a walk,' he said, although he was sure she didn't hear him.

Outside, Ikejide was plucking oranges; his uniform bunched up at the back as he nudged fruit down with a stick.

'Good morning, sah,' he said.

'*Kedu?*' Richard asked. He felt comfortable practising his Igbo with Kainene's stewards, because they were always so expressionless that it did not matter whether or not he got the tones right.

'I am well, sah.'

'*Jisie ike.*'

'Yes, sah.'

Richard went to the bottom of the orchard, where he could see, through the thicket of trees, the white foam of the sea's waves. He sat on the ground. He wished that Major Madu had not invited them to dinner; he was not at all interested in meeting the man's wife. He got up and stretched and went around to the front yard and looked at the violet bougainvillea that crept up the walls. He walked for a while down the muddy stretch of deserted road that led to the house before he turned back. Kainene was in bed reading a newspaper. He climbed in beside her and she reached out and touched his hair, her fingers gently caressing his scalp. 'Are you all right? You've been tense since yesterday.'

Richard told her about Okeoma, and because she did not respond right away, he added, 'I remember the first time I read about Igbo-Ukwu art, in an article where an Oxford don described it as having a strange rococo, almost Fabergé-like virtuosity. I never forgot that – *rococo, almost Fabergé-like virtuosity.* I fell in love even with that expression.'

She folded the newspaper and placed it on the bedside cabinet. 'Why does it matter so much what Okeoma thinks?'

'I do love the art. It was horrible of him to accuse me of disrespect.'

'And it's wrong of you to think that love leaves room for nothing else. It's possible to love something and still condescend to it.'

Richard rolled away from her. 'I don't know what I'm doing. I don't even know if I'm a writer.'

'You won't know until you write, will you?' Kainene climbed out of bed, and he noticed a metallic sheen on her thin shoulders. 'I see you don't feel up to an evening out. I'll call Madu and cancel dinner.'

She came back after making the phone call and sat on the bed, and in the silence that separated them he suddenly felt grateful that her crispness gave him no space for self-pity, gave him nothing to hide behind.

'I once spat in my father's glass of water,' she said. 'He hadn't upset me or anything. I just did it. I was fourteen. I would have been incredibly satisfied if he drank it, but of course Olanna ran and changed the water.' She stretched out beside him. 'Now you tell me something horrible you did.'

He was aroused by her silky skin rubbing against his, by how readily she had changed the evening plans with Major Madu. 'I didn't have the confidence to do horrible things,' he said.

'Well, tell me something, then.'

He thought of telling her about that day in Wentnor when he hid from Molly and felt, for the first time, the possibility of shaping his own destiny. But he didn't. Instead, he told her about his parents, how they stared at each other when they talked, forgot his birthdays, and then had Molly make a cake that said HAPPY BELATED BIRTHDAY weeks after. They never knew what and when he ate; Molly fed him when she remembered. They had not planned to have him and, because of that, they had raised him as an afterthought. But he understood even as a young boy that it was not that they did not love him, rather it was that they often forgot that they did because they loved each other too much. Kainene raised her eyebrows, sardonic, as if his reasoning did not make sense to her, and because of that he was afraid to tell her that he sometimes thought he loved her too much.

2. The Book: The World Was Silent When We Died

He discusses the British soldier-merchant Taubman Goldie, how he coerced, cajoled, and killed to gain control of the palm-oil trade and how, at the Berlin Conference of 1884 where Europeans divided Africa, he ensured that Britain beat France to two protectorates around the River Niger: the North and the South.

The British preferred the North. The heat there was pleasantly dry; the Hausa-Fulani were narrow-featured and therefore superior to the negroid Southerners, Muslim and therefore as civilized as one could get for natives, feudal and therefore perfect for indirect rule. Equable emirs collected taxes for the British, and the British, in return, kept the Christian missionaries away.

The humid South, on the other hand, was full of mosquitoes and animists and disparate tribes. The Yoruba were the largest in the Southwest. In the Southeast, the Igbo lived in small republican communities. They were non-docile and worryingly ambitious. Since they did not have the good sense to have kings, the British created 'warrant chiefs', because indirect rule cost the Crown less. Missionaries were allowed in to tame the pagans, and the Christianity and education they brought flourished. In 1914, the governor-general joined the North and the South, and his wife picked a name. Nigeria was born.

PART TWO

The Late Sixties

7

Ugwu lay on a mat in his mother's hut, staring at a dead spider squashed on the wall; its body fluids had stained the mud a deeper red. Anulika was measuring out cups of *ukwa* and the crusty aroma of roasted breadfruit seeds hung thick in the room. She was talking. She had been talking for quite a while, and Ugwu's head ached. His visit home suddenly seemed much longer than a week, perhaps because of the endless gassy churning in his stomach from eating only fruit and nuts. His mother's food was unpalatable. The vegetables were overcooked, the cornmeal was too lumpy, the soup too watery, and the yam slices coarse from being boiled without a dollop of butter. He could not wait to get back to Nsukka and finally eat a real meal.

'I want to have a baby boy first, because it will place my feet firmly in Onyeka's house,' Anulika said. She walked over to get a bag in the rafters and Ugwu noticed, again, the new suspicious roundness to her body: the breasts that filled her blouse, the buttocks that rolled with each step. Onyeka must have touched her. Ugwu could not bear to think of the man's ugly body thrusting into his sister's. It had all happened too fast; there had been talk of suitors the last time he visited, but she had spoken of Onyeka in such an indifferent way that he did not think she would accept his proposal so quickly. Now even their parents were too swift to talk about Onyeka, his good mechanic job in town, his bicycle, his good behaviour, as if he were already a member of the family. Nobody ever mentioned his stunted height and the pointed teeth that looked like they belonged to a bush rat.

'You know, Onunna from Ezeugwu's compound had a baby girl first, and her husband's people went to see a *dibia* to find out why! Of course, Onyeka's people will not do that to me, they don't dare, but I want to have a boy first anyway,' Anulika said.

Ugwu sat up. 'I have tired of stories of Onyeka. I noticed something when he came by yesterday. He should bathe more often, he smells like rotten oil beans.'

'And you, what do you smell like?' Anulika poured the *ukwa* in the bag and knotted it. 'I've finished. You better get going before it gets too late.'

Ugwu went out to the yard. His mother was pounding something in a mortar and his father was stooped near her, sharpening a knife against a stone. The scrape of metal against stone set off tiny sparks that flickered briefly before they disappeared.

'Did Anulika wrap the *ukwa* well?' his mother asked.

'She did.' Ugwu raised the bag to show her.

'Greet your master and madam,' his mother said. 'Thank them for everything they sent us.'

'Yes, Mother.' He went over and hugged her. 'Stay well. Greet Chioke when she returns.'

His father straightened up and wiped the knife blade on his palm before shaking hands. 'Go well, *ije oma*. We will send word when Onyeka's people tell us they are ready to bring palm wine. It will be in a few months' time.'

'Yes, Father.' Ugwu stood around while his little cousins and siblings, the younger ones naked and the older ones in oversized shirts, said their goodbyes and listed what they wanted him to bring on his next visit. Buy us bread! Buy us meat! Buy us fried fish! Buy us groundnuts!

Anulika escorted him to the main road. He saw a familiar figure near the grove of *ube* trees and, although he had not seen her since she went to Kano to learn a trade four years ago, he knew immediately that it was Nnesinachi.

'Anulika! Ugwu! Is it you?' Nnesinachi's voice was as husky as he remembered but she was taller now, and her skin was darker from the fierce sun in the North.

When they hugged, he felt her chest push into his.

'I would barely have recognized you, the North has changed you so,' he said, wondering if she had really pressed herself against him.

'I came back yesterday with my cousins.' She was smiling at him. She had never smiled at him so warmly in the past. Her eyebrows had been shaved and pencilled in, one thicker than the other. She turned to Anulika. 'Anuli, I was on my way to see you. I hear you are getting married!'

'My sister, it is what I hear too,' Anulika said, and they both laughed.

'Are you going back to Nsukka?' she asked Ugwu.

'Yes. But I will come back soon, for Anulika's wine-carrying.'

'Go well.' Nnesinachi's eyes met his briefly, boldly, before she walked on, and he knew he had not imagined it; she really had pressed herself against him when they hugged. He felt a rush of weakness to his legs. He held himself from turning back to look at her, just in case she turned as well, and for a moment, he forgot the uncomfortable churning in his stomach.

'Her eyes must have opened in the North. You can't marry her, so you had better take what she is offering, before she marries,' Anulika said.

'You noticed?'

'How could I not have noticed? Do I look like a sheep?'

Ugwu narrowed his eyes to look at her. 'Has Onyeka touched you?'

'Of course Onyeka has touched me.'

Ugwu slowed his pace. He knew she must have slept with Onyeka and yet he did not like her confirming it. When Chinyere, Dr Okeke's housegirl, first started to sneak across the hedge to his Boys' Quarters for hasty thrusts in the dark, he had told Anulika about it during a visit home and they had discussed it. But they had never discussed her; he had always made himself assume that there was nothing to discuss. Anulika was walking ahead of him, unbothered by his sulky slowness, and he hurried up to her, silent, their steps light on the grass where they, as children, had hunted grasshoppers.

'I'm so hungry,' he said, finally.

'You didn't even eat the yam Mama boiled.'

'We boil our yam with butter.'

'We boil our yam with *boh-tah*. Look at your mouth. When they send you back to the village, what will you do? Where will you find *boh-tah* to use to boil your yam?'

'They won't send me back to the village.'

She looked at him from the corners of her eyes, up and down. 'You have forgotten where you come from, and now you have become so foolish you think you are a Big Man.'

Master was in the living room when Ugwu came in and greeted him.

'How are your people?' Master asked.

'They are well, sah. They send greetings.'

'Very good.'

'My sister Anulika will be getting married soon.'

'I see.' Master was focused on tuning the radio.

Ugwu could hear Olanna and Baby singing in the bathroom.

London Bridge is falling down, falling down, falling down,
London Bridge is falling down, my fair lady.

Baby's *London*, in her tiny unformed voice, sounded like *bonbon*.
The bathroom door was open.

'Good evening, mah,' Ugwu said.

'Oh, Ugwu, I didn't hear you come in!' Olanna said. She was bent
over the tub, giving Baby a bath. 'Welcome, *nno*. Are your people
well?'

'Yes, mah. They send greetings. My mother said she cannot thank
you enough for the wrappers.'

'How is her leg?'

'It no longer aches. She gave me *ukwa* for you.'

'Eh! She must have known what I am craving now.' She turned to
look at him, her hands covered in bath foam. 'You look well. See your
fat cheeks!'

'Yes, mah,' Ugwu said, although it was a lie. He always lost weight
when he visited home.

'Ugwu!' Baby called. 'Ugwu, come and see!' She was pressing a
squawking plastic duck in her hand.

'Baby, you can greet Ugwu after your bath,' Olanna said.

'Anulika will be getting married soon, mah. My father said I
should let you and Master know. They do not have a date yet, but
they will be very happy if you come.'

'Anulika? Is she not a little young? About sixteen-seventeen?'

'Her mates have started to marry.'

Olanna turned back to the tub. 'Of course we will come.'

'Ugwu!' Baby said again.

'Shall I warm Baby's porridge, mah?'

'Yes. And please make her milk.'

'Yes, mah.' He would linger for a moment and then ask her if all
had gone well in the week he was away, and she would tell him which
friends had come, who had brought what, if they had finished the
stew he had put in containers in the freezer.

'Your master and I have decided that Arize should come here to have her baby in September,' Olanna said.

'That is good, mah,' Ugwu said. 'I hope the baby will resemble Aunty Arize and not Uncle Nnakwanze.'

Olanna laughed. 'I hope so too. We will start cleaning the room in time. I want it to be spotless for her.'

'It will be spotless, mah, don't worry.' Ugwu liked Aunty Arize. He remembered her wine-carrying ceremony in Umunnachi about three years ago, how plump and bubbly she had been and how he had drunk so much palm wine that he had nearly dropped the infant Baby.

'I'm going to Kano on Monday to pick her up and take her shopping in Lagos,' Olanna said. 'I'll take Baby. We'll pack that blue dress Arize made for her.'

'The pink one is better, mah. The blue one is too tight.'

'That's true.' Olanna picked up a plastic duck and threw it back into the tub, and Baby squealed and submerged it in the water.

'*Nkem!*' Master called out. '*O mego!* It has happened!'

Olanna hurried to the living room, Ugwu close behind.

Master was standing by the radio. The television was on but the volume was off so that the dancing people looked as if they were swaying drunkenly. 'There's been a coup,' Master said, and gestured to the radio. 'Major Nzeogwu is speaking from Kaduna.'

The voice on the radio was youthful, eager, confident.

> *The Constitution is suspended and the regional government and elected assemblies are hereby dissolved. My dear countrymen, the aim of the Revolutionary Council is to establish a nation free from corruption and internal strife. Our enemies are the political profiteers, the swindlers, the men in high and low places that seek bribes and demand ten per cent, those that seek to keep the country divided permanently so that they can remain in office, the tribalists, the nepotists, those that make the country look big for nothing before international circles, those that have corrupted our society.*

Olanna ran to the telephone. 'What is happening in Lagos? Did they say what is happening in Lagos?'

'Your parents are fine, *nkem*. Civilians are safe.'

Olanna was dialling. 'Operator? Operator?' She put the phone down and picked it up again. 'It isn't going through.'

Master gently took the phone from her. 'I'm sure they are fine. The lines will come back up soon. It's just for security.'

On the radio, the voice had become firmer.

> *I assure all foreigners that their rights will continue to be respected. We promise every law-abiding citizen the freedom from all forms of oppression, freedom from general inefficiency, and freedom to live and strive in every field of human endeavour. We promise that you will no more be ashamed to say that you are a Nigerian.*

'Mummy Ola!' Baby called from the bathroom. 'Mummy Ola!'

Ugwu went back to the bathroom and dried Baby with a towel and then hugged her, blew against her neck. She smelt deliciously of Pears baby soap.

'Baby chicken!' he said, tickling her. Her plaits were wet, the ends tightened in a curly kink, and Ugwu smoothed them and marvelled again at how much she looked like her father; his people would say that Master had spit this child out.

'More tickles!' Baby said, laughing. Her chubby face was slick with moisture.

'Baby baby chicken,' Ugwu murmured, in the sing-song way that always amused her.

Baby laughed and, from the living room, Ugwu heard Olanna say, 'Oh, God, what did he say? What did he say?'

He was serving Baby's porridge when the deputy president spoke briefly on the radio, the voice understated, as if he were exhausted from the effort of saying, 'The government is handing over to the military.'

There were more announcements later – the prime minister was missing, Nigeria was now a federal military government, the premiers of the North and West were missing – but Ugwu was not sure who spoke and on what station because Master sat next to the radio, turning the knob quickly, stopping, listening, turning, stopping. He had removed his glasses and looked more vulnerable with his eyes sunken deep in his face. He did not put them back on until the guests arrived. There were more today than usual, and Ugwu brought dining chairs to the living room to seat them all. Their voices were urgent and excited, each person barely waiting for the last to finish speaking.

'This is the end of corruption! This is what we have needed to happen since that general strike,' one guest said. Ugwu did not remember his name, but he tended to eat up all the *chin-chin* right after it was served, so Ugwu had taken to placing the tray as far away from him as possible. The man had large hands; a few generous handfuls from the tray and all was lost.

'Those majors are true heroes!' Okeoma said, and raised an arm.

There was excitement in their voices even when they talked about the people who were killed.

'They said the Sardauna hid behind his wives.'

'They said the finance minister shit in his trousers before they shot him.'

Some guests chuckled and so did Ugwu, until he heard Olanna say, 'I knew Okonji. He was a friend of my father's.' She sounded subdued.

'The BBC is calling it an Igbo coup,' the *chin-chin*–eating guest said. 'And they have a point. It was mostly Northerners who were killed.'

'It was mostly Northerners who were in government,' Professor Ezeka whispered, his eyebrows arched, as if he could not believe he had to say what was so obvious.

'The BBC should be asking their people who put the Northerners in government to dominate everybody!' Master said.

Ugwu was surprised that Master and Professor Ezeka seemed to agree. He was even more surprised when Miss Adebayo said, 'Those North Africans are crazy to call this an infidel versus righteous thing,' and Master laughed – not the usual derisive laugh before he shifted to the edge of his chair to challenge her; it was a laugh of approval. He agreed with her.

'If we had more men like Major Nzeogwu in this country, we would not be where we are today,' Master said. 'He actually has a vision!'

'Isn't he a communist?' It was the the green-eyed Professor Lehman. 'He went to Czechoslovakia when he was at Sandhurst.'

'You Americans, always peering under people's beds to look for communism. Do you think we have time to worry about that?' Master asked. 'What matters is whatever will make our people move forwards. Let's assume that a capitalist democracy is a good thing in principle, but if it is our kind – where somebody gives you a dress that they tell you looks like their own, but it doesn't fit you and the buttons have fallen off – then you have to discard it and make a dress that is your own size. You simply have to!'

'Too much rhetoric, Odenigbo,' Miss Adebayo said. 'You can't make a theoretical case for the military.'

Ugwu felt better; this was the sparring he was used to.

'Of course I can. With a man like Major Nzeogwu, I can,' Master said. 'Ugwu! More ice!'

'The man is a communist,' Professor Lehman insisted. His nasal voice annoyed Ugwu, or perhaps it was simply that Professor Lehman had the same fair hair as Mr Richard but none of the quiet dignity. He wished Mr Richard still came. He clearly remembered his last visit, months before Baby was born, but other memories of those tumultuous weeks were faded now, incomplete; he had been so afraid that Master and Olanna would never reunite and his world would crumble that he did not eavesdrop much. He would not even have known that Mr Richard was involved in the quarrel if Harrison had not told him.

'Thank you, my good man.' Master took the bowl of ice and clinked some into his glass.

'Yes, sah,' Ugwu said, watching Olanna. Her head was supported by her clasped hands. He wished he could truly feel sorry for her friend the politician who had been killed, but politicians were not like normal people, they were *politicians*. He read about them in the *Renaissance* and *Daily Times* – they paid thugs to beat opponents, they bought land and houses with government money, they imported fleets of long American cars, they paid women to stuff their blouses with false votes and pretend to be pregnant. Whenever he drained a pot of boiled beans, he thought of the slimy sink as *politician*.

That night, he lay in his room in the Boys' Quarters and tried to concentrate on *The Mayor of Casterbridge*, but it was difficult. He hoped Chinyere would slip under the hedge and come over; they never planned it, she just appeared on some days and didn't on others. He ached for her to come on this exciting night of the coup that had changed the order of things and throbbed with possibility, with newness. When he heard her tap on the window, he offered up a bashful thanks to the gods.

'Chinyere,' he said.

'Ugwu,' she said.

She smelt of stale onions. The light was off, and in the thin stream that came from the security bulb outside he saw the cone-shaped rise of her breasts as she pulled her blouse off, untied the wrapper around her waist, and lay on her back. There was something moist about the darkness, about their bodies close together, and he imagined that she was Nnesinachi and that the taut legs encircling him were Nnesinachi's. She was silent at first and then, hips thrashing, her hands tight around his back, she called out the same thing she said every time. It sounded like a name – Abonyi, Abonyi – but he wasn't sure. Perhaps she imagined that he was someone else too, someone back in her village.

She got up and left as silently as she came. When he saw her the next day across the hedge, hanging out clothes on the line, she said 'Ugwu' and nothing else; she did not smile.

Olanna postponed her trip to Kano because of the coup. She waited until the airports were reopened, the Post and Telegraphs up again, the military governors appointed to the regions. She waited until she was sure there was order. But the coup was in the air. Everyone was talking about it, even the taxi driver in the white hat and kaftan who drove her and Baby from the airport to Arize's compound.

'But the Sardauna was not killed, madam,' he whispered. 'He escaped with Allah's help and is now in Mecca.' Olanna smiled gently and said nothing because she knew that this man, with his prayer beads dangling from his rearview mirror, needed to believe that. The Sardauna, after all, had not only been premier of the North, he had also been the spiritual leader for this man and so many Muslims like him.

She told Arize about the taxi driver's comment, and Arize shrugged and said, 'There is nothing that they are not saying.' Arize's wrapper was pushed low, below her waist, and her blouse was loose-fitting to accommodate the swell of her belly. They sat in the living room with photos of Arize and Nnakwanze's wedding on the oily wall, while Baby played with the children in the compound. Olanna did not want Baby to touch those children in their torn clothes, milky mucus trailing from their noses, but she didn't say so; it shamed her that she felt that way.

'We'll catch the first flight to Lagos tomorrow, Ari, so you can rest before we start shopping. I don't want to do anything that will be difficult for you,' Olanna said.

'Ha, difficult! I am only pregnant, Sister, I am not sick, oh. Is it not women like me who work on the farm until the baby wants to come out?' And am I not the one sewing that dress?' Arize pointed to the corner, where her Singer sewing machine was on a table amid a pile of clothes.

'My concern is for my godchild in there, not for you,' Olanna said. She raised Arize's blouse and placed her face against the firm round-ness of Arize's belly, against the stretched-tight skin, in the gentle ritual she had been doing since Arize became pregnant; if she did it often enough, Arize said, the child would imbibe her features and look like her.

'I don't care about the outside,' Arize said. 'But she must look like you on the inside. She must have your brain and know Book.'

'Or he.'

'No, this one is a girl, you will see. Nnakwanze says it will be a boy who will resemble him, but I told him that God will not allow my child to have that flat face.'

Olanna laughed. Arize got up and opened an enamel box and brought out some money. 'See what Sister Kainene sent me last week. She said I should use it to buy things for the baby.'

'It was nice of her.' Olanna knew she sounded stilted, knew Arize was watching her.

'You and Sister Kainene should talk. What happened in the past is in the past.'

'You can only talk to the person who wants to talk to you,' Olanna said. She wanted to change the subject. She always wanted to change the subject when Kainene came up. 'I better take Baby to greet Aunty Ifeka.' She hurried out to fetch Baby before Arize could say anything else.

She washed some sand off Baby's face and hands before they walked out of the compound and down the road. Uncle Mbaezi was not yet back from the market, and they sat with Aunty Ifeka on a bench in front of her kiosk, Baby on Olanna's lap. The yard was filling with the chatter of neighbours and the shrieks of children run-ning around under the *kuka* tree. Somebody was playing loud music from a gramophone; soon, a cluster of men by the compound gate began to laugh and jostle one another, mimicking the song. Aunty Ifeka laughed, too, and clapped her hands.

'What's funny?' Olanna asked.

'That is Rex Lawson's song,' Aunty Ifeka said.

'What is funny about it?'

'Our people say that the chorus sounds like *mmee-mmee-mmee*, the bleating of a goat.' Aunty Ifeka chuckled. 'They say the Sardauna sounded like that when he was begging them not to kill him. When the soldiers fired a mortar into his house, he crouched behind his wives and bleated, "*Mmee-mmee-mmee*, please don't kill me, *mmee-mmee-mmee*!"'

Aunty Ifeka laughed again, and so did Baby, as if she understood.

'Oh.' Olanna thought about Chief Okonji and wondered if he too was said to have bleated like a goat before he died. She looked away across the street, where children were playing with car tyres, racing with one another as they rolled the tyres along. A small sandstorm was gathering in the distance, and the dust rose and fell in grey-white clouds.

'The Sardauna was an evil man, *ajo mmadu*,' Aunty Ifeka said. 'He hated us. He hated everybody who did not remove their shoes and bow to him. Is he not the one who did not allow our children to go to school?'

'They should not have killed him,' Olanna said quietly. 'They should have put him in prison.'

Aunty Ifeka snorted. 'Put him in which prison? In this Nigeria where he controlled everything?' She got up and began to close up the kiosk. 'Come, let's go inside so I can find Baby something to eat.'

The Rex Lawson song was playing loudly in Arize's compound when Olanna returned. Nnakwanze found it hilarious too. He had two huge front teeth, and when he laughed, it was as if too many teeth had been painfully crammed into his small mouth. *Mmeee-mmeee-mmeee*, a goat begging not to be killed: *mmeee-mmeee-mmeee*.

'It's not funny,' Olanna said.

'Sister, but it is funny, oh,' Arize said. 'Because of too much Book, you no longer know how to laugh.'

Nnakwanze was sitting on the floor at Arize's feet, rubbing her belly in light circular motions. He had worried a lot less than Arize when she did not get pregnant the first, second, and third year of their marriage; when his mother visited them too often, poking at Arize's belly and urging her to confess how many abortions she had had before marriage, he asked his mother to stop visiting. He asked her, too, to stop bringing foul-smelling concoctions for Arize to drink in bitter gulps. Now that Arize was pregnant, he did more overtime at the railway and asked her to cut down on her sewing.

He was still singing the song and laughing. A goat begging not to be killed: *mmeee-mmeee-mmeee*.

Olanna got up. The night breeze was unpleasantly cool. 'Ari, you should get to bed, so you are rested in the morning for Lagos.'

Nnakwanze made as if to help Arize up, but she brushed him aside. 'I have told you people that I am not sick. I am only pregnant.'

Olanna was pleased that the house in Lagos would be empty. Her father had called to say they were going overseas. She knew it was because he wanted to be away until things calmed down, because he was wary of his ten per cents and lavish parties and slick connections, but neither he nor her mother said so. They called it a holiday. It was their policy to leave things unsaid, the same way they pretended not to notice that she and Kainene no longer spoke and that she came home only when she was sure Kainene was not visiting.

In the airport taxi, Arize taught Baby a song while Olanna watched Lagos career by: the tumultuous traffic, the rusty buses and exhausted masses waiting for them, the touts, the beggars sliding on flat, wooden trolleys, the shabby hawkers thrusting trays towards people who either would not or could not buy.

The driver stopped in front of her parents' walled compound in Ikoyi. He peered at the high gate. 'The minister they killed used to live around here, *abi*, aunty?' he asked. Olanna pretended not to have heard and instead said to Baby, 'Now, look what you did to your dress! Hurry inside so we can wash it off!'

Later, her mother's driver, Ibekie, took them to Kingsway. The supermarket smelt of new paint. Arize walked from aisle to aisle, cooing, touching the plastic wrappings, picking out baby clothes, a pink pram, a plastic doll with blue eyes.

'Everything is so shiny in supermarkets, Sister,' Arize said, laughing. 'No dust!'

Olanna held up a white dress trimmed with pink lace. '*O maka*. This is lovely.'

'It's too expensive,' Arize said.

'Nobody asked you.'

Baby pulled down a doll from a low shelf and turned it upside down, and it let out a crying sound.

'No, Baby.' Olanna took the doll and placed it back.

They shopped for a while longer and then left for Yaba market, where Arize could shop for fabrics for herself. Tejuosho Road was crowded, families huddled around pots of bubbling food, women roasting corn and plantains in charred basins, bare-chested men loading bags into lorries with hand-painted wisdoms: NO CONDITION IS PERMANENT. GOD KNOWS BEST. Ibekie parked near the newspaper stands. Olanna glanced at the people standing and reading the *Daily Times* and her feet grew light with pride. They were reading Odenigbo's article, she was sure; it was easily the best there. She had edited it herself and toned down his rhetoric, so that his argument – that only a unitary government could remove the divisions of regionalism – was clearer.

She took Baby's hand and led the way past the roadside hawkers who sat under umbrellas with batteries and padlocks and cigarettes carefully arranged on enamel trays. The main market entrance was strangely empty. Then Olanna saw the crowd ahead. A man in a yellowed singlet stood at the centre while two men slapped him, one after the other, methodical, leathery-sounding slaps. 'Why now? Why are you denying?' The man stared at them, blank, bending his neck slightly after each slap. Arize stopped.

Somebody from the crowd called out, 'We are counting the Igbo people. *Oya*, come and identify yourself. You are Igbo?'

Arize muttered under her breath, '*I kwuna okwu*,' as if Olanna was thinking of saying anything, and then shook her head and started to speak fluent, loud Yoruba, all the while casually turning so they could go back the way they had come. The crowd lost interest in them. Another man in a safari suit was being slapped on the back of the head. 'You are Igbo man! Don't deny it! Simply identify yourself!'

Baby began to cry. 'Mummy Ola! Mummy Ola!'

Olanna picked Baby up. She and Arize did not talk until they got back in the car. Ibekie had already reversed and kept glancing at the rearview mirror. 'I saw people running,' he said.

'What is happening?' Olanna asked.

Arize shrugged. 'We hear rumours that they have been doing this in Kaduna and Zaria since the coup; they go out in the streets and start to harass Igbo people because they said the coup was an Igbo coup.'

'*Ezi okwu?* Really?'

'Yes, Aunty,' Ibekie said quickly, as if he had been waiting for the opportunity to speak. 'My uncle in Ebutte Metta does not sleep in his house any more since the coup. All his neighbours are Yoruba, and they said some men have been looking for him. He sleeps in different houses every night, while he takes care of his business. He has sent his children back home.'

'*Ezi okwu?* Really?' Olanna repeated. She felt hollow. She did not know that things had come to this; in Nsukka, life was insular and the news was unreal, functioning only as fodder for the evening talk, for Odenigbo's rants and impassioned articles.

'Things will calm down,' Arize said, and touched Olanna's arm. 'Don't worry.'

Olanna nodded and looked out at the words printed on a nearby lorry: NO TELEPHONE TO HEAVEN. She could not believe how easy it had been to deny who they were, to shrug off being Igbo.

'She will wear that white dress for her christening, Sister,' Arize said.

'What, Ari?'

Arize pointed at her belly. 'Your goddaughter will wear that white dress for her christening. Thank you so much, Sister.'

The light in Arize's eyes made Olanna smile; things would indeed calm down. She tickled Baby, but Baby did not laugh. Baby stared back at her with frightened eyes that were not yet dried of tears.

Richard watched as Kainene zipped up the lilac dress and turned to him. The hotel room was brightly lit, and he looked at her and at her reflection in the mirror behind her.

'*Nke a ka mma*,' he said. It *was* prettier than the black dress on the bed, the one she had earlier picked out for her parents' party. She bowed mockingly and sat down to put on her shoes. She looked almost pretty with her smoothing powder and red lipstick and relaxed demeanour, not as knotted up as she had been lately, chasing a contract with Shell-BP. Before they left, Richard brushed aside some of her wig hair and kissed her forehead, to avoid spoiling her lipstick.

There were garish balloons in her parents' living room. The party was underway. Stewards in black and white walked around with trays and fawning smiles, their heads held inanely high. The champagne sparkled in tall glasses, the chandeliers' light reflected the glitter of jewellery on fat women's necks, and the High Life band in the corner played so loudly, so vigorously, that people clumped close together to hear one another.

'I see many Big Men of the new regime,' Richard said.

'Daddy hasn't wasted any time in ingratiating himself,' Kainene said in his ear. 'He ran off until things calmed down, and now he's back to make new friends.'

Richard scanned the rest of the room. Colonel Madu stood out right away, with his wide shoulders and wide face and wide features and head that was above everyone else's. He was talking to an Arab man in a tight dinner jacket. Kainene walked over to say hello to them and Richard went to look for a drink, to avoid talking to Madu just yet.

Kainene's mother came up and kissed his cheek; he knew she was drunk, or she would have greeted him with the usual frosty 'How do you do?' Now, though, she told him he looked well and cornered him at an unfortunate end of the room, with the wall to his back and an intimidating piece of sculpture, something that looked like a snarling lion, to his side.

'Kainene tells me you are going home to London soon?' she asked. Her ebony complexion looked waxy with too much make-up. There was something nervous about her movements.

'Yes. I'll be away for about ten days.'

'Just ten days?' She half smiled. Perhaps she had hoped he would be away for longer, so she could finally find a suitable partner for her daughter. 'To visit your family?'

'My cousin Martin is getting married,' Richard said.

'Oh, I see.' The rows and rows of gold around her neck weighed her down and made her head look slumped, as if she was under great strain and, in trying so hard to hide it, made it all the more obvious. 'Maybe we'll have a drink in London then. I'm telling my husband that we should take another small holiday. Not that anything will happen, but not everybody is happy with this unitary decree the government is talking about. It's just nicer to be away until things are settled. We may leave next week but we are not telling anybody, so keep it to yourself.' She touched his sleeve playfully, and Richard saw a glimpse of Kainene in the curve of her lips. 'We are not even telling our friends the Ajuahs. You know Chief Ajuah, who owns the bottling company? They are Igbo, but they are Western Igbo. I hear they are the ones who deny being Igbo. Who knows what they will say that we have done? Who knows? They will sell other Igbo people for a tarnished penny. A tarnished penny, I'm telling you. Do you want another drink? Wait here and I'll get another drink. Just wait here.'

As soon as she lurched away, Richard went looking for Kainene. He found her on the balcony with Madu, standing and looking down at the swimming pool. The smell of roasting meat was thick in the air. He watched them for a while. Madu's head was slightly cocked to the side as Kainene spoke, her body looked frail next to his huge frame, and they seemed somehow to fit effortlessly. Both very dark, one tall and thin, the other taller and huge. Kainene turned and saw him.

'Richard,' she said.

He joined them, shook hands with Madu. 'How are you, Madu? *A na-emekwa?*' he asked, eager to speak first. 'How is life in the North?'

'Nothing to complain about,' Madu said in English.

'You didn't come with Adaobi?' He did wish the man would come out more often with his wife.

'No,' Madu said, and sipped his drink; it was clear he had not wanted anybody to disturb their chat.

'I see my mother was entertaining you, how exciting,' Kainene said. 'Madu and I were stuck with Ahmed there for a while. He wants to buy Daddy's warehouse in Ikeja.'

'Your father will not sell anything to him,' Madu declared, as if it were his decision to make. 'Those Syrians and Lebanese already own half of Lagos, and they are all bloody opportunists in this country.'

'I would sell to him if he stopped smelling so awfully of garlic,' Kainene said.

Madu laughed.

Kainene slipped her hand into Richard's. 'I was just telling Madu that you think another coup is coming.'

'There won't be another coup,' Madu said.

'You would know, wouldn't you, Madu? Big Man colonel that you are now,' Kainene teased.

Richard tightened his hold on her hand. 'I went to Zaria last week, and it seemed that all everybody was saying was second coup, second coup. Even Radio Kaduna and the *New Nigerian*,' he said in Igbo.

'What does the press know, really?' Madu replied in English. He always did that; since Richard's Igbo had become near-fluent, Madu insistently responded to it in English so that Richard felt forced to revert to English.

'The papers ran articles about jihad, and Radio Kaduna kept broadcasting the late Sardauna's speeches, and there was talk about how Igbo people were going to take over the civil service and – '

Madu cut him short. 'There won't be a second coup. There's a little tension in the army, but there always is a little tension in the army. Did you have the goat meat? Isn't it wonderful?'

'Yes,' Richard agreed, almost automatically, and then wished he hadn't. The air in Lagos was humid; standing next to Madu, it seemed suffocating. The man made him feel inconsequential.

The second coup happened a week later, and Richard's first reaction was to gloat. He was rereading Martin's letter in the orchard, sitting on the spot where Kainene often told him that a groove the exact size and shape of his buttocks had appeared.

> *Is 'going native' still used? I always knew you would! Mother tells me you have given up on the tribal art book and are pleased with this one, a sort of fictionalized travelogue? And on European Evils in Africa! I'm quite keen to hear more about it when you are in London. Pity you gave up the old title: 'The Basket of Hands'. Were hands chopped off in Africa as well? I'd imagined it was only in India. I'm intrigued!*

Richard imagined that smile Martin often had when they were schoolboys, during those years that Aunt Elizabeth had immersed them in activities with her manic determination that there be no sitting around: cricket tournaments, boxing lessons, tennis, piano lessons from a Frenchman with a lisp. Martin had thrived at them all, always with that superior smile of people who were born to belong and excel.

Richard reached out to pluck a wildflower that looked like a poppy. He wondered what Martin's wedding would be like; Martin's fiancée was a fashion designer, of all things. If only Kainene could go with him; if only she didn't have to stay to sign the new contract. He wanted Aunt Elizabeth and Martin and Virginia to see her, but most of all he wanted them to see him, the man he had become after his years here: to see that he was browner and happier.

Ikejide came up to him. 'Mr Richard, sah! Madam say make you come. There is another coup,' Ikejide said. He looked excited.

Richard hurried indoors. He was right; Madu was wrong. The moist July heat had plastered his hair limply to his head, and he ran his hand through it as he went. Kainene was on a sofa in the living room, her arms wrapped around herself, rocking back and forth. The British voice on the radio was so loud that she raised her voice when she said, 'Northern officers have taken over. The BBC says they are killing Igbo officers in Kaduna. Nigerian Radio isn't saying anything.' She spoke too fast. He stood behind her and began to rub her shoulders, kneading her stiff muscles in circular motions. On the radio, the breathless British voice said it was quite extraordinary that a second coup had occurred only six months after the first.

'Extraordinary. Extraordinary indeed,' Kainene said. She reached out, in a sudden jerky move, and pushed the radio off the table. It fell on the carpeted floor, and a dislodged battery rolled out. 'Madu is in Kaduna,' she said, and put her face in her hands. 'Madu is in Kaduna.'

'It's all right, my darling,' Richard said. 'It's all right.'

For the first time, he considered the possibility of Madu's death. He decided not to go back to Nsukka for a while and was not sure why. Was it really because he wanted to be with her when she heard Madu was dead? In the next few days, she was so taut with anxiety that he too began to worry about Madu and then resent himself for doing so, and then resent his resentment. He should not be so petty. She included him in her worry, after all, as if Madu was their friend and not just hers. She told him about the people she called, about the inquiries she made to find out what had happened. Nobody knew. Madu's wife had heard nothing. Lagos was in chaos. Her parents had left for England. Many Igbo officers were dead. The killings were organized; she told him about a soldier who said the alarm for a battalion muster parade was sounded in his barracks and after everyone assembled, the Northerners picked out all the Igbo soldiers and took them away and shot them.

Kainene was muted and quiet but never tearful, so the day she told him, 'I heard something,' with a sob in her voice, he was sure it was news of Madu. He thought about how to console her, whether he would be able to console her.

'Udodi,' Kainene said. 'They killed Colonel Udodi Ekechi.'

'Udodi?' He had been so certain it was about Madu that for a moment he was blank.

'Northern soldiers put him in a cell in the barracks and fed him his own shit. He ate his own shit.' Kainene paused. 'Then they beat him senseless and tied him to an iron cross and threw him back in his cell. He died tied to an iron cross. He died on a cross.'

Richard sat down slowly. His dislike for Udodi – loud, drunken, duplicity dripping from his pores – had only deepened in the past years. Yet hearing about his death left him sober. He thought, again, of Madu dying and realized he did not know how he would feel.

'Who told you this?'

'Maria Obele. Udodi's wife is her cousin. She said they are saying that no Igbo officer in the North escaped. But some Umunnachi people said they heard Madu escaped. Adaobi has not heard anything. How could he have escaped. How?'

'He might be hiding out somewhere.'

'How?' Kainene asked again.

Colonel Madu appeared in Kainene's house two weeks later, much taller-looking now because he had lost so much weight; the angles of his shoulder bones were visible through his white shirt.

Kainene screamed. 'Madu! Is this you? *O gi di ife a?*'

Richard was not sure who walked towards whom first, but Kainene and Madu were holding each other close, Kainene touching his arms and face with a tenderness that made Richard look away. He went to the liquor cabinet and poured a whisky for Madu and a gin for himself.

'Thank you, Richard,' Madu said, but he did not take the drink and Richard stood there, holding two glasses, before he placed one down.

Kainene sat on a side table in front of Madu. 'They said they shot you in Kaduna, then they said they buried you alive in the bush, then they said you escaped, then they said you were in prison in Lagos.'

Madu said nothing. Kainene stared at him. Richard finished his drink and poured another.

'You remember my friend Ibrahim? From Sandhurst?' Madu asked finally.

Kainene nodded.

'Ibrahim saved my life. He told me about the coup that morning. He was not directly involved, but most of them – the Northern officers – knew about it. He drove me to his cousin's house, but I didn't really understand until he asked his cousin to take me to the backyard, where he kept his domestic animals. I slept in the chicken house for two days.'

'No! *Ekwuzina!*'

'And do you know that soldiers came to search his cousin's house to look for me? Everybody knew how close Ibrahim and I were, and they suspected he helped me escape. They didn't check the chicken house, though.' Colonel Madu paused, nodding and looking into the distance. 'I did not know how bad chicken shit smelt until I slept in it for three days. On the third day, Ibrahim sent me some kaftans and money through a small boy and asked me to leave right away. I dressed as a Fulani nomad and walked through the smaller villages because Ibrahim said that artillery soldiers had set up blocks on all the major roads in Kaduna. I was lucky to find a lorry driver, an Igbo man from Ohafia, who took me to Kafanchan. My cousin lives there. You know Onunkwo, don't you?' Madu did not wait for Kainene to respond. 'He is the station master at the railway, and he told me that Northern soldiers had sealed off Makurdi Bridge. That bridge is a grave. They searched every single vehicle, they delayed passenger trains for up to eight hours, and they shot all the Igbo soldiers they discovered there and threw the bodies over. Many of the soldiers wore disguises, but they used their boots to find them.'

'What?' Kainene leaned forwards.

'Boots.' Madu glanced at his shoes. 'You know we soldiers wear boots all the time so they examined the feet of each man, and any Igbo man whose feet were clean and uncracked by harmattan, they took away and shot. They also examined their foreheads for signs of their skin being lighter from wearing a soldier's beret.' Madu shook his head. 'Onunkwo advised me to wait for some days. He did not think I would make it across the bridge because they would recognize me easily under any disguise. So I stayed ten days in a village near Kafanchan. Onunkwo found me different houses to stay in. It was not safe to stay with him. Finally, he said he had found a driver, a good man from Nnewi, who would hide me in the water tank of his goods train. The man gave me a fireman's suit to wear and I climbed into the tank. I had water up to my chin. Each time the train jerked, some of the water entered my nose. When we got to the bridge, the soldiers searched the train thoroughly. I heard footsteps on the lid of the tank and thought it was all over. But they did not open it and we passed. It was only then I knew that I was alive and I would survive. I came back to Umunnachi to find Adaobi wearing black.'

Kainene kept looking at Madu long after he finished speaking. There was another stretch of silence, which made Richard uncomfortable because he was not sure how to react, what expression to have.

'Igbo soldiers and Northern soldiers can never live in the same barracks after this. It is impossible, impossible,' Colonel Madu said. He had a glassy sheen in his eyes. 'And Gowon cannot be head of state. They cannot impose Gowon on us as head of state. It is not how things are done. There are others who are senior to him.'

'What are you going to do now?' Kainene asked.

Madu did not seem to hear her. 'So many of us are gone,' he said. 'So many solid, good men – Udodi, Iloputaife, Okunweze, Okafor – and these were men who believed in Nigeria and didn't care for tribe. After all, Udodi spoke better Hausa than he spoke Igbo, and look how they slaughtered him.' He stood up and began to pace the room. 'The problem was the ethnic balance policy. I was part of the commission that told our GOC that we should scrap it, that it was polarizing the army, that they should stop promoting Northerners who were not qualified. But our GOC said no, our *British* GOC.' Madu turned and glanced at Richard.

'I'll ask Ikejide to cook your special rice,' Kainene said.

Madu shrugged, silent, and stared out of the window.

❊ 10 ❊

U **gwu set the table** for lunch. 'I've finished, sah,' he said, although he knew Master would not touch the *okro* soup and would keep walking up and down the living room with the radio turned up high, as he had been doing since Miss Adebayo left about an hour ago. She had banged so hard on the front door that Ugwu worried the glass would crack, and then when he opened it, she pushed past him, asking, 'Where is your master? Where is your master?'

'I will call him, mah,' Ugwu said, but Miss Adebayo had hurried ahead into Master's study. He heard her say, 'There's trouble in the North,' and his mouth went dry because Miss Adebayo was not an alarmist and whatever was happening in the North had to be serious and Olanna was in Kano.

Ever since the second coup some weeks ago, when the Igbo soldiers were killed, he had struggled to understand what was happening, read the newspapers more carefully, listened more closely to Master and his guests. The conversations no longer ended in reassuring laughter, and the living room often seemed clouded with uncertainties, with unfinished knowledge, as if they all knew something would happen and yet did not know what. None of them would ever have imagined that *this* would happen, that the announcer on ENBC Radio Enugu would be saying now, as Ugwu straightened the tablecloth, 'We have confirmed reports that up to five-hundred Igbo people have been killed in Maiduguri.'

'Rubbish!' Master shouted. 'Did you hear *that*? Did you *hear* that?'

'Yes, sah,' Ugwu said. He hoped the loud noise would not wake Baby up from her siesta.

'Impossible!' Master said.

'Sah, your soup,' Ugwu said.

'Five-hundred people killed. Absolute rubbish! It can't be true.'

Ugwu took the dish into the kitchen and put it in the refrigerator. The smell of spices nauseated him, as did the sight of soup, of food. But Baby would wake up soon and he would have to make her dinner. He brought out a bag of potatoes from the storeroom and sat staring at it, thinking about two days ago, when Olanna left for Kano to fetch Aunty Arize, how her plaited hair had pulled at the skin of her forehead and made it shiny-sleek.

Baby came into the kitchen. 'Ugwu.'

'*I tetago?* Are you awake?' Ugwu asked, before he hugged her. He wondered if Master had seen her walk past the living room. 'Did you see baby chickens in your dream?'

Baby laughed, and her dimples sank deep in her cheeks. 'Yes!'

'Did you talk to them?'

'Yes!'

'What did they say?'

Baby didn't give the usual response. She let go of his neck and squatted on the floor. 'Where is Mummy Ola?'

'Mummy Ola will be back soon.' Ugwu examined the blade of the knife. 'Now, help me with the potato peels. Put them all in the dustbin, and when Mummy Ola comes back, we will tell her you helped with the cooking.'

After Ugwu put the potatoes on to boil, he gave her a bath, dusted her body over with Pears talcum powder, and brought out her pink nightdress. It was the one Olanna loved, the one she said made Baby look like a doll. But Baby said, 'I want my pyjamas,' and Ugwu was no longer sure which it was Olanna loved anyway, the nightdress or the pyjamas.

He heard a knock on the front door. Master ran out of his study. Ugwu dashed to the door and grasped the handle first and held on, so that he would be the one to open it, although he knew it couldn't be Olanna. She had her own key.

'Is it Obiozo?' Master asked, looking at one of the two men standing at the door. 'Obiozo?'

When Ugwu saw the hollow-eyed men with the dirt-smeared clothes, he knew right away that he should take Baby away, shield her. He took her food into the bedroom, set it on her play table, and told her she could pretend she was eating with Jill from the *Jack and Jill* comic that was delivered with the *Renaissance*. He stood by the door that led to the corridor and peered into the living room. One of the men was speaking, while the other drank from a bottle of water, the glass ignored on the table.

'We saw a lorry driver who agreed to carry us,' the man said, and Ugwu could tell right away that he was Master's kinsman; his Abba dialect was heavy, each *f* sounding like a *v*.

'What happened?' Master asked.

The man placed the bottle of water down and said quietly, 'They are killing us like ants. Did you hear what I said? Ants.'

'Our eyes have seen plenty, *anyi afujugo anya*,' Obiozo said. 'I saw a whole family, a father and mother and three children, lying on the road to the motor park. Just lying there.'

'What about Kano? What is happening in Kano?' Master asked.

'It started in Kano,' the man said.

Obiozo was speaking, saying something about vultures and bodies dumped outside the city walls, but Ugwu no longer listened. *It started in Kano* rang in his head. He did not want to tidy the guest room and find bedsheets and warm the soup and make fresh *garri* for them. He wanted them to leave right away. Or, if they would not leave, he wanted them to shut their filthy mouths. He wanted the radio announcers to be silent too, but they were not. They repeated the news of the killings in Maiduguri until Ugwu wanted to throw the radio out of the window, and the next afternoon, after the men left, a solemn voice on ENBC Radio Enugu recounted eyewitness accounts from the North: teachers hacked down in Zaria, a full Catholic church in Sokoto set on fire, a pregnant woman split open in Kano. The newscaster paused. 'Some of our people are coming back now. The lucky ones are coming back. The railway stations are full of our people. If you have tea and bread to spare, please take it to the stations. Help a brother in need.'

Master leapt up from the sofa. 'Go, Ugwu,' he said. 'Take tea and bread and go to the railway station.'

'Yes, sah,' Ugwu said. Before he made the tea, he fried some plantains for Baby's lunch. 'I have put Baby's lunch in the oven, sah,' he said.

He was not sure Master heard him and as he left, he worried that Baby would go hungry and Master would not know that her fried plantains were in the oven. He made himself keep worrying about it until he got to the station. Mats and dirty wrappers were spread all over the platform and people were crumpled down on them, men and women and children crying and eating bread and tending wounds. Hawkers walked around with trays on their heads. Ugwu did not want to go into that ragged bazaar but he steeled himself and walked towards a man sitting on the ground with a red-stained rag wound around his head. Flies buzzed everywhere.

'Do you want some bread?' Ugwu asked.

'Yes, my brother. *Dalu.* Thank you.'

Ugwu did not look to see how deep the knife wound on his head was. He poured the tea and held out the bread. He would not remember this man tomorrow because he would not want to.

'Do you want some bread?' Ugwu asked another man nearby, who sat hunched. '*I choro* bread?'

The man turned. Ugwu recoiled and nearly dropped the flask. The man's right eye was gone, in its place, a juicy-red pulp.

'It was the soldiers who saved us,' the first man was saying, as if he felt he had to tell his story in exchange for the bread he was eating dipped in tea. 'They told us to run to the army barracks. Those madmen were chasing us like runaway goats, but once we entered the gates of the barracks, we were safe.'

A rickety train pulled up, so full that some people held on to the outside of the coaches, clutching at metal bars. Ugwu watched as tired, dusty, bloody people climbed down, but he did not join those who rushed over to help. He could not bear to think that Olanna was one of those limping and defeated people, and yet he could not bear to think that she was not, that she was still behind, somewhere in the North. He watched until the train emptied out. Olanna was not there. He gave the rest of the bread to the one-eyed man, then turned and ran. He did not stop until he got to Odim Street and past the bush with the white flowers.

※ 11 ※

Olanna was sitting on Mohammed's veranda, drinking chilled rice milk, laughing at the delicious cold trickle down her throat, at the stickiness on her lips, when the gateman appeared and asked to speak to Mohammed.

Mohammed left and came back moments later, holding what looked like a pamphlet. 'They're rioting,' he said.

'It's the students, isn't it?' Olanna asked.

'I think it's religious. You must leave right away.' His eyes avoided hers.

'Mohammed, calm down.'

'Sule said they are blocking the roads and searching for infidels. Come, come.' He was already heading indoors. Olanna followed. He worried too much, did Mohammed. Muslim students were always demonstrating about one thing or the other, after all, and harassing people who were Western-dressed, but they always dispersed quickly enough.

Mohammed went into a room and came out with a long scarf. 'Wear this, so you can blend in,' he said.

Olanna placed it over her head and wound it round her neck. 'I look like a proper Muslim woman,' she joked.

But Mohammed barely smiled. 'Let's go. I know a short cut to the train station.'

'Train station? Arize and I are not leaving until tomorrow, Mohammed,' Olanna said. She almost ran to keep up with him. 'I'm going back to my uncle's house in Sabon Gari.'

'Olanna.' Mohammed started the car; it jerked as he took off. 'Sabon Gari is not safe.'

'What do you mean?' She tugged at the scarf; the embroidery at the edges felt coarse and uncomfortable against her neck.

'Sule said they are well organized.'

Olanna stared at him, suddenly frightened at how frightened he looked. 'Mohammed?'

His voice was low. 'He said Igbo bodies are lying on Airport Road.'

Olanna realized, then, that this was not just another demonstration by religious students. Fear parched her throat. She clasped her hands together. 'Please let us pick up my people first,' she said. 'Please.'

Mohammed headed towards Sabon Gari. A bus drove past, dusty and yellow; it looked like one of those campaign buses that politicians used to tour rural areas and give out rice and cash to villagers. A man was hanging out of the door, a loudspeaker pressed to his mouth, his slow Hausa words resonating. 'The Igbo must go. The infidels must go. The Igbo must go.' Mohammed reached out and squeezed her hand and held on to it as they drove past a crowd of young men on the roadside, chanting, *Araba, araba!* He slowed down and blew the horn a few times in solidarity; they waved and he picked up speed again.

In Sabon Gari, the first street was empty. Olanna saw the smoke rising like tall, grey shadows before she smelt the scent of burning.

'Stay here,' Mohammed said, as he stopped the car outside Uncle Mbaezi's compound. She watched him run out. The street looked strange, unfamiliar; the compound gate was broken, the metal flattened on the ground. Then she noticed Aunty Ifeka's kiosk, or what remained of it: splinters of wood, packets of groundnuts lying in the dust. She opened the car door and climbed out. She paused for a moment because of how glaringly bright and hot it was, with flames billowing from the roof, with grit and ash floating in the air, before she began to run towards the house. She stopped when she saw the bodies. Uncle Mbaezi lay facedown in an ungainly twist, legs splayed. Something creamy-white oozed through the large gash on the back of his head. Aunty Ifeka lay on the veranda. The cuts on her naked body were smaller, dotting her arms and legs like slightly parted red lips.

Olanna felt a watery queasiness in her bowels before the numbness spread over her and stopped at her feet. Mohammed was dragging her, pulling her, his grasp hurting her arm. But she could not leave without Arize. Arize was due at anytime. Arize needed to be close to a doctor.

'Arize,' she said. 'Arize is down the road.'

The smoke was thickening around her so that she was not sure if the crowd of men drifting into the yard were real or just plumes of smoke, until she saw the shiny metal blades of their axes and machetes, the bloodstained kaftans that flapped around their legs.

Mohammed pushed her into the car and then went around and got in. 'Keep your face down,' he said.

'We finished the whole family. It was Allah's will!' one of the men called out in Hausa. The man was familiar. It was Abdulmalik. He nudged a body on the ground with his foot and Olanna noticed, then, how many bodies were lying there, like dolls made of cloth.

'Who are you?' another asked, standing in front of the car.

Mohammed opened his door, the car still on, and spoke in rapid, coaxing Hausa. The man stood aside. Olanna turned to look closely, to see if it really was Abdulmalik.

'Don't raise your face!' Mohammed said. He narrowly missed a *kuka* tree; one of the large pods had fallen down and Olanna heard the crunching squash as the car ran over it. She lowered her head. It *was* Abdulmalik. He had nudged another body, a woman's headless body, and stepped over it, placed one leg down and then the other, although there was enough room to step to the side.

'Allah does not allow this,' Mohammed said. He was shaking; his entire body was shaking. 'Allah will not forgive them. Allah will not forgive the people who have made them do this. Allah will *never* forgive this.'

They drove in a frenzied silence, past policemen in blood-splattered uniforms, past vultures perched by the roadside, past boys carrying looted radios, until he parked at the train station and shoved her onto a crowded train.

Olanna sat on the floor of the train with her knees drawn up to her chest and the warm, sweaty pressure of bodies around her. Outside the train, people were strapped to the coaches and some stood on the steps holding on to the railings. She had heard muted shouts when a man fell off. The train was a mass of loosely held metal, the ride unsteady as if the rails were crossed by speed bumps, and each time it jolted, Olanna was thrown against the woman next to her, against something on the woman's lap, a big bowl, a calabash. The woman's wrapper was dotted with splotchy stains that looked like blood, but

Olanna was not sure. Her eyes burnt. She felt as if there were a mixture of peppers and sand inside them, pricking and burning her lids. It was agony to blink, agony to keep them closed, agony to leave them open. She wanted to rip them out. She wet her fingers with saliva and rubbed her eyes. She sometimes did that to Baby when Baby got a minor scratch. 'Mummy Ola!' Baby would wail, raising the offending arm or leg, and Olanna would stick a finger in her mouth and run it over Baby's injury. But the saliva only made her burning eyes worse.

A young man in front of her screamed and placed his hands on his head. The train swerved and Olanna bumped against the calabash again; she liked the firm feel of the wood. She edged her hand forwards until it was gently caressing the carved lines that crisscrossed the calabash. She closed her eyes, because they burnt less that way, and kept them closed for hours, her hand against the calabash, until somebody shouted in Igbo, '*Anyi agafeela!* We have crossed the River Niger! We have reached home!'

A liquid – urine – was spreading on the floor of the train. Olanna felt it coldly soaking into her dress. The woman with the calabash nudged her, then motioned to some other people close by. '*Bianu*, come,' she said. 'Come and take a look.'

She opened the calabash.

'Take a look,' she said again.

Olanna looked into the bowl. She saw the little girl's head with the ashy-grey skin and the plaited hair and rolled-back eyes and open mouth. She stared at it for a while before she looked away. Somebody screamed.

The woman closed the calabash. 'Do you know,' she said, 'it took me so long to plait this hair? She had such thick hair.'

The train had stopped with a rusty screech. Olanna got down and stood in the jostling crowd. A woman fainted. Motor boys were hitting the sides of lorries and chanting, 'Owerri! Enugu! Nsukka!' She thought about the plaited hair resting in the calabash. She visualized the mother plaiting it, her fingers oiling it with pomade before dividing it into sections with a wooden comb.

❧ 12 ❧

Richard was rereading Kainene's note when the plane touched down in Kano. He had only just found it while searching in his briefcase for a magazine. He wished he had known it was lying there the ten days he was in London, waiting to be read.

> *Is love this misguided need to have you beside me most of the time? Is love this safety I feel in our silences? Is it this belonging, this completeness?*

He was smiling as he read; Kainene had never written anything like this to him before. He doubted that she had ever written him anything at all, except for the generic *Love, Kainene,* on his birthday cards. He read over and over, lingering on each *I* that was so elaborately curved, it looked like a sterling sign. Suddenly he didn't mind that the flight had been delayed in London and that this stop at Kano to change planes before going on to Lagos would delay him even longer. An absurd lightness draped itself around him; all things were possible, all things were manageable. He got up and helped the woman seated next to him carry her bag down. *Is love this safety I feel in our silences?*

'You're so kind,' the woman told him in an Irish accent. The flight was full of non-Nigerians. If Kainene were here, she would certainly say something mocking – *There go the marauding Europeans.* He shook hands with the stewardess at the foot of the ramp and walked quickly across the tarmac; the sun was intense, a piercing white hotness that made him imagine his body fluids evaporating, drying out, and he was relieved to get inside the cool building. He stood in the customs queue and reread Kainene's note. *Is love this misguided need to have you beside me most of the time?* He would ask her to marry him when he returned to Port Harcourt. She would first say something like, 'A white man and no money to speak of. My parents will be scandalized.' But she would say yes. He knew she would say yes. It was something about her lately, a mellowing, a softening from which this note had come. He was not sure if she had forgiven him for the incident with Olanna – they had never talked about it – but this note, this new openness, meant that she was ready to move forwards. He was smoothing the note on his palm, when a young, very dark-skinned customs officer asked, 'Anything to declare, sir?'

'No,' Richard said, and handed over his passport. 'I'm going on to Lagos.'

'Okay, well done, sir! Welcome to Nigeria,' the young man said. He had a large, chubby body that looked sloppy in his uniform.

'You work here?' Richard asked him.

'Yes, sir. I am in training. By December, I will be a full customs officer.'

'Excellent,' Richard said. 'And where are you from?'

'I come from the Southeastern region, a town called Obosi.'

'Onitsha's little neighbour.'

'You know the place, sir?'

'I work at Nsukka University and I have travelled throughout the Eastern region. I'm writing a book about the area. And my fiancée is from Umunnachi, not too far from you.' He felt a flush of achievement, at how easily *fiancée* had slipped out of him, a sign of future uxorious bliss. He smiled, then realized that his smile threatened to grow into a giggle and that he might be slightly delirious. It was that note.

'Your fiancée, sir?' The young man looked disapproving.

'Yes. Her name is Kainene.' Richard spoke slowly, making sure to drag out the second syllable fully.

'You speak Igbo, sir?' There was a slender respect in the man's eyes now.

'*Nwanne di na mba,*' Richard said, enigmatically, hoping that he had not mixed things up and that the proverb meant that one's brother could come from a different land.

'Eh! You speak! *I na-asu Igbo!*' The young man took Richard's hand in his moist one and shook it warmly and started to talk about himself. His name was Nnaemeka.

'I know Umunnachi people well, they find too much trouble,' he said. 'My people warned my cousin not to marry an Umunnachi man, but she did not hear. Every day they beat her until she packed her things and returned to her father's house. But not everybody in Umunnachi is bad. My mother's people are from there. Have you not heard of my mother's mother? Nwayike Nkwelle? You should write about her in your book. She was a wonderful herbalist, and she had the best cure for malaria. If she had charged people big money, I will be studying medicine overseas now. But my family cannot send me overseas, and the people in Lagos are giving scholarships to the children of the people who can bribe them. It is because of Nwayike Nkwelle that I want to learn how to be a doctor. But I am not saying that this my customs work is bad. After all, we have to take exam to get the job, and many people are jealous. By the time I become a full officer, life will be better and there will be less suffering. . . .'

A voice, speaking English with an elegant Hausa accent, announced that the passengers from the London flight should proceed to board the flight for Lagos. Richard was relieved. 'It has been nice talking to you, *jisie ike*,' he said.

'Yes, sir. Greet Kainene.'

Nnaemeka turned to go back to his desk. Richard picked up his briefcase. The side entrance burst open and three men ran in holding up long rifles. They were wearing green army uniforms, and Richard wondered why soldiers would make such a spectacle of themselves, dashing in like that, until he saw how red and wildly glassy their eyes were.

The first soldier waved his gun around. '*Ina nyamiri!* Where are the Igbo people? Who is Igbo here? Where are the infidels?'

A woman screamed.

'You are Igbo,' the second soldier said to Nnaemeka.

'No, I come from Katsina! Katsina!'

The soldier walked over to him. 'Say Allahu Akbar!'

The lounge was silent. Richard felt cold sweat weighing on his eyelashes.

'Say Allahu Akbar!' the soldier repeated.

Nnaemeka knelt down. Richard saw fear etched so deeply onto his face that it collapsed his cheeks and transfigured him into a mask that looked nothing like him. He would not say Allahu Akbar because his accent would give him away. Richard willed him to say the words, anyway, to try; he willed something, anything, to happen in the stifling silence and as if in answer to his thoughts, the rifle went off and Nnaemeka's chest blew open, a splattering red mass, and Richard dropped the note in his hand.

Passengers were crouched behind the chairs. Men got on their knees to lower their heads to the floor. Somebody was shouting in Igbo, 'My mother, oh! My mother, oh! God has said no!' It was the bartender. One of the soldiers walked up close and shot him and then aimed at the bottles of liquor lined up behind and shot those. The room smelt of whisky and Campari and gin.

There were more soldiers now, more shots, more shouts of 'Nyamiri!' and 'Araba, araba!' The bartender was writhing on the floor and the gurgle that came from his mouth was guttural. The soldiers ran out to the tarmac and into the aeroplane and pulled out Igbo people who had already boarded and lined them up and shot them and left them lying there, their bright clothes splashes of colour on the dusty black stretch. The security guards folded their arms across their uniforms and watched. Richard felt himself wet his trousers. There was a painful ringing in his ears. He almost missed his flight because, as the other passengers walked shakily to the plane, he stood aside, vomiting.

Susan was still in her bathrobe. She didn't look surprised to see him arrive unannounced. 'You look exhausted,' she said, touching his cheek. Her hair was dull and matted, loosely held back to reveal her reddened ears.

'I've just got in from London. Our flight stopped first in Kano,' he said.

'Did it?' Susan said. 'And how was Martin's wedding?'

Richard sat still on the sofa; he remembered nothing of what had happened in London. Susan didn't seem to notice that he had not spoken. 'Small whisky with lots of water?' she asked, already pouring the drinks. 'Kano is interesting, isn't it?'

'Yes,' Richard said, although what he had wanted to tell her was how he had watched the hawkers and cars and buses on the crowded Lagos roads with bemusement, because life continued to hurtle on here in the normal way that it always had, as if nothing was happening in Kano.

'It's rather silly how the Northerners will pay foreigners twice more rather than hire a Southerner. But there's quite a bit of money to be made there. Nigel's just rung to tell me about his friend, John, a ghastly Scot. Anyway, John's a charter pilot and has made a small fortune flying Igbo people to safety these past few days. He said hundreds were killed in Zaria alone.'

Richard felt as if his body was gearing up to do something, to shiver, to collapse. 'You know what's happening there, then?'

'Of course I do. I just hope it doesn't spread to Lagos. One really can't predict these things.' Susan downed her drink in a gulp. He noticed the ashen tone of her skin, the tiny beads of sweat above her lip. 'There are lots and lots of Igbo people here – well, they are everywhere really, aren't they? Not that they didn't have it coming to them, when you think about it, with their being so clannish and uppity and controlling the markets. Very Jewish, really. And to think they are relatively uncivilized; one couldn't compare them to the Yoruba, for example, who have had contact with Europeans on the coast for years. I remember somebody telling me when I first came to be careful about hiring an Igbo houseboy because, before I knew it, he would own my house and the land it was built on. Another small whisky?'

Richard shook his head. Susan poured herself another drink and this time did not add any water. 'You didn't see anything at the airport in Kano, did you?'

'No,' Richard said.

'They wouldn't go to the airport, I suppose. It's quite extraordinary, isn't it, how these people can't control their hatred of each other. Of course, we all hate somebody, but it's about *control*. Civilization teaches you control.'

Susan finished her drink and poured another. Her voice echoed as he went into the bathroom and worsened the splintering pain in his head. He turned the tap on. It shocked him, how unchanged he looked in the mirror, how the hair of his eyebrows still stuck out unrestrained and his eyes were still the same stained-glass blue. He should have been transfigured by what he had seen. His shame should have left red warts on his face. What he had felt when he saw Nnaemeka killed was not shock but a great relief that Kainene was not with him because he would have been helpless to protect her and they would have known she was Igbo and they would have shot her.

He could not have saved Nnaemeka, but he should have *thought* about him first, he should have been consumed by the young man's death. He stared at himself and wondered if it really had happened, if he really had seen men die, if the lingering smells from shattered liquor bottles and bloodied human bodies were only in his imagination. But he knew it had certainly happened and he questioned it only because he willed himself to. He lowered his head to the sink and began to cry. The water hissed as it gushed out of the tap.

3. The Book: The World Was Silent When We Died

He writes about Independence. The Second World War changed the world order: Empire was crumbling, and a vocal Nigerian elite, mostly from the South, had emerged.

The North was wary; it feared domination from the more educated South and had always wanted a country separate from the infidel South anyway. But the British had to preserve Nigeria as it was, their prized creation, their large market, their thorn in France's eye. To propitiate the North, they fixed the pre-Independence elections in favour of the North and wrote a new constitution which gave the North control of the central government.

The South, too eager for independence, accepted this constitution. With the British gone, there would be good things for everyone: 'white' salaries long denied Nigerians, promotions, top jobs. Nothing was done about the clamour of the minority groups, and the regions were already competing so fiercely that some wanted separate foreign embassies.

At Independence in 1960, Nigeria was a collection of fragments held in a fragile clasp.

※ 13 ※

Olanna's Dark Swoops began the day she came back from Kano, the day her legs failed. Her legs were fine when she climbed down from the train and she did not need to hold on to the blood-smeared railings; they were fine as she stood for the three-hour drive to Nsukka in a bus so crowded she could not reach out to scratch her itching back. But at the front door of Odenigbo's house, they failed. So did her bladder. There was the melting of her legs, and there was also the wetness of hot liquid running between her thighs. Baby discovered her. Baby had walked to the front door to look out, asking Ugwu when Mummy Ola would come back, and then cried out at the crumpled form on the steps. Odenigbo carried her in, bathed her, and held Baby back from hugging her too tightly. After Baby fell asleep, Olanna told Odenigbo what she had seen. She described the vaguely familiar clothes on the headless bodies in the yard, the still-twitchy fingers on Uncle Mbaezi's hand, the rolled-back eyes of the child's head in the calabash and the odd skin tone – a flat, sallow grey, like a poorly wiped blackboard – of all the corpses that lay in the yard.

That night, she had the first Dark Swoop: A thick blanket descended from above and pressed itself over her face, firmly, while she struggled to breathe. Then, when it let go, freeing her to take in gulp after gulp of air, she saw burning owls at the window grinning and beckoning to her with charred feathers. She tried to describe these Dark Swoops to Odenigbo. She tried to tell him, also, how the pills tasted, the ones Dr Patel brought, clammy like her tongue in the morning.

But Odenigbo always said, 'Shush, *nkem*. You'll be fine.' He spoke too softly to her. His voice sounded so silly, so unlike him. He even sang when he bathed her in the tub full of water scented with Baby's bath foam. She wanted to ask him to stop being ridiculous, but her lips were heavy. Speaking was a labour. When her parents and Kainene visited, she did not say much; it was Odenigbo who told them what she had seen.

At first, her mother sat next to her father and nodded as Odenigbo spoke in that silly-soft voice. Then her mother collapsed; she simply began to slide down as if her bones had liquefied until she half lay, half sat on the floor. It was the first time Olanna saw her mother without make-up, without gold clinging to her ears, and the first time Olanna saw Kainene cry since they were children. 'You don't have to talk about it, you don't have to,' Kainene said, sobbing, although Olanna had not even tried to talk about it.

Her father walked up and down the room. He asked Odenigbo over and over where exactly Patel had read medicine and how he could claim that Olanna's inability to walk was psychological. He talked about how frustrated they felt to have to drive all the way from Lagos because the federal government blockade meant Nigeria Airways was no longer flying to the southeast. 'We wanted to come right away, right away,' he said, so often that Olanna wondered if he really thought it would have made a difference when they came. But it did make a difference that they came, especially that Kainene came. It did not mean that Kainene had forgiven her, of course, but it meant something.

In the following weeks, Olanna lay in bed and nodded when friends and relatives came by to say *ndo* – sorry – and to shake their heads and mutter about the evils of those Muslim Hausa people, those black-as-he-goats Northerners, those dirty cattle rearers with jigger-infested feet. Her Dark Swoops were worse on the days she had visitors; sometimes three came in quick succession and left her breathless and exhausted, too exhausted even to cry, and with only enough energy to swallow the pills Odenigbo slipped in her mouth. Some guests had stories to tell – the Okafors had lost a son and his family of four in Zaria, the Ibe daughter had not returned from Kaura-Namoda, the Onyekachi family had lost eight people in Kano. There were other stories, too, of how British academics at the university in Zaria encouraged the massacres and sent students out to incite the youths, how crowds at the Lagos motor parks had booed and taunted, 'Go, Igbo, go, so that *garri* will be cheaper! Go, and stop trying to own every house and every shop!' Olanna did not like to hear these stories, nor did she like the furtive way the guests glanced at her legs, as though to discover a lump that would explain why she could not walk.

There were days when she woke up from her naps feeling clear-headed, like today. Her bedroom door was open, and she could hear the rise and fall of voices from the living room. For a while Odenigbo had asked their friends not to visit. He had stopped playing tennis, too, so he could be at home and Ugwu would not have to take her to the toilet. She was pleased that they were visiting again. Sometimes she followed the conversation. She knew that the university women's association was organizing food donations for the refugees, that the markets and railways and tin mines in the North were said to be empty now that the Igbo had fled, that Colonel Ojukwu was now seen as the leader of the Igbo, that people were talking about secession and a new country, which would be named after the bay, the Bight of Biafra.

Miss Adebayo was speaking in her loud voice. 'I am saying that our students should stop making noise. Asking David Hunt to go does not make sense. Give the man a chance and see if peace will come.'

'David Hunt thinks we are all mental children.' It was Okeoma. 'The man should go home. Why is he coming to tell us how to put out a fire, when it is he and his fellow British who collected the firewood for it in the first place?'

'They may have collected the firewood, but we lit the match,' said somebody with an unfamiliar voice, perhaps it was Professor Achara, the new lecturer in physics, who had come back from Ibadan after the second coup.

'Firewood or no firewood, the important thing is to find a way to make peace before things explode,' Miss Adebayo said.

'What peace are we looking for? Gowon himself has said that a basis for unity does not exist, so what peace are we looking for?' Odenigbo asked. Olanna imagined him at the edge of his chair, pushing his glasses back as he spoke. 'Secession is the only answer. If Gowon wanted to keep this country united, he would have done something long ago. For goodness' sake, not one of them has come out to condemn the massacres, and months have passed! It is as if all our people who were killed don't matter!'

'Didn't you hear what Zik said the other day? Eastern Nigeria seethes, seethes, and will continue to seethe until the federal government addresses the massacres,' Professor Ezeka said, his hoarse voice quickly fading.

Olanna's head ached. The sun shone weakly through the curtains Ugwu had drawn when he brought her breakfast. She needed to urinate; she urinated too often these days and she kept forgetting to ask Dr Patel if her medication was the reason. She stared at the bell on the bedside cabinet, then reached out and ran a hand over the black, dome-shaped plastic, over the red button in the middle that gave out a shrill sound when she depressed it. Odenigbo had insisted on installing it himself, at first, and each time she pressed it, there was a fire spark at the wall connection. Finally, he brought an electrician, who chuckled as he did the rewiring. The bell no longer sparked, but it was too loud, and whenever she needed to go to the toilet and rang it, the echo reverberated all over the house. She let her finger linger over the red button, then drew away. She would not ring it. She lowered her legs to the floor. The sound from the living room was diminished now as if somebody had lowered the collective volume of the voices.

Then she heard Okeoma say 'Aburi'. It sounded lovely, the name of that Ghanaian town, and she imagined a sleepy cluster of homes on stretches of sweet-scented grasslands. Aburi came up often in their conversations: Okeoma would say that Gowon should have followed the agreement he and Ojukwu signed in Aburi, or Professor Ezeka would say that Gowon's reneging after Aburi meant that he did not wish the Igbo well, or Odenigbo would proclaim, 'On Aburi we stand.'

'But how can Gowon make such a turnaround?' Okeoma's voice was louder. 'He agreed to confederation at Aburi, and now he wants one Nigeria with a unitary government, but a unitary government was the very reason that he and his people killed Igbo officers.'

Olanna stood up and placed one leg forwards, then the other. She swayed. There was a tight pressure around her ankles. She was walking. The firmness of the floor beneath her feet was stirring and her legs felt as if they had vibrating vessels in them. She walked past Baby's Raggedy Ann lying on the floor, and stopped to look down at the stuffed doll for a while before she went in to the toilet.

Later, Odenigbo came in and looked searchingly into her eyes in the way he often did, as if looking for proof of something. 'You haven't rung in a while, *nkem*. Don't you have to urinate?'

'Have they all gone?'

'Yes. Don't you want to urinate?'

'I did already. I walked.'

Odenigbo stared at her.

'I walked,' Olanna said again. 'I used the toilet.'

There was something she had never seen on Odenigbo's face, something precious and frightened. She sat up and he immediately reached out to hold her, but she shrugged him off and walked a few steps to the wardrobe and then back to the bed. Odenigbo sat and looked at her.

She took his hand and touched it to her face, pressed it against her breast. 'Touch me.'

'I'm going to tell Patel. I want him to come in and take a look at you.'

'Touch me.' She knew he didn't want to, that he touched her breasts because he would do whatever she wanted, whatever would make her better. She caressed his neck, buried her fingers in his dense hair, and when he slid into her, she thought about Arize's pregnant belly, how easily it must have broken, skin stretched that taut. She started to cry.

'*Nkem*, don't cry.' Odenigbo had stopped; he was lying next to her and smoothing her forehead. Later, when he gave her more pills and some water, she took them dutifully and then lay back and waited for the strange stillness they brought.

Ugwu's gentle knock woke her up; he would open the door and come in with a tray of food that he would place next to her packets of medicine, bottle of Lucozade, and tin of glucose. She remembered the first week she came back, the week that Odenigbo sprang up whenever she stirred. She had asked for water and Odenigbo opened the bedroom door to go to the kitchen and nearly tripped on Ugwu, curled on a mat right outside their door. 'My good man, what are you doing here?' he asked, and Ugwu answered, 'You don't know where anything is in the kitchen, sah.'

She closed her eyes now and pretended she was asleep. He was standing close to her and watching her; she could hear his breathing.

'When you are ready, mah, the food is here,' he said. Olanna nearly laughed; he probably knew all the times she pretended to be asleep when he brought her food. She opened her eyes. 'What did you cook?'

'*Jollof* rice.' He raised the cover of the dish. 'I used fresh tomatoes from the garden.'

'Has Baby eaten?'

'Yes, mah. She is playing outside with Dr Okeke's children.'

Olanna picked up the fork and held it.

'I will make fruit salad for you tomorrow, mah. That pawpaw tree behind has a ripe fruit. I will give it one more day, and then I will pluck it fast before those birds come for it. I will use orange and milk.'

'Good.'

Ugwu still stood there, and she knew he would not leave until she had started to eat. She raised the fork to her mouth slowly, chewing with her eyes closed. It was as good as whatever Ugwu cooked, she was sure, but, except for the chalky pills, she had been unable to taste anything in so long. Finally, she drank some water and asked Ugwu to take the tray away.

On her bedside table, Odenigbo had placed a long sheet of paper with WE, UNIVERSITY STAFF, DEMAND SECESSION AS A MEANS OF SECURITY typewritten at the top and a patchwork of varied signatures at the bottom.

'I was waiting for you to be strong enough to sign it before I deliver it to the statehouse in Enugu,' he had said.

After Ugwu left the room, she picked up a pen and signed the letter and then checked through the text for any errors. There were none. But Odenigbo didn't need to deliver the letter because the secession was announced that evening. He sat on the bed with the radio placed on the bedside cabinet. The reception had little static, as if the radio waves understood the importance of the speech. Ojukwu's voice was unmistakable; it was vibrantly male, charismatic, smooth:

> *Fellow countrymen and women, you the people of Eastern Nige-*
> *ria: Conscious of the supreme authority of Almighty God over all*
> *mankind; of your duty over posterity; aware that you can no*
> *longer be protected in your lives and in your property by any gov-*
> *ernment based outside Eastern Nigeria; determined to dissolve*
> *all political and other ties between you and the former Republic of*

> *Nigeria; having mandated me to proclaim on your behalf and in your name that Eastern Nigeria be a sovereign independent Republic, now therefore I do hereby solemnly proclaim that the territory and region known as and called Eastern Nigeria, together with her continental shelf and territorial waters, shall henceforth be an independent sovereign state of the name and title of The Republic Of Biafra.*

'This is our beginning,' Odenigbo said. That false softness had left his voice and he sounded normal again, bracing and sonorous. He took his glasses off and grabbed Baby's little hands and began to dance around in circles with her. Olanna laughed and then felt as if she were following a script, as if Odenigbo's excitement would abide nothing but more excitement. She sat up and shivered. She had wanted the secession to happen, but now it seemed too big to conceive. Odenigbo and Baby were moving round and round, Odenigbo singing off-key, a song he had made up – '*This is our beginning, oh, yes, our beginning, oh, yes . . .*' – while Baby laughed in blissful incomprehension. Olanna watched them, her mind frozen in the present, on the cashew-juice stain on the front of Baby's dress.

The rally was held in Freedom Square, in the centre of the campus, lecturers and students shouting and singing, an endless sheet of heads and placards held high.

> *We shall not, we shall never move,*
> *Just like a tree that's planted by the water,*
> *We shall not be moved.*
> *Ojukwu is behind us, we shall never move.*
> *God is behind us, we shall never move.*

They swayed as they sang, and Olanna imagined that the mango and *gmelina* trees swayed too, in agreement, in one fluid arc. The sun felt like a flame brought too close, and yet it was drizzling and the lukewarm raindrops mixed with her sweat. Her arm brushed Odenigbo's as she raised her placard: it read WE CANNOT DIE LIKE DOGS. Baby was sitting on Odenigbo's shoulders, waving her stuffed doll, and the sun was bright through the thin drizzle, and Olanna was filled with a delicious exuberance. Ugwu was beside her. His placard read GOD BLESS BIAFRA. They were Biafrans. She was Biafran. Behind her, a man was talking about the market, how the traders were dancing to Congo music and giving away the best of their mangoes and groundnuts. A woman said she would go there right after the rally to see what she could get for free, and Olanna turned to them and laughed.

A student leader spoke into the microphone and the singing stopped. Some young men were carrying a coffin with NIGERIA written on it in white chalk; they raised it up, mock solemnity on their faces. Then they placed it down and pulled their shirts off and started to dig a shallow hole in the ground. When they lowered the coffin into the hole, a cheer rose in the crowd and spread, ripplelike, until it was one cheer, until Olanna felt that everybody there had become one. Somebody shouted, 'Odenigbo!' And it spread among the students. 'Odenigbo! Address us!'

Odenigbo climbed up to the podium waving his Biafran flag: swaths of red, black, and green and, at the centre, a luminous half of a yellow sun.

'Biafra is born! We will lead Black Africa! We will live in security! Nobody will ever again attack us! Never again!'

Odenigbo raised his arm as he spoke, and Olanna thought how awkwardly twisted Aunty Ifeka's arm had looked, as she lay on the ground, how her blood had pooled so thick that it looked like glue, not red but close to black. Perhaps Aunty Ifeka could see this rally now, and all the people here, or perhaps not, if death was a silent opaqueness. Olanna shook her head, to shake away the thoughts, and took Baby from Ugwu's neck and hugged her close.

After the rally, she and Odenigbo drove to the staff club. Students had gathered on the hockey field nearby, burning paper effigies of Gowon around a glowing bonfire; the smoke curled into the night air and mixed with their laughter and chatter. Olanna watched them and realized with a sweet surge that they all felt what she felt, what Odenigbo felt, as though it were liquid steel instead of blood that flowed through their veins, as though they could stand barefoot over red-hot embers.

❈ 14 ❈

Richard did not think it would be so easy to find Nnaemeka's family, but when he arrived at Obosi and stopped at the Anglican church to ask, the catechist told him they lived just down the road, in the unpainted house flanked by palm trees. Nnaemeka's father was small and albino, copper-coloured, his eyes a greyish-hazel that brightened as soon as Richard spoke Igbo. He was so different from the large, dark customs officer at the airport that for a moment Richard wondered if perhaps he was in the wrong house and this was not Nnaemeka's father. But the older man blessed the kola nut in a voice so similar to Nnaemeka's that it took Richard back to the airport lounge that hot afternoon and to Nnaemeka's irritating chatter before the door burst open and the soldiers ran in.

'He who brings the kola nut brings life. You and yours will live, and I and mine will live. Let the eagle perch and let the dove perch and, if either decrees that the other not perch, it will not be well for him. May God bless this kola in Jesus' name.'

'Amen,' Richard said. He could see other resemblances now. The man's gestures as he broke the kola nut apart into five lobes were eerily like Nnaemeka's, as was the set of his mouth, with the lower lip jutting out. Richard waited until they had chewed the kola nut, until Nnaemeka's mother appeared, dressed in black, before he said, 'I saw your son at the airport in Kano, the day it happened. We talked for a while. He spoke about you and his family.' Richard paused and wondered whether they would prefer to hear that their son had remained stoic in the face of death or if they would want to hear that he fought it, that he charged towards the gun. 'He told me that his grandmother from Umunnachi was a respected herbal doctor known far and wide for her cure of malaria, and that it was because of her that he first wanted to be a doctor.'

'Yes, that is so,' Nnaemeka's mother said.

'He spoke only good words about his family,' Richard said. He chose his Igbo words carefully.

'Of course he would speak good words about his family.' Nnaemeka's father gave Richard a long look as if he did not understand why Richard had to say what they already knew.

Richard shifted on the bench. 'Did you have a funeral?' he asked, and then wished he had not.

'Yes,' Nnaemeka's father said; he fixed his gaze on the enamel bowl that held the last lobe of kola nut. 'We waited for him to return from the North and he did not return, so we had a funeral. We buried an empty coffin.'

'It was not empty,' Nnaemeka's mother said. 'Did we not put that old book he used to read for the civil service exam inside?'

They sat in silence. Dust motes swam in the slice of sunlight that came through the window.

'You must take the last piece of kola nut with you,' Nnaemeka's father said.

'Thank you.' Richard slipped the lobe into his pocket.

'Shall I send the children to the car?' Nnaemeka's mother asked. It was difficult to tell what she looked like, with the black scarf that covered all of her hair and much of her forehead.

'The car?' Richard asked.

'Yes. Did you not bring us things?'

Richard shook his head. He should have brought yams and drinks. It was after all a condolence visit, and he knew how things were done. He had been caught up in himself, in thinking that his coming was enough, that he would be the magnanimous angel who brought the last hours of their son to them and, by doing so, would assuage their grief and redeem himself. But to them he was just like any other person who had come to pay condolences. His visit made no difference to the only reality that mattered: their son was gone.

He got up to leave, knowing that nothing had changed for him either; he would feel the same way he had felt since he returned from Kano. He had often wished that he would lose his mind, or that his memory would suppress itself, but instead everything took on a terrible transparence and he had only to close his eyes to see the freshly dead bodies on the floor of the airport and to recall the pitch of the screams. His mind remained lucid. Lucid enough for him to write calm replies to Aunt Elizabeth's frantic letters and tell her that he was fine and did not plan to return to England, to ask her to please stop sending flimsy airmail editions of newspapers with articles about the Nigerian pogroms circled in pencil. The articles annoyed him. 'Ancient tribal hatreds', the *Herald* wrote, was the reason for the massacres. *Time* magazine titled its piece MAN MUST WHACK, an expression printed on a Nigerian lorry, but the writer had taken *whack* literally and gone on to explain that Nigerians were so naturally prone to violence that they even wrote about the necessity of it on their passenger lorries. Richard sent a terse letter off to *Time*. In Nigerian Pidgin English, he wrote, *whack* meant *eat*. At least the *Observer* was a little more adroit, in writing that if Nigeria survived the massacres of the Igbo, it would survive anything. But there was a hollowness to all the accounts, an echo of unreality. So Richard began to write a long article about the massacres. He sat at the dining table in Kainene's house and wrote on long sheets of unlined paper. He had brought Harrison to Port Harcourt, and while he worked he could hear Harrison talking to Ikejide and Sebastian. 'You are not knowing how to bake German chocolate cake?' A cackle. 'You are not knowing what is rhubarb crumble?' Another scornful cackle.

Richard started by writing about the refugee problem, a result of the massacres, about the traders who fled their markets in the North, university lecturers who left their campuses, civil servants who fled their jobs in the ministries. He struggled over the closing paragraph.

It is imperative to remember that the first time the Igbo people were massacred, albeit on a much smaller scale than what has recently occurred, was in 1945. That carnage was precipitated by the British colonial government when it blamed the Igbo people for the national strike, banned Igbo-published newspapers, and generally encouraged anti-Igbo sentiment. The notion of the recent killings being the product of 'age-old' hatred is therefore misleading. The tribes of the North and the South have long had contact, at least as far back as the ninth century, as some of the magnificent beads discovered at the historic Igbo-Ukwu site attest. No doubt these groups also fought wars and slave-raided each other, but they did not massacre in this manner. If this is hatred, then it is very young. It has been caused, simply, by the informal divide-and-rule policies of the British colonial exercise. These policies manipulated the differences between the tribes and ensured that unity would not exist, thereby making the easy governance of such a large country practicable.

When he gave Kainene the article, she read it carefully, with her eyes narrowed, and afterwards told him, 'Very fierce'.

He was not sure what *very fierce* meant or whether she liked it. He desperately wanted her to approve. Her aura of distance had returned since she came back from visiting Olanna in Nsukka. She had put up a photograph of her murdered relatives – Arize laughing in her wedding dress, Uncle Mbaezi ebullient in a tight suit next to a solemn Aunty Ifeka in a print wrapper – but she said very little about them and nothing about Olanna. She often withdrew into silence in the middle of a conversation, and when she did, he let her be; sometimes he envied her the ability to be changed by what had happened.

'What do you think of it?' he asked, and before she could answer, he asked what he really wanted to. 'Do you like it? How do you feel about it?'

'I think it sounds exceedingly formal and stuffy,' she said. 'But what I feel about it is pride. I feel proud.'

He sent it off to the *Herald*. When he got a response two weeks later, he ripped the letter up after reading it. The international press was simply saturated with stories of violence from Africa, and this one was particularly bland and pedantic, the deputy editor wrote, but perhaps Richard could do a piece on the human angle? Did they mutter any tribal incantations while they did the killings, for example? Did they eat body parts like they did in the Congo? Was there a way of trying truly to understand the minds of these people?

Richard put the article away. It frightened him that he slept well at nights, that he was still calmed by the scent of orange leaves and the turquoise stillness of the sea, that he was sentient.

'I'm going on. Life is the same,' he told Kainene. 'I should be reacting; things should be different.'

'You can't write a script in your mind and then force yourself to follow it. You have to let yourself be, Richard,' she said quietly.

But he couldn't let himself be. He didn't believe that life was the same for all the other people who had witnessed the massacres. Then he felt more frightened at the thought that perhaps he had been nothing more than a voyeur. He had not feared for his own life, so the massacres became external, outside of him; he had watched them through the detached lens of knowing he was safe. But that couldn't be; Kainene would not have been safe if she had been there.

He began to write about Nnaemeka and the astringent scent of liquor mixing with fresh blood in that airport lounge where the bartender lay with a blown-up face, but he stopped because the sentences were risible. They were too melodramatic. They sounded just like the articles in the foreign press, as if these killings had not happened and, even if they had, as if they had not quite happened that way. The echo of unreality weighed each word down; he clearly remembered what had happened at that airport, but to write about it he would have to reimagine it, and he was not sure if he could.

The day the secession was announced, he stood with Kainene on the veranda and listened to Ojukwu's voice on the radio and afterward took her in his arms. At first he thought they were both trembling, until he moved back to look at her face and realized that she was perfectly still. Only he was trembling.

'Happy independence,' he told her.

'Independence,' she said, before she added, 'Happy independence.'

He wanted to ask her to marry him. This was a new start, a new country, *their* new country. It was not only because secession was just, considering all that the Igbo had endured, but because of the possibility Biafra held for him. He would be Biafran in a way he could never have been Nigerian – he was here at the beginning; he had shared in the birth. He would belong. He said, *Marry me, Kainene* in his head many times but he did not say it aloud. The next day, he returned to Nsukka with Harrison.

Richard liked Phyllis Okafor. He liked the verve of her bouffant wigs, the drawl of her native Mississippi, as well as the severe eyeglass frames that belied the warmth in her eyes. Since he had stopped going to Odenigbo's house, he often spent evenings with her and her husband, Nnanyelugo. It was as if she knew he had lost a social life, and she insistently invited him to the arts theatre, to public lectures, to play squash. So when she asked him to come to the 'In Case of War' seminar that the university women's association was organizing, he accepted. It was a good idea to be prepared, of course, but there would be no war. The Nigerians would let Biafra be; they would never fight a people already battered by the massacres. They would be pleased to be rid of the Igbo anyway. Richard was certain about this. He was less certain about what he would do if he ran into Olanna at the seminar. It had been easy to avoid her thus far; in four years he had driven past her only a few times, he never went to the tennis courts or the staff club, and he no longer shopped at Eastern Shop.

He stood near Phyllis at the entrance of the lecture hall and scanned the room. Olanna was sitting in front with Baby on her lap. Her lushly beautiful face seemed very familiar, as did her blue dress with the ruffled collar, as if he had seen both very recently. He looked away and could not help feeling relieved that Odenigbo had not come. The hall was full. The woman talking at the podium repeated herself over and over. 'Wrap your certificates in waterproof bags and make sure those are the first things you take if we have to evacuate. Wrap your certificates in waterproof bags . . .'

More people spoke. Then it was over. People were mingling, laughing, and talking and exchanging more 'in case of war' tips. Richard knew that Olanna was nearby, talking to a bearded man who taught music. He turned, casually, to slip away, and was close to the door when she appeared beside him.

'Hello, Richard. *Kedu?*'

'I'm well,' he said. The skin of his face felt tight. 'And you?'

'We are fine,' Olanna said. Her lips had a slight glisten of pink gloss. Richard did not miss her use of the plural. He was not sure if she meant herself and the child, or herself and Odenigbo, or perhaps *we* was meant to suggest that she had made peace with what had happened between them and what it had done to her relationship with Kainene.

'Baby, have you greeted?' Olanna asked, looking down at the child, whose hand was enclosed in hers.

'Good afternoon,' Baby said, in a high voice.

Richard bent and touched her cheek. There was a calmness about her that made her seem older and wiser than her four years. 'Hello, Baby.'

'How is Kainene?' Olanna asked.

Richard evaded her eyes, not sure what his expression should be. 'She is well.'

'And your book is going well?'

'Yes. Thank you.'

'Is it still called *The Basket of Hands*?'

It pleased him that she had not forgotten. 'No.' He paused and tried not to think about what had happened to that manuscript, about the flames that must have charred it quickly. 'It's called *In the Time of Roped Pots*.'

'Interesting title,' Olanna murmured. 'I hope there won't be war, but the seminar has been quite useful, hasn't it.'

'Yes.'

Phyllis came over, said hello to Olanna, and then tugged at Richard's arm. 'They say Ojukwu is coming! Ojukwu is coming!' There was the sound of raised voices outside the hall.

'Ojukwu?' Richard asked.

'Yes, yes!' Phyllis was walking towards the door. 'You know he dropped into Enugu campus for a surprise visit some days ago? It looks like it's our turn!'

Richard followed her outside. They joined the cluster of lecturers standing by the statue of a lion; Olanna had disappeared.

'He's at the library now,' somebody said.

'No, he's in the senate building.'

'No, he wants to address the students. He's at the admin block.'

Some people were already walking quickly towards the administration block, and Phyllis and Richard went along. They were close to the umbrella trees that lined the driveway when Richard saw the bearded man, in a severely smart, belted army uniform, striding across the corridor. A few reporters scrambled after him, holding out tape recorders like offerings. Students, so many that Richard wondered how they had congregated so quickly, began to chant. 'Power! Power!' Ojukwu came downstairs and stood on top of some cement blocks on the grassy lawn. He raised his hands. Everything about him sparkled, his groomed beard, his watch, his wide shoulders.

'I came to ask you a question,' he said. His Oxford-accented voice was surprisingly soft; it did not have the timbre that it did over the radio and it was a little theatrical, a little too measured. 'What shall we do? Shall we keep silent and let them force us back into Nigeria? Shall we ignore the thousands of our brothers and sisters killed in the North?'

'*No! No!*' The students were filling the wide yard, spilling onto the lawn and the driveway. Many lecturers had parked their cars on the road and joined the crowd. 'Power! Power!'

Ojukwu raised his hands again and the chanting stopped. 'If they declare war,' he said. 'I want to tell you now that it may become a long-drawn-out war. A long-drawn-out war. Are you prepared? Are we prepared?'

'Yes! Yes! Ojukwu, *nye anyi egbe!* Give us guns! *Iwe di anyi n'obi!* There is anger in our hearts!'

The chanting was constant now – give us guns, there is anger in our hearts, give us guns. The rhythm was heady. Richard glanced across at Phyllis, thrusting a fist in the air as she shouted, and he looked around for a little while at everyone else, intense and intent in the moment, before he too began to wave and chant. 'Ojukwu, give us guns! Ojukwu, *nye anyi egbe!*'

Ojukwu lit a cigarette and threw it down on the lawn. It flared for a while, before he reached out and squashed it underneath a gleaming black boot. 'Even the grass will fight for Biafra,' he said.

Richard told Kainene how charmed he had been by Ojukwu even though the man showed signs of early balding and was vaguely histrionic and wore a gaudy ring. He told her about the seminar. Then he wondered whether to tell her that he had run into Olanna. They were sitting on the veranda. Kainene was peeling an orange with a knife, and the slender peel dropped into a plate on the floor.

'I saw Olanna,' he said.

'Did you?'

'At the seminar. We said hello and she asked about you.'

'I see.' The orange slipped from her hand, or perhaps she dropped it, because she left it there on the terrazzo floor of the veranda.

'I'm sorry,' Richard said. 'I thought I should mention that I saw her.'

He picked up the orange and held it out to her but she did not take it. She got up and walked to the railing.

'War is coming,' she said. 'Port Harcourt is going crazy.'

She was looking in the far distance, as if she could actually see the city in its frenzy of excessive parties and frenetic couplings and speeding cars. Earlier that afternoon, a well-dressed young woman had come up to Richard at the train station and taken his hand. 'Come to my flat. I never do it with *oyinbo* man before, but I want try everything now, oh!' she had said, laughing, although the delirious desire in her eyes was serious enough. He had shrugged his hand free and walked away, strangely sad at the thought that she would end up with another stranger in her bed. It was as if the people in this city with the tall, whistling pines wanted to grab all they could before the war robbed them of choices.

Richard got up and stood beside Kainene.

'There won't be war,' he said.

'How did she ask about me?'

'She said, How is Kainene?'

'And you said I was well?'

'Yes.'

She said nothing else about it; he did not expect that she would.

Ugwu climbed out of the car and went around to the boot. He placed the bag of dried fish on top of the larger bag of *garri*, hoisted both onto his head, and followed Master up the cracked stairs and into the dim building that was the town union office. Mr Ovoko came up to meet them. 'Take the bags into the store,' he told Ugwu, pointing, as if Ugwu did not know from all the times he had come in the past to bring food for the refugees. The store was empty except for a small bag of rice in the corner; weevils crawled all over it.

'How are things? *A na-emekwa?*' Master asked.

Mr Ovoko rubbed his hands together. He had the lugubrious face of one who simply refuses to be consoled. 'Nobody is donating much these days. These people keep coming here and asking me for food, and then they start to ask for jobs. You know, they came back from the North with nothing. Nothing.'

'I know they came back with nothing, my friend! Don't lecture me!' Master snapped.

Mr Ovoko moved back. 'I am only saying that the situation is serious. In the beginning our people rushed to donate food, but now they have forgotten. It will be a disaster if war comes.'

'War will not come.'

'Then why has Gowon continued to blockade us?'

Master ignored the question and turned to leave. Ugwu followed.

'Of course people are still donating food. That dull fellow must be taking the food to his own family,' Master said, as he started the car.

'Yes, sah,' Ugwu said. 'Even his stomach is very big.'

'That ignoramus Gowon pledged a miserable, measly amount for more than two million refugees. Did he think it was chickens that died and it is the surviving relatives of those chickens who have returned home?'

'No, sah.' Ugwu looked out of the window. It filled him with sadness, coming here to give *garri* and fish to people who had fed themselves in the North, listening week after week to Master saying the same things. He reached out and straightened the rope that dangled from the rearview mirror. The plastic keepsake attached to it was a painting of half of a yellow sun on a black background.

Later, as he sat on the backyard steps reading *The Pickwick Papers*, stopping often to think and to watch the slender leaves of corn swish in the breeze, he was not surprised to hear Master's raised voice from the living room. Master was always short-tempered on days like this.

'And what about our university colleagues in Ibadan and Zaria and Lagos? Who is speaking out about this? They kept silent while white expatriates encouraged the rioters to kill Igbo people. You would be one of them if you didn't happen to be in Igboland! How much sympathy can you have?' Master shouted.

'Don't you dare say I have no sympathy! To say that secession is not the only way to security does not mean I don't have sympathy!' It was Miss Adebayo.

'Did your cousins die? Did your uncle die? You're going back to your people in Lagos next week and nobody will harass you for being Yoruba. Is it not your own people who are killing the Igbo in Lagos? Didn't a group of your chiefs go to the North to thank the emirs for sparing Yoruba people? So what are you saying? How is your opinion relevant?'

'You insult me, Odenigbo.'

'The truth has become an insult.'

There was silence and then the squeaking sound of the front door being opened and banged shut. Miss Adebayo had left. Ugwu stood up when he heard Olanna's voice. 'This is unacceptable, Odenigbo! You owe her an apology!'

It frightened him to hear her shout because she rarely did, and because the last time he had heard her shout was during those fractured weeks before Baby's birth, when Mr Richard stopped visiting and everything seemed to be on the brink of drowning. For a moment Ugwu heard nothing – perhaps Olanna, too, had walked out – and then he heard Okeoma reading. Ugwu knew the poem: *If the sun refuses to rise, we will make it rise.* The first time Okeoma read it, the same day the *Renaissance* newspaper was renamed the *Biafran Sun*,

Ugwu had listened and felt buoyed by it, by his favourite line, *Clay pots fired in zeal, they will cool our feet as we climb.* Now, though, it made him teary. It made him long for the days when Okeoma recited poems about people getting buttocks rashes after defecating in imported buckets, the days when Miss Adebayo and Master shouted and yet did not end the evening with her storming off, the days when he still served pepper soup. Now, he served only kola nut.

Okeoma left a little while later, and Ugwu heard Olanna's voice rise again. 'You must, Odenigbo. You owe her an apology!'

'It is not a question of whether or not I owe her an apology. It is a question of whether or not I spoke the truth,' Master said. Olanna said something Ugwu did not hear and then Master spoke in a calmer tone, 'All right, *nkem*, I will.'

Olanna came into the kitchen. 'We are going out,' she said. 'Come and lock the door.'

'Yes, mah.'

After they left in Master's car, Ugwu heard a tap on the back door and went to see who it was.

'Chinyere,' he said, surprised. She never came over this early, and never to the main house either.

'Me and my madam and the children are leaving tomorrow morning for the village. I came to tell you to stay well. *Ka o di.*'

Ugwu had never heard her say so much. He was not sure what to say. They looked at each other for a while.

'Go well,' he said. He watched her walk to the hedge that separated the two compounds and slip underneath it. She would no longer appear at his door at night and lie on her back and spread her legs silently, at least not for a while. He felt a strange crushing weight in his head. Change was hurtling towards him, bearing down on him, and there was nothing he could do to make it slow down.

He sat down and stared at the cover of *The Pickwick Papers*. There was a serene calm in the backyard, in the gentle wave of the mango tree and the winelike scent of ripening cashews. It belied what he saw around him. Fewer and fewer guests visited now, and in the evenings the campus streets were ghostly, covered by the pearly light of silence and emptiness. Eastern Shop had closed. Chinyere's mistress was only one of many families on campus who were leaving; houseboys bought huge cartons in the market and cars drove out of compounds with their boots sunken by heavy loads. But Olanna and Master had not packed a single thing. They said that war would not come and that people were simply panicking. Ugwu knew that families had been told they could send women and children to the hometowns, but the men could not leave, because if the men left it would mean that they were panicking and there was nothing to panic about. 'No cause for alarm' was what Master said often. 'No cause for alarm.' Professor Uzomaka who lived opposite Dr Okeke had been turned back three times by the militiamen at the campus gates. They let him pass the third day after he swore that he would come back, that he was only taking his family to their hometown because his wife worried so much.

'Ugwuanyi!'

Ugwu looked up and saw his aunty coming towards him from the front yard. He stood up.

'Aunty! Welcome.'

'I was knocking on the front door.'

'Sorry. I did not hear.'

'Are you alone at home? Where is your master?'

'They went out. They took Baby with them.' Ugwu examined her face. 'Aunty, is it well?'

She smiled. 'It is well, *o di mma*. I bring a message from your father. They will have Anulika's wine-carrying ceremony next Saturday.'

'Eh! Next Saturday?'

'It is better they do it now, before war comes, if war is going to come.'

'That is true.' Ugwu looked away, towards the lemon tree. 'So. Anulika is really getting married.'

'Did you think you would marry your own sister?'

'God forbid.'

His aunty reached out and pinched his arm. 'Look at you, a man has emerged. *Eh!* In a few years it will be your turn.'

Ugwu smiled. 'It is you and my mother who will find a good person when the time comes, Aunty,' he said, with a false demureness. There was no point in telling her that Olanna had told him they would send him to university when he finished secondary school. He would not marry until he had become like Master, until he had spent many years reading books.

'I am going,' his aunty said.

'Won't you drink some water?'

'I cannot stay. *Ngwanu*, let it be. Greet your master and give him my message.'

Even before his aunty left, Ugwu was already imagining his arrival for the ceremony. This time, he would finally hold Nnesinachi naked and pliant in his arms. His Uncle Eze's hut was a good place to take her, or perhaps even the quiet grove by the stream, as long as the little children did not bother them. He hoped she would not be silent like Chinyere; he hoped she would make the same sounds he heard from Olanna when he pressed his ear to the bedroom door.

That evening, while he was cooking dinner, a quiet voice on the radio announced that Nigeria would embark on a police action to bring back the rebels of Biafra.

Ugwu was in the kitchen with Olanna, peeling onions, watching the movement of Olanna's shoulder as she stirred the soup on the stove. Onions made him feel cleaned up, as if the tears they drew from him took away impurities. He could hear Baby's high voice in the living room, playing with Master. He did not want either of them to come into the kitchen now. They would destroy the magic he felt, the sweet sting of onions in his eyes, the glow of Olanna's skin. She was talking about the Northerners in Onitsha who had been killed in reprisal attacks. He liked the way *reprisal attacks* came out of her mouth.

'It's so wrong,' she said. 'So wrong. But His Excellency has handled it all well; God knows how many would have been killed if he did not have the Northern soldiers sent back to the North.'

'Ojukwu is a great man.'

'Yes, he is, but we are all capable of doing the same things to one another, really.'

'No, mah. We are not like those Hausa people. The reprisal killings happened because they pushed us.' His *reprisal killings* had come out sounding close to hers, he was sure.

Olanna shook her head but said nothing for a while. 'After your sister's wine-carrying, we will go to Abba to spend some time there since the campus is so empty,' she said finally. 'You can stay with your people if you want to. We will come back for you when we return; we won't be gone for more than a month, at the most. Our soldiers will drive the Nigerians back in a week or two.'

'I will come with you and Master, mah.'

Olanna smiled, as if she had wanted him to say that. 'This soup is not thickening at all,' she muttered. Then she told him about the first time she cooked soup as a young girl, how she managed to burn the bottom of the pot to a charred purple and yet the soup turned out very tasty. He was absorbed in Olanna's voice and so he did not hear the sound – *boom-boom-boom* – from somewhere distant outside the windows, until she stopped stirring and looked up.

'What is that?' she asked. 'Do you hear it, Ugwu? What is it?'

Olanna dropped the ladle and ran into the living room. Ugwu followed. Master was standing by the window, holding a folded copy of the *Biafran Sun*.

'What is that?' Olanna asked. She pulled Baby to her. 'Odenigbo!'

'They are advancing,' Master said calmly. 'I think we should plan on leaving today.'

Then Ugwu heard the loud honk of a car outside. Suddenly he was afraid to go to the door, even to go to the window and peek out.

Master opened the door. The green Morris Minor had parked so hurriedly that one tyre was outside the driveway, crushing the lilies that bordered the lawn; when the man came out of the car, Ugwu was shocked to see that he was only wearing a singlet and trousers. And bathroom slippers too!

'Evacuate now! The federals have entered Nsukka! We are evacuating now! Right now! I am going to all the houses still occupied. Evacuate now!'

It was after he had spoken and rushed back into his car and driven off, honking continuously, that Ugwu recognized him: Mr Vincent Ikenna, the registrar. He had visited a few times. He drank his beer with Fanta.

'Get a few things together, *nkem*,' Master said. 'I'll check the water in the car. Ugwu, lock up quick! Don't forget the Boys' Quarters.'

'*Gini?* What things?' Olanna asked. 'What will I take?'

Baby started to cry. There was the sound again, *boom-boom-boom*, closer and louder.

'It won't be for long, we'll be back soon. Just take a few things, clothes.' Master gestured vaguely before he grabbed the car keys from the shelf.

'I'm still cooking,' Olanna said.

'Put it in the car,' Master said.

Olanna looked dazed; she wrapped the pot of soup in a dishcloth and took it out to the car. Ugwu ran around throwing things into bags: Baby's clothes and toys, biscuits from the fridge, his clothes, Master's clothes, Olanna's wrappers and dresses. He wished he knew what to take. He wished that sound did not seem even closer. He dumped the bags in the backseat of the car and dashed back inside to lock the doors and close the window louvres. Master was honking outside. He stood in the middle of the living room, feeling dizzy. He needed to urinate. He ran into the kitchen and turned the stove off. Master was shouting his name. He took the albums from the shelves, the three photo albums Olanna so carefully put together, and ran out to the car. He had hardly shut the car door when Master drove off. The campus streets were eerie; silent and empty.

At the gates, Biafran soldiers were waving cars through. They looked distinguished in their khaki uniforms, boots shining, half of a yellow sun sewn on their sleeves. Ugwu wished he was one of them. Master waved and said, 'Well done!'

Dust swirled all around, like a see-through brown blanket. The main road was crowded; women with boxes on their heads and babies tied to their backs, barefoot children carrying bundles of clothes or yams or boxes, men dragging bicycles. Ugwu wondered why they were holding lit kerosene lanterns although it was not yet dark. He saw a little child stumble and fall and the mother bend and yank him up, and he thought about home, about his little cousins and his parents and Anulika. They were safe. They would not have to run because their village was too remote. This only meant that he would not see Anulika get married, that he would not hold Nnesinachi in his arms as he had planned. But he would be back soon. The war would last just long enough for the Biafran army to gas the Nigerians to kingdom come. He would yet taste Nnesinachi's sweetness, he would yet caress that soft flesh.

Master drove slowly because of the crowds and roadblocks, but slowest when they got to Milliken Hill. The lorry ahead of them had NO ONE KNOWS TOMORROW printed on its body. As it crawled up the steep incline, a young man jumped out and ran alongside, carrying a wood block, ready to throw it behind the back tyre if the lorry were to roll back.

When they finally arrived at Abba, it was dusk, the windscreen was coated in ochre dust, and Baby was asleep.

❧ 16 ❧

Richard was surprised when he heard the announcement that the federal government had declared a *police action to bring the rebels to order*. Kainene was not.

'It's the oil,' she said. 'They can't let us go easily with all that oil. But the war will be brief. Madu says Ojukwu has big plans. He suggested I donate some foreign exchange to the war cabinet, so that when this ends, I'll get any contract I bid for.'

Richard stared at her. She did not seem to understand that he could not comprehend a war at all, brief or not.

'It's best if you move your things to Port Harcourt until we drive the Nigerians back,' Kainene said. She was scanning a newspaper and nodding her head to the Beatles on the stereo and she made it seem normal, that war was the inevitable outcome of events and that moving his things from Nsukka was simply as it should be.

'Yes, of course,' he said.

Her driver took him. Checkpoints had sprung up everywhere, tyres and nail-studded boards placed across the road, men and women in khaki shirts with expressionless, disciplined demeanours standing by. The first two were easy to pass. 'Where are you going?' they asked, and waved the car through. But near Enugu, the civil defenders had blocked the road with tree trunks and old rusty drums. The driver stopped.

'Turn back! Turn back!' A man peered through the window; he was holding a long piece of wood carefully carved to look like a rifle. 'Turn back!'

'Good afternoon,' Richard said. 'I work at the university in Nsukka and I am on my way there. My houseboy is there. I have to get my manuscript and some personal belongings.'

'Turn back, sah. We will drive the vandals back soon.'

'But my manuscript and my papers and my houseboy are there. You see, I didn't take anything. I didn't know.'

'Turn back, sah. That is our order. It is not safe. But soon, when we drive the vandals back, you can return.'

'But you must understand.' Richard leaned farther forwards.

The man's eyes narrowed while the large eye painted on his shirt underneath the word VIGILANCE seemed to widen. 'Are you sure you are not an agent of the Nigerian government? It is you white people who allowed Gowon to kill innocent women and children.'

'*Abu m onye* Biafra,' Richard said.

The man laughed, and Richard was not sure if it was a pleasant or an unpleasant laugh. 'Eh, a white man who is saying that he is a Biafran! Where did you learn to speak our language?'

'From my wife.'

'Okay, sah. Don't worry about your things in Nsukka. The roads will be clear in a few days.'

The driver reversed, and as he drove back the way they had come, Richard kept looking back at the blocked road until he could no longer see it. He thought about how easily those Igbo words had slipped out of him. 'I am a Biafran.' He did not know why, but he hoped the driver would not tell Kainene that he had said that. He hoped, too, that the driver would not tell Kainene that he had referred to her as his wife.

Susan called some days later. It was late morning and Kainene was at one of her factories.

'I didn't know you had Kainene's number,' Richard said. Susan laughed.

'I heard Nsukka was evacuated and I knew you would be with her. So how are you? Are you all right?'

'Yes.'

'You didn't have trouble evacuating, did you?' Susan asked. 'You're all right?'

'I'm all right.' He was touched by her concern.

'Right. So what are your plans?'

'I will be here for now.'

'It's not safe, Richard. I'm not staying here longer than another week. These people never fight civilized wars, do they? So much for calling it a civil war.' Susan paused. 'I rang the British Council in Enugu and I can't believe our people there are still going off to play water polo and have cocktails at the Hotel Presidential! There's a bloody war going on.'

'It will be cleared up soon.'

'Cleared up, ha! Nigel is leaving in two days. Nothing is going to clear up; this war will drag on for years. Look what happened in the Congo. These people have no sense of peace. They'd sooner fight until the last man is down – '

Richard hung up while Susan was still speaking, surprising himself by the rudeness. There was a part of him that wished he could help her, throw away the bottles of liquor in her cabinet and wipe away the paranoia that scarred her life. Perhaps it was a good thing she was leaving. He hoped she would find happiness, with Nigel or otherwise. He was still occupied with thoughts of Susan, half hoping she would not call again and half hoping she would, when Kainene came home. She kissed his cheeks, his lips, his chin. 'Did you spend the day worrying about Harrison and *In the Time of Roped Pots*?' she asked.

'Of course not,' he said, even though they both knew it was a lie.

'Harrison will be fine. He must have packed up and gone to his village.'

'Yes, he must have,' Richard said.

'He probably took the manuscript with him.'

'Yes.' Richard remembered how she had destroyed his first real manuscript, *The Basket of Hands*, how she had led him to the orchard, to the pile of charred paper under his favourite tree, her face all the time expressionless; and how afterwards he had felt not blame or anger but hope.

'There was another rally in town today, at least a thousand people walking, and many cars covered in green leaves,' she said. 'I wish they would stick to fields instead of blocking major roads. I've already donated money and I won't be held up in the hot sun just to help further Ojukwu's ambition.'

'It's about a cause, Kainene, not a man.'

'Yes, the cause of benign extortion. You know taxi drivers no longer charge soldiers? They get offended when a soldier offers to pay the fare. Madu says there is a group of women at the barracks every other day, from all sorts of backwater villages, bringing yams and plantains and fruits to the soldiers. These are people who have nothing themselves.'

'It's not extortion. It's the cause.'

'The cause indeed.' Kainene shook her head but she looked amused. 'Madu told me today that the army has nothing, absolutely nothing. They thought Ojukwu had arms piled up somewhere, given the way he's been talking, "No power in Black Africa can defeat us!" So Madu and some of the officers who came back from the North went to tell him that we have no arms, no mobilization of troops, and that our men are training with wooden guns, for goodness' sake! They wanted him to release his stockpiled arms. But he turned around and said they were plotting to overthrow him. Apparently he has no arms at all and he plans to defeat Nigeria with his fists.' She raised a fist and smiled. 'But I do think he is terribly attractive: that beard alone.'

Richard said nothing. He wondered, fleetingly, if he should grow a beard.

Olanna leaned on the veranda railing of Odenigbo's house in
Abba, looking out at the yard. Near the gate, Baby was on her
knees playing in the sand while Ugwu watched her. The
wind rustled the leaves of the guava tree. Its bark fascinated Olanna,
the way it was discoloured and patchy, a light clay alternating with a
darker slate, much like the skin of village children with the *nlacha*
skin disease. Many of those children had stopped by to say '*nno nu,*
welcome,' on the day they arrived from Nsukka, and their parents
and uncles and aunts had come too, bearing good wishes, itching for
gossip about the evacuation. Olanna had felt a fondness for them;
their welcome made her feel protected. Her warmth had extended
even to Odenigbo's mother. She wondered now why she did not
pull Baby away from the grandmother who had rejected her at birth
and why she herself did not move away from Mama's hug. But there
was a haunting, half-finished quality to all that happened that day –
cooking in the kitchen with Ugwu, the departure so hasty that she
worried the oven was left on, the crowds on the road, the sound of
shelling – so she took Mama's hug in her stride, even hugged her
back. Now they had gone back to being civil, Mama often came over
to see Baby, through the wooden gate in the mud wall that separated
her home from Odenigbo's. Sometimes Baby went across to visit her
and run after the goats that wandered in her courtyard. Olanna was
never sure how clean were the pieces of dried fish or smoked meat
Baby came back chewing, but she tried not to mind, just as she tried
to stifle her resentment; Mama's affection for Baby had always been
half-baked, half-hearted, and it was too late for Olanna to feel anything but resentment.

Baby was laughing at something Ugwu said; her pure high-pitched laughter made Olanna smile. Baby liked it here; life was slower and simpler. Because their stove and toaster and pressure cooker and imported spices were left behind in Nsukka, their meals were simpler too, and Ugwu had more time to play with her.

'Mummy Ola!' Baby called. 'Come and see!'

Olanna waved. 'Baby, it's time for your evening bath.'

She watched the outline of the mango trees in the next yard; some of them had fruit drooping down like heavy earrings. The sun was falling. The chickens were clucking and flying up into the kola nut tree, where they would sleep. She could hear some villagers exchanging greetings, in the same loud-voiced way that the women in the sewing group did. She had joined them two weeks ago, in the town hall, sewing singlets and towels for the soldiers. She felt bitter towards them at first, because when she tried to talk about the things she had left behind in Nsukka – her books, her piano, her clothes, her china, her wigs, her Singer sewing machine, the television – they ignored her and started to talk about something else. Now she understood that nobody talked about the things left behind. Instead, they talked about the win-the-war effort. A teacher had donated his bicycle to the soldiers, cobblers were making soldiers' boots for free, and farmers were giving away yams. Win the war. It was difficult for Olanna to visualize a war happening now, bullets falling on the red dust of Nsukka while the Biafran troops pushed the vandals back. It was often difficult to visualize anything concrete that was not dulled by memories of Arize and Aunty Ifeka and Uncle Mbaezi, that did not feel like life being lived on suspended time.

She kicked off her slippers and walked barefoot across the front yard and over to Baby's sand hut. 'Very nice, Baby. Maybe it will still be standing tomorrow, if the goats don't come in the yard in the morning. Now, time for a bath.'

'No, Mummy Ola!'

'I think Ugwu is going to carry you off right now.' Olanna glanced at Ugwu.

'No!'

Ugwu picked Baby up and ran off towards the house. Baby's slipper fell off and they stopped to pick it up, Baby saying 'No!' and laughing at the same time. Olanna wondered how Baby would take their leaving the following week for Umuahia, three hours away, where Odenigbo had been deployed to the Manpower Directorate.

He had hoped to work at the Research and Production Directorate, but there were too many overqualified people and too few jobs; even she had been told there was no vacancy for her at any of the directorates. She would teach at the primary school, her own win-the-war effort. It did have a certain melody to it: win-the-war, win-the-war, win-the-war. She hoped Professor Achara had found them accommodation close to other university people so that Baby would have the right kind of children to play with.

She sat down on one of the low wooden chairs that slanted so that she had to recline in them in order to rest her back. They were chairs she saw only in the village, made by village carpenters who set up dusty signs by the corners of the dirt roads, often with CARPENTER misspelt: capinter, capinta, carpentar. You could not sit up on such chairs; they assumed a life of hard-earned rest, of evenings reclining in fresh air after a day of farmwork. Perhaps they assumed, also, a life of ennui.

It was dark and the bats were flying noisily above when Odenigbo came home. He was always out during the day, attending meeting after meeting, all of them on how Abba would contribute to the win-the-war effort, how Abba would play a major role in establishing the state of Biafra; sometimes she saw men returning from the meetings, holding mock guns carved from wood. She watched Odenigbo walk across the veranda, aggressive confidence in his stride. Her man. Sometimes when she looked at him she felt gripped by proud possession.

'*Kedu?*' he asked, bending to kiss her lips. He examined her face carefully, as if he had to do so to make sure she was well. He had been doing that since she returned from Kano. He told her often that the *experience* had changed her and made her so much more *inward*. He used *massacre* when he spoke to his friends, but never with her. It was as if what had happened in Kano was a massacre but what she had seen was an experience.

'I'm fine,' she said. 'Aren't you a little early?'

'We finished early because there's going to be a general meeting in the square tomorrow.'

'Why?' Olanna asked.

'The elders decided it was time. There are all kinds of silly rumours about Abba evacuating soon. Some ignoramuses even say the federal troops have entered Awka!' Odenigbo laughed and sat down next to Olanna. 'Will you come?'

'To the meeting?' She had not even considered it. 'I'm not from Abba.'

'You could be, if you married me. You should be.'

She looked at him. 'We are fine as we are.'

'We are at war and my mother would have to decide what will be done with my body if anything happened to me. You should decide that.'

'Stop it, nothing will happen to you.'

'Of course nothing will happen to me. I just want you to marry me. We really should marry. It no longer makes sense. It never made sense.'

Olanna watched a wasp flit around the spongy nest lodged in the wall corner. It had made sense to her, the decision not to marry, the need to preserve what they had by wrapping it in a shawl of difference. But the old framework that fit her ideals was gone now that Arize and Aunty Ifeka and Uncle Mbaezi would always be frozen faces in her album. Now that bullets were falling in Nsukka. 'You have to take wine to my father, then,' she said.

'Is that a yes?'

A bat swooped down and Olanna lowered her head. 'Yes. It is a yes,' she said.

In the morning, she heard the town crier walking past the house, beating a loud *ogene*. 'There will be a meeting of all Abba tomorrow at four p.m. in Amaeze Square!' *Gom-gom-gom*. 'There will be a meeting of all Abba tomorrow at four p.m. in Amaeze Square!' *Gom-gom-gom*. 'Abba has said that every man and every woman must attend!' *Gom-gom-gom*. 'If you do not attend, Abba will fine you!'

'I wonder how steep the fines are,' Olanna said, watching Odenigbo dress. He shrugged. He had only the two shirts and pairs of trousers that Ugwu had hurriedly packed, and she smiled, thinking of how she knew what he would wear each morning before he dressed.

They had sat down to have breakfast when her parents' Land Rover drove into the compound.

'How fortuitous,' Odenigbo said. 'I'll tell your dad right away. We can have the wedding here next week.' He was smiling. There was something boyish about him since she'd said yes on the veranda, something naively gleeful that she wished she felt too.

'You know it's not done that way,' she said. 'You have to go to Umunnachi with your people and do it properly.'

'Of course I know. I was only joking.'

Olanna walked to the door, wondering why her parents had come. They had visited only a week ago, after all, and she was not quite ready for another monologue from her jittery mother while her father stood by and nodded his agreement: Please come and stay with us in Umunnachi; Kainene should leave Port Harcourt until we know whether this war is coming or going; that Yoruba caretaker we left in Lagos will loot the house; I am telling you, we really should have arranged to bring all the cars back.

The Land Rover parked under the kola nut tree, and her mother climbed out. She was alone. Olanna felt slight relief that her father had not come. It was easier to deal with one at a time.

'Welcome, Mom, *nno*,' Olanna said, hugging her. 'Is it well?'

Her mother shrugged in the way that was meant to say so-so. She was wearing a red george wrapper and pink blouse and her shoes were flat, a shiny black. 'It is well.' Her mother looked around, the same way she had looked around, furtively, the last time before pushing an envelope of money into Olanna's hand. 'Where is he?'

'Odenigbo? He's inside, eating.'

Her mother led the way to the veranda and leaned against a pillar. She opened her handbag, gestured for Olanna to look inside. It was full of the glitter and twinkle of jewellery, corals and metals and precious stones.

'Ah! Ah! Mum, what is all that for?'

'I carry them everywhere I go now. My diamonds are inside my bra.' Her mother was whispering. '*Nne*, nobody knows what is going on. We are hearing that Umunnachi is about to fall and that the federals are very close by.'

'The vandals are not close by. Our troops are driving them back around Nsukka.'

'But how long is it taking to drive them back?'

Olanna disliked the petulant pout on her mother's face, the way her mother lowered her voice as if doing so would exclude Odenigbo. She would not tell her mother that they had decided to get married. Not yet.

'Anyway,' her mother said, 'your father and I have finalized our plans. We have paid somebody who will take us to Cameroon and get us on a flight from there to London. We will use our Nigerian passports; the Cameroonians will not give us trouble. It was not easy but it is done. We paid for four places.' Her mother patted her headgear, as if to ensure that it was still there. 'Your father has gone to Port Harcourt to tell Kainene.'

Olanna felt pity at the plea in her mother's eyes. Her mother knew she would not run away to England with them, and that Kainene would not either. But it was so like her to try, to make this doomed, grasping, well-meaning effort.

'You know I won't go,' she said gently, wanting to reach out and touch her mother's perfect skin. 'But you and Dad should go, if it will make you feel safer. I'll stay with Odenigbo and Baby. We'll be fine. We are going to Umuahia in a few weeks for Odenigbo to start work at the directorate.' Olanna paused. She wanted to say that they would have their wedding in Umuahia but instead she said, 'As soon as Nsukka is recovered, we'll go back.'

'But what if Nsukka is not recovered? What if this war drags on and on?'

'It won't.'

'How can I leave my children and run to safety?'

But Olanna knew she could and she would. 'We'll be fine, Mum.'

Her mother wiped her eyes with her palm, although there were no tears, before she brought out an airmail envelope from her handbag. 'It's a letter from Mohammed. Somebody brought it to Umunnachi. Apparently he heard Nsukka was evacuated and he thought you had come to Umunnachi. Sorry; I had to open it, to make sure there was nothing dangerous in it.'

'Nothing dangerous?' Olanna asked. '*Gini?* What are you talking about, Mum?'

'Who knows? Is he not the enemy now?'

Olanna shook her head. She was pleased her mother would be going abroad and she would not have to deal with her until this war was over. She wanted to wait until her mother left before she read the letter, so that her mother would not search her face for an expression, but she could not help pulling out the single sheet of paper right away. Mohammed's handwriting was like him – patrician and long, with elegant flourishes. He wanted to know if she was well. He gave her phone numbers to call if she needed help. He thought the war was senseless and hoped it would end soon. He loved her.

'Thank God you didn't marry him,' her mother said, watching her fold the letter. 'Can you imagine what a situation you would have been in now? *O di egwu!*'

Olanna said nothing. Her mother left soon afterwards; she did not want to come inside and see Odenigbo. 'You can still change your mind, *nne*, the four places are paid for,' she said, climbing into the car, holding tightly to her jewellery-filled bag. Olanna waved until the Land Rover drove past the compound gates.

It surprised her, how many men and women were in Abba, gathered at the square for the meeting, crowded around the ancient *udala* tree. Odenigbo had told her how, as children, he and the others, sent to sweep the village square in the mornings, would instead spend most of their time fighting over the fallen *udala* fruit. They could not climb the tree or pluck the fruit because it was taboo; *udala* belonged to the spirits. She looked up at the tree as the elders addressed the crowd and imagined Odenigbo here as a boy, looking up as she was doing, hoping to see the shadowy outline of a spirit. Had he been energetic like Baby? Probably, perhaps more so than Baby

'Abba, *kwenu!*' the *dibia* Nwafor Agbada said, the man whose medicine was said to be the strongest in these parts.

'Yaa!' everyone said.

'Abba, *kwezuenu!*'

'Yaa!'

'Abba has never been defeated by anyone. I said that Abba has never been defeated.' His voice was strong. He had only a few cotton-ball tufts of hair on his head, and his staff shook as he plunged it into the ground. 'We do not look for quarrels, but when your quarrel finds us, we will crush you. We fought Ukwulu and Ukpo and finished them. My father never told me about a war where we were defeated, and his father never told him either. We will never run from our homeland. Our fathers forbid it. We will never run from our own land!'

The crowd cheered. So did Olanna. She remembered the pro-Independence rallies at university; mass movements always made her feel empowered, the thought that for a thin slice of time all these people were united by a single possibility.

She told Odenigbo about Mohammed's letter as they walked back from the village square after the meeting. 'He must be so upset about all of this. I can't imagine how he must be feeling.'

'How can you say that?' Odenigbo said.

She slowed her pace and turned to him, startled. 'What's the matter?'

'What's the matter is that you are saying that a bloody Muslim Hausa man is upset! He is complicit, absolutely complicit, in everything that happened to our people, so how can you say he is upset?'

'Are you joking?'

'Am I joking? How can you sound this way after seeing what they did in Kano? Can you imagine what must have happened to Arize? They raped pregnant women before they cut them up!'

Olanna recoiled. She tripped on a stone in her path. She could not believe he had brought Arize up like that, cheapened Arize's memory in order to make a point in a spurious argument. Anger froze her insides. She started to walk fast, past Odenigbo, and when she got home, she lay down in the guest room and was not surprised when the Dark Swoop descended. She struggled to pull it off, to breathe, and finally lay in bed exhausted. She didn't speak to Odenigbo the next day. Or the next. And, when her mother's cousin, Uncle Osita, came from Umunnachi to tell her that she was being summoned to a meeting at her grandfather's compound, she did not tell Odenigbo about it. She simply asked Ugwu to get Baby ready and, after Odenigbo left for a meeting, she drove off with them in his car.

She thought of the way Odenigbo had said, 'I'm sorry, I'm sorry,' with an edge of impatience, as if he felt entitled to her forgiveness. He must think that if she could be forgiving of what happened around Baby's birth, she could be forgiving of anything. She resented that. Maybe it was why she didn't tell him she was going to Umunnachi. Or maybe it was because she knew why she was being summoned to Umunnachi and did not want to talk about it with Odenigbo.

She drove over the bumpy dirt roads lined by tall grasses and thought how interesting it was, that villagers could tell you something like *Umunnachi summons you*, as though Umunnachi were a person rather than a town. It was raining. The roads were marshy. She glanced at the looming three storeys of her parents' country home as she drove past it; they would be in Cameroon by now, or perhaps already in London or in Paris, reading the newspapers to learn what was happening back home. She parked in front of her grandfather's house, near the thatch fence. Her tyres skidded a little in the clumpy soil. After Ugwu and Baby had come out of the car, she sat still for a while, watching the raindrops slide down the windscreen. Her chest felt tight and she needed some time to breathe slowly to free it, to free herself so she could answer the questions the elders would present to her at the meeting. They would be gentle, formal, everyone gathered in the musty living room: her elderly uncles and granduncles, their wives, some cousins, and perhaps a baby tied on someone's back.

She would speak in a clear voice and look down at the white chalk lines all over the floor, some faded from years, some simple, straight lines, others elaborate curves, still others plain initials. As a child, she had watched her grandfather present the piece of *nzu* to his guests, and she would follow every movement of the men as they drew on the floor and the women as they smeared it on their faces and, sometimes, even nibbled it. Once, when her grandfather stepped out, Olanna had chewed the piece of chalk too and still remembered the dulling potash taste.

Her grandfather, Nweke Udene, would have led this meeting if he were alive. But Nwafor Isaiah would lead; he was now the oldest member of their *umunna*. He would say, 'Others have come back and we have kept our eyes on the road for our son Mbaezi and our wife Ifeka and our daughter Arize as well as our in-law from Ogidi. We have waited and waited and we have not seen them. Many months have passed and our eyes ache from being focused on the road. We have asked you to come today and tell us what you know. Umunnachi is asking about all her children who did not return from the North. You were there, our daughter. What you tell us, we will tell Umunnachi.'

It was mostly what happened. The only thing Olanna had not expected was the raised voice of Aunty Ifeka's sister, Mama Dozie. A fierce woman, she was said to have beat up Papa Dozie once, after he left their sick child and went off to visit his mistress. Mama Dozie herself had been away harvesting cocoyams in the *agu*. The child nearly died. Mama Dozie, it was said, had threatened to cut off Papa Dozie's penis first, before strangling him, if the child were to die.

'Do not lie, Olanna Ozobia, *i sikwana asi!*' Mama Dozie shouted. 'May chickenpox afflict you if you lie. Who told you it was my sister's body that you saw? Who told you? Do not lie here. Cholera will strike you dead.'

Her son Dozie led her away. He had grown so tall, Dozie, since the last time Olanna saw him a couple of years ago. He was holding his mother tightly and she was trying to push him aside, as if to be allowed to pummel Olanna, and Olanna wished she could let her. She wanted Mama Dozie to hit her and slap her if it would make Mama

Dozie feel better, if it would turn everything she had just told the members of her extended family gathered in this room into a lie. She wished that Odinchezo and Ekene would shout at her too, and question her for being alive, instead of dead like their sister and parents and brother-in-law. She wished that they would not sit there, quiet, looking down as men in mourning often did and later tell her they were happy she did not see Arize's body; everyone knew what those monsters did to pregnant women.

Odinchezo broke off a large leaf from the *ede* plant and gave it to her to use as a makeshift umbrella. But Olanna didn't place it above her head as she hurried to her car. She took her time unlocking the door and let the rain run over her plaited hair and past her eyes and down her cheeks. It struck her how quickly the meeting had unfolded, how little time it took to confirm four of her family dead. She had given those left behind a right to mourn and wear black and receive visitors who would come in, saying '*Ndo nu.*' She had given them a right to move on after the mourning and count Arize and her husband and parents as gone forever. The heavy weight of four muted funerals weighed on her head, funerals based not on physical bodies but on her words. And she wondered if she was mistaken, if she had perhaps imagined the bodies lying in the dust, so many bodies in the yard that recalling them made salt rush to her mouth. When she finally got the car open and Ugwu and Baby had dashed in, she sat motionless for a while, aware that Ugwu was watching her with concern and that Baby was almost falling asleep.

'Do you want me to get you water to drink?' Ugwu asked.

Olanna shook her head. Of course he knew she didn't want water. He wanted to get her out of her trance so she would start the car and drive them back to Abba.

❊ 18 ❊

Ugwu was the first to see people trooping on the dirt road that ran through Abba. They were dragging goats, carrying yams and boxes on their heads, chickens and rolled-up mats under their arms, kerosene lamps in their hands. The children carried small basins or pulled smaller children along. Ugwu watched them walk past, some silent, others talking loudly; many of them, he knew, did not know where they were going.

Master came home from a meeting early that evening. 'We'll leave for Umuahia tomorrow,' he said. 'We would have gone to Umuahia anyway. We're just leaving a week or two sooner.' He spoke too fast, looking at a point in the distance. Ugwu wondered if it was because he did not want to admit that his hometown was about to fall, or if it was because Olanna had not been speaking to him. Ugwu did not know what had happened between them but, whatever it was, it happened after the village square meeting. Olanna had come home in a strange silence. She spoke mechanically. She did not laugh. She let him make every decision about the food and about Baby, spending most of her time on the slanting wooden chair on the veranda. Once he saw her walk over to the guava tree and caress its trunk, and he told himself he would go and pull her away, after a minute, before the neighbours said she was going mad. But she didn't stay long. She turned quietly and went back and sat on the veranda.

She looked just as quiet now. 'Please pack our clothes and food for tomorrow, Ugwu.'

'Yes, mah.'

He packed their things quickly – they did not have that much anyway, it was not like Nsukka where he had been paralyzed with so many choices that he had taken very little. He put them in the car early the next morning and then went around the house to make sure he had missed nothing. Olanna had already packed the albums. She had bathed Baby. They stood waiting by the car while Master checked the oil and water. On the road, people were walking past in thick groups.

The wooden gate in the mud wall behind the house creaked open and Aniekwena came into the compound. He was Master's cousin. Ugwu disliked the sly twist of his lips; he always visited at meal-times and then said 'Oh! Oh!' in exaggerated surprise when Olanna asked him to join them in 'touching their hands to their mouths'. He looked grim now. Behind him was Master's mother.

'We are ready to go, Odenigbo, and your mother has refused to pack her things and come,' Aniekwena said.

Master closed the bonnet. 'Mama, I thought we agreed that you would go to Uke.'

'*Ekwuzikwananu nofu!* Don't say that! You told me that we have to run and that it is better that I go to Uke. But did you hear me agree? Did I say "oh" to you?'

'Do you want to come with us to Umuahia, then?' Master asked.

Mama looked at the car, packed full. 'But why are you running? Where are you running to? Can you hear any guns?'

'People are fleeing Abagana and Ukpo, which means the Hausa sol-diers are close and will soon enter Abba.'

'Did you not hear our *dibia* tell us that Abba has never been con-quered? Who am I running away from my own house for? *Alu melu!* Do you know that your father will be cursing us now?'

'Mama, you cannot stay here. Nobody will be left in Abba.'

She looked up and squinted in concentration as though looking for a ripening pod on the kola nut tree was more important than what Master was saying.

Olanna opened the car door and asked Baby to get in the back.

'The news is not good. The Hausa soldiers are close,' Aniekwena said. 'I am leaving for Uke. Send word to us when you get to Umuahia.' He turned and started to walk away.

'Mama!' Master shouted. 'Go and bring your things now!'

His mother kept looking up the kola nut tree. 'I will stay and watch over the house. After you all have run, you will come back. I will be here waiting. Who am I running away from my own house for, *gbo?*'

'Perhaps it would be a better idea to speak to her gently instead of raising your voice,' Olanna said in English. She sounded very formal, clipped. Ugwu had not heard her speak to Master like that, except during the months before Baby was born.

Master's mother was looking at them suspiciously, as if she was sure that Olanna had just insulted her in English.

'Mama, will you not come with us?' Master asked. '*Biko*. Please come with us.'

'Give me the key to your house. I might need something there.'

'Please come with us.'

'Give me the key.'

Master stared at her silently and then handed her a bunch of keys. 'Please come with us,' he said again, but she said nothing and tied the keys into one edge of her wrapper.

Master climbed into the car. As he drove out, he kept turning back to see his mother, perhaps to see if she would change her mind and dash after Aniekwena or wave to him to stop. But she didn't. She stood there, not waving. Ugwu watched her too, until they turned into the dirt road. How could she stay there all alone, not surrounded by relatives? If everybody in Abba was leaving, how would she eat since there would be no market?

Olanna touched Master's shoulder. 'She will be all right. The federal troops won't stay in Abba if they pass through.'

'Yes,' Master said. He leaned over and kissed her lips, and Ugwu felt a buoyant relief that they were speaking normally again. The stream of refugees filing past was thinning.

'Professor Achara has found us a house in Umuahia,' Master said, his voice too loud, too cheerful. 'Some old friends are already there, and everything will soon be back to normal. Everything will be perfectly normal!'

Because Olanna remained silent, Ugwu said, 'Yes, sah.'

There was nothing normal about the house. The thatch roof and cracked, unpainted walls bothered Ugwu, but not as much as the cavernous pit latrine in the outhouse with a rusting zinc sheet drawn across it to keep flies out. It terrified Baby. The first time she used it, Ugwu held her steady while Olanna cajoled her. Baby cried and cried. She cried often the following days, as if she too realized that the house was unworthy of Master, that the compound was ugly with its stubby grass and cement blocks piled in corners, that the neighbours' houses were too close, so close one smelt their greasy cooking and heard their crying children. Ugwu was certain that Professor Achara had fooled Master into renting the house; there was something wily in the man's bulging eyes. Besides, his own house down the road was large and painted a dazzling white.

'This is not a good house, mah,' Ugwu said.

Olanna laughed. 'Look at you. Don't you know many people are sharing houses now? The scarcity is serious. And here we are with two bedrooms and a kitchen and living room *and* dining room. We are lucky to know an indigene of Umuahia.'

Ugwu said nothing else. He wished she would not be so complacent about it.

'We have decided to have the wedding next month,' Olanna told him a few days later. 'It will be very small, and the reception will be here.'

Ugwu was aghast. For their wedding, he had imagined perfection, the house in Nsukka festively decorated, the crisp, white tablecloth laden with dishes. It was better they wait for the war to end, rather than have their wedding in this house with its sullen rooms and mouldy kitchen.

Even Master didn't seem to mind the house. He returned from the directorate in the evenings and sat outside, contentedly listening to Radio Biafra and the BBC, as if the veranda did not have mud-encrusted floors, as if the stark wood bench there was like the cushioned sofa back in Nsukka. His friends began to stop by as the weeks passed. Sometimes Master went with them to the Rising Sun Bar down the road. Other times he sat with them on the veranda and talked. Their visits made Ugwu overlook the indignities of the house. He no longer served pepper soup or drinks, but he could listen to the regular rise and fall of their voices, the laughter, the singing, Master's shouting. Life came close to being as it was in Nsukka just after the secession; hope swirled around once again.

Ugwu liked Special Julius, who wore sequined, knee-length tunics and was an army contractor and brought cartons of Golden Guinea beer and bottles of White Horse whisky and sometimes petrol in a black jerry can; it was Special Julius, too, who suggested that Master pile palm fronds on top of his car as camouflage and paint over his headlights with coal tar.

'Very unlikely that we will have air raids, but vigilance must be our watchword!' Master said, as he held the brush in his hand. Some tar had oozed down the fenders, marring the blue colour, and later, after Master went indoors, Ugwu carefully wiped it off, until the black glob covered only the headlights.

Ugwu's favourite guest, though, was Professor Ekwenugo. He was a member of the Science Group. The nail on his index finger was so long and tapering that it looked like a slender dagger, and he smoothed it as he spoke about what he and his colleagues were making: high-impact landmines called *ogbunigwe*, brake fluid from coconut oil, car engines from scrap metal, armoured cars, grenades. The others cheered whenever he made an announcement and Ugwu cheered too, from his stool in the kitchen. Professor Ekwenugo's announcement of the first Biafran rocket caused the loudest round of clapping.

'We launched it this afternoon, this very afternoon,' he said, caressing his nail. 'Our own home-made rocket. My people, we are on our way.'

'We are a country of geniuses!' Special Julius said to nobody in particular. 'Biafra is the land of genius!'

'The land of genius,' Olanna repeated, her face in that delicate phase between smiling and laughing.

The clapping soon gave way to singing.

> *So-lidarity forever!*
> *So-lidarity forever!*
> *Our republic shall vanquish!*

Ugwu sang along and wished, again, that he could join the Civil Defence League or the militia, who went combing for Nigerians hiding in the bush. The war reports had become the highlights of his day, the fast-paced drumming, the magnificent voice saying,

> *Eternal vigilance is the price of liberty! This is Radio Biafra Enugu! Here is the daily war report!*

After the glowing news – Biafran troops were flushing out the last remnants of the enemy, Nigerian casualties were high, mopping-up operations were concluding – he would fantasize about joining the army. He would be like those recruits who went into training camp –

while their relatives and well-wishers stood by the sidelines and cheered – and who emerged bright-eyed, in brave uniforms stiff with starch, half of a yellow sun gleaming on their sleeves.

He longed to play a role, to act. Win the war. So when the news that Biafra had captured the midwest and Biafran troops were marching to Lagos came over the radio, he felt a strange mix of relief and disappointment. Victory was theirs and he was eager to go back to the house on Odim Street, to be close to his family, to see Nnesinachi. Yet it seemed that the war had ended too soon and he had not contributed. Special Julius brought a bottle of whisky, and the guests sang and shouted drunkenly about the might of Biafra, the stupidity of the Nigerians, the foolishness of those newscasters on BBC radio.

'Look at their dirty English mouths. "Astonishing move by Biafra", indeed!'

'They are surprised because the arms Harold Wilson gave those Muslim cattle rearers have not killed us off as quickly as they had hoped!'

'It is Russia you should blame, not Britain.'

'Definitely Britain. Our boys brought us some Nigerian shell cases from the Nsukka sector for analysis. Every single one had UK WAR DEPARTMENT on it.'

'We keep intercepting British accents on their radio messages too.'

'Britain *and* Russia, then. That unholy alliance will not succeed.'

The voices rose higher and higher, and Ugwu stopped listening. He got up and went out through the back and sat on the mound of cement blocks beside the house. Some little boys in the Biafran Boys Brigade were practising on the street, with sticks shaped like guns, doing frog jumps, calling one another *captain!* and *adjutant!* in high voices.

A hawker with a tray balanced on her head ambled past. 'Buy *garri*! Buy *garri*!'

She stopped when a young woman from the opposite house called out to her. They bargained for a while and then the young woman shouted, 'If you want to rob people, then do so. Don't say you are selling *garri* for that price.'

The hawker hissed and walked off.

Ugwu knew the young woman. He had first noticed her because of how perfectly rounded her buttocks were, how they rolled rhythmically, from side to side, as she walked. Her name was Eberechi.

He had heard the neighbours talking about her; the story was that her parents had given her to a visiting army officer, as one would give kola nut to a guest. They had knocked on his door at night, opened it, and gently pushed her in. The next morning, the beaming officer thanked her beaming parents while Eberechi stood by.

Ugwu watched her go back indoors and wondered how she had felt about being offered to a stranger and what had happened after she was pushed into his room and who was to blame more, her parents or the officer. He didn't want to think too much about blame, though, because it would remind him of Master and Olanna during those weeks before Baby's birth, weeks he preferred to forget.

Master found a rain-holder on the wedding day. The elderly man arrived early and dug a shallow pit at the back of the house, made a bonfire in it, and then sat in the thick of the bluish smoke, feeding dried leaves to the fire.

'No rain will come, nothing will happen until the wedding is over,' he said, when Ugwu took him a plate of rice and meat. Ugwu smelt the harsh gin on his breath. He turned and went back indoors so the smoke would not soak into his carefully ironed shirt. Olanna's cousins Odinchezo and Ekene were sitting out on the veranda in their militia uniforms. The photographer was fiddling with his camera. Some guests were in the living room, talking and laughing, waiting for Olanna, and once in a while somebody went over and placed something – a pot, a stool, an electric fan – in the pile of presents.

Ugwu knocked on her door and opened it.

'Professor Achara is ready to take you to the church, mah,' he said.

'Okay.' Olanna looked away from the mirror. 'Where is Baby? She hasn't gone out to play, has she? I don't want any dirt on that dress.'

'She is in the living room.'

Olanna sat in front of the crooked mirror. Her hair was held up so that all of her radiant, flawlessly smooth face was exposed. Ugwu had never seen her look so beautiful, and yet there was a sad reluctance in the way she patted the ivory and pink hat on one side of her head to make sure the pins were secure.

'We'll do the wine-carrying later, when our troops recover Umunnachi,' she said, as though Ugwu did not know.

'Yes, mah.'

'I sent a message to Kainene in Port Harcourt. She won't come, but I wanted her to know.'

Ugwu paused. 'They are waiting, mah.'

Olanna got up and surveyed herself. She ran a hand over the sides of her pink and ivory dress, which flared from the waist and stopped just below her knees. 'The stitches are so uneven. Arize could have done this better.'

Ugwu said nothing. If only he could reach out and tug at her lips to remove the sad smile on her face. If only it took that little.

Professor Achara knocked on the half-open door. 'Olanna? Are you ready? They say Odenigbo and Special Julius are already at the church.'

'I'm ready; please come in,' Olanna said. 'Did you bring the flowers?'

Professor Achara handed her a plastic bouquet of multi-coloured flowers. Olanna moved back. 'What is this? I wanted fresh flowers, Emeka.'

'But nobody grows flowers in Umuahia. People here grow what they can eat,' Professor Achara said, laughing.

'I won't hold flowers, then,' Olanna said.

For an uncertain moment, neither of them knew what to do with the plastic flowers: Olanna held them half extended while Professor Achara touched but did not grasp them. Finally, he took them back and said, 'Let me see if we can find anything else,' and left the room.

The wedding was simple. Olanna didn't hold flowers. St Sebastian's Catholic Church was small and filled only halfway with the friends who had come. Ugwu did not pay close attention to who was there, though, because, as he stared at the shabby, white altar cloth, he imagined that he was getting married. At first his bride was Olanna and then she transformed into Nnesinachi and then into Eberechi with the perfectly rounded buttocks, all in the same pink and ivory dress and tiny matching hat.

It was Okeoma's appearance, back at the house, that brought Ugwu out of his imagined world. Okeoma looked nothing like Ugwu remembered: the untidy hair and rumpled shirt of the poet were gone. His smart-fitting army uniform made him look straighter, leaner, and the sleeve had a skull-and-bones image next to the half of a yellow sun. Master and Olanna hugged him many times. Ugwu wanted to hug him too, because Okeoma's laughing face brought back the past with such force that for a moment, Ugwu felt as if the room blurred with the rain-holder's smoke was the living room on Odim Street.

Okeoma had brought his lanky cousin, Dr Nwala.

'He's a chief medical officer at Albatross Hospital,' Okeoma said, introducing him. Dr Nwala kept staring at Olanna with such annoyingly open adoration that Ugwu wanted to tell him to keep his froglike eyes away from her, chief medical officer or not. Ugwu felt not just involved in, but responsible for Olanna's happiness. As she and Master danced outside, circled by clapping friends, he thought, *They belong to me.* It was like a seal of stability, their wedding, because as long as they were married, his world with them was safe. They danced body to body for a while until Special Julius changed the ball-room music to High Life, and they pulled apart and held hands and looked into each other's faces, moving to the tune of Rex Lawson's new song, 'Hail Biafra, the Land of Freedom'. In her high heels, Olanna was taller than Master. She was smiling and glowing and laughing. When Okeoma started his toast, she wiped her eyes and told the photographer standing behind the tripod, 'Wait, wait, don't take it yet.'

Ugwu heard the sound just before they cut their cake in the living room, the swift *wah-wah-wah* roar in the sky. At first it was thunderous, and then it receded for a moment and came back again, louder and swifter. From somewhere close by, chickens began to squawk wildly.

Somebody said, 'Enemy plane! Air raid!'

'Outside!' Master shouted, but some guests were running into the bedroom, screaming, 'Jesus! Jesus!'

The sounds were louder now, overhead.

They ran – Master, Olanna holding Baby, Ugwu, some guests – to the cassava patch beside the house and lay on their bellies. Ugwu looked up and saw the planes, gliding low beneath the blue sky like two birds of prey. They spurted hundreds of scattered bullets before dark balls rolled out from underneath, as if the planes were laying large eggs. The first explosion was so loud that Ugwu's ear popped and his body shivered alongside the vibrating ground. A woman from the opposite house tugged at Olanna's dress. 'Remove it! Remove that white dress! They will see it and target us!'

Okeoma yanked off his uniform shirt, buttons flying off, and wrapped it around Olanna. Baby began to cry. Master held his hand loosely over her mouth, as if the pilots might hear her. The second explosion followed and then the third and fourth and fifth, until Ugwu felt the warm wetness of urine on his shorts and was convinced that the bombs would never end; they would continue to fall until everything was destroyed and everyone died. But they stopped. The planes moved farther away in the sky. Nobody moved or spoke for a long time, until Special Julius got up and said, 'They have gone.'

'The planes were so low,' a boy said excitedly. 'I saw the pilot!'

Master and Okeoma were first to walk out to the road. Okeoma looked smaller wearing only a singlet and trousers. Olanna continued to sit on the ground holding Baby, the camouflage-print army shirt wrapped around her wedding dress. Ugwu got up and headed down the road. He heard Dr Nwala say to Olanna, 'Let me help you up. The dirt will stain your dress.'

Smoke rose from a compound near the corn-grinding station a street away. Two houses had collapsed into dusty rubble and some men were digging frantically through the jumbled cement, saying, 'Did you hear that cry? Did you?' A fine haze of silvery dust covered their entire bodies so that they looked like limbless ghosts with open eyes.

'The child is alive, I heard the cry, I heard it,' somebody said. Men and women had gathered to help and to stare; some dug through the rubble too, others stood and looked and still others shrieked and snapped their fingers. A car was on fire; the body of a woman lay next to it, her clothes burnt off, flecks of pink all over her blackened skin, and when somebody covered it with a torn jute sack, Ugwu could still see the stiff, charcoal-black legs. The sky was overcast. The wet smell of coming rain mixed with the smoky smell of burning. Okeoma and Master had joined in digging through the rubble. 'I heard the child,' somebody said again. 'I heard the child.'

Ugwu turned to leave. A stylish sandal lay on the ground and he picked it up and looked at the leather straps, the thick wedge heel, before he left it where it had been. He imagined the chic young woman who had been wearing it, who had discarded it to run to safety. He wondered where the other sandal was.

When Master came back home, Ugwu was sitting on the floor of the living room, his back against the wall. Olanna was picking at a piece of cake on a saucer. She was still wearing her wedding dress; Okeoma's uniform shirt was neatly folded on a chair. The guests had all left slowly, saying little, their faces shadowed with guilt, as if embarrassed that they had allowed the air raid to ruin the wedding.

Master poured himself a glass of palm wine. 'Did you listen to the news?'

'No,' Olanna said.

'Our troops have lost all the captured territory in the midwest and the march to Lagos is over. Nigeria now says this is war, no longer a police action.' He shook his head. 'We were sabotaged.'

'Would you like some cake?' Olanna asked. The cake sat on the centre table, whole but for the thin slice she had cut off.

'Not now.' He drank his palm wine and poured another. 'We will build a bunker in case of another air raid.' His tone was normal, calm, as if air raids were benign, as if it were not death that had come so close moments ago. He turned to Ugwu. 'Do you know what a bunker is, my good man?'

'Yes, sah,' Ugwu said. 'Like the one Hitler had.'

'Well, yes, I suppose.'

'But, sah, people are saying that bunkers are mass graves,' Ugwu said.

'Absolute nonsense. Bunkers are safer than lying in a cassava patch.'

Outside, darkness had fallen and the sky was lit once in a while by lightning. Olanna suddenly jumped up from a chair and screamed, 'Where is Baby? *Ke* Baby?' and started to run into the bedroom.

'*Nkem!*' Master went after her.

'Can't you hear it? Can't you hear them bombing us again?'

'It's thunder.' Master grabbed Olanna from behind and held her. 'It's only the thunder. What our rain-holder kept back is finally unleashing itself. It's only the thunder.'

He held her for a while longer until, finally, Olanna sat down and cut another slice of cake for herself.

4. The Book: The World Was Silent When We Died

He argues that Nigeria did not have an economy until Independence. The colonial state was authoritarian, a benignly brutal dictatorship designed to benefit

Britain. What the economy consisted of in 1960 was potential – raw materials, human beings, high spirits, some money from the marketing board reserves left over from what the British had taken to rebuild their post-war economy. And there was the newly discovered oil. But the new Nigerian leaders were too optimistic, too ambitious with development projects that would win their people's credibility, too naive in accepting exploitative foreign loans, and too interested in aping the British and in taking over the superior attitudes and better hospitals and better salaries long denied Nigerians. He gestures to complex problems facing the new country but focuses on the 1966 massacres. The ostensible reasons – revenge for the 'Igbo coup', protest against a unitary decree that would make Northerners lose out in the civil service – did not matter. Nor did the varying numbers of the dead: three thousand, ten thousand, fifty thousand. What mattered was that the massacres frightened and united the Igbo. What mattered was that the massacres made fervent Biafrans of former Nigerians.

PART THREE

The Early Sixties

❊ 19 ❊

Ugwu sat on the steps that led to the backyard. Raindrops slid down the leaves, the air smelt of wet soil, and he and Harrison were talking about his upcoming trip with Mr Richard.

'Tufia! I don't know why my master wants to see that devilish festival in your village,' Harrison said. He was a few steps below; Ugwu could see the bald patch on the middle of his head.

'Maybe Mr Richard wants to write about the devil,' Ugwu said. Of course the *ori-okpa* was not a devilish festival, but he would not disagree with Harrison. He needed Harrison to be in a good mood so he could ask him about tear gas. They were silent for a while, watching the vultures hovering overhead; the neighbours had killed a chicken.

'Ah, those lemons are ripening.' Harrison gestured to the tree. 'I'm using the fresh one for meringue pie,' he added in English.

'What is meh-rang?' Ugwu asked. Harrison would like that question.

'You don't know what it is?' Harrison laughed. 'It is an American food. I will make it for my master to bring here when your madam comes back from London. I know she will like it.' Harrison turned to glance at Ugwu. He had placed a newspaper before sitting on the step, and it rumpled as he shifted. 'Even you will like it.'

'Yes,' Ugwu said, although he had sworn never to eat Harrison's food after he dropped by Mr Richard's house and saw Harrison spooning shredded orange peels into a pot of sauce. He would have been less alarmed if Harrison had cooked with the orange itself, but to cook with the peels was like choosing the hairy skin of a goat rather than the meat.

'I also use lemons to make cake; lemons are very good for the body,'

Harrison said. 'The food of white people makes you healthy, it is not like all of the nonsense that our people eat.'

'Yes, that is so.' Ugwu cleared his throat. He should ask Harrison about tear gas now, but instead he said, 'Let me show you my new room in the Boys' Quarters.'

'Okay.' Harrison got up.

When they walked into Ugwu's room, he pointed to the ceiling, patterned black and white. 'I did that myself,' he said. He had held a candle up there for hours, flicking the flame all over the ceiling, stopping often to move the table he was standing on.

'*O maka*, it is very nice.' Harrison looked at the narrow spring bed in the corner, the table and chair, the shirts hanging on nails stuck to the wall, the two pairs of shoes arranged carefully on the floor. 'Are those new shoes?'

'My madam bought them for me from Bata.'

Harrison touched the pile of journals on the table. 'You are reading all of these?' he asked in English.

'Yes.' Ugwu had saved them from the study dustbin; the *Mathematical Annals* were incomprehensible, but at least he had read, if not understood, a few pages of *Socialist Review*.

It had started to rain again. The patter on the zinc roof was loud and grew louder as they stood under the awning outside and watched the water sliding down from the roof in parallel lines.

Ugwu slapped at his arm – he liked the rain-cooled air, but he didn't like the mosquitoes flying around. Finally he asked the question. 'Do you know how I can get tear gas?'

'Tear gas? Why do you ask?'

'I read about it in my master's newspaper, and I want to see what it is like.' He would not tell Harrison that he in fact heard of tear gas when Master talked about the members of the Western House of Assembly, who punched and kicked one another until the police came and sprayed tear gas and they all passed out, leaving orderlies to carry them, limp, to their cars. The tear gas fascinated Ugwu. If it made people pass out, he wanted to get it. He wanted to use it on Nnesinachi when he went home with Mr Richard for the *ori-okpa* festival. He would lead her to the grove by the stream and tell her the tear gas was a magic spray that would keep her healthy. She would believe him. She would be so impressed to see him arrive in a white man's car that she would believe anything he said.

'It will be very difficult to get tear gas,' Harrison said.

'Why?'

'You are too young to know why.' Harrison nodded mysteriously. 'When you are a grown man I will tell you.'

Ugwu was puzzled at first, before he realized that Harrison did not know what tear gas was either but would never admit it. He was disappointed. He would have to ask Jomo.

Jomo knew what tear gas was and laughed long and hard when Ugwu told him what he wanted to use it for. Jomo clapped his hands together as he laughed. 'You are a sheep, *aturu*,' Jomo said finally. 'Why do you want to use tear gas on a young girl? Look, go to your village, and if the time is right and the young girl likes you, she will follow you. You don't need tear gas.'

Ugwu kept Jomo's words in mind as Mr Richard drove him to his hometown the next morning. Anulika ran up the path when she saw them and boldly shook Mr Richard's hand. She hugged Ugwu and, as they walked along, told him that their parents were at the farm, their cousin gave birth only yesterday, Nnesinachi left for the North last week –

Ugwu stopped and stared at her.

'Has something happened?' Mr Richard asked. 'The festival hasn't been cancelled, has it?'

Ugwu wished it had been. 'No, sah.'

He led the way to the village square, already filling up with men and women and children, and sat under the *oji* tree with Mr Richard. Children soon surrounded them, chanting '*Onye ocha*, white man,' reaching out to feel Mr Richard's hair. He said, '*Kedu?* Hello, what's your name?' and they stared at him, giggling, nudging each other. Ugwu leaned against the tree and mourned the time he had spent thinking of seeing Nnesinachi. Now she was gone and some trader in the North would end up with his prize. He hardly noticed the *mmuo*: masculine figures covered in grass, their faces snarling wooden masks, their long whips dangling from their hands. Mr Richard took photographs, wrote in his notebook, and asked questions, one after another – what was that called and what did they say and who were those men holding back the *mmuo* with a rope and what did that mean – until Ugwu felt irritable from the heat and the questions and the noise and the enormous disappointment of not seeing Nnesinachi.

He was silent on the drive back, looking out of the window.

'You're already homesick, aren't you?' Mr Richard asked.

'Yes, sah,' Ugwu said. He wanted Mr Richard to shut up. He wanted to be alone. He hoped Master would still be at the club so he could take the *Renaissance* from the living room and curl up on his bed in the Boys' Quarters and read. Or he would watch the new television. If he was lucky, an Indian film would be on. The large-eyed beauty of the women, the singing, the flowers, the bright colours, and the crying, were what he needed now.

When he let himself in through the back door, he was shocked to find Master's mother near the stove. Amala was standing by the door. Even Master did not know they were coming, or he would have been asked to clean the guest room.

'Oh,' he said. 'Welcome, Mama. Welcome, Aunty Amala.' The last visit was fresh in his mind: Mama harassing Olanna, calling her a witch, hooting, and, worst of all, threatening to consult the *dibia* in the village.

'How are you, Ugwu?' Mama adjusted her wrapper before she patted his back. 'My son said you went to show the white man the spirits in your village?'

'Yes, Mama.'

He could hear Master's raised voice from the living room. Perhaps a visitor had dropped by and he had decided not to go to the club.

'You can go and rest, *i nugo*,' Mama said. 'I am preparing my son's dinner.'

The last thing he wanted now was for Mama to colonize his kitchen or use Olanna's favourite saucepan for her strong-smelling soup. He wished so much that she would just leave. 'I will stay in case you need help, Mama,' he said.

She shrugged and went back to shaking out black peppercorns from a pod. 'Do you cook *ofe nsala* well?'

'I have never cooked it.'

'Why? My son likes it.'

'My madam has never asked me to cook it.'

'She is not your madam, my child. She is just a woman who is living with a man who has not paid her bride price.'

'Yes, Mama.'

She smiled, as if pleased that he had finally understood something important, and gestured to two small clay pots at the corner. 'I brought fresh palm wine for my son. Our best wine-tapper brought it to me this morning.'

She pulled out the green leaves stuffed in the mouth of one pot and the wine frothed over, white and fresh and sweet-smelling. She poured some into a cup and gave it to Ugwu.

'Taste it.'

It was strong on his tongue, the kind of concentrated palm wine tapped in the dry season that made men in his village start to stagger too soon. 'Thank you, Mama. It is very good.'

'Do your people tap wine well?'

'Yes, Mama.'

'But not as well as my people. In Abba, we have the best wine-tappers in the whole of Igboland. Is that not so, Amala?'

'It is so, Mama.'

'Wash that bowl for me.'

'Yes, Mama.' Amala began to wash the bowl. Her shoulders and arms shook as she scrubbed. Ugwu had not really looked at her and now he noticed that her slender, dark arms and face were shiny-wet, as if she had bathed in groundnut oil.

Master's voice, loud and firm, came from the living room. 'Our idiot government should break ranks with Britain too. We must take a stand! Why is Britain not doing more in Rhodesia? What bloody difference will limp economic sanctions make?'

Ugwu moved closer to the door to listen; he was fascinated by Rhodesia, by what was happening in the south of Africa. He could not comprehend people that looked like Mr Richard taking away the things that belonged to people that looked like him, Ugwu, for no reason at all.

'Bring me a tray, Ugwu,' Mama said.

Ugwu brought down a tray from the cupboard and made as if to help her serve Master's food, but she waved him away. 'I am here so you can rest a little, you poor boy. That woman will start over-working you again once she returns from overseas, as if you are not somebody's child.' She unwrapped a small packet and sprinkled something into the soup bowl. Suspicion flared in Ugwu's mind; he remembered the black cat that appeared in the backyard after her last visit. And the packet was black, too, like the cat.

'What is that, Mama? That thing you put in my master's food?' he asked.

'It is a spice that is a specialty of Abba people.' She turned to smile briefly. 'It is very good.'

'Yes, Mama.' Maybe he was wrong to think she was putting her medicine from the *dibia* in the master's food. Maybe Olanna was right and the black cat meant nothing and was only a neighbour's cat, although he did not know any of the neighbours who had a cat like that, with eyes that flashed yellow-red.

Ugwu didn't think again of the strange spice or the cat because, while Master had dinner, he sneaked a glass of palm wine from the pot and then another glass, since it was so sweet, and afterwards he felt as if the inside of his head was coated in soft wool. He could hardly walk. From the living room, he heard Master say in an unsteady voice, 'To the future of great Africa! To our independent brothers in the Gambia and to our Zambian brothers who have left Rhodesia!' followed by laughter in wild bursts. The palm wine had got to Master as well. Ugwu laughed along, even though he was alone in the kitchen and did not know what was funny. Finally, he fell asleep on the stool, his head against the table that smelt of dried fish.

He woke up with stiff joints. His mouth tasted sour, his head ached, and he wished the sun were not so oppressively bright and that Master would not speak so loudly over the newspapers at breakfast. *How can more politicians return unopposed than elected? Utter rubbish! This is rigging of the worst order!* Each syllable throbbed inside Ugwu's head.

After Master left for work, Mama asked, 'Will you not go to school, *gbo*, Ugwu?'

'We are on holiday, Mama.'

'Oh.' She looked disappointed.

Later, he saw her rubbing something on Amala's back, both of them standing in front of the bathroom. His suspicions returned. There was something wrong about the way Mama's hands were moving in circular motions, slowly, as if in consonance with some ritual, and about the way Amala stood silent, with her back straight and her wrapper lowered to her waist and the outline of her small breasts visible from the side. Perhaps Mama was rubbing a potion on Amala. But it made no sense because if Mama had indeed gone to the *dibia*, the medicine would be for Olanna and not Amala. It may be, though, that the medicine worked on women and Mama would have to protect herself and Amala to make sure that only Olanna died or became barren or went mad. Perhaps Mama was performing the preliminary protections now that Olanna was in London and would bury the medicine in the yard to keep it potent until Olanna came back.

Ugwu shivered. A shadow hung over the house. He worried about Mama's cheeriness, her tuneless humming, her determination to serve all of Master's meals, her frequent hushed words to Amala. He watched her carefully whenever she went outside, to see if she would bury anything, so he could unearth it as soon as she went back indoors. But she did not bury anything. When he told Jomo that he suspected Mama had gone to a *dibia* to find a way to kill Olanna, Jomo said, 'The old woman is simply happy to have her son to herself, that is why she is cooking and singing every day. Do you know how happy my mother is when I go to see her without my wife?'

'But I saw a black cat the last time she came,' Ugwu said.

'Professor Ozumba's housegirl down the street is a witch. She flies to the top of the mango tree at night to meet with her fellow witches, because I always rake up all the leaves they throw down. She is the one the black cat was looking for.'

Ugwu tried to believe Jomo, that he was reading undue meaning into Mama's actions, until he walked into the kitchen the next evening, after weeding his herb garden, and saw the flies in a foaming mass by the sink. The window was barely open. He did not see how so many flies, more than a hundred fat, greenish flies, could have come in through that crack to buzz together in a dense, turbulent cluster. They signified something terrible. Ugwu dashed to the study to call Master.

'Quite odd,' Master said; he took off his glasses and then put them back on. 'I'm sure Prof. Ezeka will be able to explain it, some sort of migratory behaviour. Don't shut the window so you don't trap them in.'

'But, sah,' Ugwu said, just as Mama came into the kitchen.

'Flies do this sometimes,' she said. 'It is normal. They will go the same way they came.' She was leaning by the door and her tone was ominously victorious.

'Yes, yes.' Master turned to go back to the study. 'Tea, my good man.'

'Yes, sah.' Ugwu did not understand how Master could be so unperturbed, how he could not see that the flies were not normal at all. As he took the tea tray into the study, he said, 'Sah, those flies are telling us something.'

Master gestured to the table. 'Don't pour. Leave it there.'

'Those flies in the kitchen, sah, they are a sign of bad medicine from the *dibia*. Somebody has done bad medicine.' Ugwu wanted to add that he knew very well who it was, but he was not sure how Master would take that.

'What?' Master's eyes narrowed behind his glasses.

'The flies, sah. It means somebody has done bad medicine for this house.'

'Shut the door and let me do some work, my good man.'

'Yes, sah.'

When Ugwu returned to the kitchen, the flies were gone. The window was the same, open only a crack, and the wan sunlight lit up the blade of a chopping knife on the table. He was reluctant to touch anything; the mysteries around him had tainted the pans and pots. For once, he was pleased to let Mama cook, but he did not eat the *ugba* and fried fish she made for dinner, did not take so much as a sip of the leftover palm wine he served to Master and his guests, did not sleep well that night. He kept jerking awake with itchy, watering eyes, wishing he could talk to somebody who would understand: Jomo, his aunty, Anulika. Finally he got up and went into the main house to dust the furniture, something mild and mindless that would keep him occupied. The purple-grey of early dawn filled the kitchen with shadows. He turned on the light switch fearfully, expecting to find something. Scorpions, perhaps; a jealous person had sent them to his uncle's hut once, and his uncle woke up every day for weeks to find angry black scorpions crawling near his newborn twin sons. One baby had been stung and almost died.

Ugwu cleaned the bookshelves first. He had removed the papers from the centre table and was bent over dusting it when Master's bedroom door opened. He glanced at the corridor, surprised that Master was up so early. But it was Amala who walked out of the room. The corridor was dim and her startled eyes met Ugwu's more startled eyes and she stopped for a moment before she hurried on to the guest room. Her wrapper was loose around her chest. She held on to it with one hand and bumped against the door of the guest room, pushing it as if she had forgotten how to open it, before she went in. Amala, common, quiet, ordinary Amala, had slept in Master's bedroom! Ugwu stood still and tried to get his whirling head to become steady so that he could think. Mama's medicine had done this, he was sure, but his worry was not what had happened between Master and Amala. His worry was what would happen if Olanna found out.

❈ 20 ❈

Olanna sat across from her mother in the living room upstairs. Her mother called it the ladies' parlour, because it was where she entertained her friends, where they laughed and hailed each other by their nicknames – Art! Gold! Ugodiya! – and talked about whose son was messing around with women in London while his mates built houses on their fathers' land, and who had bought local lace and tried to pass it off as the latest from Europe, and who was trying to snatch so-and-so's husband, and who had imported superior furniture from Milan. Now, though, the room was muted. Her mother held a glass of tonic water in one hand and a handkerchief in the other. She was crying. She was telling Olanna about her father's mistress.

'He has bought her a house in Ikeja,' her mother said. 'My friend lives on the same street.'

Olanna watched the delicate movement of her mother's hand as she dabbed at her eyes. It looked like satin, the handkerchief; it could not possibly be absorbent enough.

'Have you talked to him?' Olanna asked.

'What am I to say to him? *Gwa ya gini?*' Her mother placed the glass down. She had not sipped from it since one of the maids brought it in on a silver tray. 'There is nothing I can say to him. I just wanted to let you know what is happening so that they will not say I did not tell somebody.'

'I'll talk to him,' Olanna said. It was what her mother wanted. She had been back from London a day, and already the glow of possibility that came after she saw the Kensington gynaecologist was dulled. Already she could not remember the hope that spread through her when he said there was nothing wrong with her and she had only to – he had winked – work harder. Already she wished she were back in Nsukka.

'The worst part of it is that the woman is common riffraff,' her mother said, twisting the handkerchief. 'A Yoruba goat from the bush with two children from two different men. I hear she is old and ugly.'

Olanna got up. As if it mattered what the woman looked like. As if 'old and ugly' did not describe her father as well. What troubled her mother was not the mistress, she knew, but the significance of what her father had done: buying the mistress a house in a neighbourhood where Lagos socialites lived.

'Maybe we should wait for Kainene to visit so she can talk to your father instead, *nne?*' her mother said, dabbing at her eyes again.

'I said I would talk to him, Mum,' Olanna said.

But that evening, as she walked into her father's room, she realized that her mother was right. Kainene was the best person for this. Kainene would know exactly what to say and would not feel the awkward ineptness that she did now, Kainene with her sharp edges and her bitter tongue and her supreme confidence.

'Dad,' she said, closing the door behind her. He was at his desk, sitting on the straight-backed chair made of dark wood. She couldn't ask him if it was true, because he had to know that her mother knew it to be true and so did she. She wondered, for a moment, about this other woman, what she looked like, what she and her father talked about.

'Dad,' she said again. She would speak mostly in English. It was easy to be formal and cold in English. 'I wish you had some respect for my mother.' That was not what she had intended to say. *My mother*, instead of *Mum*, made it seem as if she had decided to exclude him, as if he had become a stranger who could not possibly be addressed on the same terms, could not be *my father*.

He leaned back in his chair.

'It's disrespectful that you have a relationship with this woman and that you have bought her a house where my mother's friends live,' Olanna said. 'You go there from work and your driver parks outside and you don't seem to care that people see you. It's a slap to my mother's face.'

Her father's eyes were downcast now, the eyes of a man groping in his mind.

'I am not going to tell you what to do about it, but you *have* to do something. My mother isn't happy.' Olanna stressed the *have*, placed an exaggerated emphasis on it. She had never talked to her father like this before; she rarely talked to him anyway. She stood there staring at him, and he at her, and the silence between them was empty.

'*Anugo m*, I have heard you,' he said. His Igbo was low, conspiratorial, as if she had asked him to go ahead and cheat on her mother but to do it considerately. It angered her. Perhaps it was, in effect, what she had asked him to do but still she was annoyed. She looked around his room and thought how unfamiliar his large bed was; she had never seen that lustrous shade of gold on a blanket before or noticed how intricately convoluted the metal handles of his chest of drawers were. He even looked like a stranger, a fat man she didn't know.

'Is that all you have to say, that you've heard me?' Olanna asked, raising her voice.

'What do you want me to say?'

Olanna felt a sudden pity for him, for her mother, for herself and Kainene. She wanted to ask him why they were all strangers who shared the same last name.

'I will do something about it,' he added. He stood up and came towards her. 'Thank you, *ola m*,' he said.

She was not sure what to make of his thanking her, or of his calling her *my gold*, something he had not done since she was a child and which now had a contrived solemnity to it. She turned and left the room.

When Olanna heard her mother's raised voice the next morning – 'Good-for-nothing! Stupid man!' – she hurried downstairs. She imagined them fighting, her mother grasping the front of her father's shirt in a tight knot as women often did to cheating husbands. The sounds came from the kitchen. Olanna stopped at the door. A man was kneeling in front of her mother with his hands raised high, palms upward in supplication.

'Madam, please; madam, please.'

Her mother turned to the steward, Maxwell, who stood aside watching. '*I fugo?* Does he think we employed him to steal us blind, Maxwell?'

'No, mah,' Maxwell said.

Her mother turned back to the man kneeling on the floor. 'So this is what you have been doing since you came here, you useless man? You came here to steal from me?'

'Madam, please; madam, please. I am using God to beg you.'

'Mum, what is it?' Olanna asked.

Her mother turned. 'Oh, *nne*, I didn't know you were up.'

'What is it?'

'It's this wild animal here. We employed him only last month, and he already wants to steal everything in my house.' She turned back to the kneeling man. 'This is how you repay people for giving you a job? Stupid man!'

'What did he do?' Olanna asked.

'Come and see.' Her mother led her out to the backyard where a bicycle leaned against the mango tree. A woven bag had fallen from the backseat, spilling rice onto the ground.

'He stole my rice and was about to go home. It was only by God's grace that the bag fell. Who knows what else he has stolen from me in the past? No wonder I have been looking for some of my necklaces.' Her mother was breathing quickly.

Olanna stared at the rice grains on the ground and wondered how her mother could have worked herself up like this over them and if her mother really believed her own outrage.

'Aunty, please beg Madam. It is the devil that made me do it.' The driver's pleading hands faced Olanna now. 'Please beg madam.'

Olanna looked away from the man's lined face and yellowed eyes; he was older than she had first thought, certainly above sixty. 'Get up,' she said.

He looked uncertain, glancing at her mother.

'I said get up!' Olanna had not intended to raise her voice, but it had come out sharp. The man stood up awkwardly, eyes downcast.

'Mum, if you're going to sack him, then sack him and have him go right away,' Olanna said.

The man gasped, as if he had not expected her to say that. Her mother looked surprised too and glanced at Olanna, at the man, at Maxwell, before she put down the hand placed on her hip. 'I will give you one more chance, but don't ever touch anything in this house unless you are permitted. Do you hear me?'

'Yes, madam. Thank you, madam. God bless you, madam.'

The man was still singing his thanks as Olanna took a banana from the table and left the kitchen.

She told Odenigbo about it on the phone, how it repulsed her to see that elderly man abase himself so, how she was certain her mother would have fired him but only after an hour of revelling in his grovelling and in her own self-righteous outrage. 'It could not have been more than four cups of rice,' she said.

'It was still stealing, *nkem*.'

'My father and his politician friends steal money with their contracts, but nobody makes them kneel to beg for forgiveness. And they build houses with their stolen money and rent them out to people like this man and charge inflated rents that make it impossible to buy food.'

'You can't right theft with theft.' Odenigbo sounded strangely sombre; she had expected an outburst from him about the injustice of it all.

'Does inequality have to mean indignity?' she asked.

'It often does.'

'Are you all right?'

'My mother is here. I had no idea she was coming.'

No wonder he sounded that way. 'Will she be gone before Tuesday?'

'I don't know. I wish you were here.'

'I'm glad I'm not. Have you had a conversation about breaking the spell of the educated witch?'

'I'll tell her before she says anything that there's nothing to be discussed.'

'You might pacify her by telling her that we are trying to have a child. Or will she be horrified at the thought of my having a child? Some of those witchcraft genes may be passed along to her grandchild after all.'

She hoped Odenigbo would laugh, but he didn't. 'I can't wait for Tuesday,' he said, after a while.

'I can't wait either,' she said. 'Tell Ugwu to air the rug in the bedroom.'

That night, when her mother came into her room, Olanna smelt the floral Chloe perfume, a lovely scent, but she did not see why a person needed to wear perfume to bed. Her mother had too many bottles of perfume; they lined her dresser like a store shelf: stunted bottles, tapering bottles, rounded bottles. Even wearing them to bed every night, her mother could not use them all in fifty years.

'Thank you, *nne*,' she said. 'Your father is already trying to make amends.'

'I see.' Olanna did not want to know just what it was her father had done to make amends but she felt an odd sense of accomplishment to have talked to her father like Kainene, to have got him to do something, to have been useful.

'Mrs Nwizu will soon stop telephoning to tell me she saw him there,' her mother said. 'She said something catty the other day about people whose daughters have refused to marry. I think she was throwing words at me and wanted to see if I would throw them back at her. Her daughter got married last year and they could not afford to import anything for the wedding. Even the wedding dress was made here in Lagos!' Her mother sat down. 'By the way, there is somebody who wants to meet you. You know Igwe Onochie's family? Their son is an engineer. I think he has seen you somewhere, and he is very interested.'

Olanna sighed and leaned back to listen to her mother.

She got back to Nsukka in the middle of the afternoon, that still hour when the sun was relentless and even the bees perched in quiet exhaustion. Odenigbo's car was in the garage. Ugwu opened the door before she knocked, his shirt unbuttoned, slight sweat patches under his arms. 'Welcome, mah,' he said.

'Ugwu.' She had missed his loyal, smiling face. '*Unu anokwa ofuma?* Did you stay well?'

'Yes, mah,' he said, and went out to bring her luggage from the taxi.

Olanna walked in. She had missed the faint smell of detergent that lingered in the living room after Ugwu cleaned the louvres. Because she had imagined that Odenigbo's mother was already gone, she was dampened to see her on the sofa, dressed, fussing with a bag. Amala stood nearby, holding a small metal box.

'*Nkem!*' Odenigbo said, and hurried forwards. 'It's good to have you back! So good!'

When they hugged, his body did not relax against hers and the brief press of his lips felt papery. 'Mama and Amala are just leaving. I'm taking them to the motor park,' he said.

'Good afternoon, Mama,' Olanna said, but did not make an attempt to go any closer.

'Olanna, *kedu?*' Mama asked. It was Mama who initiated their hug; it was Mama who smiled warmly. Olanna was puzzled but pleased.

Perhaps Odenigbo had spoken to her about how serious their relationship was, and their planning to have a child had finally won Mama over.

'Amala, how are you?' Olanna asked. 'I didn't know you came too.'

'Welcome, Aunty,' Amala mumbled, looking down.

'Have you brought everything?' Odenigbo asked his mother. 'Let's go. Let's go.'

'Have you eaten, Mama?' Olanna asked.

'My morning meal is still heavy in my stomach,' Mama said. She had a happily speculative look on her face.

'We have to go now,' Odenigbo said. 'I have a scheduled game later.'

'What about you, Amala?' Olanna asked. Mama's smiling face suddenly made her want them to stay a little longer. 'I hope you ate something.'

'Yes, Aunty, thank you,' Amala said, her eyes still focused on the floor.

'Give Amala the key to put the things in the car,' Mama said to Odenigbo.

Odenigbo moved towards Amala, but stopped a little way away so that he had to stretch out and lengthen his arm to give her the key. She took it carefully from his fingers; they did not touch each other. It was a tiny moment, brief and fleeting, but Olanna noticed how scrupulously they avoided any contact, any touch of skin, as if they were united by a common knowledge so monumental that they were determined not to be united by anything else.

'Go well,' she said. She watched the car ease out of the compound and stood there, telling herself she was mistaken; there had been nothing in that gesture. But it bothered her. She felt something similar to what she had felt while waiting for the gynaecologist: convinced that something was wrong with her body and yet willing him to tell her that all was well.

'Mah, will you eat? Should I warm rice?' Ugwu asked.

'Not now.' For a moment, she wanted to ask Ugwu if he too had observed that gesture, if he had observed anything at all. 'Go and see if any avocados are ripe.'

'Yes, mah.' Ugwu hesitated ever so slightly before he left.

She stood at the front door until Odenigbo came back. She was not sure what the shrivelling in her stomach and the racing in her chest meant. She opened the door and searched his face.

'Did anything happen?' she asked.

'What do you mean?' He held some newspapers in his hand. 'One of my students missed the last test, and this morning he came and offered me some money to pass him, the ignoramus.'

'I didn't know Amala came with Mama,' she said.

'Yes.' He began to rearrange the newspapers, avoiding her eyes. And, slowly, shock spread over Olanna. She knew. She knew from the jerky movements he made, from the panic on his face, from the hasty way he was trying to look normal again, that something that should not have happened had happened.

'You touched Amala,' Olanna said. It was not a question, and yet she wanted him to respond as if it were; she wanted him to say *no* and get upset with her for even thinking that. But Odenigbo said nothing. He sat down on his armchair and looked at her.

'You touched Amala,' Olanna repeated. She would always remember his expression, him looking at her as if he could never have imagined this scene and so did not know how to think about thinking about what to say or do.

She turned towards the kitchen and nearly fell beside the dining table because the weight in her chest was too large, not measured to fit her size.

'Olanna,' he said.

She ignored him. He would not come after her because he was frightened, full of the fear of the guilty. She did not get in her car right away and drive to her flat. Instead, she went outside and sat on the backyard steps and watched a hen near the lemon tree, guarding six chicks, nudging them towards crumbs on the ground. Ugwu was plucking avocados from the tree near the Boys' Quarters. She was not sure how long she sat there before the hen began to squawk loudly and spread its wings to shield the chicks, but they did not run into the shelter quickly enough. A kite swooped down and carried one of them off, a brown-and-white chick. It was so fast, the descent of the kite and the gliding away with the chick grasped in hooked claws, that Olanna thought she might have imagined it. She couldn't have, though, because the hen was running around in circles, squawking, raising clouds of dust. The other chicks looked bewildered. Olanna watched them and wondered if they understood their mother's mourning dance. Then, finally, she started to cry.

*   *   *

The blurred days crawled into one another. Olanna grasped for thoughts, for things to do. The first time Odenigbo came to her flat she was unsure whether to let him in. But he knocked and knocked and said, '*Nkem*, please open, *biko*, please open,' until she did. She sat sipping some water while he told her that he had been drunk, that Amala had forced herself on him, that it had been a brief rash lust. Afterwards, she told him to get out. It was grating that he remained self-assured enough to call what he had done a *brief rash lust*. She hated that expression and she hated the firmness of his tone the next time he came and said, 'It meant nothing, *nkem*, nothing.' What mattered to her was not what it meant but what had happened: his sleeping with his mother's village girl after only three weeks away from her. It seemed too easy, the way he had broken her trust. She decided to go to Kano because, if there was a place where she could think clearly, it was in Kano.

Her flight stopped first in Lagos, and as she sat waiting in the lounge a tall, thin woman hurried past. She stood up and was about to call out *Kainene!* when she realized it could not be. Kainene was darker-skinned than the woman and would never wear a green skirt with a red blouse. She wished so much that it were Kainene, though. They would sit next to each other and she would tell Kainene about Odenigbo and Kainene would say something clever and sarcastic and comforting all at once.

In Kano, Arize was furious.

'Wild animal from Abba. His rotten penis will fall off soon. Doesn't he know he should wake up every morning and kneel down and thank his God that you looked at him at all?' she said, while showing Olanna sketches of bouffant wedding gowns. Nnakwanze had finally proposed. Olanna looked at the drawings. She thought them all to be ugly and overdesigned, but she was so pleased by the rage felt on her behalf that she pointed at one of them and murmured, '*O maka*. It's lovely.'

Aunty Ifeka said nothing about Odenigbo until a few days had passed. Olanna was sitting on the veranda with her; the sun was fierce and the zinc awning crackled as if in protest. But it was cooler here than in the smoke-filled kitchen, where three neighbours were cooking at the same time. Olanna fanned herself with a small raffia mat. Two women were standing near the gate, one shouting in Igbo – 'I said you will give me my money today! *Tata!* Today, not tomorrow! You heard me say so because I did not speak with water in my mouth!' – while the other made pleading gestures with her hands and glanced skyward.

'How are you?' Aunty Ifeka asked. She was stirring a doughy paste of ground beans in a mortar.

'I'm fine, Aunty. I'm finer for being here.'

Aunty Ifeka reached inside the paste to pick out a small black insect. Olanna fanned herself faster. Aunty Ifeka's silence made her want to say more.

'I think I will postpone my programme at Nsukka and stay here in Kano,' she said. 'I could teach for a while at the institute.'

'No.' Aunty Ifeka put the pestle down. '*Mba*. You will go back to Nsukka.'

'I can't just go back to his house, Aunty.'

'I am not asking you to go back to his house. I said you will go back to Nsukka. Do you not have your own flat and your own job? Odenigbo has done what all men do and has inserted his penis in the first hole he could find when you were away. Does that mean somebody died?'

Olanna had stopped fanning herself and could feel the sweaty wetness on her scalp.

'When your uncle first married me, I worried because I thought those women outside would come and displace me from my home. I now know that nothing he does will make my life change. My life will change only if I want it to change.'

'What are you saying, Aunty?'

'He is very careful now, since he realized that I am no longer afraid. I have told him that if he brings disgrace to me in any way, I will cut off that snake between his legs.'

Aunty Ifeka went back to her stirring, and Olanna's image of their marriage began to come apart at the seams.

'You must never behave as if your life belongs to a man. Do you hear me?' Aunty Ifeka said. 'Your life belongs to you and you alone, *soso gi*. You will go back on Saturday. Let me hurry up and make some *abacha* for you to take.'

She tasted a little of the paste and spat it out.

Olanna left on Saturday. The man sitting next to her on the plane, across the aisle, had the shiniest, darkest ebony complexion she had ever seen. She had noticed him earlier, in his three-piece wool suit, staring at her as they waited on the tarmac. He had offered to help her with her carry-on bag and, later, had asked the flight attendant if he could take the seat next to hers since it was vacant. Now, he offered her the *New Nigerian* and asked, 'Would you like to read this?' He wore a large opal ring on his middle finger.

'Yes. Thank you.' Olanna took the paper. She skimmed through the pages, aware that he was watching her and that the newspaper was his way of starting conversation. Suddenly she wished she could be attracted to him, that something mad and magical would happen to them both and, when the plane landed, she would walk away with her hand in his, into a new bright life.

'They have finally removed that Igbo vice chancellor from the University of Lagos,' he said.

'Oh.'

'It's on the back cover.'

Olanna turned to the back cover. 'I see.'

'Why should an Igbo man be the vice chancellor in Lagos?' he asked and, when Olanna said nothing, only half smiling to show she was listening, he added, 'The problem with Igbo people is that they want to control everything in this country. Everything. Why can't they stay in their East? They own all the shops; they control the civil service, even the police. If you are arrested for any crime, as long as you can say *keda* they will let you go.'

'We say *kedu*, not *keda*,' Olanna said quietly. 'It means *How are you?*'

The man stared at her and she stared back and thought how beautiful he would have been if he had been a woman, with that perfectly shiny, near-black skin.

'Are you Igbo?' he asked.

'Yes.'

'But you have the face of Fulani people.' He sounded accusing.

Olanna shook her head. 'Igbo.'

The man mumbled something that sounded like *sorry* before he turned away and began to look through his briefcase. When she handed the newspaper to him, he seemed reluctant to take it back, and although she glanced at him from time to time, his eyes did not meet hers again until they landed in Lagos. If only he knew that his prejudice had filled her with possibility. She did not have to be the wounded woman whose man had slept with a village girl. She could be a Fulani woman on a plane deriding Igbo people with a good-looking stranger. She could be a woman taking charge of her own life. She could be anything.

As they got up to leave, she looked at him and smiled but kept herself from saying *thank you* because she wanted to leave him with both his surprise and his remorse intact.

Olanna hired a pick-up truck and a driver and went to Odenigbo's house. Ugwu followed her around as she packed books and pointed at things for the driver to pick up.

'Master looks like somebody that is crying every day, mah,' Ugwu said to her in English.

'Put my blender in a carton,' she said. *My* blender sounded strange; it had always been *the* blender, unmarked by her ownership.

'Yes, mah.' Ugwu went to the kitchen and came back with a carton. He held it tentatively. 'Mah, please forgive Master.'

Olanna looked at him. He had known; he had seen this woman share his master's bed; he too had betrayed her. '*Osiso!* Put my blender in the car!'

'Yes, mah.' Ugwu turned to the door.

'Do the guests still come in the evenings?' Olanna asked.

'It's not like before when you were around, mah.'

'But they still come?'

'Yes.'

'And your master still plays tennis and goes to the staff club?'

'Yes.'

'Good.' She did not mean that. She had wanted to hear that Odenigbo could no longer bear to live the life that had been theirs.

When he visited her, she tried not to feel disappointment at how normal he looked. She stood at the door and gave noncommittal answers, resentful of his effortless volubility, of how casually he said, 'You know I will never love another woman, *nkem*,' as if he was certain that, with time, everything would be the same again. She resented, too, the romantic attention of other men. The single men took to stopping by her flat, the married ones to bumping into her outside her department. Their courting upset her because it – and they – assumed that her relationship with Odenigbo was permanently over. 'I am not interested,' she told them, and even as she said it, she hoped that it would not get back to Odenigbo because she did not want him to think she was pining. And she did not pine: she added new material to her lectures, cooked long meals, read new books, bought new records. She became secretary of the St Vincent de Paul Society, and after they donated food to the villages she wrote the minutes of their meetings in a notebook. She cultivated zinnias in her front yard and, finally, she cultivated a friendship with her black American neighbour, Edna Whaler.

Edna had a quiet laugh. She taught music and played jazz records a little too loudly and cooked tender pork chops and talked often about the man who had left her a week before their wedding in Montgomery and the uncle who had been lynched when she was a child. 'You know what always amazed me?' she would ask Olanna, as if she had not told her only a day previously. 'That civilized white folk wore nice dresses and hats and gathered to watch a white man hang a black man from a tree.'

She would laugh her quiet laugh and pat her hair, which had the greasy shine of hot-pressing. At first, they did not talk about Odenigbo. It was refreshing for Olanna to be with somebody who was far removed from the circle of friends she had shared with Odenigbo. Then, once, as Edna sang along to Billie Holiday's 'My Man', she asked, 'Why do you love him?'

Olanna looked up. Her mind was a blank board. 'Why do I love him?'

Edna raised her eyebrows, mouthing but not singing Billie Holiday's words.

'I don't think love has a reason,' Olanna said.

'Sure it does.'

'I think love comes first and then the reasons follow. When I am with him, I feel that I don't need anything else.' Olanna's words surprised her, but the startling truth brought the urge to cry.

Edna was watching her. 'You can't keep lying to yourself that you're okay.'

'I'm not lying to myself,' Olanna said. Billie Holiday's plaintively scratchy voice had begun to irritate her. She didn't know how transparent she was. She thought her frequent laughter was authentic and that Edna had no idea that she cried when she was alone in her flat.

'I'm not the best person to talk to about men, but you need to talk this through with somebody,' Edna said. 'Maybe the priest, as payback for all those St Vincent de Paul charity trips you've made?'

Edna laughed and Olanna laughed along, but already she was thinking that perhaps she did need to talk to somebody, somebody neutral who would help her reclaim herself, deal with the stranger she had become. She started to drive to St Peter's many times in the next few days but stopped and changed her mind. Finally, on a Monday afternoon, she went, driving quickly, ignoring speed bumps, so that she would not give herself any time to stop. She sat on a wooden bench in Father Damian's airless office and kept her eyes focused on the filing cabinet labeled LAITY as she talked about Odenigbo.

'I don't go to the staff club because I don't want to see him. I've lost my interest in tennis. He betrayed and hurt me, and yet it seems as if he's running my life.'

Father Damian tugged at his collar, adjusted his glasses, and rubbed his nose, and she wondered if he was thinking of something, anything, to do since he had no answers for her.

'I didn't see you in church last Sunday,' he said finally.

Olanna was disappointed, but he was a priest after all and this had to be his solution: Seek God. She had wanted him to make her feel justified, solidify her right to self-pity, encourage her to occupy a larger portion of the moral high ground. She wanted him to condemn Odenigbo.

'You think I need to go to church more often?' she asked.

'Yes.'

Olanna nodded and brought her bag closer, ready to get up and leave. She should not have come. She should not have expected a round-faced, voluntary eunuch in white robes to be in a position to understand how she felt. He was looking at her, his eyes large behind the lenses.

'I also think that you should forgive Odenigbo,' he said, and pulled at his collar as though it was choking him. For a moment, Olanna felt contempt for him. What he was saying was too easy, too predictable. She did not need to have come to hear it.

'Okay.' She got up. 'Thank you.'

'It's not for him, you know. It's for you.'

'What?' He was still sitting, so she looked down to meet his eyes.

'Don't see it as forgiving him. See it as allowing yourself to be happy. What will you do with the misery you have chosen? Will you eat misery?'

Olanna looked at the crucifix above the window, at the face of Christ serene in agony, and said nothing.

* * *

Odenigbo arrived very early, before she had had breakfast. She knew that something was wrong even before she unlocked the door and saw his sombre face.

'What is it?' she asked, and felt a sharp horror at the hope that sneaked into her mind: that his mother had died.

'Amala is pregnant,' he said. There was a selfless and steely tone to his voice, that of a person delivering bad news to other people while remaining strong on their behalf.

Olanna clutched the door handle. 'What?'

'Mama just came to tell me that Amala is pregnant with my child.'

Olanna began to laugh. She laughed and laughed and laughed because the present scene, the past weeks, suddenly seemed fantastical.

'Let me come in,' Odenigbo said. 'Please.'

She moved back from the door. 'Come in.'

He sat down on the edge of the chair, and she felt as if she had been gumming back the pieces of broken chinaware only to have them shatter all over again; the pain was not in the second shattering but in the realization that trying to put them back together had been of no consequence from the beginning.

'*Nkem*, please, let's deal with this together,' he said. 'We will do whatever you want. Please let's do it together.'

Olanna went to the kitchen to turn the kettle off. She came back and sat down opposite him. 'You said it happened just once. Just once and she got pregnant? Just once?' She wished she had not raised her voice. But it was so implausible, so theatrically implausible, that he would sleep with a woman once in a drunken state and get her pregnant.

'It was just once,' he said. 'Just once.'

'I see.' But she did not see at all. The urge came then, to slap his face, because the self-entitled way he stressed *once* made the act seem inevitable, as if the point was how many times it had happened rather than that it should not have happened at all.

'I told Mama I'll send Amala to Dr Okonkwo in Enugu, and she said it would be over her dead body. She said Amala will have the child and she will raise the child herself. There is a young man doing timber work in Ondo that Amala is to marry.' Odenigbo stood up. 'Mama planned this from the beginning. I see now how she made sure I was dead drunk before sending Amala to me. I feel as if I've been dropped into something I don't entirely understand.'

Olanna looked at him, from his halo of hair to his slender toes in leather sandals, alarmed that she could feel this burst of dislike for someone she loved. 'Nobody dropped you into anything,' she said.

He made to hold her but she shrugged him off and asked him to leave. Later, in the bathroom, she stood in front of the mirror and savagely squeezed her belly with both hands. The pain reminded her of how useless she was; reminded her that a child nestled now in a stranger's body instead of in hers.

Edna knocked for so long that Olanna had to get up and unlock the door.

'What's wrong?' Edna asked.

'My grandfather used to say that other people just farted but his own fart always released shit,' Olanna said. She had wanted to sound funny, but her voice was too hoarse, too tear-lined.

'What's wrong?'

'The girl he slept with is pregnant.'

'What the hell is wrong with you?'

Olanna squinted; what was wrong with *her*?

'Get ahold of yourself!' Edna said. 'You think he's spending his day crying like you are? When that bastard left me in Montgomery, I tried to kill myself and you know what he was doing? He had gone off and was playing in a band in Louisiana!' Edna patted her hair irritably. 'Look at you. You're the kindest person I know. Look how beautiful you are. Why do you need so much outside of yourself? Why isn't what you *are* enough? You're so damned weak!'

Olanna moved back; the tumultuous crowding of pain and thoughts and anger that shot through her made the words flow out of her mouth with quiet precision. 'It is not my fault that your man deserted you, Edna.'

Edna first looked surprised, then disgusted, before she turned and walked out of the flat. Olanna watched her go, sorry to have said what she said. But she would not apologize yet. She would give Edna a day or two. She felt suddenly hungry, bitingly hungry; her insides had been emptied out by her tears. She did not let her leftover *jollof* rice warm properly but ate it all from the pot, drank two cold bottles of beer, and still did not feel sated. She ate the biscuits in the cupboard and some oranges from the fridge, and then decided to go to Eastern Shop for some wine. She would drink. She would drink as much wine as she could.

The two women standing at the shop entrance, the Indian in the Faculty of Science and the Calabar woman who taught anthropology, smiled and said good afternoon, and she wondered if their covert glances shielded their pity, if they thought she was falling apart and weak.

She was examining wine bottles when Richard came up to her.

'I thought it was you,' he said.

'Hello, Richard.' She glanced at his basket. 'I didn't know you did your own shopping.'

'Harrison has gone to his hometown for a few days,' he said. 'How are you? Are you all right?'

She disliked the pity in his eyes. 'I'm very well. I can't decide which of these two to buy.' She gestured to the wine bottles. 'Why don't I buy both and if you'll share them with me, we can decide which is better. Can you spare an hour? Or do you have to run back to your writing?'

Richard looked taken aback by her cheer. 'I would hate to impose, really.'

'Of course you wouldn't be imposing. Besides, you've never visited me' – she paused – 'in my flat.'

She would be her normal, gracious self and they would drink wine and talk about his book and her new zinnias and Igbo-Ukwu art and the Western Region elections fiasco. And he would go back and tell Odenigbo that she was fine. She *was* fine.

When they got to her flat, Richard sat upright on the sofa, and she wished he would sit in that relaxed, semi-sprawling way he did in Odenigbo's house; even the way he held his wine glass was stiff. She sat on the carpeted floor. They toasted Kenya's independence.

'You really must write about the horrible things the British did in Kenya,' Olanna said. 'Didn't they cut off testicles?'

Richard murmured something and looked away, as if the word *testicles* had made him shy. Olanna smiled and watched him. 'Didn't they?'

'Yes.'

'You should write about it then.' She drank her second glass slowly, raising her head to enjoy the cold liquid flowing down her throat. 'Do you have a title for the book?'

'"The Basket of Hands."'

' "The Basket of Hands." ' Olanna tilted her glass and finished her drink. 'It sounds macabre.'

'It's about labour. The good things that were achieved – the railways, for example – but also how labour was exploited and the lengths the colonial enterprise went to.'

'Oh.' Olanna got up and uncorked the second bottle. She bent down to fill her glass first. She felt light, as if it were much easier to carry her own weight, but she was clear-headed; she knew what she wanted to do and what she was doing. Richard's almost-damp smell filled her nose when she stood before him with the bottle.

'My glass isn't quite empty,' he said.

'No, it's not.' She placed the wine bottle on the floor and sat next to him and touched the hair that lay on his skin and thought how fair and soft it was, not assertively brittle like Odenigbo's, nothing like Odenigbo at all. He looked at her and she wondered if his eyes had really turned grey or if she was imagining it. She touched his face, left her hand resting on his cheek.

'Come, sit on the floor with me,' she said finally.

They sat side by side, their backs resting on the sofa seat. Richard said, in a mumble, 'I should leave,' or something that sounded like it. But she knew he would not leave and that when she stretched out on the bristly carpet he would lie next to her. She kissed his lips. He pulled her forcefully close, and then, just as quickly, he let go and moved his face away. She could hear his rapid breathing. She unbuckled his trousers and moved back to pull them down and laughed because they got stuck at his shoes. She took her dress off. He was on top of her and the carpet pricked her naked back and she felt his mouth limply enclose her nipple. It was nothing like Odenigbo's bites and sucks, nothing like those shocks of pleasure. Richard did not run his tongue over her in that flicking way that made her forget everything; rather, when he kissed her belly, she was aware that he was kissing her belly.

Everything changed when he was inside her. She raised her hips, moving with him, matching his thrusts, and it was as if she was throwing shackles off her wrists, extracting pins from her skin, freeing herself with the loud, loud cries that burst out of her mouth. Afterwards, she felt filled with a sense of well-being, with something close to grace.

21

Richard was almost relieved to learn of Sir Winston Churchill's death. It gave him an opportunity to avoid going to Port Harcourt for the weekend. He could not face Kainene yet.

'You'll have to lay your awful Churchill joke to rest now, won't you?' Kainene said on the phone, when he told her that he would be going to Lagos for the memorial at the British High Commission. He laughed and then thought of what it would be like if she found out and left him and he never heard that sardonic voice over the phone.

It was only days ago, but even the memory of Olanna's flat was hazy: he had fallen asleep afterwards, on her living-room floor, and woken up with a dry headache and a keenly uncomfortable sense of his own nudity. She was sitting on the sofa, dressed and silent. He felt awkward, not sure whether they were supposed to talk about what had happened. Finally, he turned to leave without saying a word because he did not want what he imagined to be regret on her face to turn into dislike. He had not been chosen; it could have been any man. He had sensed this even while holding her naked, but it had not marred the pleasure he found in her curvy body, her moving with him, her taking as much as she gave. He had never been so firm, never lasted so long as he had with her.

Now, though, he was bereft. His admiration had thrived on her being unattainable, a worship from afar, but now that he had tasted the wine on her tongue, pressed himself so close against her that he too smelt of coconuts, he felt a strange loss. He had lost his fantasy. But what he worried most about losing was Kainene. He was determined that Kainene would never know.

*　　*　　*

Susan sat next to him at the memorial service, and when parts of a speech delivered by Sir Winston Churchill were played, she clasped her gloved hands together, tightly, and leaned against him. Richard felt tears in his eyes. This was perhaps the only thing they had in common, their admiration for Churchill. Afterwards, she asked him to have a drink with her at the Polo Club. She had taken him once before and had said, while they sat by the expanse of green lawn, 'Africans have been allowed in for only a few years, but you wouldn't believe how many come now, and they show such little appreciation, really.'

They were seated at the same spot again, near the whitewashed railing, by a Nigerian waiter in a tight black suit. The club was almost empty, although a polo game was on at the other side. The sounds of eight shouting, swearing men galloping at full speed after a ball filled the air. Susan spoke quietly, full of the dulled grief of mourning a person she had never known. She said how interesting it was that the last commoner to get a state funeral was the Duke of Wellington, as if it was news to him, and how sad it was that some people still didn't know how much Churchill had done for Britain, and how horrible it was that somebody at the memorial had suggested that his mother had some Red Indian blood. She looked a little more tan than he remembered; he had not seen her since he moved to Nsukka. She became animated after a few glasses of gin and talked about a marvellous film on the royal family that had been screened at the British Council.

'You're not paying much attention, are you?' she asked after a while. Her ears were red.

'Of course I am.'

'I heard about your lady love, Chief Ozobia's daughter,' Susan said, *lady love* in the comic caricature that she assumed was an uneducated accent.

'Her name is Kainene.'

'Will you make sure always to use a rubber? One must be careful, even with the most educated of these people.'

Richard looked out at the calm, unending greenness. He would never have been happy with her – life would be gossamer, all his days merging into one long sheer sheet of nothingness.

'I had an affair with John Blake,' she said.

'Did you?'

Susan laughed. She was playing with her glass, running it along the table, smearing the water that had collected on it. 'You seem surprised.'

'I'm not,' he said, although he was. Not because she had an affair but because it was with John, who was married to her good friend Caroline. But this was expatriate life. All they did, as far as he was concerned, was have sex with one another's wives and husbands, illicit couplings that were more a way of passing heat-blanched time in the tropics than they were genuine expressions of passion.

'It means nothing, absolutely nothing,' Susan said. 'But I did want you to know that I shall keep busy while I wait for you to finish with your dusky affair.'

Richard wanted to say something about her disloyalty to her friend and then realized how hypocritical it would sound, even if only to himself.

5. The Book: The World Was Silent When We Died

He writes about starvation. Starvation was a Nigerian weapon of war. Starvation broke Biafra and brought Biafra fame and made Biafra last as long as it did. Starvation made the people of the world take notice and sparked protests and demonstrations in London and Moscow and Czechoslovakia. Starvation made Zambia and Tanzania and Ivory Coast and Gabon recognize Biafra, starvation brought Africa into Nixon's American campaign and made parents all over the world tell their children to eat up. Starvation propelled aid organizations to sneak-fly food into Biafra at night since both sides could not agree on routes. Starvation aided the careers of photographers. And starvation made the International Red Cross call Biafra its gravest emergency since the Second World War.

22

U gwu's diarrhoea was cramping and painful. It did not get better
when he chewed the bitter tablets in Master's cabinet or the
sour leaves Jomo gave him, and it had nothing to do with food
because the sudden dashes to the Boys' Quarters happened with
whatever he ate. It was about his worry. Master's fear worried him.

Since Mama brought the news of Amala's pregnancy, Master half
stumbled around as if his glasses were blurred, called for his tea in a
subdued voice, and asked Ugwu to tell the guests he had gone out,
even though his car was in the garage. He stared into space often. He
listened to High Life often. He spoke of Olanna often. 'We'll leave
that for when your madam moves back' or 'Your madam would prefer
it in the corridor,' he would say, and Ugwu would say, 'Yes, sah,'
although he knew Master would not bother saying any of that if
Olanna were really coming back.

Ugwu's diarrhoea got worse when Mama visited with Amala. He
watched Amala carefully; she did not look pregnant, still slender and
flat-bellied, and he hoped that the medicine had not worked after all.
But Mama told him, as she peeled hot cocoyams, 'When this baby boy
comes, I will have somebody to keep me company and my fellow
women will no longer call me the mother of an impotent son.'

Amala sat in the living room. Her pregnancy had elevated her, so
she could sit idly listening to the radiogram, no longer Mama's help
but now the woman who would give birth to Mama's grandchild.
Ugwu watched her from the kitchen door. It was a good thing she
had not chosen Master's armchair or Olanna's favourite puff because
he would have asked her to get up right away. She sat with her knees
pressed together, her eyes focused on the pile of newspapers on the
centre table, her face blank. It was so wrong that such an ordinary

person in a nondescript dress and a cotton scarf around her forehead was in the middle of all this. She was neither beautiful nor ugly; she was like the many young women he used to watch going to the stream in his village every morning. Nothing distinguished her. Watching her, Ugwu suddenly felt angry. His anger was not directed at Amala, though, but at Olanna. She should not have run away from her own house because Mama's medicine had pushed Master into the arms of this common slip of a girl. She should have stayed and showed Amala and Mama who was truly mistress here.

The days were suffocating and repetitive, Mama cooking strong-smelling soups that she ate alone because Master stayed out late and Amala felt nauseated and Ugwu had diarrhoea. But Mama did not seem to mind; she hummed and cooked and cleaned and praised herself when she finally learned to turn the stove on. 'One day I will have my own stove; my grandson will buy one for me,' she said, and laughed.

She finally decided to go back to the village after more than a week and said she would leave Amala behind. 'You see how ill she is?' she asked Master. 'My enemies want to harm the pregnancy, they do not want somebody to carry on our family name, but we will defeat them.'

'You must take her with you,' Master said. It was past midnight. Mama had stayed up until Master came home and Ugwu was in the kitchen, half asleep, waiting to lock up.

'Did you not hear me say that she is ill?' Mama said. 'It is better for her to stay here.'

'She will see a doctor, but you must take her with you.'

'You are refusing your child and not Amala,' Mama said.

'You must take her with you,' Master repeated. 'Olanna may return soon, and things will not stand right if Amala is here.'

'Your own child,' Mama said, shaking her head mournfully, but she did not argue. 'I will leave tomorrow because I must attend an *umuada* meeting. I will return at the end of the week to fetch her.'

The afternoon Mama left, Ugwu found Amala in the vegetable garden, crouched on the ground with her knees drawn up, arms around her legs. She was chewing peppers.

'Is it well?' Ugwu asked. Perhaps the woman was a spirit person and had come here to perform rituals with her fellow *ogbanje*.

Amala said nothing for a while; she spoke so seldom that her voice always surprised Ugwu by how childishly high it was. 'Pepper can remove pregnancy,' she said.

'What?'

'If you eat plenty of hot peppers, they will remove pregnancy.' She was huddled in the mud like a pathetic animal, chewing slowly, tears streaming down her face.

'Peppers cannot do that,' Ugwu said. Yet he hoped that she was right, that peppers would indeed abort the pregnancy and his life would return to what it was before: Olanna and Master securely together.

'If you eat enough, they can,' she insisted, and reached out to pluck another one.

Ugwu did not want her to finish the peppers he so carefully cultivated for his stews, but if she was right about what the peppers could do, perhaps it was worth it to let her be. Her face was slick with the moisture of tears and mucus, and once in a while she opened her mouth and extended her pepper-burned tongue to pant like a dog. He wanted to ask why she had gone along with it if she did not want the baby. She had gone to Master's room herself, after all, and she must have known about Mama's plan. But he did not ask; he did not want her friendship. He turned and went back inside.

Days after Amala left, Olanna visited. She sat upright on the sofa, legs crossed like an unfamiliar guest, and refused the *chin-chin* Ugwu brought on a saucer.

'Take it back to the kitchen,' she said to Ugwu, at the same time as Master said, 'Leave it on the table.'

Ugwu stood uncertainly, holding the saucer.

'Take it back to the kitchen, then!' Master snapped, as if Ugwu were somehow responsible for the tension that had settled in the room. Ugwu did not shut the kitchen door, so that he could stand by it and listen, but he might as well have closed it because Olanna's raised voice was audible enough. 'It's *you* and not your mother. It happened because *you* let it happen! You must take responsibility!'

It startled Ugwu, how that soft voice could change to something so fierce.

'I am not a philandering man, and you know that. This would not have happened if my mother didn't have a hand!' Master should have lowered his voice; he should know very well that a beggar did not shout.

'Did your mother pull out your penis and insert it into Amala as well?' Olanna asked.

Ugwu felt the sudden rumbling rush in his stomach and he ran out to the toilet in the Boys' Quarters. When he came out, he saw Olanna standing by the lemon tree. He searched her face to see how the conversation had ended, if it had ended; why she was out here. But he could make nothing of her face. There were tight lines around her mouth and a sleek confidence to the way she stood, wearing a new wig that made her seem much taller.

'You want anything, mah?' he asked.

She walked over to look at the *anara* plants. 'These look very well. Did you use fertilizer?'

'Yes, mah. From Jomo.'

'And on the peppers?'

'Yes, mah.'

She turned to walk away. It was incongruous to see her there in her black shoes and her knee-length dress. She, who was always in a wrapper or a housecoat in the garden.

'Mah?'

She turned.

'I have one uncle who is trading in the North. People have been jealous of him because he is doing well. One day he washed his clothes, and when he brought them in from the sun, he saw that somebody had cut off a piece of his shirtsleeve.'

Olanna was watching him; there was something in her expression that made him realize she would not be patient enough to listen much longer.

'The person who cut it used it for bad medicine, but it did not work because my uncle burnt the shirt immediately. That day, there were many flies near his hut.'

'What are you talking about, for heaven's sake?' Olanna asked in English. Because she hardly ever spoke English to him, it sounded cold, distancing.

'Mama used bad medicine on my master, mah. I saw flies in the kitchen. I saw her putting something in his food. Then I saw her rubbing something on Amala's body, and I know it is the medicine that she used to tempt my master.'

'Rubbish,' Olanna said. It came out sounding like a hiss, *rubbish*, and Ugwu's stomach tightened. She was different; her skin and clothes were crisper. She bent and flicked away a green aphid that had perched on her dress before she walked away. But she did not go around the house, past Master's garage to her own car parked in front. Instead she went back into the house. He followed. In the kitchen, he heard her voice from the study, shouting a long string of words that he could not make out and did not want to. Then silence. Then the opening and closing of the bedroom door. He waited for a while before he tiptoed across the corridor and pressed his ear against the wood. She sounded different. He was used to her throaty moans but what he heard now was an outward, gasping *ah-ah-ah*, as if she was gearing up to erupt, as if Master was pleasing and angering her at the same time and she was waiting to see how much pleasure she could take before she let out the rage. Still, hope surged inside Ugwu. He would cook a perfect *jollof* rice for their reconciliation meal.

Later, when he heard her car start and saw the glaring headlights near the bush with the white flowers, he thought she was going to collect a few things from her flat. He set two places for dinner but did not serve the food because he wanted to keep it warm in the pot.

Master came into the kitchen. 'Do you intend to eat alone today, my good man?'

'I am waiting for madam.'

'Serve my food, *osiso!*'

'Yes, sah,' Ugwu said. 'Will madam come again soon, sah?'

'Serve my food!' Master repeated.

23

Olanna stood in Richard's living room. Its austere emptiness made her nervous; she wished he had pictures or books or Russian dolls that she could look at. There was only a small photo of an Igbo-Ukwu roped pot on the wall, and she was peering at it when Richard came out. The uncertain half smile on his lips softened his face. She sometimes forgot what a handsome man he was, in that fair-haired, blue-eyed sort of way.

She spoke immediately. 'Hello, Richard.' Without waiting for his response and the lull that came with greetings, she added, 'Did you see Kainene last weekend?'

'No. No, I didn't.' His eyes avoided hers, focused on her glossy wig. 'I was in Lagos. Sir Winston Churchill has died, you see.'

'What happened was stupid of both of us,' Olanna said and noticed that his hands were shaking.

Richard nodded. 'Yes, yes.'

'Kainene doesn't forgive easily. It would make no sense at all to tell her.'

'Of course not.' Richard paused. 'You had emotional problems, and I should not have – '

'What happened took two, Richard,' Olanna said, and suddenly felt contempt for his trembling hands and pale shyness and the vulnerabilities he wore so openly knotted at his throat like a tie.

Harrison came in with a tray. 'I am bringing drinks, sah.'

'Drinks?' Richard turned quickly, jerkily, and Olanna was relieved that there was nothing close or he would have knocked it over. 'Oh, no, really. Would you like something?'

'I'm just leaving,' Olanna said. 'How are you, Harrison?'

'Fine, madam.'

Richard followed her to the door.

'I think we should keep things normal,' she said, before she hurried out to her car.

She wondered if she should have been less histrionic and given them both the chance to have a calm conversation about what happened. But it would have achieved little, digging up the dirt of yesterday. They had both wanted it to happen and they both wished it had not; what mattered now was that nobody else should ever know.

She surprised herself, then, when she told Odenigbo. She was lying down while he sat next to her on his bed – she thought of the bedroom itself now as his rather then theirs – and it was the second time they had slept together since she left. He was asking her to please move back to the house.

'Let's get married,' he said. 'Mama will leave us alone then.'

It may have been his smug tone or the flagrant way he continued to sidestep responsibility and blame his mother that made Olanna say, 'I slept with Richard.'

'No.' Odenigbo looked incredulous, shaking his head.

'Yes.'

He got up and walked to the wardrobe and looked at her, as if he could not be close to her at that moment because he was afraid of what he would do if he were. He took his glasses off and rubbed the bridge of his nose. She sat up and realized that distrust would always lie between them, that disbelief would always be an option for them.

'Do you have feelings for the man?' he asked.

'No,' she said.

He came back and sat next to her. He looked torn between shoving her off the bed and pulling her close, and then he got up abruptly and left the room. When she knocked later on his study door to say she was leaving, he did not respond.

Back in her flat, she paced up and down. She should not have told him about Richard. Or she should have told him more: that she regretted betraying Kainene and him but did not regret the act itself. She should have said that it was not a crude revenge, or a score keeping, but took on a redemptive significance for her. She should have said the selfishness had liberated her.

The loud knocking on her front door the next morning filled her with relief. She and Odenigbo would sit down and talk properly, and this time she would make sure that they did not circle each other without meeting. But it was not Odenigbo. Edna came in crying, her eyes swollen red, to tell her that white people had bombed the black

Baptist church in her hometown. Four little girls had died. One of them was her niece's schoolmate. 'I saw her when I went back home six months ago,' Edna said. 'Just six months ago I saw her.'

Olanna made tea and sat next to Edna, their shoulders touching, while Edna cried in loud gasps that sounded like choking. Her hair did not have its usual greasy shine; it looked like the matted head of an old mop.

'Oh, my God,' she said, between sobs. 'Oh, my God.'

Olanna reached out often to squeeze her arm. The rawness of Edna's grief made her helpless, brought the urge to stretch her hand into the past and reverse history. Finally, Edna fell asleep. Olanna gently placed a pillow beneath her head and sat thinking about how a single act could reverberate over time and space and leave stains that could never be washed off. She thought about how ephemeral life was, about not choosing misery. She would move back to Odenigbo's house.

They had dinner in silence the first night. Odenigbo's chewing irritated her, his bulging cheek and the grinding motion of his jaw. She ate little and looked across often at her box of books in the living room. Odenigbo was absorbed in separating his chicken from the bone, and for once he ate all of his rice until his plate was clean. When he finally spoke, he talked about the chaos in the Western Region.

'They should never have reinstalled the premier. Why are they surprised now that thugs are burning cars and killing opponents in the name of elections? A corrupt brute will always behave like a corrupt brute,' he said.

'He has the prime minister behind him,' Olanna said.

'It's the Sardauna who's really in charge. The man is ruling this country like his personal Muslim fiefdom.'

'Are we still trying to have a child?'

Behind his lenses, his eyes looked startled. 'Of course we are,' he said. 'Or aren't we?'

Olanna said nothing. A foggy sadness overwhelmed her, thinking of what they had allowed to happen between them and yet there was the new excitement of freshness, of a relationship on different terms. She would no longer be alone in her struggle to preserve what they shared; he would join her. His certainty had been rocked.

Ugwu came in to clear the table.

'Get me some brandy, my good man,' Odenigbo said.

'Yes, sah.'

Odenigbo waited for Ugwu to serve the brandy and leave before he said, 'I asked Richard to stop coming here.'

'What happened?'

'I saw him on the road near my faculty building, and there was an expression on his face that really annoyed me, so I followed him back to Imoke Street and told him off.'

'What did you say to him?'

'I don't remember.'

'You don't want to tell me.'

'I don't remember.'

'Was anybody else there?'

'His houseboy came out.'

They sat on the sofa in the living room. He had no right to harass Richard, to direct his anger at Richard, and yet she understood why he had.

'I never blamed Amala,' she said. 'It was to you that I had given my trust and the only way a stranger could tamper with that trust was with your permission. I blamed only you.'

Odenigbo placed his hand on her thigh.

'You should be angry with me, not with Richard,' she said.

He was silent for so long that she thought he was not going to respond and then he said, 'I *want* to be angry with you.'

His defencelessness moved her. She knelt down before him and unbuttoned his shirt to suck the soft-firm flesh of his belly. She felt his intake of breath when she touched his trousers' zipper. In her mouth, he was swollen stiff. The faint ache in her lower jaw, the pressure of his widespread hands on her head, excited her, and afterwards she said, 'Goodness, Ugwu must have seen us.'

He led her to the bedroom. They undressed silently and showered together, pressing against each other in the narrow bathroom and then clinging together in bed, their bodies still wet and their movements slow. She marvelled at the comforting compactness of his weight on top of her. His breath smelt of brandy and she wanted to tell him how it was almost like old times again, but she didn't because she was sure he felt the same way and she did not want to ruin the silence that united them.

She waited until he fell asleep, his arm flung over her, his snoring loud through parted lips, before she got up to call Kainene. She had to make sure that Richard had said nothing to Kainene. She didn't really think that Odenigbo's shouting would have rattled him into confessing but she could not be entirely sure.

'Kainene, it's me,' she said, when Kainene picked up the phone.

'*Ejima m*,' Kainene said. Olanna could not remember the last time Kainene had called her *my twin*. It warmed her, as did Kainene's unchanged voice, the dry-toned drawl that suggested speaking to Olanna was the slightest of bothers, but a bother all the same.

'I wanted to say *kedu*,' Olanna said.

'I'm well. Do you know what time it is?'

'I didn't realize it was so late.'

'Are you back with the revolutionary lover?'

'Yes.'

'You should have heard Mum talking about him. He's given her perfect ammunition this time.'

'He made a mistake,' Olanna said, and then wished she hadn't because she didn't want Kainene to think she was excusing Odenigbo.

'Isn't it against the tenets of socialism, though, impregnating people of the lower classes?' Kainene asked.

'I'll let you sleep.'

There was a slight pause, before Kainene said, with an amused tone, '*Ngwanu*. Good night.'

Olanna put the phone down. She should have known that Richard would not tell Kainene; his own relationship with her might not survive it. And perhaps it was best that he would no longer visit in the evenings.

Amala had a baby girl. It was a Saturday and Olanna was making banana fritters with Ugwu in the kitchen, and when the doorbell rang, she knew right away that a message had come from Mama.

Odenigbo came to the kitchen door, his hands held behind his back. '*O mu nwanyi*,' he said quietly. 'She had a girl. Yesterday.'

Olanna did not look up from the bowl smeared with mashed bananas because she did not want him to see her face. She did not know how it would look, if it could capture the cruel mix of emotions she felt, the desire to cry and slap him and steel herself all at once.

'We should go to Enugu this afternoon to see that everything is fine,' she said briskly, and stood up. 'Ugwu, please finish.'

'Yes, mah.' Ugwu was watching her; she felt the responsibility of an actress whose family members expected the best performance.

'Thank you, *nkem*,' Odenigbo said. He placed his arm around her, but she shrugged it off.

'Let me take a quick bath.'

In the car, they were silent. He looked across at her often, as if he wanted to say something but did not know how to begin. She kept her eyes straight ahead and glanced at him only once, at the tentative way he held the steering wheel. She felt morally superior to him. Perhaps it was unearned and false, to think she was better than he was, but it was the only way she could keep her disparate emotions together, now that his child with a stranger was born.

He finally spoke as he parked in front of the hospital.

'What are you thinking?' he asked.

Olanna opened the car door. 'About my cousin Arize. She hasn't even been married a year and she is desperate to get pregnant.'

Odenigbo said nothing. Mama met them at the entrance of the maternity ward. Olanna had expected Mama to dance and look at her with mocking eyes, but the lined face was dour, the smile as she hugged Odenigbo was strained. Chemical hospital smells were thick in the air.

'Mama, *kedu?*' Olanna asked. She wanted to seem in control, to determine how things would proceed.

'I am well,' Mama said.

'Where is the baby?'

Mama looked surprised by her briskness. 'In the newborn ward.'

'Let's see Amala first,' Olanna said.

Mama led them to a cubicle. The bed was covered in a yellowed sheet and Amala lay on it with her face to the wall. Olanna pulled her eyes away from the slight swell of her belly; it was newly unbearable, the thought that Odenigbo's baby had been in that body. She focused on the biscuits, glucose tin, and glass of water on the side table.

'Amala, they have come,' Mama said.

'Good afternoon, *nno*,' Amala said, without turning to face them.

'How are you?' Odenigbo and Olanna asked, almost at the same time.

Amala mumbled a response. Her face was still to the wall. In the silence that followed, Olanna heard quick footfalls on the corridor outside. She had known this was coming for months now, and yet looking at Amala she felt an ashy hollowness. A part of her had hoped this day would never arrive.

'Let's see the baby,' she said. As she and Odenigbo turned to leave, she noticed that Amala did not turn, did not move, did not do anything to show she had heard.

At the newborn ward a nurse asked them to wait on one of the benches that lined the wall. Olanna could see, through the louvres, the many cots and many crying infants, and she imagined that the nurse would be confused and would bring the wrong baby. But it was the right baby; the full head of softly curled black hair and the dark skin and the widely spaced eyes were unmistakable. Only two days old, and she looked like Odenigbo.

The nurse made to give Olanna the baby, wrapped in a white, woolly blanket, but she gestured to Odenigbo. 'Let her father hold her.'

'You know her mother has refused to touch her,' the nurse said, as she handed the baby to Odenigbo.

'What?' Olanna asked.

'She has not touched her at all. We are using a wet nurse.'

Olanna glanced at Odenigbo, holding the baby with his arms outstretched as if he needed some distance. The nurse was about to say something else when a young couple came in and she hurried over to them.

'Mama just told me,' Odenigbo said. 'She said Amala won't hold the baby.'

Olanna said nothing.

'I should go and see to the bill,' he said. He sounded apologetic.

She held out her arms and as soon as he handed her the baby, the high-pitched crying began. From across the room, the nurse and the couple watched and Olanna was certain that they could tell that she did not know what to do with a howling infant in her arms, that she was incapable of getting pregnant.

'Shush, shush, *o zugo*,' she said, feeling a little theatrical. But the tiny mouth remained open and twisted, and the crying was so shrill, she wondered if it hurt the tiny body. Olanna fit her small finger in the baby's fist. Slowly the crying stopped but the little mouth remained open, showing pink gums, and the round eyes scrunched up and peered at her. Olanna laughed. The nurse walked across.

'Time to take her in,' she said. 'How many do you have?'

'I don't have children,' Olanna said, pleased that the nurse had assumed that she did.

Odenigbo came back and they walked to Amala's cubicle, where Mama sat by the bedside, holding a covered enamel bowl. 'Amala has refused to eat,' she said. '*Gwakwa ya.* Tell her to eat.'

Olanna sensed Odenigbo's discomfort before he spoke in a voice that was too loud. 'You should eat, Amala.'

Amala mumbled something. Finally, she turned her face towards them and Olanna looked at her: a plain village girl curled up on the bed as if she were cringing from one more furious blow from life. She never once looked at Odenigbo. What she must feel for him was an awed fear. Whether or not Mama had told her to go to his room, she had not said no to Odenigbo because she had not even considered that she could say no. Odenigbo made a drunken pass and she submitted willingly and promptly: He was the master, he spoke English, he had a car. It was the way it should be.

'Did you hear what my son said?' Mama asked. 'He said you should eat.'

'I heard, Mama.' Amala sat up and took the enamel plate, her eyes focused on the floor. Olanna was watching her. Perhaps it was hate she felt for Odenigbo. How much did one know of the true feelings of those who did not have a voice? Olanna moved closer to Amala, but she was unsure what she wanted to say and so she picked up the tin of glucose, examined it, and placed it back. Mama and Odenigbo had stepped outside.

'We are leaving,' Olanna said.

'Go well,' Amala said.

Olanna wanted to say something to her but she could not find the words, so she patted Amala's shoulder and left the cubicle. Odenigbo and Mama were talking beside a water tank, for so long that mosquitoes began to bite Olanna as she stood waiting, so she climbed into the car and pressed the horn.

'Sorry,' Odenigbo said, when he got in. He did not say anything about what he and his mother had talked about until they were driving past the campus gates in Nsukka, an hour later. 'Mama doesn't want to keep the baby.'

'She doesn't want to keep the baby?'

'No.'

Olanna knew why. 'She wanted a boy.'

'Yes.' Odenigbo removed a hand from the steering wheel to roll his window farther down. She found a guilty pleasure in the humility he had cloaked himself in since Amala gave birth. 'We've agreed that the baby will stay with Amala's people. I'll go to Abba next week to see them and discuss – '

'We'll keep her,' Olanna said. She startled herself by how clearly she had articulated the desire to keep the baby and how right it felt. It was as if it was what she had always wanted to do.

Odenigbo turned to her with eyes widened behind his glasses. He was driving so slowly over a speed bump that she feared the car would stall. 'Our relationship is the most important thing to me, *nkem*,' he said quietly. 'We have to make the right decision for us.'

'You were not thinking about us when you got her pregnant,' Olanna said, before she could help herself; she hated the malice in her tone, the renewed resentment she felt.

Odenigbo parked the car in the garage. He looked tired. 'Let's think about this.'

'We'll keep her,' Olanna said firmly.

She could raise a child, his child. She would buy books about motherhood and find a wet nurse and decorate the bedroom. She shifted this way and that in bed that night. She had not felt sorry for the child. Instead, holding that tiny, warm body, she had felt a conscious serendipity, a sense that this may not have been planned but had become, the minute it happened, what was meant to be. Her mother did not think so; her mother's voice over the phone line the next day was grave, the solemn tone that would be used to talk about somebody who had died.

'*Nne*, you will have your own child soon. It is not right for you to raise the child he had with a village girl he impregnated as soon as you travelled. Raising a child is a very serious thing to undertake, my daughter, but in this case it is not the right thing.'

Olanna held the phone and stared at the flowers on the centre table. One of them had fallen off; it was surprising that Ugwu had forgotten to remove it. There was truth in her mother's words, she knew, and yet she knew, also, that the baby had looked like she had always imagined her and Odenigbo's child would, with the lush hair and widely spaced eyes and pink gums.

'Her people will give you trouble,' her mother said. 'The woman herself will give you trouble.'

'She doesn't want the child.'

'Then leave it with her people. Send them what is needed but leave the child there.'

Olanna sighed. '*Anugo m*, I'll give this more thought.'

She put the phone down and picked it up again and gave the operator Kainene's number in Port Harcourt. The woman sounded lazy, made her repeat the number a few times and giggled before connecting her.

'How noble of you,' Kainene said when Olanna told her.

'I'm not being noble.'

'Will you adopt her formally?'

'Yes. I think so.'

'What will you tell her?'

'What will I tell her?'

'Yes, when she's older.'

'The truth: that Amala is her mother. And I'll have her call me Mummy Olanna or something, so that if Amala ever comes back, she can be Mummy.'

'You're doing this to please your revolutionary lover.'

'I'm not.'

'You're always pleasing other people.'

'I'm not doing this for him. This is not his idea.'

'Why are you doing it then?'

'She was so helpless. I felt as if I knew her.'

Kainene said nothing for a while. Olanna pulled at the phone wire.

'I think this is a very brave decision,' Kainene said finally.

Although Olanna heard her clearly, she asked, 'What did you say?'

'It's very brave of you to do this.'

Olanna leaned back on the seat. Kainene's approval, something she had never felt before, was like a sweetness on her tongue, a surge of ability, a good omen. Suddenly her decision became final; she would bring the baby home.

'Will you come for her baptism?' Olanna asked.

'I still haven't visited that dusty hell, so yes, maybe I will.'

Olanna hung up, smiling.

Mama brought the baby, wrapped in a brown shawl that had the unpleasant smell of *ogiri*. She sat in the living room and cooed to the baby until Olanna came out. Mama got up and handed the baby over.

'*Ngwanu*. I will visit again soon,' she said. She seemed in an uncomfortable hurry, as if the whole business was one that she was quick to finish.

After she left, Ugwu examined the baby, his expression slightly worried. 'Mama said the baby looks like her mother. It is her mother come back.'

'People just look alike, Ugwu, it doesn't mean they reincarnate.'

'But they do, mah. All of us, we will come back again.'

Olanna waved him away. 'Go and throw this shawl into the dustbin. It smells terrible.'

The baby was crying. Olanna hushed her and bathed her in a small basin and glanced at the clock and worried that the wet nurse, a large woman that Ugwu's aunty had found, would be late. Later, after the nurse arrived and the baby fed at her breast and fell asleep, Olanna and Odenigbo looked down at her, lying face up in the cot near their bed. Her skin was a radiant brown.

'She has so much hair, like you,' Olanna said.

'You'll look at her sometimes and hate me.'

Olanna shrugged. She did not want him to think she was doing this for him, as a favour to him, because it was more about herself than it was about him.

'Ugwu said your mother went to a *dibia*,' she said.

'What?'

'Ugwu thinks all this happened because your mother went to a *dibia* and his medicine charmed you into sleeping with Amala.'

Odenigbo was silent for a moment. 'I suppose it's the only way he can make sense of it.'

'The medicine should have produced the desired boy, shouldn't it?' she said. 'It is all so irrational.'

'No more irrational than belief in a Christian God you cannot see.'

She was used to his gentle jibes about her social-service faith and she would have responded to say that she was not even sure she believed in a Christian God that could not be seen. But now, with a helpless human being lying in the cot, one so dependent on others that her very existence had to be proof of a higher goodness, things had changed.

'I do believe,' she said. 'I believe in a good God.'

'I don't believe in any gods at all.'

'I know. You don't believe in anything.'

'Love,' he said, looking at her. 'I believe in love.'

She did not mean to laugh, but the laughter came out anyway. She wanted to say that love, too, was irrational. 'We have to think of a name,' she said.

'Mama named her Obiageli.'

'We can't call her that.' His mother had no right to name a child she had rejected. 'We'll call her Baby for now until we find the perfect name. Kainene suggested Chiamaka. I've always loved that name: God is beautiful. Kainene will be her godmother. I have to go and see Father Damian about her baptism.' She would go shopping at Kingsway. She would order a new wig from London. She felt giddy.

Baby stirred and a new wave of fear enveloped Olanna. She looked at the hair shining with Pears oil and wondered if she could really do it, if she could raise a child. She knew it was normal, the way the baby was breathing too fast, as if panting in her sleep, and yet even that worried her.

The first few times she called Kainene that evening, there was no answer. Perhaps Kainene was in Lagos. She called again at night and when Kainene said, 'Hello,' she sounded hoarse.

'*Ejima m,*' Olanna said. 'Do you have a cold?'

'You fucked Richard.'

Olanna stood up.

'You're the good one.' Kainene's voice was controlled. 'The good one shouldn't fuck her sister's lover.'

Olanna sank back down on the puff and realized that what she felt was relief. Kainene knew. She would no longer have to worry about Kainene's finding out. She was free to feel real remorse.

'I should have told you, Kainene,' she said. 'It meant nothing.'

'Of course it meant nothing. It was just fucking my lover, after all.'

'I didn't mean it like that.' Olanna felt the tears in her eyes. 'Kainene, I'm so sorry.'

'Why did you do it?' Kainene sounded frighteningly calm. 'You're the good one and the favourite and the beauty and the Africanist revolutionary who doesn't like white men, and you simply did not need to fuck him. So why did you?'

Olanna was breathing slowly. 'I don't know, Kainene, it wasn't something I planned. I am so sorry. It was unforgivable.'

'It *was* unforgivable,' Kainene said and hung up.

Olanna put down the phone and felt a sharp cracking inside her. She knew her twin well, knew how tightly Kainene held on to hurt.

24

Richard wanted to cane Harrison. It had always appalled him, the thought that some colonial Englishmen flogged elderly black servants. Now, though, he felt like doing just as they had done. He longed to make Harrison lie down on his belly and flog, flog, flog him until the man learned to keep his mouth shut. If only he had not brought Harrison with him to Port Harcourt. But he was spending a whole week and did not want to leave him alone in Nsukka. The first day they arrived, Harrison, as if to justify his visit, cooked a complicated meal: a bean and mushroom soup, a pawpaw medley, chicken in a cream sauce speckled with greens, and a lemon tart as pudding.

'This is excellent, Harrison,' Kainene said, with a teasing sparkle in her eyes. She was in a good mood; she had pulled Richard into her arms after he arrived and mock-danced with him over the polished floor of the living room.

'Thank you, madam.' Harrison bowed.

'And do you cook this in your home?'

Harrison looked wounded. 'I am not cooking in my home, madam. My wife is cooking native food.'

'Of course.'

'I am cooking any type of European food, anything my master is eating in his country.'

'You must have difficulty eating *native* food when you go home then.' Kainene stressed the word *native*, and Richard held back his laughter.

'Yes, madam.' Harrison bowed again. 'But I must manage.'

'This tart tastes better than one I had the last time I was in London.'

'Thank you, madam.' Harrison beamed. 'My master is telling me that everybody in Mr Odenigbo's house is saying the same thing. I used to make it for my master to take there, but I am not making anything again for Mr Odenigbo's house since that time he is shouting on my master. Shouting like madman and the whole street is hearing. The man's head is not correct.'

Kainene turned to Richard and raised her eyebrows. Richard knocked his glass of water over.

'I will get rag, sah,' Harrison said, and Richard restrained himself from leaping across to strangle him.

'Whatever is Harrison talking about?' Kainene asked, after the water had been wiped up. 'The revolutionary shouted at you?'

He could have lied. Even Harrison himself did not know exactly why Odenigbo had driven into the compound that evening and shouted at him. But he did not lie, because he was scared that he would fail at lying and would eventually have to tell her the truth and that way make it all doubly damaging. So he told her everything. He told her about the good white Burgundy he and Olanna drank and how, afterwards, he was overwhelmed with regret.

Kainene pushed away her plate and sat with her elbows on the table, her chin lightly supported on her clasped hands. She said nothing for many long minutes. He could not read the expression on her face.

'I hope you won't say *forgive me*,' she said, finally. 'There is nothing more trite.'

'Please don't ask me to leave.'

She looked surprised. 'Leave? That would be too easy, wouldn't it?'

'I'm sorry, Kainene.'

Richard felt transparent; she was looking at him but he felt as if she could see the wood carving that hung on the wall behind him. 'So you have been lusting after my sister. How unoriginal,' she said.

'Kainene,' he said.

She stood up. 'Ikejide!' she called. 'Come and clear this place.'

They were leaving the dining room when the phone rang. She ignored it. It rang again and again and finally she went to it. She came back into the bedroom and said, 'That was Olanna.'

Richard looked at her, pleaded with his eyes.

'It would be forgivable if it were somebody else. Not my sister,' she said.

'I am so sorry.'

'You should sleep in the guest room.'

'Yes, yes, of course.'

He did not know what she was thinking. It was what frightened him the most, that he had no idea what she was thinking. He patted his pillow and rearranged his blanket and sat up in bed and tried to read. But his mind was too active for his body to be still. He worried that Kainene would call Madu and tell him what had happened, and Madu would laugh and say, 'He was a mistake from the beginning, leave him, leave him, leave him.' Finally, before he fell asleep, Molière's words came to him, strangely comforting: *Unbroken happiness is a bore; it should have ups and downs.*

Kainene greeted him with a stoic face in the morning.

The rain was heavy on the roof and the overcast sky cast a pallor over the dining room. Kainene sat drinking a cup of tea and reading a newspaper with the light on.

'Harrison is making pancakes,' she said, and turned back to her paper. Richard sat opposite her, unsure of what to do, too guilty even to pour his tea. Her silence and the noises and smells from the kitchen made him feel claustrophobic.

'Kainene,' he said. 'Can we speak, please?'

She looked up, and he noticed, first, that her eyes were swollen and raw, and then he saw the wounded rage in them. 'We will talk when I want to talk, Richard.'

He looked down, like a child being reprimanded, and felt, again, afraid that she would ask him to get out of her life forever.

The doorbell rang before noon and, when Ikejide came in to say that madam's sister was at the door, Richard thought that Kainene would ask him to shut the door in Olanna's face. But she didn't. She asked Ikejide to serve drinks and went down to the living room and from the top of the stairs where he stood, Richard tried to hear what was said. He heard Olanna's tearful voice but could not make out what she was saying. Odenigbo spoke briefly, in a tone that was unusually calm. Then Richard heard Kainene's voice, clear and crisp. 'It is stupid to expect me to forgive this.'

There was a short silence and then the sound of the door being opened. Richard hurried to the window to see Odenigbo's car backing out, the same blue Opel that had parked in his own compound on Imoke Street before Odenigbo bounded out, a stocky man in well-ironed clothes shouting, 'I want you to stay away from my house! Do you understand me? Stay away! Don't ever come to my house again!' He had stood in front of the veranda and wondered if Odenigbo would punch him. Later, he realized that Odenigbo did not intend to punch him, perhaps did not consider him worthy of a punch, and the thought had depressed him.

'Did you eavesdrop?' Kainene asked, walking into the room. Richard turned away from the window, but she didn't wait for his response before she added, mildly, 'I'd forgotten how much the revolutionary looks like a wrestler, really – but one with finesse.'

'I will never forgive myself if I lose you, Kainene.'

Her face was expressionless. 'I took your manuscript from the study this morning and I burnt it,' she said.

Richard felt a soar in his chest of emotions he could not name. 'The Basket of Hands', the collection of pages that he was finally confident could become a book, was gone. He could never duplicate the unbridled energy that had come with the words. But it did not matter. What mattered was that by burning his manuscript she had shown him that she would not end the relationship; she would not bother to cause him pain if she was not going to stay. Perhaps he was not a true writer after all. He had read somewhere that, for true writers, nothing was more important than their art, not even love.

•

6. The Book: The World Was Silent When We Died

He writes about the world that remained silent while Biafrans died. He argues that Britain inspired this silence. The arms and advice that Britain gave Nigeria shaped other countries. In the United States, Biafra was 'under Britain's sphere of interest'. In Canada, the prime minister quipped, 'Where is Biafra?' The Soviet Union sent technicians and planes to Nigeria, thrilled at the chance to influence Africa without offending America or Britain. And from their white-supremacist positions, South Africa and Rhodesia gloated at further proof that black-run governments were doomed to failure.

Communist China denounced the Anglo-American-Soviet imperialism but did little else to support Biafra. The French sold Biafra some arms but did not give the recognition that Biafra most needed. And many Black African countries feared that an independent Biafra would trigger other secessions and so supported Nigeria.

PART FOUR

The Late Sixties

25

Olanna jumped each time she heard the thunder. She imagined another air raid, bombs rolling out of a plane and exploding in the compound before she and Odenigbo and Baby and Ugwu could reach the bunker down the street. Sometimes she imagined the bunker itself collapsing, squashing them all into mud. Odenigbo and some of the neighbourhood men had built it in a week; after they dug the pit, as wide as a hall, and after they roofed it with clay-layered palm trunks, he told her, 'We're safe now, *nkem*. We're safe.' But the first time he showed her how to climb down the jagged steps, Olanna saw a snake coiled in a corner. Its black skin glistened with silver markings and tiny crickets hopped about and, in the silence of the damp underground that made her think of a grave, she screamed.

Odenigbo bashed the snake with a stick and told her he would make sure the zinc sheet at the entrance of the bunker was more secure. His calmness bewildered her. The tranquil tone he used to confront their new world, their changed circumstances, bewildered her. When the Nigerians changed their currency and Radio Biafra hurriedly announced a new currency too, Olanna stood in the bank queue for four hours, dodging flogging men and pushing women, until she exchanged their Nigerian money for the prettier Biafran pounds. Later, during breakfast, she held up the medium-sized envelope of notes and said, 'All the cash we have.'

Odenigbo looked amused. 'We're both earning money, *nkem*.'

'This is the second month the directorate has delayed your salary,' she said, and put the tea bag on his saucer in her own cup. 'And you can't call what they pay me at Akwakuma earning money.'

'We'll get our life back soon, in a free Biafra,' he said, his usual words lined with his usual forceful reassurance, and sipped his tea.

Olanna placed her cup against her cheek, to warm it, to delay the first sip of weak tea made from a reused tea bag. When he stood up and kissed her goodbye, she wondered why he was not frightened by how little they had. Perhaps it was because he did not go to the market himself. He did not notice how a cup of salt cost a shilling more each week and how chickens were chopped into bits that were still too expensive and how nobody sold rice in large bags any more because nobody could buy them. That night, she was silent as his thrusts became faster. It was the first time she felt detached from him; while he was murmuring in her ear, she was mourning her money in the bank in Lagos.

'*Nkem?* Are you all right?' he asked, raising himself to look at her.

'Yes.'

He sucked her lower lip before he rolled off and fell asleep. She had never known his snoring to be so rasping. He was tired. The long walk to the Manpower Directorate, the sheer mindlessness of compiling names and addresses day after day, exhausted him, she knew, yet he came home each day with lit-up eyes. He had joined the Agitator Corps; after work, they went into the interior to educate the people. She often imagined him standing in the middle of a gathering of rapt villagers, talking in that sonorous voice about the great nation that Biafra would be. His eyes saw the future. And so she did not tell him that she grieved for the past, different things on different days, her tablecloths with the silver embroidery, her car, Baby's strawberry cream biscuits. She did not tell him that sometimes when she watched Baby running around with the neighbourhood children, so helpless and happy, she wanted to gather Baby in her arms and apologize. Not that Baby would understand.

Ever since Mrs Muokelu, who taught Elementary One at Akwakuma, had told her about the children forced into a truck by soldiers and returned at night with their palms chafed and bleeding from grinding cassava, she had asked Ugwu never to let Baby out of his sight. But she did not really believe the soldiers would have much use for a child as young as Baby. She worried, instead, about air raids. She had a recurring dream: She forgot about Baby and ran to the bunker and after the bombs had fallen, she tripped on the burnt body of a child with its features so blackened that she could not be certain it was Baby. The dream haunted her. She made Baby practise running to the bunker. She asked Ugwu to practise picking Baby up and running. She taught Baby how to take cover if there was no time for the bunker – to lie flat on her belly, hands wrapped around her head.

Still, she worried that she had not done enough and that the dream portended some negligence of hers that would harm Baby. When, towards the end of the rainy season, Baby began to cough in drawn-out whistles, Olanna felt relief. *Something* had happened to Baby. If the heavens were fair, war-time misfortunes would be mutually exclusive; since Baby was sick, she could not be harmed in an air raid. A cough was something Olanna could exercise control over, an air raid was not.

She took Baby to Albatross Hospital. Ugwu removed the palm fronds piled on top of Odenigbo's car, but each time she turned the key, the engine wheezed and died out. Finally, Ugwu pushed it before it started. She drove slowly and stepped on the brake when Baby started to cough. At the checkpoint, where a huge tree trunk lay across the road, she told the civil defenders that her child was very sick and they said *sorry* and did not search the car or her handbag. The dim hospital corridor smelt of urine and penicillin. Women were sitting with babies on their laps, standing with babies on their hips, and their chatter mixed with crying. Olanna remembered Dr Nwala from the wedding. She had barely noticed him until after the bombing, when he said, 'The mud will stain your dress,' and helped her up, Okeoma's shirt still wrapped around her.

She told the nurses that she was an old colleague of his.

'It's terribly urgent,' she said, and kept her English accent crisp and her head held high. A nurse showed her into his office promptly. One of the women sitting in the corridor cursed. '*Tufiakwa!* We have been waiting since dawn! Is it because we don't talk through our nose like white people?'

Dr Nwala raised his willowy body from his seat and came around to shake her hand. 'Olanna,' he said, looking into her eyes.

'How are you, doctor?'

'We are managing,' he said, and patted Baby's shoulder. 'How are you?'

'Very well. Okeoma visited us last week.'

'Yes, he stayed a day with me.' He was staring at her, but she felt as if he were not listening, as if he were not really there. He looked lost.

'Baby has been coughing for some days now,' Olanna said loudly.

'Oh.' He turned to Baby. He placed the stethoscope on her chest and murmured *ndo* as she coughed. When he walked over to the cupboard to look through some bottles and packets of medicine, Olanna felt sorry for him and was not sure why. He spent too long looking through so few things.

'I'll give you a cough syrup, but she needs antibiotics and I'm afraid we've run out,' he said, staring at her again, in that odd way that locked his eyes with hers. His expression was filled with melancholy fatigue. Olanna wondered if perhaps he had recently lost a person he loved.

'I'll write a prescription and you can try one of those people who trade, but it should be somebody reliable, of course.'

'Of course,' Olanna repeated. 'I have a friend, Mrs Muokelu, who can help.'

'Very good.'

'You should come and visit us when you have time,' Olanna said, standing up.

'Yes.' He took her hand in his and held it for a little too long.

'Thank you, doctor.'

'For what? I can't do much.' He gestured towards the door, and Olanna knew he meant the women who were waiting outside. As she left, she glanced at the near-empty cupboard of medicine.

Olanna ran past the town square on her way to Akwakuma Primary School in the morning. She always did that in open spaces, running until she got to the thick shade of trees that would give good cover in case of an air raid. Some children were standing under the mango tree in the school compound, throwing stones up at the fruit. She shouted, 'Go to your classes, *osiso!*' and they scattered briefly before coming back to aim at the mangoes. She heard a cheer when one fell, and then the raised voices as they quarrelled over whose throw had brought the fruit down.

Mrs Muokelu was in front of her classroom fiddling with the bell. The thick, black hair on her arms and legs, the fuzz on her upper lip, the curled strands on her chin, and the squat, muscular limbs often made Olanna wonder if perhaps Mrs Muokelu would have been better off being born a man.

'Do you know where I can buy antibiotics, my sister?' Olanna asked, after they hugged. 'Baby has a cough, and they did not have any at the hospital.'

Mrs Muokelu hummed for a while to show that she was thinking. His Excellency's face glared from the fabric of the boubou she wore everyday; she often announced that she would wear nothing else until the state of Biafra was fully established.

'Anybody can sell medicine, but you don't know who is mixing chalk in his backyard and calling it Nivaquine,' she said. 'Give me the money and I will go to Mama Onitsha. She is authentic. She will sell you Gowon's dirty pant if you pay the right price.'

'Let her keep the pant and just give us medicine.' Olanna was laughing.

Mrs Muokelu smiled and picked up the bell. 'I saw a vision yesterday,' she said. Her boubou was too long for her short body; it dragged along the ground and Olanna feared that she would trip on it and fall.

'What was the vision?' Olanna asked. Mrs Muokelu always had visions. In the last one, she had seen Ojukwu personally leading the battle in the Ogoja sector, which meant that the enemy had been completely wiped out there.

'Traditional warriors from Abiriba used their bows and arrows and finished the vandals in the Calabar sector. *I makwa*, children were walking over their bones to go to the stream.'

'Really,' Olanna said, and kept her face serious.

'It means Calabar will never fall,' Mrs Muokelu said, and began to ring the bell. Olanna watched the swift movements of the masculine arm. They really had nothing in common, herself and this barely educated primary-school teacher from Eziowelle who believed in visions. Yet Mrs Muokelu had always seemed familiar. It was not because Mrs Muokelu plaited her hair and went with her to the Women's Voluntary Services meetings and taught her how to preserve vegetables, but because Mrs Muokelu exuded fearlessness, a fearlessness that reminded Olanna of Kainene.

That evening, when Mrs Muokelu brought the antibiotic capsules wrapped in newspaper, Olanna asked her to come inside and showed her a photo of Kainene, sitting by the pool with a cigarette between her lips.

'This is my twin sister. She lives in Port Harcourt.'

'Your twin!' Mrs Muokelu exclaimed, fingering the plastic half of a yellow sun that she wore on a string around her neck. 'Wonders shall never end. I did not know you were a twin, and, *nekene*, she does not look like you at all.'

'We have the same mouth,' Olanna said.

Mrs Muokelu glanced at the photo again and shook her head. 'She does not look like you at all,' she repeated.

The antibiotics yellowed Baby's eyes. Her coughing got better, less chesty and less whistling, but her appetite disappeared. She pushed her *garri* around her plate and left her pap uneaten until it congealed in a waxy lump. Olanna spent most of the cash in the envelope and bought biscuits and toffees in shiny wrappers from a woman who traded behind enemy lines, but Baby only nibbled at them. She placed Baby on her lap and forced bits of mashed yam into her mouth, and when Baby choked and started to cry, Olanna, too, fought tears. Her greatest fear was that Baby would die. It was there, the festering fear, underlying everything she thought and did. Odenigbo skipped the Agitator Corps activities and rushed home earlier, and Olanna knew he shared her fear. But they did not talk about it, as though verbalizing it would make Baby's death imminent, until the morning she sat watching Baby sleep while Odenigbo got dressed for work. The resonating voice on Radio Biafra filled the room.

> *These African states have fallen prey to the British–American imperialist conspiracy to use the committee's recommendations as a pretext for a massive arms support for their puppet and tottering neocolonialist regime in Nigeria. . . .*

'That's right!' Odenigbo said, buttoning his shirt with quick movements.

On the bed, Baby stirred. Her face had lost its fat and was eerily adult, sunken and thin-skinned. Olanna watched her.

'Baby won't make it,' she said quietly.

Odenigbo stopped and looked at her. He turned the radio off and came over and held her head against his belly. Because he said nothing at first, his silence became a confirmation that Baby would die. Olanna shifted away.

'It's only normal that she doesn't have an appetite,' he said finally. But his tone lacked the certitude she was used to.

'Look how much weight she's lost!' Olanna said.

'*Nkem*, her cough is getting better and her appetite will come back.' He began to comb his hair. She was angry with him for not saying what she wanted to hear, for not assuming the power of fate and telling her that Baby would be well, for being normal enough to continue to dress for work. His kiss before he left was quick, not the usual lingering press of lips, and that, too, she held against him. Tears filled her eyes. She thought about Amala. Amala had made no contact with them since the day at the hospital but she wondered now if she would be expected to tell Amala if Baby were to die.

Baby yawned and woke up. 'Good morning, Mummy Ola.' Even her voice was thin.

'Baby, *ezigbo nwa*, how are you?' Olanna picked her up, hugged her, blew onto her neck, and struggled with her tears. Baby felt so slight, so light. 'Will you eat some pap, my baby? Or some bread? What do you want?'

Baby shook her head. Olanna was trying to cajole Baby into drinking some Ovaltine when Mrs Muokelu arrived with a knotted raffia bag and a self-satisfied smile.

'They have opened a relief centre on Bishop Road and I went very early this morning,' she said. 'Ask Ugwu to bring me a bowl.'

She poured some yellow powder into the bowl Ugwu brought.

'What is that?' Olanna asked.

'Dried egg yolk.' Mrs Muokelu turned to Ugwu. 'Fry it for Baby.'

'Fry it?'

'Is something wrong with your ears? Mix it with some water and fry it, *osiso*! They say children love the taste of this thing.'

Ugwu gave her a slow look before he went into the kitchen. The dried egg yolk, fried in red palm oil, looked soggy and unnervingly bright-coloured on the plate. Baby ate all of it.

The relief centre used to be a girls' secondary school. Olanna imagined the grassy, walled compound before the war, young women hurrying to classes in the morning and sneaking to the gate in the evening to meet young men from the government college down the road. Now it was dawn and the gate was locked. A large crowd had gathered outside. Olanna stood awkwardly among the men and women and children, who all seemed used to standing and waiting for a rusted iron gate to be opened so they could go in and be given food donated by foreign strangers. She felt discomfited. She felt as if she were doing something improper, unethical: expecting to get food in exchange for nothing. Inside the compound, she could see people moving about, tables set out with sacks of food, a board that said WORLD COUNCIL OF CHURCHES. Some of the women clutched their baskets and peered over the gate and muttered about these relief people wasting time. The men were talking among themselves; the oldest-looking man wore his red chieftaincy hat with a feather stuck in it. A young man's voice stood out from the others, high-pitched, shouting gibberish, like a child learning to speak.

'He has serious shell shock,' Mrs Muokelu whispered, as if Olanna did not know. It was the only time Mrs Muokelu spoke. She had slowly edged her way to the front of the gate, nudging Olanna to follow her each time. Somebody behind had begun a story about a Biafran victory. 'I am telling you, all of the Hausa soldiers turned and ran, they had seen what was bigger than them. . . .' The voice trailed away as a man inside the compound strode towards the gate. His T-shirt, LAND OF THE RISING SUN written on it in black, was loose around his slim body and he carried a sheaf of papers. He walked with an air of importance, his shoulders held high. He was the supervisor.

'Order! Order!' he said, and opened the gate.

The swift scrambling rush of the crowd surprised Olanna. She felt jostled; she swayed. It was as if they all shoved her aside in one calculated move since she was not one of them. The firm elbow of the elderly man beside her landed painfully on her side as he launched his run into the compound. Mrs Muokelu was ahead, dashing towards one of the tables. The old man in the feathered hat fell down, promptly picked himself up, and continued his lopsided run to the queue. Olanna was surprised, too, by the militia members flogging with long whips and shouting 'Order! Order!' and by the stern faces of the women at the tables, who bent and scooped into the bags held out before them and then said, 'Yes! Next!'

'Join that one!' Mrs Muokelu said, when Olanna moved to stand some way behind her. 'That is the egg-yolk queue! Join it! This one is stockfish.'

Olanna joined the queue and held herself from pushing back at the woman who tried to nudge her out. She let the woman stand in front of her. The incongruity of queuing to beg for food made her feel uncomfortable, blemished. She folded her arms, then let them lie by her sides, and then folded them again. She was close to the front when she noticed that the powder being scooped into bags and bowls was not yellow but white. Not egg yolk but cornmeal. The egg-yolk queue was the next one. Olanna hurried over to join it, but the woman who was dishing out the yolk stood up and said, 'Egg yolk is finished! *O gwula!*'

Panic rose in Olanna's chest. She ran after the woman. 'Please,' she said.

'What is it?' the woman asked. The supervisor, standing close by, turned to stare at Olanna.

'My little child is sick – ' Olanna said.

The woman cut her short. 'Join that queue for milk.'

'No, no, she has not been eating anything, but she ate egg yolk.' Olanna held the woman's arm. '*Biko*, please; I need the egg yolk.'

The woman pulled her arm away and hurried into the building and slammed the door. Olanna stood there. The supervisor, still staring, fanned himself with his sheaf of papers and said, '*Ehe!* I know you.'

His bald head and bearded face did not look familiar at all. Olanna turned to walk away because she was sure he was one of those men who claimed to have met her before only to have a chance to make a pass.

'I have seen you before,' he said. He moved closer, smiling now, but without the leer she expected; his face was frank and delighted. 'Some years ago at Enugu Airport when I went to meet my brother who was returning from overseas. You talked to my mother. *I kasiri ya obi.* You calmed her down when the plane landed and did not stop right away.'

That day at the airport came back to Olanna hazily. It had to be about seven years ago. She remembered his bush accent and his nervous excitement and that he had seemed older than he looked now.

'Is it you?' she asked. 'But how did you recognize me?'

'How can anybody forget a face like your own? My mother has always told the story of a beautiful woman who held her hand. All the members of my family know the story. Every time somebody talks about my brother's return, she will tell it.'

'And how is your brother?'

Pride lit up his face. 'He is a senior man in the directorate. He is the one who gave me this job with relief.'

Olanna immediately wondered whether he could help her get some egg yolk. But what she asked was, 'And your mother is well?'

'Very well. She is at Orlu in my brother's house. She was very ill when my elder sister did not return from Zaria at first; we all thought those animals had done to her what they did to the others, but my sister returned – she had Hausa friends who helped her – so my mother got better. She will be happy when I tell her that I saw you.'

He paused to glance at one of the food tables where two young girls were fighting, one saying, 'I am telling you that this stockfish is mine,' and the other saying, '*Ngwanu*, both of us will die today.'

He turned back to her. 'Let me go and see what is going on there. But wait by the gate. I will send somebody to you with egg yolk.'

'Thank you.' Olanna was relieved that he had offered and yet felt awkward at the exchange. At the gate, she skulked; she felt like a thief.

'Okoromadu sent me to you,' a young woman said beside her, and Olanna almost jumped. The woman slid a bag into her hand and walked back into the compound. 'Thank him for me,' Olanna called out. If the woman heard, she did not turn. The weight of the bag felt reassuring as she waited for Mrs Muokelu; later, as she watched Baby eat until only the palm oil grease was left on the plate, she wondered how Baby could stand the awful plastic taste of the dried egg yolk.

The next time Olanna went to the relief centre, Okoromadu was talking to the crowd at the gate. Some women held rolled-up mats under their arms; they had spent the night outside the gates.

'We have nothing for you today. The lorry carrying our supplies from Awomama was hijacked on the road,' he said, in the measured tone of a politician addressing his supporters. Olanna watched him. He enjoyed this, the power that came with knowing whether or not a group of people would eat. 'We have military escorts, but it is soldiers who are hijacking us. They set up roadblocks and take everything from the lorry; they even beat the drivers. Come on Monday, and maybe we will be open.'

A woman walked briskly up to him and thrust her baby boy into his arms. 'Then take him! Feed him until you open again!' She began to walk away. The baby was thin, jaundiced, squalling.

'*Bia nwanyi!* Come back, woman!' Okoromadu was holding the baby with stiff arms, away from his body.

The other women in the crowd began to chide the mother – Are you throwing your child away? *Ujo anaghi atu gi?* Are you walking in

God's face? – but it was Mrs Muokelu who went over and took the baby from Okoromadu and placed it back in the mother's arms.

'Take your child,' she said. 'It is not his fault that there is no food today.'

The crowd dispersed. Olanna and Mrs Muokelu walked slowly.

'Who knows if it is true that soldiers really hijacked their lorry?' Mrs Muokelu said. 'Who knows how much they have kept for themselves to sell? We never have salt here because they keep all the salt to trade.'

Olanna was thinking of the way that Mrs Muokelu had returned the baby to the mother. 'You remind me of my sister,' she said.

'How?'

'She's very strong. She's not afraid.'

'She was smoking in that picture you showed me. Like a common prostitute.'

Olanna stopped and stared at Mrs Muokelu.

'I am not saying she is a prostitute,' Mrs Muokelu said hastily. 'I am only saying that it is not good that she smokes because women who smoke are prostitutes.'

Olanna looked at her and saw a malevolence in the beard and hairy arms. She walked faster, silent, ahead of Mrs Muokelu, and did not say goodbye before she turned in to her street. Baby was sitting outside with Ugwu.

'Mummy Ola!'

Olanna hugged her, smoothed her hair. Baby was holding her hand, looking up at her. 'Did you bring egg yolk, Mummy Ola?'

'No, my baby. But I will bring some soon,' she said.

'Good afternoon, mah. You didn't bring anything?' Ugwu asked.

'Can't you see that my basket is empty?' Olanna snapped. 'Are you blind?'

On Monday, she went alone to the relief centre. Mrs Muokelu did not come by to call her before dawn and was not there among the crowd. The gate was locked, the compound empty, and she waited around for an hour until the crowd began to disperse. On Tuesday, the gate was locked. On Wednesday, there was a new padlock on the gate. It was not until Saturday that the gate swung open and Olanna surprised herself by how easily she joined in the inward rush of the crowd, how she moved nimbly from queue to queue, dodged the swinging canes of the militia, pushed back when somebody pushed her. She was leaving with small bags of cornmeal and egg yolk and two pieces of stockfish when Okoromadu arrived.

He waved. 'Beautiful woman. *Nwanyi oma!*' he said. He still did not know her name. He came over and slipped a tin of corned beef into her basket and then hurried away as if he had done nothing. Olanna looked down at the long, red tin and nearly burst out laughing from sheer unexpected pleasure. She brought it out, examined it, ran a hand over the cold metal, and looked up to find a shell-shocked soldier watching her. His stare was blunt; it did not care to disguise itself. She put the corned beef back into her basket and covered it with a bag. She was pleased Mrs Muokelu was not with her, so she would not have to share it. She would ask Ugwu to make a stew with it. She would save some to make sandwiches and she and Odenigbo and Baby would have an English-style tea with corned beef sandwiches.

The shell-shocked soldier followed her out of the gate. She quickened her pace on the dusty stretch that led to the main road, but five of them, all in tattered army uniforms, soon surrounded her. They babbled and gestured towards her basket, their movements disjointed, their tones raised, and Olanna made out some of the words. 'Aunty!' 'Sister!' 'Bring am now!' 'Hungry go kill all of us!'

Olanna clutched her basket tightly. A hot, childish urge to cry rose in her. 'Go away! Come on, go away!'

They looked surprised at her outburst and for a moment, they were still. Then they began to come closer, all together, as if some internal voice were directing them. They were bearing down on her. They could do anything; there was something desperately lawless about them and their noise-deadened brains. Olanna's fear came with rage, a fierce and emboldening rage, and she imagined fighting them, strangling them, killing them. The corned beef was hers. Hers. She moved a few steps back. In a flash, done so quickly that she did not realize it until afterwards, the one wearing a blue beret grasped her basket, took the tin of corned beef, and ran off. Others followed. The last stood there watching her, his slack mouth hanging open, before he turned to run too, but in the opposite direction, away from the others. The basket lay on the ground. Olanna stood still and cried silently because the corned beef had never been hers. Then she picked up the basket, dusted some sand from her bag of cornmeal, and walked home.

Olanna and Mrs Muokelu had avoided each other in school for almost two weeks and so the afternoon Olanna came home and saw Mrs Muokelu sitting outside with a metal bucket full of grey wood ash, she was surprised.

Mrs Muokelu stood up. 'I came to teach you how to make soap. Do you know how much they are selling common bar soap now?'

Olanna looked at the threadbare cotton boubou plastered with His Excellency's glowering face and realized that this unsolicited lesson was an apology. She took the bucket of ash. She led the way to the backyard, and after Mrs Muokelu had explained and demonstrated how to make soap she stowed the ash near the pile of cement blocks.

Later, Odenigbo shook his head when she told him about it. They were under the thatch awning of the veranda, on a wood bench placed against the wall.

'She didn't need to teach you how to make soap. I don't see you making soap anyway.'

'You think I can't?'

'She should simply have apologized.'

'I think I overreacted because it was about Kainene.' Olanna shifted. 'I wonder if Kainene got my letters.'

Odenigbo said nothing. He took her hand and she felt grateful that there were things she did not need to explain to him.

'How much hair does Mrs Muokelu have on her chest?' he asked. 'Do you know?'

Olanna was not sure if he began to laugh first or if she did, but suddenly they were laughing, raucously, almost falling off the bench. Other things became hilarious. Odenigbo said that the sky was completely cloudless and Olanna told him that it was perfect weather for bomber planes, and they laughed. A little boy walking past wearing a pair of shorts with large holes that showed his dry-skinned buttocks greeted them and they had hardly responded *good afternoon* before they burst into more laughter. The laughter had not died on their faces and their hands were still clasped on the bench when Special Julius walked into the compound. His tunic glittered with sequins.

'I've brought the best palm wine in Umuahia! Ask Ugwu to bring some glasses,' he said, and put a small jerry can down. There was an optimistic affluence about him and his flamboyant clothes, as if there were no problem he could not solve. After Ugwu brought the glasses, Special Julius said, 'Have you heard that Harold Wilson is in Lagos? He is bringing the British army to finish us off. They say he came with two battalions.'

'Sit down, my friend, and stop talking rubbish,' Odenigbo said.

Special Julius laughed and slurped his drink noisily. 'I am talking rubbish, *okwa ya*? Where is the radio? Lagos may not tell the world that the British prime minister has come to help them kill us, but maybe those crazy people in Kaduna will.'

Baby came out. 'Uncle Julius, good afternoon.'

'Baby-Baby. How is your cough? Is it better?' He dipped a finger into his palm wine and put it in her mouth. 'This should help your cough.'

Baby licked her lips, looking pleased.

'Julius!' Olanna said.

Special Julius waved airily. 'Never underestimate the power of alcohol.'

'Come and sit with me, Baby,' Olanna said. Baby's dress was frayed, worn too often. Olanna settled her on her lap and held her close. At least Baby was not coughing so much now; at least Baby was eating.

Odenigbo picked up the radio from underneath the bench. A shrill sound pierced the air, and at first Olanna thought it had come from the radio before she realized it was the air-raid alarm. She sat still. Somebody from the house nearby screamed, 'Enemy plane!' at the same time as Special Julius shouted, 'Take cover!' and leapt across the veranda, overturning the palm wine. Neighbours were running, shouting words that Olanna could not understand because the stubborn searing sound had shrilled its way into her head. She slipped on the wine and fell on her knee. Odenigbo pulled her up before he grabbed Baby and ran. The strafing had started – pellets raining down from above – as Odenigbo held the zinc sheet open while they all crawled down into the bunker. Odenigbo climbed in last. Ugwu was clutching a spoon smeared with soup. Olanna slapped at the crickets; their faintly moist bodies felt slimy against her fingers, and even when they were no longer perched on her, she still slapped her arms and legs. The first explosion sounded distant. Others followed, closer, louder, and the earth shook. Voices around her were shouting,

'Lord Jesus! Lord Jesus!' Her bladder felt painfully, solidly full, as though it would burst and release not urine but the garbled prayers she was muttering. A woman was crumpled next to her, holding a child, a little boy younger than Baby. The bunker was dim but Olanna could see crusty-white ringworm marks all over the child's body. Another explosion shook the ground. Then the sounds stopped. The air was so still that, as they climbed out of the bunker, they could hear the *caw-caw-caw* of some birds far off. Burning smells filled the air.

'Our anti-aircraft fire was wonderful! *O di egwu!*' somebody said.

'Biafra win the war!' Special Julius started the song and soon most of the people on the street had gathered to join in.

> *Biafra win the war.*
> *Armoured car, shelling machine,*
> *Fighter and bomber,*
> *Ha enweghi ike imeri Biafra!*

Olanna watched as Odenigbo sang lustily, and she tried to sing too, but the words lay stale on her tongue. There was a sharp pain in her knee; she took Baby's hand and went indoors.

She was giving Baby an evening bath when the siren alarm sounded again and she grabbed Baby naked and ran from the out-house. Baby nearly slipped from her grasp. The swift roar of planes and the sharp *ka-ka-ka* of anti-aircraft gunfire came from above and from below and from the sides and made her teeth chatter. She slumped in the bunker and ignored the crickets.

'Where is Odenigbo?' she asked, after a while, grabbing Ugwu's arm. 'Where is your master?'

'He is here, mah,' Ugwu said, looking around.

'Odenigbo!' Olanna called. But he did not answer. She did not remember seeing him come into the bunker. He was still up there somewhere. The explosion that followed shook the inside of her ear loose; she was sure that if she bent her head sideways, something hard-soft like cartilage would fall out. She moved to the entrance of the bunker. Behind her, she heard Ugwu say, 'Mah? Mah?' A woman from down the street said, 'Come back! Where are you going? *Ebe ka I na-eje?*' but she ignored them both and scrambled out of the bunker.

The sun's brilliance was startling; it made her feel faint. She ran, her heart hurting her chest, shouting, 'Odenigbo! Odenigbo!' until she saw him bent over somebody on the ground. She looked at his bare, hairy chest and his new beard and his torn slippers, and suddenly his mortality – their mortality – struck her with a clutch at her throat, a squeeze of alarm. She held him tightly. A house down the road was on fire.

'*Nkem*, it's okay,' Odenigbo said. 'A bullet hit him but it looks like a flesh wound.' He pushed her away and went back to the man, whose arm he was tying up with his shirt.

In the morning, the sky was like a calm sea. Olanna told Odenigbo that he would not go to the directorate and that she would not teach; they would spend the day in the bunker.

He laughed. 'Don't be silly.'

'Nobody will send their children to school,' she said.

'What will you do then?' His tone was as normal as his snoring throughout the night had been, while she lay awake, sweating, imagining the sound of bombing.

'I don't know.'

He kissed her. 'Just head for the bunker if the alarm goes off. Nothing will happen. I may be a little late if we go educating in Mbaise today.'

At first she was annoyed by his casualness and then she felt comforted by it. She believed his words, but only for as long as he was there. After he left, she felt vulnerable, exposed. She did not take a bath. She was afraid to go outside to the pit latrine. She was afraid to sit down because she might doze off and be unprepared when the siren went off. She drank cup after cup of water until her belly swelled up, yet she felt as if all the saliva had been sucked out of her mouth and she was about to choke on clumps of dry air.

'We are going to stay in the bunker today,' she told Ugwu.

'The bunker, mah?'

'Yes, the bunker. You heard me.'

'But we cannot just stay in the bunker, mah.'

'Did I speak with water in my mouth? I said we will stay in the bunker.'

Ugwu shrugged. 'Yes, mah. Should I bring Baby's food?'

She did not respond. She would slap him if he so much as smiled, because she could see the muted amusement on his face at the thought of taking a dish with Baby's pap and crawling into a damp hole in the ground to spend the day.

'Get Baby ready,' she said, and turned the radio on.

'Yes, mah,' Ugwu said. '*O nwere igwu*. I found lice eggs in her hair this morning.'

'What?'

'Lice eggs. But there were only two and I did not find any others.'

'Lice? What are you saying? How can Baby have lice? I keep her clean. Baby! Baby!'

Olanna pulled Baby forwards and began to loosen her plaits and search through her thick hair. 'It must be those dirty neighbours you play with, those dirty neighbours.' Her hands were shaking and she yanked at a tuft of hair to maintain her grip. Baby began to cry.

'Stay still!' Olanna said.

Baby wriggled free, ran to Ugwu, and stood there looking at Olanna with baffled eyes as if she no longer recognized her. From the radio, the Biafran national anthem burst out and filled the silence.

> *Land of the rising sun, we love and cherish,*
> *Beloved homeland of our brave heroes;*
> *We must defend our lives or we shall perish.*
> *We shall protect our hearts from all our foes;*
> *But if the price is death for all we hold dear,*
> *Then let us die without a shred of fear. . . .*

They listened until it ended.

'Take her outside and stay in the veranda and be on the alert,' Olanna said finally, wearily, to Ugwu.

'We are not staying in the bunker again?'

'Just take her outside to the veranda.'

'Yes, mah.'

Olanna tuned the radio; it was too early for the war broadcasts, for the fire-filled monologues on Biafra's greatness that she desperately needed to hear. On BBC, there was a news update on the war – emissaries from the Pope, from the Organization of African Unity, from the Commonwealth, were coming to Nigeria to propose peace. She listened listlessly and turned it off when she heard Ugwu talking to somebody. She went outside to see who it was. Mrs Muokelu was standing behind Baby, rebraiding the plaits Olanna had loosed. The hair on her arms shone glossily, as if she had used too much palm kernel oil.

'You did not go to school as well?' Olanna asked.

'I knew that parents would keep their children at home.'

'Who wouldn't? What kind of nonstop bombing campaign is this?'

'It is because Harold Wilson came.' Mrs Muokelu snorted. 'They want to impress him so he will bring in the British army.'

'Special Julius said that too, but it's impossible.'

'Impossible?' Mrs Muokelu smiled as though Olanna had no idea what she was talking about. 'That Special Julius, by the way – you know he sells forged passes?'

'He is an army contractor.'

'I am not saying he does not do small-small contracts with the army, but he sells forged passes. His brother is a director and they do it together. It is because of them that all sorts of crooks are running around with special passes.' Mrs Muokelu finished a plait and patted Baby's hair. 'That his brother is a criminal. They say he gave army exemption passes to all his male relatives, everyone in his *umunna*. And you need to hear what he does with those young-young girls that crawl around looking for sugar daddies. They say he takes up to five of them into his bedroom at the same time. *Tufia!* It is people like him who must be executed when the state of Biafra is fully established.'

Olanna jumped. 'Was that a plane? Was that a plane?'

'Plane, *kwa*?' Mrs Muokelu laughed. 'Somebody closed their door in the next house and you say it is a plane?'

Olanna sat down on the floor and stretched out her legs. She was exhausted from fear.

'Did you hear that we shot down their bomber around Ikot-Ekpene?' Mrs Muokelu asked.

'I didn't hear.'

'And this was done by a common civilian with his hunting gun! You know, it is as if the Nigerians are so stupid that whoever works for them becomes stupid too. They are too stupid to fly the planes that Russia and Britain gave them, so they brought in white people, and even those white people can't hit any target. Ha! Half their bombs don't even explode.'

'The half that explodes is enough to kill us,' Olanna said.

Mrs Muokelu kept speaking as though she had not heard Olanna. 'I hear that our *ogbunigwe* is putting the fear of God into them. In

Afikpo, it killed only a few hundred men, but the entire Nigerian battalion withdrew from fear. They have never seen a weapon like that. They don't know what we still have for them.' She chuckled and shook her head and tugged at the half of a yellow sun around her neck. 'Gowon sent them to bomb Awgu Market in the middle of the afternoon while women were buying and selling. He has refused to let the Red Cross bring us food, refused *kpam-kpam*, so that we will starve to death. But he will not succeed. If we had people pouring guns and planes into our hands as they pour into Nigeria, this thing would have ended a long time ago and everybody would be in his own house now. But we will conquer them. Is God sleeping? No!' Mrs Muokelu laughed. The siren went off. Olanna had been expecting the harsh sound for so long that a prescient shiver went through her just before she heard it. She turned to Baby but Ugwu had already picked her up and begun to run for the bunker. Olanna could hear the sound of the planes far off, like gathering thunder, and soon the scattered sharp cracks of anti-aircraft fire. Before she crawled into the bunker, she looked up and saw the gliding bomber jets, hawklike, flying startlingly low, with balls of grey smoke around them.

As they climbed out of the bunker later, somebody said, 'They targeted the primary school!'

'Those heathens have bombed our school,' Mrs Muokelu said.

'Look! Another bomber!' a young man said, laughing, and pointed at a vulture flying overhead.

They joined the crowd hurrying towards Akwakuma Primary School. Two men walked past, in the opposite direction, carrying a blackened corpse. A bomb crater, wide enough to swallow a lorry, had split the road at the school entrance in two. The roof of the classroom block was crushed into a jumble of wood and metal and dust. Olanna did not recognize her room. All the windows were blown out, but the walls still stood. Just outside, where her pupils played in the sand, a piece of shrapnel had drilled an elegant hole in the ground. And as she joined in carrying out the few salvageable chairs, it was the hole she thought about: how hot, carnivorous metal could draw such pretty ringlets in the soil.

The siren did not go off early in the morning, and so when the fierce *wah-wah-wah* sounds of the bombers appeared from nowhere, as

Olanna dissolved corn flour to make Baby's pap, she knew this was it. Somebody would die. Perhaps they would all die. Death was the only thing that made any sense as she hunched underground, plucked some soil, rubbed it between her fingers, and waited for the bunker to explode. The bombing was louder and closer. The ground pulsed. She felt nothing. She was floating away from inside herself. Another explosion came and the earth vibrated, and one of the naked children crawling after crickets giggled. Then the explosions stopped and the people around her began to move. If she had died, if Odenigbo and Baby and Ugwu had died, the bunker would still smell like a freshly tilled farm and the sun would still rise and the crickets would still hop around. The war would continue without them. Olanna exhaled, filled with a frothy rage. It was the very sense of being inconsequential that pushed her from extreme fear to extreme fury. She had to matter. She would no longer exist limply, waiting to die. Until Biafra won, the vandals would no longer dictate the terms of her life.

She was first to climb out of the bunker. A woman had thrown herself down near the body of a child and was rolling around in the dirt, crying. 'Gowon, what have I done to you? Gowon, *olee ihe m mere gi?*' A few women gathered around and helped her up. 'Stop crying, it is enough,' they said. 'What do you want your other children to do?'

Olanna went to the backyard and began to sift through the metal bucket of ash. She coughed as she started a fire; the wood smoke stung.

Ugwu was watching her. 'Mah? Do you want me to do it?'

'No.' She dissolved the ash in a basin of cold water, stirring with a force that made the water splatter on her legs. She put the drippings on the fire and ignored Ugwu. He must have sensed the anger that was rising up her body and making her light-headed because he went back indoors silently. From the street, the crying woman's voice rose again and again, hoarser and thinner than the last time. Gowon, what have I done to you? Gowon, *olee ihe m mere gi?* Olanna poured some palm oil into the cooled mixture and stirred and stirred until her arms stiffened from fatigue. There was something delicious in the sweat that trickled under her arms, in the surge of vigour that made her heart thump, in the odd-smelling mash that emerged after cooling. It lathered. She had made soap.

Olanna did not run across the square on her way to school the following day. Caution had become, to her, feeble and faithless. Her steps were sturdy and she looked up often at the clear sky to search for bomber jets, because she would stop and hurl stones and words up at them. About a quarter of her class attended school. She taught them about the Biafran flag. They sat on wooden planks and the weak morning sun streamed into the roofless class as she unfurled Odenigbo's cloth flag and told them what the symbols meant. Red was the blood of the siblings massacred in the North, black was for mourning them, green was for the prosperity Biafra would have, and, finally, the half of a yellow sun stood for the glorious future. She taught them to raise their hand in the flying salute like His Excellency and she asked them to copy her drawings of the two leaders: His Excellency was burly, sketched with double lines, while Gowon's effete body was outlined in single lines.

Nkiruka, her brightest student, shaded contours into the faces and, with a few strokes of her pencil, gave Gowon a snarl and His Excellency a grin.

'I want to kill all the vandals, miss,' she said, when she came up to hand in her drawing. She was smiling the smile of a precocious child who knew she had said the right thing.

Olanna stared at her and did not know what to say. 'Nkiruka, go and sit down,' she said at last.

The first thing she told Odenigbo when he got home was how banal the word *kill* had sounded from the child's mouth and how guilty she had felt. They were in their bedroom and the radio was turned on low and she could hear Baby's high-pitched laughter from the next room.

'She doesn't actually want to kill anybody, *nkem*. You just taught her patriotism,' Odenigbo said, slipping off his shoes.

'I don't know.' But his words emboldened her, as did the pride in his face. He liked that she had spoken so forcefully, for once, about the cause; it was as if she had finally become an equal participant in the war effort.

'The Red Cross people remembered our directorate today,' he said and pointed at the small carton he had brought back.

Olanna opened it and placed the squat cans of condensed milk and the slender tin of Ovaltine and the packet of salt on the bed. They seemed luxurious. On the radio, a vibrant voice said that gallant Biafran soldiers were flushing out the vandals around Abakaliki.

'Let's have a party,' she said.

'A party?'

'A small dinner party. You know, that's what we had often in Nsukka.'

'This will be over soon, *nkem*, and we'll have all the parties in a free Biafra.'

She liked the way he said that, *in a free Biafra*, and she stood up and squashed her lips against his. 'Yes, but we can have a war-time party.'

'We hardly have enough for ourselves.'

'We have more than enough for ourselves.' Her lips were still against his and her words suddenly took on a different meaning and she moved back and pulled her dress over her head in one fluid gesture. She unbuckled his trousers. She did not let him take them off. She turned her back and leaned on the wall and guided him into her, excited by his surprise, by his firm hands on her hips. She knew she should lower her voice because of Ugwu and Baby in the next room and yet she had no control over her own moans, over the raw primal pleasure she felt in wave after wave that ended with both of them leaning against the wall, gasping and giggling.

26

Ugwu hated the relief food. The rice was puffy, nothing like the slender grains in Nsukka, and the cornmeal never emerged smooth after being stirred in hot water, and the powdered milk ended up as stubborn clumps at the bottom of teacups. He squirmed now as he scooped up some egg yolk. It was difficult to think of the flat powder coming from the egg of a real chicken. He poured it into the dough mix and stirred. Outside, a pot half filled with white sand sat on the fire; he would give it a little more time to heat up before he placed the dough inside. He had been sceptical when Mrs Muokelu first taught Olanna this baking method; he knew enough about Mrs Muokelu's ideas – Olanna's home-made soap, that blackish-brown mash that reminded him of a child's diarrhoea, had come from her, after all. But the first pastry Olanna baked had turned out well; she laughed and said it was ambitious to call it a cake, this mix of flour and palm oil and dried egg yolk, but at least they had put their flour to good use.

The Red Cross irritated Ugwu; the least they could do was ask Biafrans their preferred foods rather than sending so much bland flour. When the new relief centre opened, the one Olanna went to wearing a rosary around her neck because Mrs Muokelu said the Caritas people were more generous to Catholics, Ugwu hoped the food would be better. But what she brought back was familiar, the dried fish even saltier, and she sang, with an amused expression, the song the women sang at the centre.

Caritas, thank you,
Caritas si anyi taba okporoko
na kwashiorkor ga-ana.

She did not sing on the days she came back with nothing. She would sit on the veranda and look up at the thatch roof and say, 'Do you remember, Ugwu, how we used to throw away soup with meat after only a day?'

'Yes, mah,' Ugwu would say. If only he could go to the relief centre himself. He suspected that Olanna, with her English-speaking properness, waited her turn until everything was gone. But he could not go because she no longer allowed him out during the day. Stories of forced conscription were everywhere. He did not doubt that a boy down the street had been dragged away in the afternoon and taken, with a shaved head and no training, straight to the front in the evening. But he thought Olanna was overreacting. Surely he could still go to the market. Surely he did not have to wake up before dawn to fetch water.

He heard voices in the living room. Special Julius sounded almost as loud as Master. He would take the cake out and then weed the vegetable patch with its gnarled greens or perhaps go and sit on the pile of cement blocks and look across at the opposite house, to see if Eberechi would come out and shout, 'Neighbour, how are you?' He would wave back a hello and imagine himself grasping those buttocks. It surprised him, how happy he was when she greeted him. The cake turned out crisp on the outside and moistly soft inside, and he cut slim slices and took them out in saucers. Special Julius and Olanna were sitting down while Master was standing, gesturing, talking about the last village he visited, how the people had sacrificed a goat at the shrine of *oyi* to keep the vandals away.

'A whole goat! All that wasted protein!' Special Julius said and laughed.

Master did not laugh. 'No, no, you must never underestimate the psychological importance of such things. We never ask them to eat the goat instead.'

'Ah, cake!' Special Julius said. He ignored the fork and stuffed the piece in his mouth. 'Very good, very good. Ugwu, you have to teach the people in my house because all they do with our flour is *chin-chin*, every day is *chin-chin, chin-chin*, and it is the hard kind with no taste! My teeth have finished.'

'Ugwu is a wonder at everything,' Olanna said. 'He would easily put that woman in Rising Sun Bar out of business.'

Professor Ekwenugo knocked on the open door and walked in. His hands were swathed in cream-coloured bandages.

'*Dianyi*, what happened to you?' Master asked.

'Just a little burn.' Professor Ekwenugo stared at his bandaged hands as if he had only just realized that they meant he no longer had a long nail to stroke. 'We are putting together something very big.'

'Is it our first Biafran-built bomber jet?' Olanna teased.

'Something very big that will reveal itself with time,' Professor Ekwenugo said, with a mysterious smile. He ate clumsily; bits of cake fell away before they got to his mouth.

'It should be a saboteur-detecting machine,' Master said.

'Yes! Bloody saboteurs.' Special Julius made the sound of spitting. 'They sold Enugu out. How can you leave civilians to defend our capital with mere machetes? This is the same way they lost Nsukka, by pulling back for no reason. Doesn't one of the commanding officers have a Hausa wife? She has put medicine in his food.'

'We will recapture Enugu,' Professor Ekwenugo said.

'How can we recapture Enugu when the vandals have occupied it?' Special Julius said. 'They are even looting toilet seats! Toilet seats! A man who escaped from Udi told me. And they choose the best houses and force people's wives and daughters to spread their legs for them and cook for them.'

Images of his mother and Anulika and Nnesinachi splayed out underneath a dirty, sun-blackened Hausa soldier came to Ugwu so clearly that he shivered. He went out and sat on a cement block and wished, desperately, that he could go home, if only for a minute, to make sure that nothing had happened to them. Perhaps the vandals were already there and had taken over his aunty's hut with the corrugated-iron roof. Or perhaps his family had fled with their goats and chickens, like all the people streaming into Umuahia. The refugees: Ugwu saw them, more and more each day, new faces on the streets, at the public borehole, in the market. Women knocked on the door often to ask if there was any work they could do in exchange for food. They came with their thin, naked children. Sometimes, Olanna gave them *garri* soaked in cold water before telling them she had no work. Mrs Muokelu had taken in a family of eight relatives. She brought the children to play with Baby, and each time, after they left Olanna asked Ugwu to search Baby's hair carefully for lice. The neighbours took in relatives. Master's cousins came for a few weeks and slept in the living room until they left to join the army. There were so many fleeing, tired, homeless people that Ugwu was not surprised the afternoon Olanna came home and said that Akwakuma Primary School would be turned into a refugee camp.

'They have brought bamboo beds and cooking utensils already. And the new Director for Mobilization is coming next week.' She sounded tired. She opened the pot on the stove and stared at the slices of boiled yam.

'What about the children, mah?'

'I was asking Headmistress if we could be relocated, and she looked at me and started laughing. We are the last. All the schools in Umuahia have become refugee camps or army training camps.' She closed the pot. 'I'm going to organize classes here in the yard.'

'With Mrs Muokelu?'

'Yes, and you too, Ugwu. You will teach a class.'

'Yes, mah.' The thought excited and flattered him. 'Mah?'

'Yes?'

'Do you think the vandals are in my hometown?'

'Of course not,' Olanna said sharply. 'Your hometown is too small. If they stay anywhere, it will be in the university.'

'But if they took the Opi road into Nsukka –'

'I said your hometown is too small! They will not be interested in staying there. There is nothing there to stay for, you see. It is just a small bush.'

Ugwu looked at her and she looked at him. The silence was heavy and accusing.

'I'm going to sell my brown shoes to Mama Onitsha, and I will make a new pretty dress for Baby,' Olanna said finally and Ugwu thought her voice was forced.

He began to wash the plates.

Ugwu saw the black Mercedes-Benz gliding down the road; the word DIRECTOR written on its metallic numberplate sparkled in the sun. Near Eberechi's house, it slowed down, shiny and enormous, and Ugwu hoped they would stop and ask him where the primary school was so he would get a good look at the dashboard. They did not just stop, though; they drove past him and into the compound. An orderly in a stiff uniform jumped out to open the back door before the car came to a complete halt. He saluted as the director climbed out.

It was Professor Ezeka. He did not look as tall as Ugwu remembered; he had put on some weight and his thin neck had filled out. Ugwu stared. There was something sleek and new about him, about the fine cut of his suit, but his supercilious expression was the same, as was his hoarse voice. 'Young man, is your master in?'

'No, sah,' Ugwu said. In Nsukka, Professor Ezeka had called him Ugwu; now he looked as if he did not recognize him. 'He has gone to work, sah.'

'And your madam?'

'She has gone to the relief centre, sah.'

Professor Ezeka motioned for his orderly to bring a piece of paper and he scribbled a note and gave it to Ugwu. His silver pen gleamed. 'Tell them the Director for Mobilization came.'

'Yes, sah.' Ugwu remembered his fastidious peering at glasses in Nsukka, his thin legs always crossed, disagreeing with Master. After the car drove down the street very slowly, as if the driver knew how many people were watching, Eberechi walked across. She was wearing that tight skirt that moulded her buttocks to a perfect roundness.

'Neighbour, how are you?' she asked.

'I am well. How are you?'

She shrugged to say she was so-so. 'Was that the Director for Mobilization himself who just left?'

'Professor Ezeka?' he asked breezily. 'Yes, we knew him well in Nsukka. He used to come to our house every day to eat my pepper soup.'

'Eh!' She laughed, wide-eyed. 'He is a Big Man. *Ihukwara moto?* Did you see that car?'

'Original imported chassis.'

They were silent for a while. He had never had a conversation this long with her before and had never seen her so close up. It was difficult to keep his eyes from moving down to that magnificent flare of buttocks. He struggled to focus on her face, her large eyes, the rash of pimples on her forehead, her hair plaited in thread-covered spikes. She was looking at him, too, and he wished he was not wearing the trousers with the hole near the knee.

'How is the small girl?' she asked.

'Baby is fine. She's asleep.'

'Are you coming to do the primary school roof?'

Ugwu knew that an army contractor had donated some corrugated iron for replacing the blown-off roof and that volunteers were camouflaging it with palm fronds. But he had not planned to join them.

'Yes, I shall come,' he said.

'See you then.'

'Bye-bye.' Ugwu waited for her to turn so that he could stare at her retreating backside.

When Olanna came back, her basket empty, she read Professor Ezeka's note with a half smile on her face. 'Yes, we just heard yesterday that he's the new director. And how like him to write something like this.'

Ugwu had read the note – *Odenigbo and Olanna, dropped by to say hello. Shall drop by again next week, if this tedious new job allows. Ezeka –* but he asked, 'How, mah?'

'Oh, he's always felt a bit better than everybody else.' Olanna placed the note on the table. 'Professor Achara is going to help get us some books and benches and blackboards. Many women have told me they will send their children to us next week.' She looked excited.

'That is good, mah.' Ugwu shifted on his feet. 'I'm going down to help with the school roof. I'll be back to make Baby's food.'

'Oh,' Olanna said.

Ugwu knew she was thinking about the conscriptions. 'I think it is important to help in something like this, mah,' he said.

'Of course. Yes, you should help. But please be careful.'

Ugwu saw Eberechi right away; she was with some men and women who were bent over a pile of palm fronds, cutting, matting, passing them on to a man on a wooden ladder.

'Neighbour!' she said. 'I have been telling everyone that your people know the director personally.'

Ugwu smiled and said a general *good afternoon*. The men and women murmured *good afternoon* and *ehe, kedu,* and *nno* with the admiring respect that came with knowing who he knew. He felt suddenly important. Somebody gave him a cutlass. A woman sat on the stairs grinding melon seeds, and some little girls were playing cards under the mango tree, and a man was carving a walking stick whose handle was the carefully realized bearded face of His Excellency. There was a rotten smell in the air.

'Imagine living in this kind of place.' Eberechi leaned close to him to whisper. 'And many more will come now that Abakaliki has fallen. You know that since Enugu fell, accommodation has been a big problem. Some people who work in the directorates are even sleeping in their cars.'

'That is true,' Ugwu agreed, although he did not know this for sure. He loved that she was talking to him, loved her familiar friendliness. He began to trim some palm fronds with firm strokes. From the classroom, someone turned the radio on: gallant Biafran soldiers were completing a mopping-up operation in a sector Ugwu did not hear clearly.

'Our boys are showing them!' the woman grinding melon seeds said.

'Biafra will win this war, God has written it in the sky,' said a man with a beard plaited in a single thin strand.

Eberechi giggled and whispered to Ugwu, 'Bush man. He does not know it is Bee-afra, not Ba-yafra.'

Ugwu laughed. Fat black ants were crawling all over the palm fronds, and she squealed and looked helplessly at him when one crawled onto her arm. Ugwu brushed it off and felt the warm moistness of her skin. She had wanted him to brush it off; she did not seem like the kind of person who was truly afraid of ants.

One of the women had a baby boy tied to her back. She adjusted the wrapper that held him and said, 'We were on our way back from the market when we discovered the vandals had occupied the junction and were shelling inside the village. We could not go home. We had to turn and run. I had only this wrapper and blouse and the small money from selling my pepper. I don't know where my two children are, the ones I left at home to go to the market.' She started to cry. The abruptness of her tears, the way they gushed out of her, startled Ugwu.

'Woman, stop crying,' the man with the plaited beard said curtly.

The woman continued to cry. Her baby, too, began to cry.

When Ugwu took a batch of fronds across to the ladder, he stopped to peer into one of the classrooms. Cooking pots, sleeping mats, metal boxes, and bamboo beds cluttered it so completely that the room did not look as though it had ever been anything else but a home for disparate groups of people with nowhere else to go. A bright poster on the wall read: IN CASE OF AIR RAID, DO NOT PANIC. IF YOU SEE THE ENEMY, MOW HIM DOWN. Another woman with a baby tied to her back was washing peeled cassava tubers in a pan of filthy water. Her baby's face was wrinkled. Ugwu nearly choked when he came close and realized that the rotten smell came from her water: it had previously been used to soak cassava, perhaps for days, and was being reused. The smell was awful, nose-filling, the smell of a dirty toilet and rancid steamed beans and boiled eggs gone bad.

He held his breath and went back to the palm fronds. The crying woman was nursing her baby on a drooping breast.

'Our town would not have fallen but for the saboteurs in our midst!' the man with the plaited beard said. 'I was a Civil Defender. I know how many infiltrators we discovered, and all of them were Rivers people. What I am telling you is that we can no longer trust these minorities who don't speak Igbo.' He paused and turned when he heard a shout from some young boys playing war in the middle of the school compound. They looked about ten or eleven years old, wore banana leaves on their heads, and held mock guns made from bamboo. The longest gun belonged to the commander of the Biafran side, a tall, stern child with sharp cheekbones. 'Advance!' he shouted.

The boys crept forwards.

'Fire!'

They flung stones with wide sweeps of their arms and then, clutching their guns, they rushed towards the other boys, the Nigerian side, the losers.

The bearded man began to clap. 'These boys are wonderful! Just give them arms and they will send the vandals back.'

Other people clapped and cheered the boys. The palm fronds were ignored for a while.

'You know I kept trying to join the army when this war started,' the bearded man said. 'I went everywhere but they kept rejecting me because of my leg so I had to join the Civil Defenders.'

'What is wrong with your leg?' the woman grinding melon seeds asked.

He raised his leg. Half of his foot was gone and what was left looked like a shrivelled piece of old yam. 'I lost it in the North,' he said.

In the silence that followed, the crackling of the palm fronds was too loud. Then a woman came out of a classroom, after a small child, slapping the child's head again and again. 'So you broke only one plate? No, go ahead and break all my plates. Break them! *Kuwa ha!* We have many, don't we? We came with all our plates, didn't we? Break them!' she said. The little girl ran off towards the mango tree. Before the mother went back into the classroom, she stood there and cursed for a while, muttering that those spirits that had sent the child to break her few plates would not succeed.

'Why should the child not break a plate? What food is there to eat from it anyway?' the breast-feeding woman asked sourly, still sniffling. They laughed, and Eberechi leaned towards Ugwu and whispered that the bearded man had bad breath, which was probably why they did not take him in the army. Ugwu ached to press his body against hers.

They left together and Ugwu looked back to make sure that everyone had noticed that they were together. A soldier in a Biafran Army uniform and a helmet walked past them, speaking a mangled Pidgin English that made little sense, his voice too loud. He swayed as he walked, as if he would tip over sideways. He had one full arm, the other was a stump that stopped before his elbow. Eberechi watched him.

'His people do not know,' she said quietly.

'What?'

'His people think he is well and fighting for our cause.'

The soldier was shouting, 'Don't waste your bullet! I say one vandal one bullet with immediate effect!' while the little boys gathered around him, taunting him, laughing at him, singing praise names for him.

Eberechi was walking a little faster. 'My brother joined the army in the beginning.'

'I didn't know.'

'Yes. He has come home only once. Everybody on the street came out to greet him and the children were fighting to touch his uniform.'

She said nothing else until they got to the front of her house and she turned away. 'Let the day break,' she said.

'See you tomorrow,' Ugwu said. He wished he had said more to her.

Ugwu arranged three benches on the veranda for Olanna's class and two by the compound entrance for Mrs Muokelu's; for his own class with the youngest pupils, he placed two benches near the pile of cement blocks.

'We will teach mathematics, English, and civics every day,' Olanna said to Ugwu and Mrs Muokelu a day before the classes began. 'We have to make sure that when the war is over, they will all fit back easily into regular school. We will teach them to speak perfect English and perfect Igbo, like His Excellency. We will teach them pride in our great nation.'

Ugwu watched her and wondered if she had tears in her eyes or if it was simply the glare of the sun. He wanted to learn all he could from her and Mrs Muokelu, to excel at teaching, to show her that he could do it. He was arranging his blackboard against a tree stump on the first day of classes when a woman, some relative of Special Julius's, brought her daughter. She stared at Ugwu.

'Is this one a teacher?' she asked Olanna.

'Yes.'

'Is he not your houseboy?' Her voice was shrill. 'Since when has a servant started to teach, *bikokwa*?'

'If you do not want your child to learn, take her home,' Olanna said.

The woman pulled her daughter by the hand and left. Ugwu was certain that Olanna would look at him with a sympathy that would annoy him more than the woman had. But she shrugged and said, 'Good riddance. Her daughter has lice. I saw the eggs in her hair.'

Other parents were different. They looked at Olanna, her beautiful face, her undemanding fees, and her perfect English, with awe-filled respect. They brought palm oil and yams and *garri*. A woman who traded across enemy lines brought a chicken. An army contractor brought two of his children and a carton of books – early readers, six copies of *Chike and the River*, eight simplified editions of *Pride and Prejudice*; when Olanna opened the carton and threw her arms around him, Ugwu resented the startled, leering pleasure on the man's face.

After the first week, Ugwu became quietly convinced that Mrs Muokelu knew very little. She calculated simple divisions with uncertainty, spoke in a low mumble when she read, as though she was afraid of the sentences, and scolded her pupils for getting something wrong without telling them what the correct thing was. And so he watched only Olanna. 'Enunciate! Enunciate!' Olanna would say to her students, her voice rising. 'Set-tle. Set-tle. The word has no *R*!' Because she made each of her students read aloud every day, Ugwu made his own class recite simple words aloud. Baby often went first. She was the youngest, not yet six in a class of seven-year-olds, but she flawlessly read *cat, pan, bed* in an accent that was like Olanna's. She did not remember, though, to call him *teacher* like everyone else and Ugwu hid his amusement when she said, 'Ugwu!'

At the end of the second week, after the children left, Mrs Muokelu asked Olanna to sit down with her in the living room. She pulled the edges of her too-long boubou together and tucked them between her legs.

'I have twelve people to feed,' she said. 'And that is not counting my husband's relatives who have just come from Abakaliki. My husband has returned from the war front with one leg. What can he do? I am going to start *afia attack* and see if I can buy salt. I can no longer teach.'

'I understand,' Olanna said. 'But must you join them in buying from enemy territory?'

'What is there to buy in Biafra? They have blockaded us *kpam-kpam.*'

'But how will you go?'

'There is a woman I know. She supplies *garri* to the army, so they give her lorry a military escort. The lorry will take us to Ufuma and then we will walk across to where the border is porous in Nkwerre-Inyi.'

'How long is the walk?'

'About fifteen or twenty miles, nothing a determined person cannot do. We will carry our Nigerian coins and buy salt and *garri* and then walk back to the lorry.'

'Please be careful, my sister.'

'Many are doing it and nothing has happened to them.' She got up. 'Ugwu will have to handle my class. But I know he can manage.'

From the dining table where he was giving Baby her *garri* and soup, Ugwu pretended not to have heard them.

He took over her class the next day. He loved the light of recognition in the older children's eyes when he explained the meaning of a word, loved the loud way Master said to Special Julius, 'My wife and Ugwu are changing the face of the next generation of Biafrans with their Socratic pedagogy!' and loved, most of all, the teasing way Eberechi called him *teacher*. She was impressed. When he saw her standing by her house and watching him teach, he would raise his voice and pronounce his words more carefully. She began to come over after classes. She would sit in the backyard with him, or play with Baby, or watch him weed the vegetable patch. Sometimes Olanna asked her to take some corn down to the grinding station down the road.

Ugwu stole some of the milk and sugar that Master brought home from the directorate and put them in old tins and gave them to her. She said *thank you* but she looked unimpressed, and so, in the middle of a searing afternoon, he sneaked into Olanna's room and poured some scented talcum powder into a folded piece of paper. He had to impress her. Eberechi sniffed it and dabbed a little on her neck before she said, 'I did not ask you for powder.'

Ugwu laughed. He felt, for the first time, completely at ease in her presence. She told him about her parents' pushing her into the army officer's room, and he listened as if he had not heard it before.

'He had a big belly,' she said, in a detached tone. 'He did it quickly and then told me to lie on top of him. He fell asleep and I wanted to move away and he woke up and told me to stay there. I could not sleep so the whole night I looked at the saliva coming down the side of his mouth.' She paused. 'He helped us. He put my brother in essential services in the army.'

Ugwu looked away. He felt angry that she had gone through what she had, and he felt angry with himself because the story had involved imagining her naked and had aroused him. He thought, in the following days, about him and Eberechi in bed, how different it would be from her experience with the colonel. He would treat her with the respect she deserved and do only what she liked, only what she wanted him to do. He would show her the positions he had seen in Master's *Concise Couples Handbook* in Nsukka. The slender book had been squashed into a dusty corner of the study shelf, and the first time Ugwu saw it while he was cleaning, he looked through it hurriedly, sweeping past the pencil-sketched diagrams that somehow became more exciting because they were unreal. Later, he realized that Master probably didn't remember that the book existed so he took it to the Boys' Quarters to study over a few nights. He had thought about trying some of the positions out with Chinyere but never did: there was something about the methodical silence of her night visits that made any novelty impossible. He wished so much that he had brought the book from Nsukka. He wanted to remember some finer details, what the woman had done with her hands in the sideways-from-behind position, for example. He searched in Master's bedroom and felt foolish because he knew there was no way the *Concise Couples Handbook* would be there. Then he felt a deep sadness at how few books there were on the table, in the whole house.

*   *   *

Ugwu was making Baby's breakfast and Master was taking a bath when Olanna began to shout from the living room. The radio was turned on very loud. She ran out to the back, to the outhouse, carrying it in her hand. 'Odenigbo! Odenigbo! Tanzania has recognized us!'

Master came out with his moist wrapper barely tied around his waist, his chest covered in lustrous wet hair. His smiling face without the thick glasses looked funny. '*Gini?* What?'

'Tanzania has recognized us!' Olanna said.

'Eh?' Master said and they hugged and pressed their lips, their faces, close together as though inhaling each other's breath.

Then Master took the radio and tuned it. 'Let's make sure. Let's hear it from others.'

Voice of America was reporting it, as was French radio, which Olanna translated: Tanzania was the first country to recognize the existence of the independent nation of Biafra. Finally, Biafra existed. Ugwu tickled Baby and she laughed.

'Nyerere will go down in history as a man of truth,' Master said. 'Of course, many other countries want to recognize us but they won't because of America. America is the stumbling block!'

Ugwu was not sure how America was to blame for other countries not recognizing Biafra – he thought Britain really was to blame – but he repeated Master's words to Eberechi that afternoon, with authority, as though they were his. It was hot and he found her asleep on a mat in the shade of their veranda.

'Eberechi, Eberechi,' he said.

She sat up with the red-eyed, wounded look of a person jerked from sleep. But she smiled when she saw him. 'Teacher, have you finished for today?'

'You heard that Tanzania has recognized us?'

'Yes, yes.' She rubbed her eyes and laughed, a happy sound that made Ugwu happier.

'America is the reason many other countries will not recognize us; America is the stumbling block,' he said.

'Yes,' she said. They were sitting side by side on the stairs. 'We got double good news today. My aunty is now the provincial representative of Caritas. She said she will give me a job at the relief centre in St John's. It means I will get extra stockfish!'

She reached out and playfully pinched the skin of his neck, a gentle pressure between her fingers. He looked at her. He not only wanted to squeeze her naked buttocks, he also wanted to wake up next to her and know he would sleep next to her every day, wanted to talk to her and listen to her laughter. She was nothing like Chinyere, a fond convenience, but rather like a real Nnesinachi, one he had come to care for because of what she said and did, and not what he imagined she would say and do. He was welling up with a surge of recognition and wanted to say, over and over, that he loved her. He loved her. But he didn't. They sat and praised Tanzania and dreamed about stockfish and were still talking desultorily when a Peugeot 403 sped across the street. It reversed, in loud screeches, as if the driver wanted to make as much of an impression as possible, and stopped in front of the house. BIAFRAN ARMY was roughly handwritten on it in red paint. A soldier climbed out, holding a gun, wearing a uniform so smart that the lines of ironing were visible down the front. Eberechi stood up as he walked up to them.

'Good afternoon,' she said.

'Are you Eberechi?'

She nodded. 'Is it about my brother? Has something happened to my brother?'

'No, no.' There was a knowing leer on his face that Ugwu instantly disliked. 'Major Nwogu is calling you. He is at the bar down the road.'

'Oh!' Eberechi left her mouth open, her hand on her chest. 'I am coming, I am coming.' She turned and ran indoors. Ugwu felt betrayed by her excitement. The soldier was staring at him.

'Good afternoon,' Ugwu said.

'Who are you?' the soldier asked. 'Are you an idle civilian?'

'I am a teacher.'

'A teacher? *Onye nkuzi?*' He swung his gun back and forth.

'Yes,' Ugwu responded in English. 'We organize classes in this neighbourhood and teach the young ones the ideals of the Biafran cause.' He hoped his English sounded like Olanna's; he hoped, too, that his affectation would frighten this soldier into not asking him any more questions.

'Which classes?' the soldier asked, in a near mumble. He looked both impressed and uncertain.

'We focus on civics and mathematics and English. The Director of Mobilization has sponsored our efforts.'

The soldier stared.

Eberechi hurried out; her face wore a thin coat of white powder, her eyebrows were darkened, her lips a red gash.

'Let's go,' she said to the soldier. Then she bent and whispered to Ugwu, 'I am coming. If they look for me, please say I went to get something from Ngozi's house.'

'Okay, Mr Teacher! See you!' The soldier said and Ugwu thought he saw a glimmer of triumph in his eyes, the illiterate fool. Ugwu could not bear to watch them go; he studied his nails instead. The mix of hurt and confusion and embarrassment weakened him. He could not believe she had just asked him to lie for her while she ran off to see a man she had never mentioned to him. His legs were sluggish as he walked across the road. Everything he did for the rest of the day was coloured with a bitter dye, and he thought, more than once, about walking down to the bar to see what was going on.

It was dark when she knocked on the back door.

'Do you know they have already renamed the Rising Sun Bar?' she asked, laughing. 'It is now called Tanzania Bar!'

He looked at her and said nothing.

'People were playing Tanzanian music and dancing, and one businessman came and ordered chicken and beer for everybody,' she said.

His jealousy was visceral; it clutched at his throat and tried to strangle him.

'Where is Aunty Olanna?' she asked.

'She is reading with Baby,' Ugwu managed to say. He wanted to shake her until she told him the full truth of the afternoon, what she had done with the man, why the lipstick was gone from her lips.

Eberechi sighed. 'Is there some water? I am thirsty. I drank beer today.'

Ugwu could not believe how casual and comfortable she was. He poured some water into a cup and she drank it slowly.

'I met the major some weeks ago; he gave me a lift when I went to Orlu, but I did not think he would even remember me. He is such a nice man.' Eberechi paused. 'I told him you are my brother. He said he will make sure nobody comes here to conscript you.' She looked proud of what she had accomplished, and Ugwu felt as if she were deliberately pulling out his teeth, one after the other.

He turned away. He needed no favours from her lover. 'I have to clean up,' he said stiffly.

She drank another cup of water before she said, '*Ngwanu*; let the day break,' and left.

* * *

Ugwu stopped going over to Eberechi's house. He ignored her greetings, was angered by her wide-eyed look and her asking, 'What is it, Ugwu? What did I do to offend you?' Eventually, she stopped asking or speaking to him. He didn't care. Yet when he heard a car drive past, he rushed to see if it was the BIAFRAN ARMY Peugeot 403. He saw her leave in the mornings and thought perhaps she and the major had arranged a regular meeting place until she came by one evening to give some stockfish to Olanna. He opened the door and took the small package without a word.

'Such a nice girl, *ezigbo nwa*,' Olanna said. 'She must be doing well at that relief centre.'

Ugwu said nothing. Olanna's affection offended him, as did the way Baby asked when Aunty Eberechi would come and play with her. He wanted them to feel the same sense of angry betrayal that he did. He would tell Olanna what had happened. It was true that he had never spoken of such personal things to her before but he felt that he could. He planned it carefully for Friday, the day Master went to Tanzania Bar with Special Julius after work. Olanna had taken Baby to visit Mrs Muokelu, and while he waited for them to come back Ugwu weeded the garden and worried that his story was insubstantial. Olanna would laugh at him in that patient way she laughed at Master when he said something ridiculous. Eberechi had never spoken about her feelings for him, after all. But surely she could not pretend not to know how he felt about her. It was callous to have thrown her army-officer lover in his face like that, even if she did not feel the same way about him.

He steeled himself and went inside when he heard Olanna. They were in the living room, Baby was sitting on the floor and unwrapping something in an old newspaper.

'Welcome, mah,' Ugwu said.

Olanna turned to look at him, and the blankness in her eyes startled him. Something was wrong. Perhaps she had discovered that he had given some of the condensed milk to Eberechi. But her eyes were too hollow, too depthless, to be just about her anger at his milk theft of weeks ago. Something was very wrong. Was Baby sick again? Ugwu glanced at Baby, who was occupied with the newspaper wrapping. His stomach cramped at the prospect of bad news.

'Mah? Did something happen?'

'Your master's mother is dead.'

Ugwu moved closer because her words had solidified, become suspended objects hovering just above his reach. It took him a moment to understand.

'His cousin sent a message,' Olanna said. 'They shot her in Abba.'

'Hei!' Ugwu placed his hand on his head and struggled to remember what Mama had looked like the last time he saw her, standing by the kola nut tree, refusing to leave home. But he could not visualize her. Instead he recalled a blurred image of her in the kitchen in Nsukka, opening a pod of peppercorns. His eyes filled with tears. He wondered what other calamities he was yet to learn of. Perhaps the Hausa vandals had stayed back in his hometown; perhaps they had killed his own mother too.

When Master came home and went into his bedroom, Ugwu was unsure whether to go to the bedroom or wait for him to come out. He decided to wait. He lit the kerosene stove and mixed Baby's pap. He wished that he had been less resentful of Mama's strong-smelling soups.

Olanna walked into the kitchen.

'Why are you using the kerosene stove?' she shouted. '*I na-ezuzu ezuzu?* Are you stupid? Haven't I told you to save our kerosene?'

Ugwu was startled. 'But mah, you said I should cook Baby's food on the stove.'

'I did not say that! Go outside and light a fire!'

'Sorry, mah.' But she had indeed said that; only Baby ate three times a day now – the rest of them ate twice – and Olanna had asked him to cook her food on the kerosene stove because the smell of firewood smoke made Baby cough.

'Do you know how much kerosene costs? Just because you don't pay for the things you use you think you can do with them as you like? Is firewood itself not a luxury where you come from?'

'Sorry, mah.'

Olanna sat down on a cement block in the backyard. Ugwu made a fire and finished making Baby's dinner. He was aware of her eyes on him.

'Your master won't talk to me,' she said.

The long pause that followed filled Ugwu with a deeply uncomfortable sense of intimacy; she had never before spoken to him about Master like this.

'Sorry, mah,' he said, and sat next to her; he wanted to place a hand on her back to comfort her but he couldn't and so he left his hand suspended, inches from touching her, until she sighed and got up and went inside.

Master came out to go to the outhouse.

'My madam told me what happened, sah,' Ugwu said. '*Ndo*. Sorry.'

'Yes, yes,' Master said, and walked on briskly.

It was inadequate to Ugwu, their exchange; he felt as if Mama's death required more words, more gestures, more shared time between them. But Master had barely glanced at him. And when Special Julius came by later to say *ndo*, Master was just as brisk and brief.

'Certainly one must expect casualties. Death is the price of our liberty,' he said, and abruptly got up and went back into the bedroom, leaving Olanna to shake her head at Special Julius, her eyes tear-filled.

Ugwu thought Master would stay home from work the next day, but he took a bath earlier than he usually did. He did not drink his tea or touch the yam slices Ugwu had warmed up from the night before. He did not tuck in his shirt.

'You just can't cross to Biafra-Two, Odenigbo,' Olanna said, as she followed him out to the car. Master pushed down the palm fronds piled on top of it. Olanna kept saying something that Ugwu could not hear while Master silently bent over the open bonnet. He climbed in and drove off with a slight wave. Olanna ran off down the road. Ugwu thought, for one absurd moment, that she was chasing after Master's car but she came back to say that she had asked Special Julius to follow him and bring him back.

'He said he has to go and bury her. But the roads are occupied. The roads are occupied,' she said. Her eyes were focused on the compound entrance. With each sound she heard – a lorry rumbling past, a chirping bird, a child's cry – she ran from the veranda bench to peer down the road. A group of people armed with machetes walked past, singing. Their leader had one arm.

'Teacher! Well done!' one of them called, when they saw Olanna. 'We are going combing! We are going to root out the infiltrators!'

They had almost passed when Olanna jerked up and shouted, 'Please look out for my husband in a blue Opel.'

One of them turned and waved with a slightly puzzled look.

Ugwu could feel the heat of the bright afternoon sun even under the thatch awning. Baby was playing barefoot in the front yard. Special Julius's long American car drove in and Olanna leapt up.

'He's not back?' Special Julius asked from the car.

'You didn't see him,' Olanna said.

Special Julius looked worried. 'But who told Odenigbo that he can make it past occupied roads? Who told him?'

Ugwu wanted the man to shut up. He had no right to criticize Master, and rather than sitting there in his ugly tunic he might turn around and go search properly for Master.

After Special Julius left, Olanna sat down and leaned forwards and placed her head in her hands.

'Do you want some water, mah?' Ugwu asked.

She shook her head. Ugwu watched the sun fall. Darkness came swiftly, brutally; there was no gradual change from light to dark.

'What am I going to do?' Olanna asked. 'What am I going to do?'

'Master will come back, mah.'

But Master did not come back. Olanna sat on the veranda until past midnight, resting her head against the wall.

27

Richard was at the dining table when the doorbell rang. He reduced the volume of the radio and rearranged the sheets of writing paper before he opened the door. Harrison stood there, his forehead, his neck, his arms, and his legs beneath his khaki shorts all wrapped in bloody bandages.

The red wetness made Richard feel faint. 'Harrison! Good God. What happened to you?'

'Good afternoon, master.'

'Were you attacked?' Richard asked.

Harrison came inside and placed his tattered bag down and began to laugh. Richard stared at him. When Harrison raised his hands to untie the bloody bandage on his head, Richard said, 'No, no, there's no need to do that. No need at all. I'll call the driver right away. We'll take you to the hospital.'

Harrison yanked the bandage off. His head was smooth; there was no gash, no mark to show where the blood had come from.

'It is beets, sah,' Harrison said, and laughed again.

'Beets?'

'Yes, sah.'

'It isn't blood then, you mean?'

'No, sah.' Harrison moved farther into the living room and made to stand at the corner, but Richard asked him to sit. He perched on the edge of the chair. The smile left his face as he began to speak.

'I am coming from my hometown, sah. I am not telling anybody that our hometown is falling soon so that they are not saying I am saboteur. But everybody is knowing that the vandals are close. Even two days ago we are hearing shelling, but the town council say it is our troops practising. So I'm taking my family and our goats to the inside-inside farm. Then I begin coming Port Harcourt because I am not knowing what happened to Master. Even I am sending message with the driver of Professor Blyden since many weeks ago.'

'I didn't get any message.'

'Foolish man,' Harrison muttered, before he continued. 'I am soaking cloth in fresh beet water and tying them in bandage and I am saying I am survivor of air raid. It is only how the militia people are allowing me to enter lorry. Only men with wounds is following the women and children.'

'So what happened in Nsukka? How did you leave?'

'It is many months now, sah. When I am hearing shelling I am packing your things and I am burying the manscrit inside box in the garden, near that small flower Jomo is planting the last time.'

'You buried the manuscript?'

'Yes, sah, because if not they are taking it from me on the road.'

'Yes, of course,' Richard said. It was unreasonable to hope that Harrison had brought 'In the Time of Roped Pots' with him. 'So how have you been getting on?'

Harrison shook his head. 'Hunger is bad, sah. My people are watching the goats.'

'Watching the goats?'

'To see what they are eating, and after seeing they are boiling the same leaves and giving their children to drink. It is stopping kwashiorkor.'

'I see,' Richard said. 'Now go to the Boys' Quarters and have a wash.'

'Yes, sah.' Harrison stood up.

'And what are your plans now?'

'Sah?'

'Do you plan to go back to your hometown?'

Harrison fiddled with the arm bandage, thick with false blood. 'No, sah. I am waiting until the war is ending so I am cooking for Master.'

'Of course,' Richard said. It was a good thing two of Kainene's stewards had gone off to join the army and only Ikejide was left.

'But, sah, they are saying that Port Harcourt is falling soon. The vandals are coming with many ships from Britain. They are shelling outside Port Harcourt now.'

'Go on and have a bath, Harrison.'

'Yes, sah.'

After Harrison left, Richard turned up the volume of the radio. He liked the cadence of the Arabic-inflected voice on Radio Kaduna, but he did not like the gleeful certitude with which it said 'Port Harcourt is liberated! Port Harcourt is liberated!' They had been talking about the fall of Port Harcourt for the past two days. So had Lagos radio, although with a little less glee. The BBC, too, had announced that the imminent fall of Port Harcourt was the fall of Biafra; Biafra would lose its viable seaport, its airport, its control of oil.

Richard pulled the bamboo stopper from the bottle on the table and poured himself a drink. The pink liquid spread a pleasant warmth through his body. Emotions swirled in his head – relief that Harrison was alive, disappointment that his manuscript was buried in Nsukka, anxiety about the fate of Port Harcourt. Before he poured a second drink, he read the label on the bottle: REPUBLIC OF BIAFRA, RESEARCH AND PRODUCTION DIRECTORATE, NENE SHERRY, 45%. He sipped slowly. Madu had brought two cartons the last time he visited, joking that locally made liquor in old beer bottles was part of the win-the-war effort.

'The RAP people claim that Ojukwu drinks this, though I doubt it,' he said. 'I drink only the clear ones myself because I don't trust that colouring.'

Madu's irreverence, calling His Excellency *Ojukwu*, always bothered Richard but he said nothing because he did not want to see Madu's amused smirk, the same smirk Madu had when he told Kainene, 'We are running our cars with a mix of kerosene and palm oil' or 'We've perfected the flying *ogbunigwe*' or 'We've made an armoured car from scrap'. His *we* was edged with exclusion. The deliberate emphasis, the deepened voice, meant that Richard was not part of *we*; a visitor could not take the liberties of the homeowners.

And so, weeks ago, Richard was confused when Kainene first told him, 'Madu would like you to write for the Propaganda Directorate. He'll get you a special pass and petrol supplies so you can move around. They'll send your pieces to our public relations people over-seas.'

'Why me?'

Kainene shrugged. 'Why not?'

'The man hates me.'

'Don't be so dramatic. I think they want experienced insiders to do stories that are about more than just the number of Biafran dead.'

At first the word *insider* thrilled Richard. But doubts soon crawled out; *insider* had been Kainene's word, after all, and not Madu's. Madu saw him as a foreigner, which perhaps was why he thought he would be good at this. When Madu called and asked if he would do it, Richard said no.

'Have you thought about it?' Madu asked.

'You would not have asked me if I were not white.'

'Of course I asked because you are white. They will take what you write more seriously because you are white. Look, the truth is that this is not your war. This is not your cause. Your government will evacuate you in a minute if you ask them to. So it is not enough to carry limp branches and shout *power, power* to show that you support Biafra. If you really want to contribute, this is the way that you can. The world has to know the truth of what is happening, because they simply cannot remain silent while we die. They will believe a white man who lives in Biafra and who is not a professional journalist. You can tell them how we continue to stand and prevail even though Nigerian MiG-Seventeens, Il-Twenty-eights, and L-Twenty-nine Delfins flown by Russians and Egyptians are bombing us every day, and how some of them are using transport planes and just crudely rolling out bombs to kill women and children, and how the British and the Soviets are in an unholy alliance giving more and more arms to Nigeria, and how the Americans have refused to help us, and how our relief flights come in at night with no lights because the Nigerians will shoot them down during the day. . . .'

Madu paused to catch his breath, and Richard said, 'Yes, I'll do it.' *They simply cannot remain silent while we die* rang in his head.

His first article was about the fall of Onitsha. He wrote that the Nigerians had tried many times to take this ancient town but the Biafrans fought valiantly, that hundreds of popular novels had been published here before the war, that the thick, sad smoke of the burning Niger Bridge had risen like a defiant elegy. He described the Holy Trinity Catholic Church, where soldiers of the Nigeria Second Division first defecated on the altar before killing two hundred civilians. He quoted a calm eyewitness: 'The vandals are people who shit on God. We will overcome them.'

As he wrote the article, he felt as if he were a schoolboy again, writing letters to Aunt Elizabeth while his headmaster monitored them. Richard remembered him clearly, his mottled complexion, how he called science 'muck', how he ate his porridge walking about in the dining hall because he said it was what gentlemen did. Richard was still not sure which he hated more at the time, being forced to write letters home or having the letter-writing session monitored. And he was not sure what he disliked more now, imagining Madu as his monitor or realizing that he cared very much what Madu thought. A note came from Madu some days later. *It was very well done (perhaps a little less flowery next time?) and they have sent it off to Europe.* Madu's handwriting was crabbed, and on the writing paper the NIGERIAN of NIGERIAN ARMY had been crossed out in ink and BIAFRAN written in hasty block letters. But Madu's words convinced Richard that he had made the right decision. He imagined himself as the young Winston Churchill covering Kitchener's battle at Omdurman, a battle of superior versus inferior arms, except that, unlike Churchill, he sided with the moral victor.

Now, weeks later, after more articles, he felt a part of things. He found pleasure in the new respect in the driver's eyes, jumping out to open the door although Richard told him not to bother. He found pleasure in how quickly the civil defenders' suspicious glances at his special duties pass changed to wide grins when he greeted them in Igbo, in how willing people were to answer his questions. He found pleasure in the superiority he adopted with foreign journalists, speaking vaguely about the background to the war – the implications of the national strike and the census and the Western Region chaos – knowing all the while they had no idea what he was talking about.

But his greatest pleasure had come from meeting His Excellency. It was at the staging of a play in Owerri. An air raid had shattered all the louvres in the windows of the theatre and the evening breeze blew some of the actors' words away. Richard sat some rows behind His Excellency, and, after the play, a top man at the Mobilization Directorate introduced them. The solid handshake, the 'Thank you for the good work you're doing' in that soft, Oxford-accented voice had filled Richard with equanimity. Even though he found the political play too obvious, he did not say so. He agreed with His Excellency: It was wonderful, just wonderful.

Richard could hear Harrison in the kitchen. He tuned to Radio Biafra, to the ending of an announcement about the enemy's being wedged in Oba, before he turned the radio off. He poured a smaller drink and reread his last sentence. He was writing about Commando Special Forces, how popular and revered they were by civilians, but his dislike of their commander, a German mercenary, made his words stiff. The writing was stilted. The sherry had sharpened his anxiety rather then deadened it. He got up and picked up the phone and called Madu.

'Richard,' Madu said. 'How lucky. I just stepped in.'

'Is there news on Port Harcourt?'

'News?'

'Is it threatened? There's been shelling in Umuokwurusi, hasn't there?'

'Oh, we have secure information that some saboteurs got their hands on some shells. You think if the vandals were really that close they would do that kind of half-hearted shelling?'

The amused tone in Madu's voice made him feel instantly foolish. 'Sorry for the bother. I just thought . . .' He let his voice trail off.

'Not at all. Greet Kainene when she comes back,' Madu said, before hanging up.

Richard finished his drink and made to pour himself another but decided not to. He forced the stopper back into the mouth of the bottle and went out to the veranda. The sea was still. He stretched and ran a quick hand though his hair, as if to shrug off the foreboding. If Port Harcourt fell, he would lose the town he had come to love, the town in which he loved; he would lose a bit of himself. But Madu had to be right. Madu would not be in denial about a town that was about to fall, certainly not a town where Kainene lived. If he said Port Harcourt was not under threat, it was not.

Richard looked at his hazy reflection in the glass door. He had a tan and his hair looked fuller, slightly tousled, and he thought of Rimbaud's words: *I is someone else.*

Kainene laughed when Richard told her about Harrison's beets. Then she touched his arm and said, 'Don't worry, if he put the manuscript in a box, it will be safe from termites.' She slipped out of her work clothes and stretched languorously, and he admired the lean grace of her arched back. Desire reeled inside him, but he would wait for evening, after dinner, after they had entertained any guests, after Ikejide had retired. They would go out to the veranda and he would push the table aside and spread out the soft rug and lie on his naked back. When she climbed astride, he would hold her hips and stare up at the night sky and, for those moments, be sure of the meaning of bliss. It was their new ritual since the war started, the only reason he was grateful for the war.

'Colin Williamson stopped by my office today,' Kainene said.

'I didn't know he was back,' Richard said, and Colin's sunburnt face came to his mind, the flash of discoloured teeth as he talked, too often, about how he left the BBC because his editors were supportive of Nigeria.

'He brought a letter from my mother,' Kainene said.

'From your mother!'

'She read his story in the *Observer* and contacted him to ask whether he would be returning to Biafra and would he deliver a letter to her daughter in Port Harcourt. She was surprised when he said he knew us.'

Richard loved the way she said *us*. 'Are they all right?'

'Of course they are; nobody is bombing London. She says she has nightmares about Olanna and me dying, she's saying prayers, and they're involved with the Save Biafra Campaign in London – which must mean they sent a small donation.' Kainene paused and handed him an envelope. 'She rather cleverly taped some British pounds into the inner lining of a card. Quite impressive. She sent one for Olanna too.'

He read the letter quickly. *Regards to Richard* was the only reference to him, at the bottom of the blue paper. He wanted to ask Kainene how she planned to deliver Olanna's but he would not. Silence had enshrined the subject of Olanna with each month, each year, that passed without their bringing it up. When Kainene received the three letters Olanna had written since the war started, she had said nothing except that she received them. And she had not replied.

'I'll send somebody to Umuahia next week to deliver Olanna's,' Kainene said.

He gave the letter back to her. The silence was becoming curdled.

'The Nigerians won't stop talking about Port Harcourt,' he said.

'They won't take Port Harcourt. Our best battalion is here.' Kainene sounded casual enough, but there was a new wariness in her eyes, the same wariness she had when she told him, months ago, that she wanted to buy an uncompleted house in Orlu. She had said it was better to own property rather than cash but he suspected that, for her, it was a safety net in case Port Harcourt fell. For him, considering the fall of Port Harcourt was blasphemous. Every weekend, when they inspected the house to make sure her builders were not stealing the materials, he never spoke of their living there, as though to absolve himself from the blasphemy.

And he no longer wanted to travel. He wanted to guard Port Harcourt with his presence; as long as he was there, he felt, nothing would happen. But the public relations people in Europe had asked for an article about the airstrip in Uli, so he left reluctantly, very early in the morning, so he would be back before midday when Nigerian planes strafed vehicles driving on major roads. A wide bomb crater loomed ahead on Okigwe Road. The driver swerved to avoid it and Richard felt a familiar foreboding, but his thoughts lightened as they approached Uli. It was his first visit to Biafra's only link to the outside world, this wonder of an airstrip where food and arms evaded Nigerian bombers. He climbed out of the car and looked at the strip of tarmac with thick bush on either side and thought of the people who did so much with so little. A tiny jet was parked at the far end. The morning sun was hot; three men were spreading palm fronds on the tarmac, working swiftly and sweating, pushing along large carts piled with fronds. Richard went over to say, 'Well done, *jisienu ike.*'

An official came out of the unfinished terminal building nearby and shook Richard's hand. 'Don't write too much, oh! Don't give away our secrets,' he joked.

'Of course not,' Richard said. 'Can I interview you?'

The man beamed and flexed his shoulders and said, 'Well, I am in charge of customs and immigration.' Richard hid a smile; people always felt important when he asked for an interview. They talked standing by the tarmac, and shortly after the man returned to the building, a tall, fair-haired man walked out. Richard recognized him: Count Von Rosen. He looked older than in the picture Richard had seen, closer to seventy than sixty, but his was an elegant ageing; his strides were long and his chin firm.

'They told me you were out here and I thought I'd say hello,' he said, his handshake as unwavering as his green eyes. 'I've just read your excellent article on the Biafran Boys Brigade.'

'A pleasure to meet you, Count Von Rosen,' Richard said. And it *was* a pleasure. Ever since he read about this Swedish aristocrat who bombed Nigerian targets with his own small plane, he had wanted to meet him.

'Remarkable men,' the count said, glancing at the workers who were making sure that, from above, the black stretch of tarmac would look like bush. 'Remarkable country.'

'Yes,' Richard said.

'Do you like cheese?' the count asked.

'Cheese? Yes. Yes, of course.'

The count dug into his pocket and brought out a small packet. 'Excellent cheddar.'

Richard took it and tried to shield his surprise. 'Thank you.'

The count fumbled in his pocket again and Richard worried that he might be bringing out more cheese. But he pulled out a pair of sunglasses and put them on. 'I'm told your wife is a wealthy Igbo, one of those who stayed back to fight for the cause.'

Richard had never thought about it like that, Kainene staying back to fight for the cause, but he was pleased that the count had been told this and told also that he and Kainene were married. He felt a sudden fierce pride for Kainene. 'Yes. She's an extraordinary woman.'

There was a pause. The intimacy of the cheese present required a reciprocating gesture, so Richard opened his diary and showed the count first a photo of Kainene, taken by the pool with a cigarette between her lips, and then the photo of the roped pot.

'I fell in love with Igbo-Ukwu art and then fell in love with her,' he said.

'Beautiful, both,' the count said, before he took his sunglasses off to examine the photos.

'Are you going on a mission today?' Richard asked.

'Yes.'

'Why are you doing this, sir?'

He put his glasses back on. 'I worked with the freedom fighters in Ethiopia and before that I flew in relief to the Warsaw ghetto,' he said with a slight smile, as if that answered the question. 'Now I must get on. Keep up the good work.'

Richard watched him walk away, a straight-backed courtier, and thought how different he was from the mercenary. 'I love the Biafrans,' the red-faced German had said. 'Nothing like the bloody kaffirs in Congo.' He had spoken to Richard in his house in the middle of the bush, drinking from a large bottle of whisky, watching his adopted child – a pretty Biafran toddler – playing with a collection of old shrapnel on the floor. Richard had felt annoyed by the affectionate contempt with which he treated the child and by the exception he made of Biafrans. It was as though the mercenary felt that here finally were black people he could like. The count was different. Richard glanced at the tiny jet again before he climbed into the car.

On the way back, just outside Port Harcourt, he heard the distant rattle of gunfire. It was not long before it stopped. It worried him. And when Kainene suggested they go to Orlu the next day to find a carpenter for her new house, Richard wished they did not have to go. Two consecutive days away from Port Harcourt worried him.

The new house was surrounded by cashew trees. Richard remembered how dejected it had looked when Kainene bought it – half-finished with layers of green mould on the unpainted walls – how the flies and bees clustered over the fallen cashews had nauseated him. The owner had been principal of the community secondary school down the road. Now that the school was a refugee camp, now that his wife had died, he was going into the interior with his goats and his children. He repeated, 'This house is out of shelling range, completely out of shelling range,' until Richard wondered how he could possibly know where the Nigerians would shell from. There was an unobtrusive charm about the bungalow, Richard conceded, as they walked through the empty, newly painted rooms. Kainene hired two carpenters from the refugee camp, made sketches on a sheet of paper, and, back in the car, told Richard, 'I don't trust them to make a decent table.'

A shrill sound went off as they drove out of Orlu. The driver stopped with a jerk, in the middle of the road, and they jumped out of the car and into the thick, green bush. Some women who ,had been walking along the road ran too, looking up as they did, twisting their necks. It was the first time Richard had taken cover with Kainene; she lay flat and rigid on the ground next to him. Their shoulders touched. The driver was a little way behind them. The silence was absolute. A loud rustling nearby made Richard tense until a red-headed lizard crawled out. They waited and waited and finally got up when they heard the revving of a car engine and rising voices from nearby, 'My money is gone! My money is gone!' There was a market only yards away. Somebody had stolen from one of the traders while she was taking cover. Richard could see her and some other women underneath open stalls, shouting and gesticulating. It was difficult to believe how silent it all had been a moment ago, and how Biafran markets now thrived so easily in the bush since the Nigerians bombed the open-air Awgu market.

'False alarm is worse than the real one,' the driver said.

Kainene dusted herself down carefully, but the ground was wet and the mud had stuck to her clothes; her blue dress looked designed with chocolate-coloured smudges. They climbed into the car and continued the journey. Richard sensed that Kainene was angry.

'Look at the tree,' he told her, pointing. It had been cleanly split in two, from the branches down to the stem. One half still stood, slightly tilted, while the other lay on the ground.

'It seems recent,' Kainene said.

'My uncle flew a plane in the war. He bombed Germany. It's strange to think of him doing something like this.'

'You don't talk about him.'

'He died. He was shot down.' Richard paused. 'I'm going to write about our new forest markets.'

The driver had stopped at a checkpoint. A lorry loaded with sofas and shelves and tables was parked by the side, and a man stood beside it talking to a young female civil defender wearing khaki jeans and canvas shoes. She left him and came up and peered at Richard and Kainene. She asked the driver to open the boot, looked inside the glove compartment, and then extended her hand for Kainene's handbag.

'If I had a bomb, I would not hide it in my bag,' Kainene muttered.

'What did you say, madam?' the young woman asked.

Kainene said nothing. The woman looked through the bag carefully. She brought out a small radio. 'What is this? Is this a transmitter?'

'It is not a transmitter. It is a ra-di-o,' Kainene said, with a mocking slowness. The young woman examined their special duties passes, smiled, and adjusted her beret. 'Sorry, madam. But you know we have many saboteurs who use strange gadgets to transmit to Nigeria. Vigilance is our watchword!'

'Why have you stopped that man with the lorry?' Kainene asked.

'We are turning back people evacuating furniture.'

'Why?'

'Evacuations like this cause panic in the civil population.' She sounded as if she were reciting something rehearsed. 'There is no cause for alarm.'

'But what if his town is about to fall? Do you know where he has come from?'

She stiffened. 'Good day, madam.'

As soon as the driver started the car, Kainene said, 'It's such an awful joke, isn't it?'

'What?' Richard asked, although he knew what she meant.

'This fear we are whipping up in our people. Bombs in women's bras! Bombs in tins of baby milk! Saboteurs everywhere! Watch your children because they could be working for Nigeria!'

'It's normal for wartime.' He sometimes wished she would not be so arch about things. 'It's important for people to be aware that there are saboteurs in our midst.'

'The only saboteurs we have are the ones Ojukwu invented so he can lock up his opponents and the men whose wives he wants. Did I ever tell you about the Onitsha man who bought up all of the cement we had in the factory shortly after the refugees started coming back? Ojukwu is having an affair with the man's wife and has just had the man arrested for nothing.'

She was tapping her foot on the car floor. She always sounded like Madu when she spoke about His Excellency. Her disdain did not convince Richard; it began when Madu complained that His Excellency had bypassed him and made his junior a commanding officer. If His Excellency had not bypassed Madu, perhaps she would be less critical.

'Do you know how many officers he's locked up? He is so suspicious of his officers that he's using civilians to buy arms. Madu said they just bought some miserable bolt-action rifles in Europe. Really, when Biafra is established, we will have to remove Ojukwu.'

'And replace him with who, Madu?'

Kainene laughed, and it pleased and surprised him that she had enjoyed his sarcasm. His foreboding returned, a rumbling rush in his stomach, as they approached Port Harcourt.

'Stop so that we can buy *akara* and fried fish,' Kainene said to the driver, and even the driver's stepping on the brake made Richard nervous.

When they got home, Ikejide said Colonel Madu had called four times.

'I hope nothing is wrong,' Kainene said, opening the oil-smeared newspaper package of fried fish and bean cakes. Richard took a still-hot *akara* and blew on it and told himself that Port Harcourt was safe. Nothing was wrong. The phone rang and he grabbed it and felt his heart begin to jog when he heard Madu's voice.

'How are you? Any problems?' Madu asked.

'No. Why?'

'There's a rumour that Britain supplied five warships to Nigeria, so youths have been burning British shops and houses all over Port Harcourt today. I wanted to be sure you hadn't been bothered. I can send one or two of my boys down.'

First, Richard was irritated at the thought that he still was a foreigner who could be attacked, and then he felt grateful for Madu's concern.

'We're fine,' he said. 'We've just come back from seeing the house in Orlu.'

'Oh, good. Let me know if anything develops.' Madu paused and spoke to somebody in muffled tones before he came back on the line. 'You should write about what the French ambassador said yesterday.'

'Yes, of course.'

'*I was told that Biafrans fought like heroes, but now I know that heroes fight like Biafrans,*' Madu intoned proudly, as if the compliment was one given him personally and he wanted to make sure Richard knew it.

'Yes, of course,' Richard said again. 'Port Harcourt is safe, isn't it?'

There was a pause on Madu's end. 'Some saboteurs have been arrested and all of them are non-Igbo minorities. I don't know why these people insist on aiding the enemy. But we will overcome. Is Kainene there?'

Richard handed Kainene the phone. The sacrilege of it, that some people could betray Biafra. He remembered the Ijaw and Efik men he had spoken to at a bank in Owerri, who said the Igbo would dominate them when Biafra was established. Richard had told them that a country born from the ashes of injustice would limit its practice of injustice. When they looked at him doubtfully, he mentioned the army general who was Efik, the director who was Ijaw, the minority soldiers who were fighting so brilliantly for the cause. Still, they looked unconvinced.

Richard stayed at home the following days. He wrote about the forest markets and stood often on the veranda, looking down the stretch of road, half expecting a mob of youths to rush towards the house with flaming torches. Kainene had seen one of the burnt houses on her way to work. A mild effort, she had called it; they had only blackened the walls. Richard wanted to see it too, to write about it and perhaps link it to the burning of effigies of Wilson and Kosygin he had seen recently at the government field, but he waited for a week to make sure it was safe to be a British man on the road before he left very early in the morning for a tour of the city.

He was surprised to see a new checkpoint on Aggrey Road and even more surprised that it was guarded by soldiers. Perhaps it was because of the burnt houses. The road was empty, all the shouting hawkers with their groundnuts and newspapers and fried fish were gone. A soldier stood in the middle of the road, swinging his gun as they approached, motioning that they go back. The driver stopped and Richard held out his pass. The soldier ignored the pass and kept swinging his gun. 'Turn back! Turn back!'

'Good morning,' Richard began. 'I am Richard Churchill and I am –'

'Turn back or I shoot! Nobody is leaving Port Harcourt! There is no cause for alarm!'

The man's fingers were twitchy on the gun. The driver turned around. Richard's foreboding had become hard pebbles in his nostrils, but he made himself sound casual when he got back home and told Kainene what had happened.

'I'm sure it's nothing,' he said. 'There are so many rumours flying around, the army probably wants to put a stop to the panic.'

'Certainly a fine way to do it,' Kainene said, and there was that wary expression of hers again. She was placing some papers in a file. 'We should call Madu and find out what's going on.'

'Yes,' Richard said. 'Well, I'll go and shave. I didn't have time to shave before I left.'

He heard the first boom from the bathroom. He kept running the stick over his chin. It came again: *boom, boom, boom*. The window louvres shattered and the glass shards clinked as they fell to the floor. Some of them landed close to his feet.

Kainene opened the bathroom door. 'I've asked Harrison and Ike-jide to put a few things in the car,' she said. 'We'll leave the Ford and take the Peugeot.'

Richard turned and stared at her and felt the urge to cry. He wished he were as calm as she was, that his hands would not shake as he washed them. He took his shaving cream, her soaps, and some sponges and threw them in a bag.

'Richard, we should hurry, the shelling sounds very close by,' Kainene said, and again there was a series of *boom, boom, boom*. She was putting her things and his into a suitcase. The drawers that held his shirts and his underwear were pulled out, and her packing was quick and methodical. He ran a hand over his books lined on the shelf and then began to search for the sheets where he had written notes for his piece about *ogbunigwe*, the fantastic, Biafran-made land-mines. He had left them on the table, he was sure. He looked inside the drawers.

'Have you seen my papers?' he asked.

'We have to get past the main raid before they advance, Richard,' Kainene said. She stuffed two fat envelopes into her bag.

'What are those envelopes?' he asked.

'Emergency cash.'

Harrison and Ikejide came in and began to drag the two packed suitcases out. Richard heard the roar of planes above. It couldn't possibly be. There had never been an air raid in Port Harcourt and it made no sense that there would be one now, when Port Harcourt was about to fall and the vandals were shelling close by. But the sound was unmistakable, and when Harrison shouted, 'Enemy plane, sah!' his words felt redundant.

Richard ran towards Kainene, but she was already running out of the room, and he followed. She said, 'Come out to the orchard!' when she ran past Harrison and Ikejide crouched under the kitchen table.

Outside, the air was humid. Richard looked up and saw them, two planes flying low, with an ominously streamlined efficiency to their shape, trailing silver-white lines in the sky. Fear spread helplessness throughout his body. They lay under the orange trees, he and Kainene, side by side, silent. Harrison and Ikejide had run out of the house; Harrison threw himself flat on the ground while Ikejide kept running, his body arched slightly forwards, his arms flying around, his head bobbing. Then came the cold whistle of a mortar in the air and the crash as it landed and the boom as it exploded. Richard pressed Kainene to him. A piece of shrapnel, the size of a fist, wheezed past. Ikejide was still running and, in the moment that Richard glanced away and back, Ikejide's head was gone. The body was running, arched slightly forwards, arms flying around, but there was no head. There was only a bloodied neck. Kainene screamed. The body crashed down near her long American car, the planes receded and disappeared into the distance, and they all lay still for long minutes, until Harrison got up and said, 'I am getting bag.'

He came back with a raffia bag. Richard did not look as Harrison went over to pick up Ikejide's head and put it in the bag. Later, as he grasped the still-warm ankles and walked, with Harrison holding the wrists, to the shallow grave at the bottom of the orchard, he did not once look directly at it.

Kainene sat on the ground and watched them.

'Are you all right?' Richard asked her. She did not respond. There was an eerie blankness in her eyes. Richard was not sure what to do. He shook her gently but the blank look remained, so he went to the tap and splashed a bucket of cold water on her.

'Stop it, for heaven's sake,' she said, and got up. 'You've wet my dress.'

She pulled out another dress from a suitcase and changed in the kitchen before they left for Orlu. She no longer hurried; slowly, she straightened the collar, smoothed down the rumpled bodice with her hands. The jumble of sounds jarred Richard as he drove – the *boom-boom-boom* of mortars, the quickening rattle of gunshots – and he expected to see a Nigerian soldier stop them or attack them or throw a grenade at them at any time. Nothing happened. The roads were crowded. The checkpoints were gone. From the backseat, Harrison said in a cowed whisper, 'They are using everything they are having to take Port Harcourt.'

Kainene said little when they arrived in Orlu and saw no carpenter and no furniture; the men had disappeared with the advance payment. She simply walked to the refugee camp down the road and found another carpenter, a sallow-skinned man who wanted to be paid in food. In the following days, she was mostly silent, withdrawn, as they sat outside and watched the carpenter cutting, hammering, smoothing.

'Why don't you want money?' Kainene asked him.

'What will I buy with the money?' he asked.

'You must be a foolish man,' Kainene said. 'There is much you can buy with money.'

'Not in this Biafra.' The man shrugged. 'Just give me *garri* and rice.'

Kainene did not respond. A bird's dropping fell on the floor of the veranda, and Richard picked up a cashew leaf and wiped it off.

'You know Olanna saw a mother carrying her child's head,' Kainene said.

'Yes,' Richard said, although he did *not* know. She had never told him about Olanna's experience during the massacres.

'I want to see her.'

'You should go.' Richard took a deep breath to steady himself and stared at one of the finished chairs. It was sharp-angled and ugly.

'How could shrapnel cut off Ikejide's head so completely?' Kainene asked, as if she wanted him to tell her that she was mistaken about the whole thing. He wished he could. At nights, she cried. She told him she wanted to dream of Ikejide but she woke up every morning and remembered his running headless body clearly while, in the safer blurred territory of her dreams, she saw herself smoking a cigarette in an elegant gold holder.

A van delivered bags of *garri* to the house, and Kainene asked Harrison not to touch them because they were for the refugee camp. She was the new food supplier.

'I'll distribute the food to the refugees myself and I'm going to ask the Agricultural Research Centre for some shit,' she told Richard.

'Shit?'

'Manure. We can start a farm at the camp. We'll grow our own protein, soya beans, and *akidi*.'

'Oh.'

'There's a man from Enugu who has a fantastic talent for making baskets and lamps. I'll have him teach others. We can create income here. We can make a difference! And I'll ask the Red Cross to send us a doctor every week.'

There was a manic vibrancy about her, about the way she left for the refugee camp each day, about the exhaustion that shadowed her eyes when she returned in the evenings. She no longer spoke of Ikejide. Instead, she spoke about twenty people living in a space meant for one and about the little boys who played war and the women who nursed babies and the selfless Holy Ghost priests Father Marcel and Father Jude. But it was Inatimi she spoke about the most. He was in the Biafran Organization of Freedom Fighters, had lost his entire family in the massacres, and often infiltrated enemy camps. He came by to educate the refugees.

'He thinks it's important for our people to know that our cause is just and to understand why this is true. I've told him not to bother teaching them about federalism and the Aburi accord and whatnot. They will never grasp it. Some of them didn't even go to primary school. But he just ignores me and goes on spending time with little groups of people.' Kainene sounded admiring, as if his ignoring her was further proof of his heroism. Richard resented Inatimi. In his mind, Inatimi became perfect, brave and bracing, made intrepid and sensitive by loss. When he finally met Inatimi he nearly laughed in the face of this small, pimpled man with a bulb of a nose. But he could see, right away, that Inatimi's god was Biafra. His was a fervent faith in the cause.

'When I lost my whole family, every single one, it was as if I had been born all over again,' Inatimi told Richard in his quiet way. 'I was a new person because I no longer had family to remind me of what I had been.'

The priests, too, were nothing like Richard had expected. He was surprised by their quiet cheer. When they told him, 'We are amazed at the good work God is doing here,' Richard wanted to ask why God had allowed the war to happen in the first place. Yet their faith moved him. If God could make them care so genuinely, God was a worthy concept.

Richard was talking to Father Marcel about God on the morning the doctor arrived. Her dusty Morris Minor had RED CROSS painted on it in red. Even before she said 'I'm Dr Inyang,' with an easy hand-shake, Richard knew she was from one of the minority tribes. He prided himself on his ability to recognize an Igbo person. It was nothing to do with how they looked; it was, instead, a fellow feeling.

Kainene led Dr Inyang straight to the sickroom, the classroom at the end of the block. Richard followed; he watched while Kainene talked about the refugees lying on bamboo pallets. A pregnant young woman sat up and held her chest and began to cough, unending chesty coughing that was painful to hear.

Dr Inyang bent over her with a stethoscope and said, in gentle Pidgin English, 'How are you? How you dey?'

First the pregnant young woman recoiled and then she spat with a vicious intensity that wrinkled her forehead. The watery smear of saliva landed on Dr Inyang's chin.

'Saboteur!' the pregnant woman said. 'It is you non-Igbo who are showing the enemy the way! *Hapu m!* It is you people that showed them the way to my hometown!'

Dr Inyang's hand rested on her chin, too stunned to wipe the saliva off. The silence was thickened by uncertainty. Kainene walked over briskly and slapped the pregnant woman, two hard smacks in quick succession on her cheek.

'We are all Biafrans! *Anyincha bu Biafra!*' Kainene said. 'Do you understand me? We are all Biafrans!'

The pregnant woman fell back on her bed.

Richard was startled by Kainene's violence. There was something brittle about her, and he feared she would snap apart at the slightest touch; she had thrown herself so fiercely into this, the erasing of memory, that it would destroy her.

28

Olanna had a happy dream. She did not remember what it was about but she remembered that it had been happy, and so she woke up warming herself with the thought that she could still have a happy dream. She wished Odenigbo had not gone to work so she could tell him about it and trace his gently indulgent smile as he listened, the smile that said he did not need to agree with her to believe her. But she had not seen that smile since his mother died, since he tried to go to Abba and came back clutching a shadow, since he began to leave for work too early and to stop at Tanzania Bar on his way home. If only he had not tried to cross the occupied roads, he would not be so gaunt and withdrawn now; his grief would not be burdened by failure. She should never have let him go. But his determination had been quietly hostile, as though he felt she had no right to stop him. His words – 'I have to bury what the vultures left behind' – dug a gully between them that she had not known how to bridge. Before he climbed into the car and drove off, she had told him, 'Somebody must have buried her.'

And later, as she sat on the veranda waiting for him, she loathed herself for not finding better words. *Somebody must have buried her.* It sounded so trivial. What she meant was that surely his cousin Aniekwena buried her. Aniekwena's message, sent through a soldier on leave, was brief: Abba was occupied and he had sneaked back to try and evacuate some property and found Mama lying dead from gunshot wounds near the compound wall. He had said nothing more, but Olanna assumed he must have dug a grave. He could not have left her lying there, decaying.

Olanna no longer remembered the hours of waiting for Odenigbo to come back, but she did remember the sensation of blindness, of cold sheaths being drawn over her eyes. She had worried from time to

time about Baby and Kainene and Ugwu dying, vaguely acknowl-
edged the possibilities of future grief, but she had never conceived of
Odenigbo's death. Never. He was her life's constant. When he came
back, long after midnight, with his shoes covered in mud, she knew
he would not be the same again. He asked Ugwu for a glass of water
and told her in a calm voice, 'They kept asking me to go back, so I
parked the car and hid it and began to walk. Finally, one Biafran
officer cocked his gun and said he would shoot and save the vandals
the trouble if I didn't turn around.'

She held him close to her and sobbed. Her relief was stained with
desolation.

'I'm fine, *nkem*,' he said. But he no longer went into the interior
with the Agitator Corps, no longer returned with lit-up eyes. Instead,
he went to Tanzania Bar every day and came back with a taciturn set
to his mouth. When he did talk, he spoke of his unpublished research
papers left behind in Nsukka, how they were almost enough to make
him a full professor, and heaven knew what the vandals would do
with them. She wanted him to truly talk to her, help her to help him
grieve, but each time she told him, he said, 'It's too late, *nkem*.' She
was not sure what he meant. She sensed the layers of his grief – he
would never know how Mama had died and would always struggle
with old resentments – but she did not feel connected to his mourning. Sometimes, she wondered if this was her own failure rather than
his, if perhaps she lacked a certain strength that would compel him to
include her in his pain.

Okeoma visited to pay condolences.

'I heard what happened,' he said, when Olanna opened the door.
She hugged him and looked at the jagged, swollen scar that ran from
his chin to his neck and thought how quickly it spread, news of death.

'He has not really spoken to me,' she said. 'What he says to me
makes no sense.'

'Odenigbo has never known how to be weak. Be patient with him.'
Okeoma spoke in a near whisper because Odenigbo had come out.
After they hugged and thumped each other's backs, Okeoma looked
at him.

'*Ndo*,' he said. 'Sorry.'

'I think she must have been surprised when they shot her,'

Odenigbo said. 'Mama never understood that we were really at war and that her life was in danger.'

Olanna stared at him.

'What has happened has happened,' Okeoma said. 'You must be strong.'

A short and shabby silence fell across the room.

'Julius brought some fresh palm wine,' Odenigbo said finally. 'You know, they mix in too much water these days, but this one is very good.'

'I'll drink that later. Where is that White Horse whisky you save for special occasions?'

'It is almost finished.'

'Then I will finish it,' Okeoma said.

Odenigbo brought the bottle and they sat in the living room, the radio turned low and the aroma of Ugwu's soup in the air.

'My commander drinks this like water,' Okeoma said, and shook the bottle to see how much was left.

'And how is he, your commander, the white-man mercenary?' Odenigbo asked.

Okeoma darted an apologetic glance at Olanna before he said, 'He throws girls on their backs in the open, where the men can see him, and does them, all the time holding his bag of money in one hand.' Okeoma drank from the bottle and scrunched up his face for a moment. 'We could easily have retaken Enugu if the man only listened, but he thinks he knows more about our own land than we do. He has started commandeering relief cars. He threatened His Excellency last week that he would leave if he doesn't get his balance.'

Okeoma took another swig from the bottle.

'Two days ago I went out in mufti and a ranger stopped me on the road and accused me of deserting. I warned him never to try that again or I would show him why we commandos are different from regular soldiers. I heard him laughing as I walked away. Imagine that! Before, he would never have dared to laugh at a commando. If we don't reorganize soon we will lose our credibility.'

'Why should white people be paid to fight our war anyway?' Odenigbo leaned back on the chair. 'There are many of us who can truly fight because we are willing to give ourselves for Biafra.'

Olanna stood up. 'Let's eat,' she said. 'I'm sorry our soup has no meat, Okeoma.'

'*I'm sorry our soup has no meat,*' Okeoma mimicked. 'Does this place look like a meat shop? I did not come looking for meat.'

Ugwu placed the plates of *garri* on the table.

'Please remove your grenade while we eat, Okeoma,' Olanna said.

He dislodged it from his waist and placed it in the corner. They ate in silence for a while, moulding their *garri* into balls, dipping in soup, swallowing.

'What is that scar?' Olanna asked.

'Oh, it's nothing,' Okeoma said, and ran his hand lightly over it. 'It looks more serious than it is.'

'You should join the Biafran Writers' League,' she said. 'You should be one of those going abroad to publicize our cause.'

Okeoma started to shake his head while Olanna was still speaking. 'I am a soldier,' he said.

'Do you still write?' Olanna asked.

He shook his head again.

'Do you have a poem for us, though? From your head?' she asked, and sounded desperate even to herself.

Okeoma swallowed a ball of *garri*, his Adam's apple bobbing up and down. 'No,' he said. He turned to Odenigbo. 'Did you hear what our shore batteries did to the vandals in the Onitsha sector?'

After lunch, Odenigbo went into the bedroom. Okeoma finished the whisky and then drank glass after glass of palm wine and fell asleep in the living room chair. His breathing was laboured; he mumbled and twice flayed his arms as if to shake some invisible attackers off. Olanna patted his shoulder to wake him up.

'*Kunie.* Come and lie down inside,' she said.

He opened reddened, bewildered eyes. 'No, no, I'm really not sleeping.'

'Look at you. You were gone.'

'Not at all.' Okeoma stifled a yawn. 'I do have a poem in my head.' He sat up and straightened his back and began to recite. He sounded different. In Nsukka, he had read his poetry dramatically, as though convinced that his art mattered more than anything else. Now he had a tone of unwilling banter, but still banter.

'*Brown
With the fish-glow sheen of a mermaid,
She appears,*

Bearing silver dawn;
And the sun attends her,
The mermaid
Who will never be mine.'

'Odenigbo would have said, "The voice of a generation!" ' Olanna said.

'What would you say?'

'The voice of a man.'

Okeoma smiled shyly, and she remembered how Odenigbo teased her about his being secretly infatuated with her. The poem was about her, and he had wanted her to know it. They sat in silence until his eyes began to close and soon his snoring became regular. She watched him and wondered what he was dreaming about. He was still sleeping, often mumbling and rolling his head from side to side, when Professor Achara arrived in the evening.

'Oh, your friend the commando is here,' he said. 'Please call Odenigbo. Let's go out to the veranda.'

They sat on the bench on the veranda. Professor Achara kept glancing down, clasping and unclasping his hands.

'I have come on a difficult matter,' he said.

Fear constricted Olanna's chest: something had happened to Kainene and they had sent Professor Achara to tell her. She wanted Professor Achara to leave right away without telling her, because what she did not know would not hurt her.

'What is it?' Odenigbo asked sharply.

'I have tried to make your landlord change his mind. I have done everything I can. But he refused. He wants you to pack out in two weeks.'

'I'm not sure I understand,' Odenigbo said.

But Olanna was sure he did. They were being asked to move out of the house because the landlord had found somebody who would pay him twice or perhaps three times the rent.

'I'm so sorry, Odenigbo. He is usually a most reasonable man, but I suppose the times have taken away a bit of our reason.'

Odenigbo sighed.

'I will help find another place,' Professor Achara said.

*   *   *

They were lucky to find one room, now that Umuahia was thronged with refugees. The long strip of a building had nine rooms, side by side, with doors that led out onto a narrow veranda. The kitchen was at one end and the bathroom at the other, next to a grove of banana trees. Their room was closer to the bathroom and, on the first day, Olanna looked at it and could not imagine how she would *live* here with Odenigbo and Baby and Ugwu, eat and dress and make love in a single room. Odenigbo set about separating their sleeping area with a thin curtain, and afterwards Olanna looked at the sagging string he had tied to nails on the wall, remembered Uncle Mbaezi and Aunty Ifeka's room in Kano, and began to cry.

'We'll get something better soon,' Odenigbo said, and she nodded and did not tell him that she was not crying about their room.

Mama Oji lived next door. She had a hard face and blinked so rarely that Olanna was disconcerted by her wide-eyed stare the first time they spoke.

'Welcome, *nno*,' she said. 'Your husband is not here?'

'He's at work,' Olanna said.

'I wanted to see him before the others do; it is about my children.'

'Your children?'

'The landlord called him doctor.'

'Oh, no. He has a doctorate.'

Mama Oji's cool, uncomprehending eyes drilled holes into Olanna.

'He is a doctor of books', Olanna said, 'not a doctor for sick people.'

'Oh.' Mama Oji's expression did not change. 'My children have asthma. Three have died since the war started. Three are left.'

'Sorry. *Ndo*,' Olanna said.

Mama Oji shrugged and then told her that all the neighbours were accomplished thieves. If she left a container of kerosene in the kitchen, it would be empty when she came out. If she left her soap in the bathroom it would walk away. If she hung out her clothes and did not keep an eye on them, they would fly off the lines.

'Be very careful,' she said. 'And lock your door even when you are just going to urinate.'

Olanna thanked her and wished, for her sake, that Odenigbo really was a medical doctor. She thanked the other neighbours who came to the door to greet and gossip. There were too many people in the yard; a family of sixteen lived in the room next to Mama Oji. The bathroom floor was slimy with too much dirt washed off too many bodies, and the toilet was thick with the smells of strangers. On humid evenings when the odours sat heavy in the moist air, Olanna longed for a fan, for electricity. Their house in the other part of town had had electricity until 8 p.m., but here in the interior, there was none. She bought oil lamps made from milk tins. Whenever Ugwu lit them, Baby squealed and ran back at the leap of naked flame. Olanna watched her, grateful that Baby did not look at yet another move, yet another new life, with any confusion at all; that instead she played with her new friend Adanna every day, shouting 'Take cover!' and laughing and hiding among the banana leaves to avoid imaginary planes. Olanna worried, though, that Baby would pick up Adanna's bush Umuahia accent or some disease from the liquid-looking boils on Adanna's arms or fleas from Adanna's scrawny dog Bingo.

The first day Olanna and Ugwu cooked in the kitchen, Adanna's mother came in and held out an enamel bowl and said, 'Please, give me small soup.'

'No, we don't have enough,' Olanna said. Then she thought of Adanna's only dress, which was made from the sack used to package relief food so that FLOU was plastered on her back, with the R swallowed into the seam, and she scooped some of the thin, meatless soup into the enamel bowl. The next day, Mama Adanna came in and asked for small *garri*, and Olanna gave her half a cup. The third day, she came in when the kitchen was full of other women and again asked Olanna for soup.

'Stop giving her your food!' Mama Oji screamed. 'This is what she does with every new tenant. She should go and farm cassava and feed her family and stop disturbing people! After all, she is an indigene of Umuahia! She is not a refugee like us! How can she be begging a refugee for food?' Mama Oji hissed loudly and then continued to pound palm fruit in her mortar. The efficient set to her fleshless face fascinated Olanna. She had never seen Mama Oji smile.

'But is it not you refugees who have finished all our food?' Mama Adanna said.

'Shut up your stinking mouth!' Mama Oji said. And Mama Adanna promptly did, as if she knew there was no way she could outshout Mama Oji, with her shrill swiftness, the way she never lacked for words or the speed with which to say them.

In the evenings, when Mama Oji fought with her husband, her voice tore across the yard. 'You castrated sheep! You call yourself a man, and yet you deserted the army! Let me just hear you tell anybody again that you were wounded in battle! Just open that dirty mouth one more time, and I will go and call the soldiers and show them where you have been hiding!'

Her tirade was a staple of the yard. So was Pastor Ambrose's loud praying as he walked up and down. So was the piano playing from the room right next to the kitchen. Olanna was startled when she first heard the melancholy tones, music so pure and so confidently played that it charged the air and held the swaying banana trees still.

'That is Alice,' Mama Oji said. 'She came here when Enugu fell. She was not even talking to anybody before. At least now she responds to greetings. She lives alone in that room. She never comes out and she never cooks. Nobody knows what she eats. The other time when we went combing, she felt too big to join us. Everybody else in the compound came out and went into the bushes and looked for vandals hiding there, but she did not come out. Some of the women even said they would report her to the militia.'

The music still floated out. It sounded like Beethoven, but Olanna was not certain. Odenigbo would know. Then the tones changed to something faster, with an angry urgency that soared higher and higher until it stopped. Alice came out of her room. She was small-boned, petite, and Olanna felt gawkily overgrown just looking at her; there was something childlike about her light-skinned, almost translucent complexion and tiny hands.

'Good evening,' Olanna said. 'I'm Olanna. We just moved into that room.'

'Welcome. I've seen your daughter.' Alice's handshake was a weak clasp, as if she handled herself with much care, as if she would never scrub herself too vigorously.

'You play so well,' Olanna said.

'Oh, no, I'm no good.' Alice shook her head. 'Where did you come from?'

'Nsukka University. And you?'

Alice hesitated. 'I came from Enugu.'

'We had friends there. Did you know anybody in the Nigerian College of Arts?'

'Oh, the bathroom is free.' She turned and hurried away. Her abruptness surprised Olanna. When she came out, she walked past with a vague nod and went into her room. Soon, Olanna heard the piano, something stretched out and slow, and she felt a desire to walk across and open Alice's door and watch her play.

She thought often about Alice, the delicate quality to her smallness and fairness, the incredible strength of her piano playing. When she gathered Baby and Adanna and a few other children in the compound and read to them, she hoped Alice would come out and join her. She wondered whether Alice liked High Life. She wanted to talk about music and art and politics with Alice. But Alice came out of her room only to hurry to the bathroom and did not respond when Olanna knocked on her door. 'I must have been asleep,' she would say later, but would not ask Olanna to come by another time.

Finally, they met again in the market. It was just after dawn and the air was heavy with dew and Olanna wandered around in the damp coolness, under the green foliage of the forest, sidestepping thick roots. She haggled quietly, consistently, with a hawker before she bought cassava tubers with pinkish skin that she had once thought were poisonous, because the pink was so bright, until Mrs Muokelu assured her they were not. A bird cawed from a tree above. Once in a while, a leaf would flutter down. She stood before a table with greying pieces of raw chicken and imagined grabbing them and running away as fast as she could. If she bought the chicken, it would be all she would buy. So she bought four medium-sized snails instead. The smaller, spiral-shelled snails were cheaper, piled high in baskets, but she could not buy them, could not think of them as food; they had always been, to her, playthings for village children. She was leaving when she saw Alice.

'Good morning, Alice,' she said.

'Good morning,' Alice said.

Olanna made to hug her, the usual brief greeting hug, but Alice extended her hand for a formal shake as though they were not neighbours.

'I cannot find salt anywhere, no salt at all,' Alice said. 'And the people who put us in this thing have all the salt they want.'

Olanna was surprised; of course she would not find salt here; there was hardly salt anywhere. Alice looked precise and petite in a neatly belted wool dress that Olanna imagined hanging in a London shop. Nothing like a Biafran woman in a forest market at dawn.

'They said the Nigerians have been bombing and bombing Uli and no relief plane has been able to land in a week,' Alice said.

'Yes, I heard,' Olanna said. 'Are you going home?'

Alice looked away, towards the thick wood. 'Not right away.'

'I'll wait for you so we can walk back together.'

'No, don't bother,' Alice said. 'Bye-bye.'

Alice turned and walked back to the cluster of stalls, her gait dainty and contrived, as though a misguided person had taught her how to walk 'like a lady'. Olanna stood watching her, wondering what lay underneath her surface, before she headed home. She stopped by the relief centre to see if there was any food, if a plane had finally managed to land. The compound was deserted and she peered through the locked gate for a while. A half-torn poster was nailed to the wall. Somebody had run charcoal over the WCC: WORLD COUNCIL OF CHURCHES and scribbled WCC: WAR CAN CONTINUE.

She was close to the corn-grinding station when a woman ran out of a roadside house, crying, following two soldiers who were pulling a tall boy along with them. 'I said you should take me!' she screamed. 'Take me instead! Have we not sacrificed Abuchi to you people already?' The soldiers ignored her and the boy kept his posture straight-backed, as if he could not trust himself to look back at his mother.

Olanna stood aside as they passed and, back home, she was furious to see Ugwu standing in front of the yard, talking to some elderly neighbours. Any soldier on a conscripting mission could see him there.

'*Bia nwoke m*, is something wrong with your head? Haven't I told you not to be out here?' she asked him in a hiss.

Ugwu took her basket and mumbled, 'Sorry, mah.'

'Where is Baby?'

'In Adanna's room.'

'Give me the key.'

'Master is inside, mah.'

Olanna glanced at her watch although she did not need to. It was too early for Odenigbo to be home. He was sitting on their bed, his back hunched, his shoulders heaving silently.

'*O gini?* What happened?' she asked.

'Nothing happened.'

She went to him. '*Ebezi na*, stop crying,' she murmured. But she did not want him to stop. She wanted him to cry and cry until he dislodged the pain that clogged his throat, until he rinsed away his sullen grief. She cradled him, wrapped her arms around him, and slowly he relaxed against her. His arms circled her. His sobs became audible. With each intake of breath, they reminded her of Baby; he cried like his daughter.

'I never did enough for Mama,' he said finally.

'It's okay,' she murmured. She, too, wished she had tried harder with his mother before settling for easy resentment. There was so much she would take back if she could.

'We never *actively* remember death,' Odenigbo said. 'The reason we live as we do is because we do not remember that *we will die*. We will all die.'

'Yes,' Olanna said; there was a slump to his shoulders.

'But perhaps it is the whole point of being alive? That life is a state of death denial?' he asked.

Olanna cradled him closer.

'I've been thinking of the army, *nkem*,' he said. 'Maybe I should join His Excellency's new S-brigade.'

Olanna said nothing for a while. She felt the urge to yank at his new beard and pull out hair and draw blood. 'You might as well find a sturdy tree and a rope, Odenigbo, because that's an easier way to commit suicide,' she said.

He moved back to look at her, but she kept her gaze averted and got up and turned on the radio and increased the volume, filling the room with the sound of a Beatles song; she would no longer discuss this desire to join the army.

'We should build a bunker,' he said, and went to the door. 'Yes, we certainly need a bunker here.'

The flat glassiness in his eyes, the slump to his shoulders, worried her. If he had to do something, though, better he build a bunker than join the army.

Outside, he was talking to Papa Oji and some of the other men who were standing by the compound entrance.

'Don't you see those banana trees?' Papa Oji asked. 'All the air raids we have had, we went there, and nothing happened to us. We don't need a bunker. Banana trees absorb bullets and bombs.'

Odenigbo's eyes were as cold as his response. 'What does an army deserter know about bunkers?'

He left the men and, moments later, he and Ugwu started to map out and dig an area behind the building. Soon, the young men joined in the work and, when the sun fell, the older ones did too, including

Papa Oji. Olanna watched them work and wondered what they thought of Odenigbo. When the other men cracked jokes and laughed, he did not. He spoke only about the work. No, *mba*, move it farther down. Yes, let's hold it there. No, shift it a little. His sweaty singlet clung to his body and she noticed, for the first time, how much weight he had lost, how shrunken his chest looked.

That night, she lay with her cheek against his. He had not told her what made him stay home to cry for his mother. She hoped, though, that whatever it was would loosen some of the knots that had tightened inside him. She kissed his neck, his ear, in the way that always made him pull her close on the nights that Ugwu slept out on the veranda. But he shrugged her hand off and said, 'I'm tired, *nkem.*' She had never heard him say that before. He smelt of old sweat, and she felt a sudden piercing longing for that Old Spice left behind in Nsukka.

Even the miracle of Abagana did not loosen his knots. Before, they would have celebrated it as if it were a personal triumph. They would have held each other and kissed and she would have tickled her cheek with his new beard. But when they heard the first radio announcement, he simply said, 'Excellent, excellent', and later he watched the dancing neighbours with a blank expression.

Mama Oji started the song, *'Onye ga-enwe mmeri?'* and the other women responded *'Biafra ga-enwe mmeri, igba!'* and formed a circle and swayed with graceful motions and stamped down hard as they said *igba!* Billows of dust rose and fell. Olanna joined them, buoyed by the words – *Who will win? Biafra will win, igba!* – and wishing Odenigbo would not just sit there with that empty expression.

'Olanna dances like white people!' Mama Oji said, laughing. 'Her buttocks do not move at all!'

It was the first time Olanna had seen Mama Oji laugh. The men were telling and retelling the story – some said the Biafran forces had laid ambush and set fire to a column of one hundred vehicles, while others said there had in fact been a thousand destroyed armoured cars and trucks – but they all agreed that if the convoy had reached its destination, Biafra would have been finished. Radios were turned on loud, placed on the veranda in front of the rooms. The news was broadcast over and over, and each time it ended, many of the neighbours joined the voice intoning, *To save Biafra for the free world is a task that must be done!* Even Baby knew the words. She repeated them while patting Bingo's head. Alice was the only neighbour who had not come out, and Olanna wondered what she was doing.

'Alice thinks she is too good for all of us in this yard,' Mama Oji said. 'Look at you. Did they not say that you are a Big Man's daughter? But you treat people like people. Who does she think she is?'

'Maybe she's asleep.'

'Asleep indeed. That Alice is a saboteur. It is on her face. She is working for the vandals.'

'Since when have saboteurs had it written on their faces?' Olanna asked, amused.

Mama Oji shrugged, as though she would not bother convincing Olanna of something she was sure of.

Professor Ezeka's driver arrived hours later when the yard was emptier and quieter. He handed Olanna a note and then went around and opened the boot and carried out two cartons. Ugwu hurried indoors with them.

'Thank you,' Olanna said. 'Greet your master.'

'Yes, mah.' He stood there still.

'Is there anything else?'

'Please, mah, I am to wait until you check that everything is complete.'

'Oh.' Ezeka's crabbed handwriting had listed all he had sent on the front of the sheet. *Please make sure the driver has not tampered with anything* was scrawled at the back. Olanna went inside to count the cans of dried milk, tea, biscuits, Ovaltine, sardines, the cartons of sugar, the bags of salt – and she could not help the gasp when she saw the toilet tissue. At least Baby would not have to use old newspapers for a while. She wrote a quick, effusive thank-you note and gave it to the driver; if Ezeka had done this to further show how superior he was, it did not dampen her pleasure. Ugwu's pleasure seemed even greater than hers.

'This is like Nsukka, mah!' he said. 'Look at the sardines!'

'Please put some salt in a bag. A quarter of that packet.'

'Mah? For who?' Ugwu looked suspicious.

'For Alice. And don't tell the neighbours what we have. If they ask, say an old friend sent books to your master.'

'Yes, mah.'

Olanna felt Ugwu's disapproving eyes following her as she took the bag over to Alice's room. There was no response to her knock. She had turned to walk away when Alice opened the door.

'A friend of ours brought us some provisions,' Olanna said, holding out the bag of salt.

'*Hei!* I can't take all of this,' Alice said, as she reached out and took it. 'Thank you. Oh, thank you so much!'

'We haven't seen him in a while. It came as a surprise.'

'And you are bothering with me. You shouldn't have.' Alice was clutching the bag of salt to her chest. Her eyes were darkly shadowed, traces of green veins crawled just underneath her pale skin, and Olanna wondered if she was sick.

But Alice looked different, fresher-skinned, in the evening, when she came outside and sat next to Olanna on the floor of the veranda and stretched out her legs. Perhaps she had put on some powder. Her feet were tiny. She smelt of a familiar body cream. Mama Adanna walked past and said, 'Eh! Alice, we have never seen you sitting outside before!' and Alice's lips moved slightly in a smile. Pastor Ambrose was praying by the banana trees. His red, long-sleeved robe shimmered in the waning sun. 'Holy Jehovah destroy the vandals with holy-ghost fire! Holy Jehovah fight for us!'

'God is fighting for Nigeria,' Alice said. 'God always fights for the side that has more arms.'

'God is on our side!' Olanna surprised herself by how sharp she sounded. Alice looked taken aback and, from somewhere behind the house, Bingo howled.

'I only think that God fights with the just side,' Olanna added gently.

Alice slapped away a mosquito. 'Ambrose is pretending to be a pastor to avoid the army.'

'Yes, he is.' Olanna smiled. 'Do you know that strange church on Ogui Road in Enugu? He looks like one of those pastors.'

'I am not really from Enugu.' Alice drew up her knees. 'I am from Asaba. I left after I finished at the Teacher Training College there and went to Lagos. I was working in Lagos before the war. I met an army colonel and in a few months he asked me to marry him, but he did not tell me that he was already married and his wife was abroad. I got pregnant. He kept postponing going to Asaba to do the traditional ceremonies. But I believed him when he said that he was busy and under pressure with all that was happening in the country. After they killed the Igbo officers, he escaped and I came to Enugu with him. I had my baby in Enugu. I was with him in Enugu when his wife came back just before the war started and he left me. Then my baby died. Then Enugu fell. So here I am.'

'I'm so sorry.'

'I am a stupid woman. I am the one who believed all his lies.'

'Don't say that.'

'You are lucky. You have your husband and daughter. I don't know how you do it, keeping everything together and teaching children and all that. I wish I were like you.'

Alice's admiration warmed and surprised her. 'There is nothing special about me,' Olanna said.

Pastor Ambrose was getting frenzied. 'Devil, I shoot you! Satan, I bomb you!'

'How did you manage evacuating Nsukka?' Alice asked. 'Did you lose much?'

'Everything. We left in a rush.'

'It was the same for me in Enugu. I don't know why they will never tell us the truth so we can prepare. The people in the Ministry of Information took their public-address van all over the city telling us everything was okay, it was only our boys practising with the shelling. If they had told us the truth, many of us would have been better prepared and would not have lost so much.'

'But you brought your piano.' Olanna didn't like the way Alice said *they*, as if she was not on their side.

'It is the only thing I took from Enugu. He sent me money and a van to help me on the very day Enugu fell. His guilty conscience was working overtime. The driver told me later that he and his wife had moved their own things to their hometown some weeks before. Imagine!'

'Do you know where he is now?'

'I don't want to know. If I see that man again, *ezi okwu m*, I will kill him with my own hands.' Alice raised her tiny hands. She was speaking Igbo for the first time, and in her Asaba dialect, the *F*'s sounded like *W*'s. 'When I think of what I went through for that man. I gave up my job in Lagos, I kept telling lies to my family, and I cut off my friends who told me he was not serious.' She bent down to pick up something from the sand. 'And he could not even do.'

'What?'

'He would jump on top of me, moan *oh-oh-oh* like a goat, and that was it.' She raised her finger. 'With something this small. And afterwards he would smile happily without ever wondering if I had known when he started and stopped. Men! Men are hopeless!'

'No, not all of them. My husband knows how to do, and with something like this.' Olanna raised a clenched fist. They laughed and she sensed, between them, a vulgar and delicious female bond.

Olanna waited for Odenigbo to come home so that she could tell him about her new friendship with Alice, about what she had told Alice. She wanted him to come home and pull her forcefully to him in the way he had not done in a long time. But when he did come home from Tanzania Bar, it was with a gun. The double-barrelled gun, long and black and dull, lay on the bed. '*Gini bu ife a?* What is this?' Olanna asked.

'Somebody at the directorate gave it to me. It's quite old. But it's good to have just in case.'

'I don't want a gun here.'

'We're fighting a war. There are guns everywhere.' He slipped out of his trousers and tied a wrapper around his waist before he took his shirt off.

'I talked to Alice today.'

'Alice?'

'The neighbour that plays the piano.'

'Oh, yes.' He was staring at the separating curtain.

'You look tired,' she said. What she wanted to say was, *You look sad.* If only he was better occupied, if only he had something to do in which the moments of grief that sneaked up on him could be immersed.

'I'm fine,' he said.

'I think you should go and see Ezeka. Ask him to help move you somewhere else. Even if it isn't his directorate, he must have some influence with the other directors.'

Odenigbo hung his trousers on a nail in the wall.

'Did you hear me?' Olanna asked.

'I won't ask Ezeka.'

She recognized his expression: He was disappointed. She had

forgotten that they had high ideals. They were people of principle; they did not ask favours of highly placed friends.

'You can serve Biafra better if you work somewhere else where you can use your brain and talent,' she said.

'I'm serving Biafra well enough at the Manpower Directorate.'

Olanna glanced at the clutter that was their room and home – the bed, two yam tubers, and the mattress that leaned against the dirt-smeared wall, the cartons and bags piled in a corner, the kerosene stove that she took to the kitchen only when it was needed – and felt a surge of revulsion, the urge to run and run and run until she was far away from it all.

They slept with their backs turned to each other. He was gone when she woke up. She touched his side of the bed, ran her hand over it, savoured the last of the rumpled warmth that lingered on the sheet. She would go and see Ezeka herself. She would ask him to do something for Odenigbo. She went outside to the bathroom, saying 'Good morning' and 'Did you come out well this morning?' to some neighbours as she went. Baby was with the younger children, crowded near the banana trees, listening to Papa Oji telling a story of how he shot down an enemy plane in Calabar with his pistol. The older children were sweeping the yard and singing.

> *Biafra, kunie, buso Nigeria agha,*
> *Anyi emelie ndi awusa,*
> *Ndi na-amaro chukwu,*
> *Tigbue fa, zogbue fa,*
> *Nwelu nwude Gowon.*

When their singing stopped, Pastor Ambrose's morning prayers sounded even louder. 'God bless His Excellency! God give Tanzania and Gabon strength! God destroy Nigeria and Britain and Egypt and Algeria and Russia! In the mighty name of Jesus!'

Some people shouted *Amen!* from their rooms. Pastor Ambrose held his Bible up, as if some solid miracle would fall on it from the sky, and shouted nonsensical words: *she baba she baba she baba.*

'Stop babbling, Pastor Ambrose, and go and join the army! How is your speaking-in-tongues helping our cause?' Mama Oji said. She was in front of her room with her son, his cloth-covered head bent over a steaming bowl. When he raised his head to get a breath of air,

Olanna looked at the concoction of urine and oils and herbs and God knew what else that Mama Oji had decided was the cure for asthma.

'Was the night bad for him?' she asked Mama Oji.

Mama Oji shrugged. 'It was bad but not too bad.' She turned to her son. 'Do you want me to slap you before you inhale it? Why are you letting the thing evaporate and waste?'

He bent his head over the bowl again.

'Jehovah destroy Gowon and Adekunle!' Pastor Ambrose screamed.

'Be quiet and join the army!' Mama Oji said.

Somebody shouted from one of the rooms. 'Mama Oji, leave Pastor alone! First let your husband go back to the army he ran away from!'

'At least he went!' Mama Oji's retort was swift. 'While your own husband lives the shivering life of a coward in the forest of Ohafia so that the soldiers will not see him.'

Baby came around from behind the house; the dog trailed behind her. 'Mummy Ola! Bingo can see spirits. When he barks at night it means he sees spirits.'

'There are no such things as spirits, Baby,' Olanna said.

'Yes, there are.'

It troubled Olanna, the things Baby was picking up here. 'Did Adanna tell you that?'

'No, Chukwudi told me.'

'Where is Adanna?'

'She's sleeping. She's sick,' Baby said, and began to shoo away the flies that circled over Bingo's head.

Mama Oji muttered, 'I have been telling Mama Adanna that the child's illness is not malaria. But she keeps giving her neem medicine that does nothing for her. If nobody else will say it, then I will: What Adanna has is Harold Wilson Syndrome, *ho-ha*.'

'Harold Wilson Syndrome?'

'Kwashiorkor. The child has kwashiorkor.'

Olanna burst out laughing. She did not know they had renamed kwashiorkor after the British prime minister, but her amusement dissipated when she went to Adanna's room. Adanna was lying on a mat, her eyes half-closed. Olanna touched her face with the back of a palm, to check for a fever, although she knew there would be none. She should have realized it earlier; Adanna's belly was swollen and her skin was a sickly tone, much lighter than it was only weeks ago.

'This malaria is very stubborn,' Mama Adanna said.

'She has kwashiorkor,' Olanna said quietly.

'Kwashiorkor,' Mama Adanna repeated, and looked at Olanna with frightened eyes.

'You need to find crayfish or milk.'

'Milk, *kwa?* From where?' Mama Adanna asked. 'But we have anti-kwash nearby. Mama Obike was telling me the other day. Let me go and get some.'

'What?'

'Anti-kwashiorkor leaves,' Mama Adanna said, already on her way out.

Olanna was surprised by how quickly she hitched up her wrapper and began to wade into the bush on the other side of the road. She came back moments later holding a bunch of slender green leaves. 'I will cook porridge now,' she said.

'Adanna needs milk,' Olanna said. 'Those won't cure kwashiorkor.'

'Leave Mama Adanna alone. The anti-kwash leaves will work as long as she does not boil them for too long,' Mama Oji said. 'Besides, the relief centres have nothing. And did you not hear that all the children in Nnewi died after drinking relief milk? The vandals had poisoned it.'

Olanna called Baby and took her inside and undressed her.

'Ugwu already gave me a bath,' Baby said, looking puzzled.

'Yes, yes, my baby,' Olanna said, examining her carefully. Her skin was still the dark colour of mahogany and her hair was still black and, although she was thinner, her belly was not swollen. Olanna wished so much that the relief centre was open and that Okoromadu was still there, but he had moved to Orlu after the World Council of Churches gave his job to one of the many pastors who no longer had parishes.

Mama Adanna was cooking the leaves in the kitchen. Olanna took a tin of sardines and some dried milk from the carton Ezeka sent and gave them to her. 'Don't tell anybody I gave you this. Give it to Adanna little by little.'

Mama Adanna grasped Olanna. 'Thank you, thank you, thank you. I will not tell anybody.'

But she did tell because, as Olanna left for Professor Ezeka's office later, Mama Oji called out, 'My son has asthma and milk will not kill him!'

Olanna ignored her.

*　　*　　*

She walked to the major road and stood under a tree. Each time a car drove past, she tried to flag it down. A soldier in a rusty station wagon stopped. She saw the leer in his eyes even before she climbed in beside him, so she exaggerated her English accent, certain that he did not understand all she said, and spoke throughout the drive about the cause and mentioned that her car and driver were at the mechanic. He said very little until he dropped her off at the directorate building. He did not know who she was or who she knew.

Professor Ezeka's hawk-faced secretary slowly looked at Olanna, from her carefully brushed wig to her shoes, and said, 'He's not in!'

'Then ring him right now and tell him I am waiting. My name is Olanna Ozobia.'

The secretary looked surprised. 'What?'

'Do I need to say it again?' Olanna asked. 'I'm sure Prof will want to hear about this. Where shall I sit while you ring him?'

The secretary stared at her and Olanna stared back steadily. Then she mutely gestured to a chair and picked up the phone. A half hour later, Professor Ezeka's driver came in to take her to his house, tucked onto a hidden dirt road.

'I thought a VIP like you would live in the Government Reserved Area, Prof,' Olanna said, after she greeted him.

'Oh, certainly not. It's too obvious a target for bombings.' He had not changed. His fastidious sense of superiority lined his voice as he waved her in and asked her to wait for him while he finished up in his study.

Olanna had seen little of Mrs Ezeka in Nsukka; she was timid and barely educated, the kind of wife his village had found him, Odenigbo had said once. Olanna struggled to hide her surprise, then, when Mrs Ezeka came out and hugged her twice in the spacious living room.

'It's so nice to see old friends! Our socializing these days is so official, this government-house event today and another one tomorrow.' Mrs Ezeka's gold pendant hung low on a chain around her neck. 'Pamela! Come and greet Aunty.'

The little girl who came out holding a doll was older than Baby, perhaps about eight years old. She had her mother's fat-cheeked face, and the pink satin ribbons in her hair swayed.

'Good afternoon,' she said. She was undressing her doll, prising the skirt off the plastic body.

'How are you?' Olanna asked.

'Fine, thank you.'

Olanna sank into a plush red sofa. A dollhouse, with tiny, exquisite doll plates and teacups, was set out on the centre table.

'What will you drink?' Mrs Ezeka asked brightly. 'I remember Odenigbo loved his brandy. We do have some rather good brandy.'

Olanna looked at Mrs Ezeka. She could not possibly remember what Odenigbo drank because she had never visited in the evenings with her husband.

'I'd like some cold water, please,' Olanna said.

'Just cold water?' Mrs Ezeka asked. 'Anyway, we can have something else after lunch. Steward!'

The steward appeared right away, as if he had been standing by the door. 'Bring cold water and Coke,' Mrs Ezeka said.

Pamela began to whine, still tugging at the doll's clothes.

'Come, come, let me do it for you,' Mrs Ezeka said. She turned to Olanna. 'She's so restless now. You see, we should have gone abroad last week. The two older ones have gone. His Excellency gave us permission ages ago. We were supposed to leave on a relief plane, but none of them landed. They said there were too many Nigerian bombers. Can you imagine? Yesterday, we waited in Uli, inside that unfinished building they call a terminal, for more than two hours and no plane landed. But hopefully we'll leave on Sunday. We will fly to Gabon and then on to England – on our Nigerian passports, of course! The British have refused to recognize Biafra!' Her laughter filled Olanna with a resentment as fine, as painful, as the prick of a new pin.

The steward brought the water on a silver tray.

'Are you sure that water is properly cold?' Mrs Ezeka asked. 'Was it in the new freezer or the old one?'

'The new one, mah, like you tell me.'

'Will you eat cake, Olanna?' Mrs Ezeka asked, after the steward left. 'We made it today.'

'No, thank you.'

Professor Ezeka came in holding some files. 'Is that all you're drinking? Water?'

'Your house is surreal,' Olanna said.

'What a choice of words, *surreal*,' Professor Ezeka said.

'Odenigbo is very unhappy in his directorate. Can you help transfer him somewhere else?' The words moved slowly out of Olanna's mouth and she realized how much she hated to ask, how much she wanted to get it over with and leave this house with the red rug and the matching red sofas and the television set and the fruity scent of Mrs Ezeka's perfume.

'Everything is tight now, really, very tight,' Professor Ezeka said. 'Requests pour in from everywhere.' He sat down, placed the files on his lap, and crossed his legs. 'But I'll see what I can do.'

'Thank you,' Olanna said. 'And thank you again for the provisions.'

'Have some cake,' Mrs Ezeka said.

'No, I don't want any cake.'

'Maybe after lunch.'

Olanna stood up. 'I can't stay for lunch. I must go. I teach some children in the yard and I told them to come in an hour's time.'

'Oh, how lovely,' Mrs Ezeka said, walking her to the door. 'If only I wasn't going overseas so soon, we would have done something together, too, for the win-the-war effort.'

Olanna forced her lips to form a smile.

'The driver will take you back,' Professor Ezeka said.

'Thank you,' Olanna said.

Before she climbed into the car, Mrs Ezeka asked her to come to the back and see the new bunker her husband had had built; it was concrete, sturdy.

'Imagine what these vandals have reduced us to. Pamela and I sometimes sleep here when they bomb us,' Mrs Ezeka said. 'But we shall survive.'

'Yes,' Olanna said and stared at the smooth floor and two beds, a furnished underground room.

When she got back to the yard, Baby was crying. Mucus ran thinly down her nose.

'They ate Bingo,' Baby said.

'What?'

'Adanna's mummy ate Bingo.'

'Ugwu, what happened?' Olanna asked, taking Baby in her arms.

Ugwu shrugged. 'That is what the people in the yard are saying. Mama Adanna took the dog out some time ago and does not answer when they ask her where it is. And she has just cooked her soup with meat.'

Olanna hushed Baby, wiped her eyes and nose, and thought for a moment about the dog with its head full of sores.

Kainene came in the middle of a hot afternoon. Olanna was in the kitchen soaking some dried cassava in water when Mama Oji called, 'There is a woman in a car asking for you!'

Olanna hurried out and stopped when she saw her sister standing near the banana trees. She looked elegant in a knee-length tan dress.

'Kainene!' Olanna extended her arms slightly, uncertainly, and Kainene moved forwards; their embrace was brief, their bodies barely touching before Kainene stepped back.

'I went to your old house and somebody told me to come here.'

'Our landlord kicked us out, we were not good for business.' Olanna laughed at her poor joke, although Kainene did not laugh. Kainene was peering into the room. Olanna wished so much that Kainene had come when they were still in a house, wished she did not feel so painfully self-conscious.

'Come in and sit down.'

Olanna dragged the bench in from the veranda and Kainene looked warily at it before she sat down and placed her hands on the leather bag that was the same earth-brown shade as her coiffed wig. Olanna raised the dividing curtain and sat on the bed and smoothed her wrapper. They did not look at each other. The silence was charged with things unsaid.

'So how have you been?' Olanna asked, finally.

'Things were normal until Port Harcourt fell. I was an army contractor, and I had a licence to import stockfish. I'm in Orlu now. I'm in charge of a refugee camp there.'

'Oh.'

'Are you silently condemning me for profiteering from the war? Somebody had to import the stockfish, you know.' Kainene raised her eyebrows; they were pencilled in, thin, fluid arcs. 'Many contractors were paid and didn't deliver. At least I did.'

'No, no, I wasn't thinking that at all.'

'You were.'

Olanna looked away. There were too many things swirling around in her head. 'I was so worried when Port Harcourt fell. I sent messages.'

'I got the letter you sent to Madu.' Kainene rearranged the straps of her handbag. 'You said you were teaching. Do you still? Your noble win-the-war effort?'

'The school is a refugee centre now. I sometimes teach the children in the yard.'

'And how is the revolutionary husband?'

'He's still with the Manpower Directorate.'

'You don't have a wedding photo.'

'There was an air raid during our reception. The photographer threw his camera down.'

Kainene nodded, as if there were no need to feel sympathy at this news. She opened her bag. 'I came to give you this. Mum sent it through a British journalist.'

Olanna held the envelope in her hand, unsure whether to open it in front of Kainene.

'I also brought two dresses for Baby,' Kainene said, and gestured to the bag she had placed on the floor. 'A woman who came back from São Tomé had some good children's clothes for sale.'

'You bought clothes for Baby?'

'How shocking, indeed. And it's about time the girl began to be called Chiamaka. This Baby business is tiresome.'

Olanna laughed.

To think that her sister was sitting across from her, that her sister had come to visit her, that her sister had brought clothes for her child. 'Will you drink water? It's all we have.'

'No, I'm fine.' Kainene got up and walked to the wall, where the mattress leaned, and then came back and sat down. 'You didn't know my steward, Ikejide, did you?'

'Isn't he the one Maxwell brought from his hometown?'

'Yes.' Kainene got up again. 'He was killed in Port Harcourt. They were bombing and shelling us, and a piece of shrapnel cut off his head, completely beheaded him, and his body kept running. His body kept running and it didn't have a head.'

'Oh, God.'

'I saw him.'

Olanna got up and sat next to Kainene on the bench and put an arm around her. Kainene smelt of home. They said nothing for long minutes.

'I thought about changing your money for you,' Kainene said. 'But you can do it at the bank and then deposit, can't you?'

'Haven't you seen the bomb craters all around the bank? My money is staying under my bed.'

'Make sure the cockroaches don't get to it. Life is harder for them these days.' Kainene leaned against Olanna and then, as if she had suddenly remembered something, she got up and straightened her dress; Olanna felt the slow sadness of missing a person who was still there.

'Goodness. I didn't know how much time had passed,' Kainene said.

'Will you visit again?'

There was a pause before Kainene said, 'I spend most of the day at the refugee camp. Maybe you can come and see it.' She fumbled for a piece of paper in her handbag and wrote down the directions to her house.

'Yes, I'll come. I'll come next Wednesday.'

'Will you drive?'

'No. Because of the soldiers. And we never have much petrol.'

'Greet the revolutionary for me.' Kainene climbed into the car and started it.

'Your number plates are different,' Olanna said, looking at the VIG printed before the numbers.

'I paid extra to stamp my patriotism on my car. Vigilance!' Kainene raised her eyebrows and a hand before she drove off. Olanna watched the Peugeot 404 disappear down the road and stood there for a while, feeling as if she had swallowed a sparkling sliver of light.

On Wednesday, Olanna arrived early. Harrison opened the door and stared, so surprised he seemed to have forgotten his usual bow. 'Madam, good morning! It is a long time!'

'How are you, Harrison?'

'Fine, madam,' he said, and bowed, finally.

Olanna sat on one of the two sofas in the bright and bare living room with flung-open windows. A radio was turned on high somewhere inside, and when she heard approaching footsteps, she forced her mouth to relax, not sure what she would say to Richard. But it was Kainene, in a rumpled black dress, holding her wig in her hand.

'Ejima m,' she said, hugging Olanna. Their embrace was close, their bodies pressed warmly against each other. 'I was hoping you would come in time so we could go together to the research centre first before the refugee camp. Will you have some rice? I didn't realize how long it's been since I ate rice until the relief people gave me a bag last week.'

'No, not now.' Olanna wanted to hold her sister for much longer, to smell that familiar scent of home.

'I was listening to Nigerian radio. Lagos says Chinese soldiers are fighting for us and Kaduna says every Igbo woman deserves to be raped,' Kainene said. 'Their imagination impresses me.'

'I never listen to them.'

'Oh, I listen more to Lagos and Kaduna than to Radio Biafra. You have to keep your enemy close.'

Harrison came in and bowed. 'Madam? I am bringing drinks?'

'The way he goes on you would think we had a grand cellar in this half-built house in the middle of nowhere,' Kainene muttered, combing her wig with her fingers.

'Madam?'

'No, Harrison, don't bring drinks. We're leaving now. Remember, lunch for two.'

'Yes, madam.'

Olanna wondered where Richard was.

'Harrison is the most pretentious peasant I have ever seen,' Kainene said, as she started the car. 'I know you don't like the word *peasant*.'

'No.'

'But he is, you know.'

'We are all peasants.'

'Are we? It's the sort of thing Richard would say.'

Olanna's throat felt instantly parched.

Kainene glanced at her. 'Richard left very early today. He's going to Gabon to visit the kwashiorkor centre next week and he said he needed to see to the arrangements. But I think he left so early because he felt awkward about seeing you.'

'Oh.' Olanna pursed her lips.

Kainene steered with a careless confidence, past potholes on the road, past palm trees stripped of fronds, past a thin soldier pulling along a thinner goat.

'Do you ever dream of that child's head in the calabash?' she asked.

Olanna looked out of the window and remembered the slanting lines crisscrossing the calabash, the white blankness of the child's eyes. 'I don't remember my dreams.'

'Grandpapa used to say, about difficulties he had gone through, "It did not kill me, it made me knowledgeable." *O gburo m egbu, o mee ka m malu ife.*'

'I remember.'

'There are some things that are so unforgivable that they make other things easily forgivable,' Kainene said.

There was a pause. Inside Olanna, something calcified leaped to life.

'Do you know what I mean?' Kainene asked.

'Yes.'

At the research centre, Kainene parked under a tree and Olanna waited in the car. She hurried back moments later. 'The man I want isn't there,' she said, and started the car. Olanna said nothing else until they arrived at the refugee camp. It was a primary school before the war. The buildings looked faded, most of the once-white paint peeled off. Some refugees who were standing outside stopped to stare at Olanna and to say *nno* to Kainene. A young, lean priest in a discoloured soutane came up to the car.

'Father Marcel, my twin sister, Olanna,' Kainene said.

The priest looked surprised. 'Welcome,' he said, and then added, unnecessarily, 'You are not identical.'

They stood under a flame tree while he told Kainene that the bag of crayfish had been delivered, that the Red Cross really had suspended relief flights, that Inatimi had come earlier with somebody else from the Biafran Organization of Freedom Fighters and said he would return later. Olanna watched Kainene speak. She did not hear much of what Kainene said, because she was thinking of how unrelenting Kainene's confidence was.

'Let's give you a tour,' Kainene said to Olanna, after Father Marcel left. 'I always start with the bunker.' Kainene showed her the bunker, a roughly dug pit covered with logs, before she began to walk towards the building at the far end of the compound. 'Now to the Point of No Return.'

Olanna followed. The smell hit her at the first door. It went straight from her nose to her stomach, turning it, churning the boiled yam she'd had for breakfast.

Kainene was watching her. 'You don't have to go in.'

'I want to,' Olanna said, because she felt she should. She didn't want to. She didn't know what the smell was but it was enlarging and she could almost see it, a foul, brown cloud. She felt faint. They went into the first classroom. About twelve people were lying on bamboo beds, on mats, on the floor. Not one of them reached out to slap away the fat flies. The only movement Olanna saw was that of a child sitting by the door: he unfolded and refolded his arms. His bones were clearly outlined and the wrap of his arms was flat, in a way that would be impossible if he had some flesh underneath the skin. Kainene scanned the room quickly and then turned to the door. Outside, Olanna gulped in air. In the second classroom, she felt that even the air inside her was becoming soiled and she wanted to press her nostrils shut to stop the mingling of the air outside and that inside her. A mother was sitting on the floor with two children lying next to her. Olanna could not tell how old they were. They were naked; the taut globes that were their bellies would not fit in a shirt anyway. Their buttocks and chests were collapsed into folds of rumpled skin. On their head, spurts of reddish hair. Olanna's eyes met their mother's steady stare and Olanna looked away quickly. She slapped a fly away from her face and thought how healthy all the flies looked, how alive, how vibrant.

'That woman is dead. We have to get her removed,' Kainene said.

'No!' Olanna blurted, because that woman with the steady stare could not be dead. But Kainene meant another woman, who lay face-down on the floor, with a thin baby clutching her back. Kainene walked over and plucked the baby away. She went outside and called out, 'Father! Father! One for burial,' and then sat on the steps outside and held the baby. The baby should have cried. Kainene was trying to force a soft, yeast-coloured pill into its mouth.

'What is that?' Olanna asked.

'Protein tablet. I'll give you some for Chiamaka. They taste horrible. I finally got the Red Cross to give me some last week. We don't have enough, of course, so I save them for the children. If I gave it to most of the people in there it would make no difference. But maybe it will for this baby. Maybe.'

'How many die a day?' Olanna asked.

Kainene looked down at the baby. 'His mother came from somewhere that fell very early. They had gone through about five refugee camps before they came here.'

'How many die a day?' Olanna asked again. But Kainene did not respond. The baby finally let out a thin squall and Kainene forced the powdery tablet into the small, open mouth. Olanna watched Father Marcel and another man carry the dead woman, by her ankles and wrists, out of the classroom and to the back of the building.

'Sometimes I hate them,' Kainene said.

'The vandals.'

'No, them.' Kainene pointed back at the room. 'I hate them for dying.'

Kainene took the baby inside and gave it to another woman, a relative of the dead woman's whose bony body was quivering; because her eyes were dry, it took Olanna a moment to realize that she was crying, the baby pressed against her flattened, dry breasts.

Later, as they walked to the car, Kainene slipped her hand into Olanna's.

29

Ugwu knew the story from Pastor Ambrose was implausible, that some people from a foundation abroad had set up a table at the end of St John's Road and were giving away boiled eggs and bottles of refrigerated water to anyone who passed by. He knew, too, that he should not leave the compound; Olanna's warnings echoed in his head. But he was bored. It was sticky hot and he hated the ashy taste of the water stored in a clay pot behind the house. He longed for water, for anything, cooled by electricity. And the story could well be true; anything was possible. Baby was playing with Adanna and he could take the short cut and be back before she even noticed he was gone.

He had just rounded the corner past the Church of St John when he saw, farther down the road, a group of men standing in a single line with their hands placed on their heads. The two soldiers with them were very tall and one held his gun pointed forwards. Ugwu stopped. The soldier with the gun began to shout something and to run towards him. Ugwu's heart jumped in his chest; he looked at the bush by the roadside but it was too thin to hide in. He looked back and the road was clear and unending; there was nothing to shield him from the soldier's bullet. He turned and dashed into the church compound. An elderly priest wearing white was standing at the top of the steps by the main door. Ugwu bounded up, relieved, because the soldier would not come inside the church to take him. Ugwu tugged at the door but it was locked.

'*Biko*, Father, let me go inside,' he said.

The priest shook his head. 'Those outside who are being conscripted, they are God's children too.'

'Please, please.' Ugwu yanked at the door.

'God's blessings will go with you,' the priest said.

'Open this door!' Ugwu shouted.

The priest shook his head and backed away.

The soldier ran into the church compound. 'Stop or I shoot!'

Ugwu stood staring, his mind blank.

'You know what they call me?' the soldier shouted. 'Kill And Go!' He was too tall for the tattered trousers that stopped long before his black boots started. He spat on the ground and pulled Ugwu's arm. 'Bloody civilian! Follow me!'

Ugwu stumbled along. Behind them, the priest said, 'God bless Biafra.'

Ugwu did not look at the faces of the other men as he joined the queue and raised his hands to his head. He was dreaming; he had to be dreaming. A dog was barking from somewhere close by. Kill And Go shouted at one of the men, cocked his gun, and shot into the air. Some women had gathered a little way away and one of them was speaking to Kill And Go's partner. At first, she spoke in low, pleading tones, then she raised her voice and gesticulated wildly. 'Can't you see he cannot talk well? He is an imbecile! How will he carry a gun?'

Kill And Go tied the men up in pairs, their hands behind their backs and the rope stretched taut between them. The man Ugwu was tied to jerked at the rope as if to see how strong it was and Ugwu was almost thrown off balance.

'Ugwu!'

The voice had come from the group of women. He turned. Mrs Muokelu was looking at him with shocked eyes. He nodded at her, in a way that he hoped was respectful, because he could not take the risk of talking. She began to half-walk, half-run down the road and he watched her go, disappointed and yet not sure what he had expected her to do.

'Get ready to move!' Kill And Go shouted. He looked up and saw a boy at the end of the road and ran off after him. His partner pointed a gun at the queue. 'Anybody run, I shoot.'

Kill And Go came back with the boy walking ahead of him.

'Shut up!' he said, as he tied the boy's hands behind his back. 'Everybody move! Our van is on the next road!'

They had just begun to walk at an awkward pace, Kill And Go shouting, '*Lep! Ai!*', when Ugwu saw Olanna. She was hurrying, panicky, wearing her wig, which she hardly wore these days, and she had hastily put it on because it was lopsided on her head. She smiled and motioned to Kill And Go, and he shouted, 'Stop!' before he went over to her. They talked with his back to the men and, moments later, he turned around and slashed at the rope that bound Ugwu's hands.

'He is already serving our nation. We are only interested in idle civilians,' he called out to the other soldier, who nodded.

Ugwu's relief made him dizzy. He rubbed his wrists. Olanna did not say a word to him as they walked home, and he sensed her silent fury only in the force with which she unlocked and threw open the door.

'I'm sorry, mah,' he said.

'You are so stupid you do not deserve the luck you had today,' she said. 'I bribed that soldier with all the money I have. Now you will produce what I will feed my child, do you understand?'

'I'm sorry, mah,' he said again.

She said little to him in the following days. She made Baby's pap herself as if she no longer trusted him. Her responses to his greetings were frosty nods. And he woke up earlier to fetch water and scrubbed the room floor harder and waited to win back her friendship.

Finally, he won it back with the help of roasted lizards. It was the morning that she and Baby were getting ready to go to Orlu to visit Kainene. A hawker walked into the compound with an enamel tray covered in newspapers, holding up a browned lizard on a stick, chanting, '*Mme mme suya! Mme mme suya!*'

'I want some, Mummy Ola, please,' Baby said.

Olanna ignored her and continued to brush her hair. Pastor Ambrose had come out of his room and was bargaining with the lizard hawker.

'I want some, Mummy Ola,' Baby said.

'Those things are not good for you,' Olanna said.

Pastor Ambrose went back to his room with a newspaper-wrapped package.

'Pastor bought some,' Baby said.

'But we are not buying any.'

Baby began to cry. Olanna turned and looked at Ugwu in exasperation and suddenly they were both smiling at the situation: Baby was crying to be allowed to eat a lizard.

'What do lizards eat, Baby?' Ugwu asked.

Baby mumbled, 'Ants.'

'If you eat one, all the ants the lizard ate will crawl around inside your stomach and bite you,' Ugwu said calmly.

Baby blinked. She looked at him for a while, as if deciding whether or not to believe him, before she wiped her tears.

On the day that Olanna and Baby left to spend a week with Kainene in Orlu, Master came home from work earlier than usual and did not go to Tanzania Bar; Ugwu hoped that their absence had pulled him out of the ditch he sunk into when his mother died. He sat on the veranda listening to the radio. Ugwu was surprised to see Alice stop by on her way to the bathroom. He assumed Master would give her his distant yes-and-no answers and she would go back to her piano. But they spoke in low tones, most of which Ugwu did not hear; once in a while he heard her giggly laughter. The next day, she was sitting on the bench beside Master. Then she stayed until the whole yard was asleep. Then Ugwu came around from the backyard, days later, and found the veranda empty and the room door firmly shut. His stomach tightened; memories of those days of Amala left a difficult-to-swallow lump in his throat. Alice was different. There was a deliberate childlike aura to her that Ugwu distrusted. He could see why she would not need any medicine from a *dibia* to tempt Master; she would do it with that pale skin and helpless manner. Ugwu walked to the banana trees and back and then went to the door and knocked loudly. He was determined to stop them, to stop it. He heard sounds inside. He knocked again. And again.

'Yes?' Master's voice was muffled.

'It is me, sah. I want to ask if I can take the kerosene stove, sah.' After he took the cooker, he would pretend to have forgotten the *garri* cup, the last bit of yam, the ladle. He was prepared to fake a seizure, an epileptic fit, anything that would keep Master from continuing what he was doing with that woman. It took long minutes before Master opened the door. His glasses were off and his eyes looked swollen.

'Sah?' Ugwu asked, looking past him. The room was empty. 'Is it well, sah?'

'Of course it's not well, you ignoramus,' Master said, staring at the pair of slippers on the floor. He looked lost in his own mind. Ugwu waited. Master sighed. 'Professor Ekwenugo was on his way to lay landmines with the Science Group when they went over some pot-holes and the mines went off.'

'The mines went off?'

'Ekwenugo was blown up. He's dead.'

Blown up rang in Ugwu's ears.

Master moved back. 'Take the stove, then.'

Ugwu came in and picked up the kerosene stove that he did not need and thought of Professor Ekwenugo's long, tapering nail. *Blown up.* Professor Ekwenugo had always been his proof that Biafra would triumph, with the stories of rockets and armoured cars and fuel made from nothing. Would Professor Ekwenugo's body parts be charred, like bits of wood, or would it be possible to recognize what was what? Would there be many dried fragments, like squashing a harmattan-dried leaf? *Blown up.*

Master left moments later for Tanzania Bar. Ugwu changed into his good trousers and hurried to Eberechi's house. It seemed the most natural thing, the only thing, to do. He refused to think of how upset Olanna would be if Mama Oji told her that he had gone out, or of what Eberechi's reaction would be, whether she would ignore him or welcome him or shout at him. He needed to see her.

She was sitting on the veranda alone, wearing that buttocks-moulding tight skirt he remembered, but her hair was different, cut in a short, rounded shape rather than plaited with thread.

'Ugwu!' she said, surprised, and stood up.

'You cut your hair.'

'Is there thread anywhere, talk less of the money to buy it?'

'It suits you,' he said.

She shrugged.

'I should have come since,' he said. He should never have stopped speaking to her because of an army officer he did not know. 'Forgive me. *Gbaghalu.*'

They looked at each other, and she reached out and pinched the skin of his neck. He slapped her hand away, playfully, and then held onto it. He did not let go when they both sat on the steps, and she told him how the family renting Master's former house was wicked, how the boys on the street hid in the ceiling when the conscripting soldiers came, how the last air raid had left a hole in their wall that rats came through.

Finally, Ugwu said that Professor Ekwenugo had died. 'You

remember I told you about him? The one in the Science Group, the one who made great things,' he said.

'I remember,' she said. 'The one with the long nail.'

'It was cut,' Ugwu said and started to cry; his tears were sparse and itchy. She placed a hand on his shoulder and he sat very still so as not to move her hand, so as to keep it where it was. There was a newness to her, or perhaps it was his perception of things that had become new. He believed now in preciousness.

'You said he cut his long nail?' she asked.

'He cut it,' Ugwu said. It was suddenly a good thing he had cut his nail; Ugwu could not bear the thought of that nail being blown up.

'I should go,' he said. 'Before my master comes home.'

'I shall come and visit you tomorrow,' she said. 'I know a short cut to your place.'

Master was not back when Ugwu got home. Mama Oji was screaming, 'Shame on you! Shame on you!' at her husband, and Pastor Ambrose was praying that God scatter Britain with holy-spirit dynamite, and a child was crying. Slowly, one after the other, the sounds ceased. Darkness fell. Oil lamps went off. Ugwu sat outside the room and waited until, finally, Master walked in with a small smile on his face and his eyes a glaring red.

'My good man,' he said.

'Welcome, sah. *Nno.*' Ugwu stood up. Master was unsteady on his feet, swaying ever so slightly to the left. Ugwu hurried forwards and placed his arm around him and supported him. They had just stepped inside the room when Master doubled over with a fierce jerk and threw up. The foaming vomit splattered on the floor. Sour smells filled the room. Master sat down on the bed. Ugwu brought a rag and some water and, while he cleaned, he listened to Master's uneven breathing.

'Don't tell any of this to your madam,' Master said.

'Yes, sah.'

Eberechi visited often, and her smile, a brush of her hand, or her pinching his neck became exquisite joys. The afternoon he first kissed her, Baby was asleep. They were inside, sitting on the bench and playing Biafran *whot* and she had just said 'Check up!' and placed down her last card when he leaned closer and tasted the tart dirt behind her ear. Then he kissed her neck, her jaw, her lips; under the pressure of his tongue, she opened her mouth and the gushing warmth of it overwhelmed him. His hand moved to her chest and enclosed her small breast. She pushed it away. He lowered it to her belly and kissed her mouth again before quickly slipping his hand under her skirt.

'Just let me see,' he said, before she could stop him. 'Just see.'

She stood up. She did not hold him back as he raised her skirt and pulled down the cotton underwear with a small tear at the waistband and looked at the large, rounded lobes of her buttocks. He pulled the underwear back up and let go of her skirt. He loved her. He wanted to tell her that he loved her.

'I am going,' she said, and straightened her blouse.

'What of your friend the army officer?'

'He is in another sector.'

'What did you do with him?'

She rubbed the back of her hand against her lips as if to wipe something off.

'Did you do anything with him?' Ugwu asked.

She walked to the door, still silent.

'You like him,' Ugwu said, feeling desperate now.

'I like you more.'

It didn't matter that she was still seeing the officer. What mattered was the *more*, whom she preferred. He pulled her to him but she moved away.

'You will kill me,' she said, and laughed. 'Let me go.'

'I'll escort you halfway,' he said.

'No need. Baby will be alone.'

'I'll be back before she wakes up.'

He wanted to hold her hand; instead, he walked so close to her that, once in a while, their bodies brushed against each other. He didn't go far before turning back. He was a short pathway away from home when he saw two soldiers standing next to a van and holding guns.

'You! Stop there!' one of them called.

Ugwu began to run until he heard the gunshot, so deafening, so alarmingly close that he fell to the ground and waited for the pain to drill into his body, certain he had been hit. But there was no pain. When the soldier ran up to him, the first thing Ugwu saw was the pair of canvas shoes, before he looked up at the wiry body and scowling face. A rosary hung around his neck. The burnt smell of gunpowder came from his gun.

'Come on, stand up, you bloody civilian! Join them there!'

Ugwu stood up and the soldier slapped the back of his head and a splintering light spread to his eyes; he dug his feet into the loose sand to steady himself for a moment before he walked over to join the two men standing with their arms raised high. One was elderly, at least sixty-five, while the other was a teenager of perhaps fifteen. Ugwu mumbled a 'good afternoon' to the elderly man and stood next to him, arms raised.

'Enter the van,' the second soldier said. His thick beard covered most of his cheeks.

'If it has come to this, that you are conscripting somebody my age, then Biafra has died,' the elderly man said quietly.

The second soldier was watching him.

The first soldier shouted, 'Shut up your stinking mouth, *agadi*!' and slapped the elderly man.

'Stop that!' the second soldier said. He turned to the elderly man. 'Papa, go.'

'Eh?' The elderly man looked uncertain.

'Go, *gawa*.'

The elderly man began to walk away, at first slowly and uncertainly, his hand rubbing the cheek where he had been slapped; then he broke into an unsteady run. Ugwu watched him disappear down the road and wished he could leap across and clutch his hand and be propelled along to freedom.

'Get into the van!' the first soldier said. It was as if the elderly man's leaving had angered him and that he held not the second soldier but the new conscripts responsible. He shoved the teenager and Ugwu. The teenager fell and quickly scrambled to his feet before they climbed into the back of the van. There were no seats; old raffia bags and rawhide canes and empty bottles lay scattered on the rusting floor. Ugwu was startled to see a boy sitting there, humming a song and drinking from an old beer bottle. Ugwu smelt the harshness of local gin as he lowered himself next to the boy and thought that perhaps he was a stunted man and not a boy.

'I am High-Tech,' he said, and the scent of local gin became stronger.

'I am Ugwu.' Ugwu glanced at his oversized shirt, tattered shorts, boots, and beret. He was indeed a boy. No more than thirteen. But the dry cynicism in his eyes made him seem much older than the teenager crumpled down opposite them.

'*Gi kwanu?* What is your own name?' High-Tech asked the teenager.

The teenager was sobbing. He looked familiar; perhaps he was one of the neighbourhood boys who had fetched water at the borehole before dawn. Ugwu felt sorry for him and yet angry, too, because the teenager's crying made the hopelessness of their situation stark and final. They really had been conscripted. They really would be sent to the war front with no training.

'Aren't you a man?' High-Tech asked the teenager. '*I bu nwanyi?* Why are you behaving like a woman?'

The teenager had his hand pressed against his eyes as he cried. High-Tech's sneer turned into mocking laughter. 'This one doesn't want to fight for our cause!'

Ugwu said nothing; High-Tech's laughter and the smell of gin nauseated him.

'I do rayconzar meechon,' High-Tech announced, speaking English for the first time. Ugwu wanted to correct his pronunciation of *reconnaissance mission*; the boy certainly would benefit from Olanna's class.

'Our battalion is made up of field engineers and we use only the mighty *ogbunigwe.*' High-Tech paused and belched, as if he expected delight from his listeners. The teenager kept crying. Ugwu listened without expression. He suspected it would be important to win High-Tech's respect, and he would succeed only by showing nothing of the fear that was crawling all over him.

'I am the one who detects where the enemy is. I move close by and climb trees and find out the exact location and then our commander will use my information to decide where to set up for our operation.' High-Tech watched Ugwu and Ugwu kept his face indifferent. 'With my last battalion I used to pretend that I was an orphan and infiltrate the enemy camp. They call me High-Tech because my first commander said I am better than any high-technology spying gadget.' He sounded eager to impress Ugwu. Ugwu stretched out his legs.

'That word you call *re-con-zar* is *reconnaissance*,' he said.

High-Tech looked at him for a moment and laughed and offered the bottle, but Ugwu shook his head. High-Tech shrugged and drank and hummed 'Biafra Win the War', tapping his foot on the floor of the van. The teenager kept crying. The first soldier was at the wheel, smoking dried leaves rolled in paper and the smoke was pungent and the drive took so long that Ugwu could no longer hold his urge to urinate.

'Please, I want to piss!' he called out.

The soldier stopped the van and pointed his gun. 'Step down and piss. You run, I shoot.'

It was the same soldier who, when they arrived at the training camp, a former primary school with buildings sheathed in palm fronds, shaved Ugwu's hair with a piece of broken glass. The rough scraping left his scalp tender, littered with nicks. The mats and mattresses arranged in the classrooms crawled with vicious bedbugs. The skinny soldiers – with no boots, no uniforms, no half of a yellow sun on their sleeves – kicked and slapped and mocked Ugwu during physical training. The parade left Ugwu's arms stiff. The obstacles training left his calves throbbing. The rope climbing left his palms bleeding. The wraps of *garri* he stood in a queue to receive, the thin soup scooped from a metal basin once a day, left him hungry. And the casual cruelty of this new world in which he had no say grew a hard clot of fear inside him.

A family of birds had nested on the roof of the classroom. In the mornings, their chirping was interrupted by the sharp trill of the commander's whistle, a voice shouting 'Fall in, fall in!' and the running and scrambling of men and boys. In the afternoons, the sun sapped energy and goodwill and the soldiers quarrelled and played Biafran *whot* and spoke of the vandals they had blown up in past operations. When one of them said, 'Our next operation will be very soon!' Ugwu's fear mixed with excitement at the thought that he was a soldier fighting for Biafra. If only he was with a real battalion, fighting with a gun. He remembered Professor Ekwenugo describing the *ogbunigwe:* 'high-impact landmine'. How glamorous it sounded, this Biafran-made mine, this Ojukwu Bucket, this wonder that was so perplexing to the vandals that they were said to send cattle herds ahead to understand just how the *ogbunigwe* killed so many. But when he went to the first training session, he stared at what was before him: a dull metal container full of scrap metal.

He wished he could tell Eberechi about his disappointment. He wanted to tell her, too, about the commander, the only one with a full uniform, sharply ironed and stiff, how he often barked into a two-way radio, and how, when the teenager tried to run away during a training session, he beat him with his bare hands until blood ran down the teenager's nose and then screamed, 'Lock him in the guardroom!' Ugwu thought most about Eberechi when the village women came with wraps of *garri*, thin soup, and, once in a while, win-the-war rice cooked with some palm oil and little else. Sometimes younger women came and went in the commander's quarters and emerged with sheepish smiles. The sentries at the entrance always raised the barriers to let the women in, although they did not have to, since the women could easily walk in by the sides. Once Ugwu saw a figure with rounded, rolling buttocks leaving the compound and he wanted to call out, *Eberechi!* although he knew it was not her. It was while looking for bits of paper on which he could write down what he did from day to day, for whenever he saw Eberechi again, that he found the book *Narrative of the Life of Frederick Douglass, An American Slave: Written by Himself* slipped into a tight corner beneath the blackboard. On the front page, PROPERTY OF GOVERNMENT COLLEGE was printed in dark blue. He sat on the floor and read. He finished it in two days and started again, rolling the words round his tongue, memorizing some sentences:

> The slaves became as fearful of the tar as of the lash. They find less difficulty from the want of beds, than from the want of time to sleep.

High-Tech liked to sit next to him while he read. Sometimes he would hum Biafran songs in an annoying monotone, and other times he would chatter about this and that. Ugwu ignored him. But one afternoon, the women did not bring any food, and a whole day went by with the grumbling of men. High-Tech nudged Ugwu at night and held out a tin of sardines. Ugwu grasped it. High-Tech laughed. 'We have to share it,' he said and Ugwu wondered how he managed to get it, how a child so young seemed so flexibly in control. They went to the back of the building and shared the oily fish.

'The vandals eat well, oh!' High-Tech said. 'The last camp I infiltrated, when I was with the battalion at Nteje, their women were cooking soup with big-big pieces of meat. They even gave some to our men when they stopped fighting for one week to celebrate Easter.'

'They stopped fighting to celebrate Easter?' Ugwu asked.

High-Tech looked pleased to have finally caught his attention. 'Yes. They even played cards together and drank whisky. Sometimes they agree not to fight so that everybody will rest.' High-Tech glanced at Ugwu and laughed. 'Your haircut is so ugly.'

Ugwu touched his head, with the odd tufts of hair that the jagged glass had missed. 'Yes.'

'It is because they shaved it dry,' High-Tech said. 'I can do it better for you with a razor and soap.'

High-Tech produced a bar of green soap and lathered Ugwu's head and shaved it with a razor blade until it was smooth and soft to the touch. Later, when High-Tech told him, 'Operation in two days,' in a whisper, Ugwu thought about the people who shaved their hair off as an act of mourning. Shaving as a memorial to death. He lay face up on his thin mattress and listened to the ugly sounds of snoring around him. He had proved himself to the other men by how well he did at training, how he scaled the obstacles and shimmied up the rough rope, but he had made no friend. He said very little. He did not want to know their stories. It was better to leave each man's load unopened, undisturbed, in his own mind. He thought about the upcoming operation, about blowing up vandals with his *ogbunigwe*, about Professor Ekwenugo's blown-up body. He imagined himself getting up in the moonlit quiet, leaping out, running until he got back to the yard in Umuahia and greeted Master and Olanna and hugged Baby. But he would not even try, he knew, because a part of him wanted to be here.

In the trench, the earth felt like soaked bread. Ugwu lay still. A spider clambered up his arm but he did not slap it away. The darkness was black, complete, and Ugwu imagined the spider's hairy legs, its surprise to find not cold underground soil but warm human flesh. The moon floated out once in a while, and the thick trees ahead became dimly outlined. The vandals were somewhere there. Ugwu hoped for a little more light; the moon had been more generous earlier when he buried his *ogbunigwe* about thirty yards ahead. Now the darkness brooded. The cable felt cold in his hand. Next to him, a soldier was mumbling prayers in the softest voice, so soft that Ugwu felt he was whispering in his ear. 'Mother of God pray for us sinners now and at the hour of our death.' He shook the spider off and stood up when the vandals started shooting. The rattle of gunfire was scattered, loud then faint; the infantry was returning the vandals' fire from different directions and those vandals, those dirty cattle rearers, would be confused and would have no idea that the *ogbunigwe* mines were waiting for them.

Ugwu thought of Eberechi's fingers pulling the skin of his neck, the wetness of her tongue in his mouth. The vandals began to shell. There was first the whistle of a mortar in the air and then the boom as the mortar fell and hot shrapnel flew around. A patch of grass caught fire, lit up, and Ugwu saw a ferret by the cluster of trees ahead, hunched like a giant tortoise. Then he saw them: crouched silhouettes moving forwards, a herd of men. They were in his killing range and it felt too soon, he had expected more to happen before they delivered themselves to him, before he detonated his *ogbunigwe* and it pushed outward in a spray of violent metal. He took a deep breath. Carefully, firmly, he connected the cable and the plug in his hands and the immediate, forceful blow-up startled him, although he had expected it. For the briefest moment, fear clenched his bowels. Perhaps he had not calculated well enough. Perhaps he had missed them. But he heard somebody close to him shout, 'Target!' The word reverberated in his head as they waited for long minutes before hauling themselves out of the trench and going over to the scattered corpses of the vandals.

'Naked them! Take the trousers and shirts!' somebody shouted.

'Boots and guns only!' another voice shouted. 'No time. No time. *Ngwa-ngwa!* Their reinforcements are on the way!'

Ugwu bent over a lean body. He yanked off the boots. In the pockets, he felt a cold, hard kola nut and warm, thick blood. The second body, close by, stirred when Ugwu touched it and he moved back. There was a forced gasping breath before it became still. Ugwu shivered. Beside him, a soldier held up a few guns and was shouting.

'Let's go!' Ugwu called out, wiping his bloodied hands on his trousers.

The others thumped him on the back and called him 'Target Destroyer!' as they trooped to headquarters to hand in their cables.

'You learn this from that book you read?' they teased. Success hauled him up above the ground. He floated through the following days as they played Biafran *whot* and drank gin and waited for the next operation. He lay face up on the ground while High-Tech rolled up some wee-wee, the leaves crisply dried, in old paper and they smoked together. He preferred Mars cigarettes; the wee-wee made him feel disjointed, created a thin slice of space between his legs and hips. They didn't bother to hide their smoking because the commander was happy and the news was hope-filled now that Biafra had recaptured Owerri from the vandals. Rules relaxed; they could go out to the bar near the expressway.

'It's a long walk,' somebody said, and High-Tech laughed and said, 'We will commandeer a car, of course.'

When High-Tech laughed, Ugwu remembered he was a child. Only thirteen. Among nine men he looked incongruously small, Ugwu thought, as they walked along. The sound of rubber slippers echoed on the silent road. Two of them were barefoot. They waited awhile before a dusty Volkswagen Beetle drove towards them and then spread across the road and blocked it. The car stopped, and a few of them banged on the bonnet.

'Get out! Bloody civilians!'

The man who was driving looked stern, as if determined to show that he could not be intimidated. Beside him, his wife began to cry and plead. 'Please, we are going to look for our son.'

A soldier was violently hitting the bonnet of the car. 'We need this for an operation!'

'Please, please, we are going to look for our son. They told us he was seen in the refugee camp.' The woman stared at High-Tech for a while, her brows furrowed. Perhaps she thought he might be her son.

'We are dying for you and you are here driving a pleasure car?' a soldier asked, pulling her out of the car. Her husband climbed out himself, but still stood by the car. His fist was tight with the key inside.

'This is wrong, officers. You have no right to take this car. I have my pass. I am working for our government.'

One of the soldiers slapped him. The man staggered and the soldier slapped him again and again and again and he crashed to the ground and the key slipped out of his hand.

'It is enough!' Ugwu said.

Another soldier touched the man's neck and wrist to make sure he was breathing. The wife was bent over her husband as the soldiers squashed into the car and drove to the bar.

The bar girl greeted them and said there was no beer.

'Are you sure you don't have beer? Are you hiding it because you think we will not pay you?' one of the soldiers said to her.

'No, there is no beer.' She was thin and sharp-featured and un-smiling.

'We destroyed the enemy!' he said. 'Give us beer!'

'She has said there is no beer,' Ugwu snapped. The soldier's loud-ness annoyed him; this was a man who had abandoned his *ogbunigwe* and run off long before the vandals were close. 'Let her bring *kai-kai.*'

As the girl set out the local gin and small metal cups, the soldiers talked about the Nigerian officers, about how they would hang Danjuma, Adekunle, and Gowon upside down after Biafra's victory. High-Tech began to roll some wee-wee. Ugwu thought he made out something familiar on an unrolled portion of paper, the word *narrative*, but it could not be. He looked again. 'What paper is that?' he asked.

'It is only the first page of your book.' High-Tech smiled and offered Ugwu the joint.

Ugwu did not take it. 'You tore my book?'

'It is only the first page. My paper finished.'

Rage pumped through Ugwu. His slap was swift, powerful, furious, but High-Tech avoided the full impact because he moved back at the last second and Ugwu's hand only scraped his cheek. Ugwu raised his hand again but the other soldiers held him, dragged him away, said it was just a book after all, told him to drink some more gin.

'Sorry,' High-Tech mumbled.

Ugwu's head ached. Everything was moving so fast. He was not living his life; life was living him. He drank steadily and watched the others, their mouths opening and closing, rancid jibes and conceited boasts and magnified memories coming out of them. Soon the bar itself, the benches placed around a table, became a sour-scented blur. The bar girl changed the bottles one after the other; Ugwu thought the gin was probably brewed in their backyard down the road. He got up to urinate outside and, afterwards, leaned against a tree and breathed in the fresh air. It was like sitting in the backyard in Nsukka, looking at the lemon tree and his herb garden and Jomo's manicured plants. He stayed there for awhile until he heard loud shouts from the bar. Perhaps somebody had won some bet or other. They tired him. The war tired him. When he finally went back inside, he stopped at the door. The bar girl was lying on her back on the floor, her wrapper bunched up at her waist, her shoulders held down by a soldier, her legs wide, wide ajar. She was sobbing, 'Please, please, *biko.*' Her blouse was still on. Between her legs, High-Tech was moving. His thrusts were jerky, his small buttocks darker-coloured than his legs. The soldiers were cheering.

'High-Tech, enough! Discharge and retire!'

High-Tech groaned before he collapsed on top of her. A soldier pulled him off and was fumbling at his own trousers when somebody said, 'No! Target Destroyer is next!'

Ugwu backed away from the door.

'*Ujo abiala o!* Target Destroyer is afraid!'

Ugwu shrugged and moved forwards. 'Who is afraid?' he said disdainfully. 'I just like to eat before others, that is all.'

'The food is still fresh!'

'Target Destroyer, aren't you a man? *I bukwa nwoke?*'

On the floor, the girl was still. Ugwu pulled his trousers down, surprised at the swiftness of his erection. She was dry and tense when he entered her. He did not look at her face, or at the man pinning her down, or at anything at all as he moved quickly and felt his own climax, the rush of fluids to the tips of himself: a self-loathing release. He zipped up his trousers while some soldiers clapped. Finally he looked at the girl. She stared back at him with a calm hate.

There were more operations. Ugwu's fear sometimes overwhelmed him, froze him. He unwrapped his mind from his body, separated the two, while he lay in the trench, pressing himself into the mud, luxuriating in how close and connected he was to the mud. The *ka-ka-ka* of shooting, the cries of men, the smell of death, the blasts of explosions above and around him were distant. But back at the camp his memory became clear; he remembered the man who placed both hands on his blown-open belly as though to hold his intestines in, the one who mumbled something about his son before he stiffened. And, after each operation, everything became new. Ugwu looked at his daily wrap of *garri* in wonder. He read pages of his book over and over. He touched his own skin and thought of its decay.

One afternoon, the commander's jeep drove in with a sickly goat lying on its side, legs tied together. It had been commandeered from an idle civilian. It bleated meekly and the soldiers gathered, excited at the thought of meat. Two of them killed it and made a fire and when the large-cut chunks had been cooked, the commander asked that all of it be brought to his quarters. He spent long minutes checking through the basin to make sure the goat was complete: the legs, the head, the balls. Later, two village women came and were taken in to the commander's quarters; much later, the soldiers threw stones at them as they left. Ugwu dreamed that the commander had given half of the goat to the soldiers and that they had chewed everything and swallowed the bones.

When he woke up, a radio was turned on high and High-Tech was sobbing. Umuahia had fallen. Biafra's capital was lost. A soldier threw his hands up and said, 'That goat, that goat was a bad omen! All is lost! We have to surrender!' The other soldiers were subdued. Even the commander's saying that he was aware of a secret counter-attack plan to recover Umuahia did not lift their spirits. But the announcement that His Excellency would be visiting did. The soldiers swept the compound, washed their clothes, lined themselves on benches to welcome him. When the convoy of jeeps and Pontiacs drove into the compound, they all stood up and saluted.

Ugwu's salute was slack, because he was worried about Olanna and Master and Baby in Umuahia, because he was not interested in His Excellency, because he did not care for the commander. He did not care for any of the officers, with their superior sneers and the way they treated their soldiers like sheep. But there was a captain he admired, a solitary and disciplined man called Ohaeto. And so the day that Ugwu found himself in the trench next to Captain Ohaeto, he was determined to impress him. The trench was not wet; there were more ants than spiders. Ugwu could tell that the vandals were closer, from the clatter of gunfire and the boom of mortars. But there was not enough light to see for certain. He really wanted to impress Captain Ohaeto; if only the light were not so poor. He was about to connect the cable and plug when something whistled past his ear and then, right afterwards, a stinging pain burnt into his back. Beside him, Captain Ohaeto was a bloodied, mangled mass. Then Ugwu felt himself lifted up above the trench, helplessly, haplessly. And when he landed, it was the force of his own weight, rather than the pain firing up his whole body, that stunned him into silence.

Richard shifted as far away as he could from the two American journalists in the car, pressing himself against the door of the Peugeot. He really should have sat in front and asked the orderly to sit in back with them. But he had not imagined that they would smell so bad, Charles the plump one wearing a squashed hat and Charles the redhead with his chin covered in ginger hair.

'One Midwestern and one New York journalist coming to Biafra, and we're both named Charles. What were the odds?' the plump one said, laughing, after they introduced themselves. 'And both our moms call us Chuck!'

Richard was not sure how long they had waited before boarding their flight at Lisbon, but the wait at São Tomé for a relief flight to Biafra had stretched to seventeen hours. They needed a bath. When the plump one, sitting next to Richard, began to talk about his first visit to Biafra at the beginning of the war, Richard thought he needed mouthwash, too.

'I came in a real plane and we landed at Port Harcourt airport,' he said. 'But this time I was sitting on the floor of a plane flying with no lights, alongside twenty tons of dried milk. We flew so fucking low, I looked out and could see the orange bursts of the Nigerian anti-aircraft. I was scared shitless.' He laughed, his fat-padded face broad and pleasant.

The redhead did not laugh. 'We don't know for sure that it was Nigerian fire. The Biafrans could have put it on.'

'Oh, come on!' The plump one glanced at Richard, but Richard kept his face straight. 'Of course it was Nigerian fire.'

'The Biafrans are mixing up food and guns in their planes, anyway,' the redhead said. He turned to Richard. 'Aren't they?'

Richard disliked him. He disliked his washed-out green eyes and his red-freckled face. When he had met them at the airport and handed them their passes and told them he would be their guide and that the Biafran government welcomed them, he had disliked the redhead's expression of scornful amusement. It was as if he were saying, *You* are speaking for the Biafrans?

'Our relief planes carry only food supplies,' Richard said.

'Of course,' the redhead said. 'Only food supplies.'

The plump one leaned across Richard to look out of the window. 'I can't believe people are driving cars and walking around. It's not like there's a war going on.'

'Until an air raid happens,' Richard said. He had moved his face back and was holding his breath.

'Is it possible to see where the Biafran soldiers shot the Italian oil worker?' the redhead asked. 'We've done something on that at the *Tribune*, but I'd like to do a longer feature.'

'No, it's not possible,' Richard said sharply.

The redhead was watching him. 'Okay. But can you tell me anything new?'

Richard exhaled. It was like somebody sprinkling pepper on his wound: Thousands of Biafrans were dead, and this man wanted to know if there was anything new about one dead white man. Richard would write about this, the rule of Western journalism: One hundred dead black people equal one dead white person. 'There is nothing new to tell,' he said. 'The area is occupied now.'

At the checkpoint, Richard spoke Igbo to the civil defender. She examined their passes and smiled suggestively and Richard smiled back; her thin, tall, breastlessness reminded him of Kainene.

'She looked like she was real interested,' the plump one said. 'I hear there's a lot of free sex here. But the girls have some kind of sexually transmitted disease? The Bonny disease? You guys have to be careful so you don't take anything back home.'

His presumptuousness annoyed Richard. 'The refugee camp we are going to is run by my wife.'

'Really? She been here long?'

'She's Biafran.'

The redhead had been staring out of the window; he turned now towards Richard. 'I had an English friend at college who really went for coloured girls.'

The plump one looked embarrassed. He spoke quickly. 'You speak Igbo pretty well?'

'Yes,' Richard said. He wanted to show them the photos of Kainene and the roped pot, but then he thought better of it.

'I'd love to meet her,' the plump one said.

'She's away today. She's trying to get more supplies for the camp.'

He climbed out of the car first and saw the two interpreters waiting. Their presence annoyed him. It was true that idioms and nuances and dialects often eluded him in Igbo, but the directorate was always too prompt in sending interpreters. Most of the refugees sitting outside watched them with vague curiosity. An emaciated man was walking around, a dagger strapped to his waist, talking to himself. Rotten smells hung heavy in the air. A group of children was roasting two rats around a fire.

'Oh, my God.' The plump one removed his hat and stared.

'Niggers are never choosy about what they eat,' the redhead muttered.

'What did you say?' Richard asked.

But the redhead pretended not to have heard and hurried ahead with one interpreter, to speak to a group of men playing draughts.

The plump one said, 'You know there's food piled in São Tomé crawling with cockroaches because there's no way to bring it in.'

'Yes.' Richard paused. 'Would it be all right if I gave you some letters? They're to my wife's parents in London.'

'Sure, I'll put them in the mail as soon as I get out of here.' The plump one brought out a large chocolate bar from his knapsack, unwrapped it, and took two bites. 'Listen, I wish I could do more.'

He walked over to the children and gave them some sweets and took photographs of them and they clamoured around him and begged for more. Once, he said, 'That's a lovely smile!' and after he left them, the children went back to their roasting rats.

The redhead walked across quickly, the camera around his neck swinging as he moved. 'I want to see the real Biafrans,' he said.

'The real Biafrans?' Richard asked.

'I mean, look at them. They can't have eaten a meal in two years. I don't see how they can still talk about the cause and Biafra and Ojukwu.'

'Do you usually decide what answers you will believe before you do an interview?' Richard asked mildly.

'I want to go to another refugee camp.'

'Of course, I will take you to another one.'

The second refugee camp, farther inside the town, was smaller, smelt better, and used to be a town hall. A woman with one arm was sitting on the stairs telling a story to a group of people. Richard caught the end of it – 'But the man's ghost came out and spoke to the vandals in Hausa and they left his house alone' – and he envied her belief in ghosts.

The redhead lowered himself on the step next to her and began to talk through the interpreter.

Are you hungry? Of course, we are all hungry.

Do you understand the cause of the war? Yes, the Hausa vandals wanted to kill all of us, but God was not asleep.

Do you want the war to end? Yes, Biafra will win very soon.

What if Biafra does not win?

The woman spat on the ground and looked at the interpreter first and then at the redhead, a long, pitying look. She got up and went inside.

'Unbelievable,' the redhead said. 'The Biafran propaganda machine is great.'

Richard knew his type. He was like President Nixon's fact finders from Washington or Prime Minister Wilson's commission members from London who arrived with their firm protein tablets and their firmer conclusions: that Nigeria was not bombing civilians, that the starvation was overflogged, that all was as well as it should be in the war.

'There isn't a propaganda machine,' Richard said. 'The more civilians you bomb, the more resistance you grow.'

'Is that from Radio Biafra?' the redhead asked. 'It sounds like something from the radio.'

Richard did not respond.

'They are eating everything,' the plump one said, shaking his head. 'Every fucking green leaf has become a vegetable.'

'If Ojukwu wanted to stop the starving, he could simply say yes to a food corridor. Those kids don't have to be eating rodents,' the redhead said.

The plump one had been taking photographs. 'But it's really not that simple,' he said. 'He's got to think of security too. He's fighting a fucking war.'

'Ojukwu will have to surrender. This is Nigeria's final push, and there's no way Biafra will recover all the lost territory,' the redhead said.

The plump one brought out a half-eaten chocolate bar from his pocket.

'So what's Biafra doing about oil now that they've lost the port?' the redhead asked.

'We are still extracting from some fields we control in Egbema,' Richard said, not bothering to explain where Egbema was. 'We move the crude to our refineries at night, in tankers with no headlights, to avoid the bombers.'

'You keep saying *we*,' the redhead said.

'Yes, I keep saying *we*.' Richard glanced at him. 'Have you been to Africa before?'

'No, first visit. Why?'

'I just wondered.'

'Am I supposed to feel inexperienced in jungle ways? I covered Asia for three years,' the redhead said, and smiled.

The plump one fumbled in his knapsack and brought out a bottle of brandy. He gave it to Richard. 'I bought it in São Tomé. Never got to take a shot. Great stuff.'

Richard took the bottle.

Before he drove them to Uli to catch their flight out, they went to a guesthouse and ate a dinner of rice and chicken stew; he hated to think that the Biafran government had paid for the redhead's meal. A few cars were leaving and arriving at the terminal building; farther ahead, the airstrip was pitch-black. The airport manager in his tight-fitting khaki suit came out and shook their hands and said, 'The plane is expected any minute now.'

'It's ridiculous that they still follow protocol in this shithole,' the redhead said. 'They stamped my passport when I got here and asked if I had anything to declare.'

A loud explosion shattered the air. The airport manager shouted, 'This way!' and they ran after him to the uncompleted building. They lay flat on the ground. The window louvres rattled and clattered. The ground quivered. The explosions stopped and scattered gunfire followed, and the airport manager stood up and brushed his clothes down. 'No more problems. Let's go.'

'Are you crazy?' the redhead screamed.

'They start shooting only when the bombs run out, nothing to worry about now,' the airport manager said airily, already on his way out.

On the tarmac, a lorry was repairing the bomb craters, filling them in with gravel. The runway lights blinked on and off and the darkness was complete again, absolute; in the blue-blackness Richard felt his head swimming. The lights came on for a little longer and then off. On again and then off. A plane was descending; there was the bumpy trailing sound on the tarmac.

'It's landed?' the plump one asked.

'Yes,' Richard said.

The lights blinked on and off. Three planes had landed and it amazed Richard how quickly some lorries, without headlights, had already driven up to them. Men were hauling sacks from the planes. The lights went on and off. Pilots were screaming. 'Hurry up, you lazy boys! Get them off! We're not going to be bombed here! Get a move on, boys! Hurry up, damn it!' There was an American accent, an Afrikaans accent, an Irish accent.

'The bastards could be a little more gracious,' the plump one said. 'They're fucking paid thousands of dollars to fly the relief in.'

'Their lives are at risk,' the redhead said.

'So are the lives of the men who are fucking unloading the planes.'

Somebody lit a hurricane lamp and Richard wondered if the Nigerian bomber hovering above could see it, wondered how many Nigerian bombers were hovering above.

'Some of our men have walked into the propellers in the dark,' Richard said calmly. He was not sure why he had said that, perhaps to shock the redhead out of his complacent superiority.

'And what happened to them?' the plump one asked.

'What do you think happened to them?'

A car was driving in towards them, slowly, with no headlights. It parked close by, doors opened and shut, and soon five emaciated children and a nun in a blue-and-white habit joined them. Richard greeted her. 'Good evening. *Kee ka I me?*'

She smiled. 'Oh, you are the *onye ocha* who speaks Igbo. You are the one who is writing wonderful things about our cause. Well done.'

'Are you going to Gabon?'

'Yes.' She asked the children to sit on the wood slabs. Richard went closer to look at them. In the dim light, the milky foam of mucus in their eyes was thick. The nun cradled the smallest, a shrivelled doll with stick legs and a pregnant belly. Richard could not tell if the child was a boy or a girl and suddenly that made him angry, so angry that when the redhead asked, 'How do we know when to get on the plane?' Richard ignored him.

One of the children made to get up. She toppled over and fell and lay face down and unmoving. The nun placed the smallest down on the ground and picked up the fallen child. 'Sit here. If you go anywhere I will smack you,' she said to the others before she hurried away.

The plump man asked. 'The kid fell asleep or what?'

Richard ignored him, too.

Finally, the plump man muttered, 'Fucking American policy.'

'Nothing wrong with our policy,' the redhead said.

'Power comes with responsibility. Your government knows that people are dying!' Richard said, his voice rising.

'Of course my government knows people are dying,' the redhead said. 'People are dying in Sudan and Palestine and Vietnam. People are dying everywhere.' He sat down on the floor. 'They brought my kid brother's body back from Vietnam last month, for God's sake.'

Neither Richard nor the plump one said anything. In the long silence that followed, even the pilots and the sounds of unloading dimmed. Later, after they had been driven hurriedly to the tarmac and dashed into the planes and the planes took off in the on-again, off-again lighting, the title of the book came to Richard: 'The World Was Silent When We Died'. He would write it after the war, a narrative of Biafra's difficult victory, an indictment of the world. Back in Orlu, he told Kainene about the journalists and how he had felt both angry with and sorry for the redhead and how he had felt incredibly alone in their presence and how the book title had come to him.

She arched her eyebrows. 'We? The world was silent when *we* died?'

'I'll make sure to note that the Nigerian bombs carefully avoided anybody with a British passport,' he said.

Kainene laughed. She laughed often these days. She laughed as she told him about the motherless baby who still clung to life, about the young girl that Inatimi was falling in love with, about the women who sang in the evenings. She laughed, too, on the morning that he and Olanna finally saw each other. Olanna spoke first. 'Hello,

Richard,' she said and he said, 'Olanna, hello,' and Kainene laughed and said, 'Richard couldn't invent any more trips.'

He watched Kainene's face carefully for withdrawal, for returning anger, for *something*. But there was nothing; her laughter softened the angles of her chin. And the tension he had expected, the weight of memory and regret that would come with seeing Olanna again in her presence, were absent.

7. The Book: The World Was Silent When We Died

For the epilogue, he writes a poem, modelled after one of Okeoma's poems. He calls it:

'WERE YOU SILENT WHEN WE DIED?'

> Did you see photos in sixty-eight
> Of children with their hair becoming rust:
> Sickly patches nestled on those small heads,
> Then falling off, like rotten leaves on dust?
>
> Imagine children with arms like toothpicks,
> With footballs for bellies and skin stretched thin.
> It was kwashiorkor – difficult word,
> A word that was not quite ugly enough, a sin.
>
> You needn't imagine. There were photos
> Displayed in gloss-filled pages of your *Life*.
> Did you see? Did you feel sorry briefly,
> Then turn round to hold your lover or wife?
>
> Their skin had turned the tawny of weak tea
> And showed cobwebs of vein and brittle bone;
> Naked children laughing, as if the man
> Would not take photos and then leave, alone.

31

Olanna saw the four ragged soldiers carrying a corpse on their shoulders. Wild panic made her woozy. She stopped, certain it was Ugwu's body, until the soldiers walked quickly, silently, past and she realized that the dead man was too tall to be Ugwu. His feet were cracked and caked in dried mud; he had fought without shoes. Olanna stared at the soldiers' retreating backs and tried to calm her queasiness, to shrug off the foreboding that had fogged her mind for days.

Later, she told Kainene how afraid she was for Ugwu, how she felt as if she were about to turn a corner and be flattened by tragedy. Kainene placed an arm around her and told her not to worry. Madu had sent word to all battalion commanders to look for Ugwu; they would find out where he was. But when Baby asked, 'Is Ugwu coming back today, Mummy Ola?' Olanna imagined it was because Baby, too, had the same premonition. When she returned to Umuahia and Mama Oji gave her a package somebody had delivered, she immediately wondered if it contained a message about Ugwu. Her hands shook as she held the brown-wrapped carton creased with excessive handling. Then she noticed Mohammed's writing, addressed to her in care of the University of Biafra, in long, elegant sweeps. Inside, she unfolded handkerchiefs, crisp, white underwear, bars of Lux soap, and chocolate, and she marvelled that they had reached her intact, even sent through the Red Cross. His letter was three months old but still smelt faintly of sweet musk. Detached sentences stuck to her mind.

> *I have sent so many letters and am unsure which has reached you. My sister, Hadiza, got married in June. I think constantly of you. My polo game is much improved. I am well and know you and Odenigbo must be too. Do try and send word back.*

She turned a chocolate bar around in her hand, stared at the MADE IN SWITZERLAND, fiddled with the silver foil. Then she flung the bar across the room. Mohammed's letter incensed her; it insulted her reality. But he could not possibly know that they had no salt and Odenigbo drank *kai-kai* every day and Ugwu was conscripted and she had sold her wig. He could not possibly know. Yet she felt angry that the patterns of his old life remained in place, so unquestioningly in place that he could write to her about his polo game.

Mama Oji knocked; Olanna took a deep, calming breath before she opened the door and gave her a bar of soap.

'Thank you.' Mama Oji held the soap with both hands and raised it to her nose and sniffed it. 'But that package was big. Is this the only thing you will give me? Is there no canned food there? Or are you saving it for your saboteur friend Alice?'

'*Ngwa*, give me back the soap,' Olanna said. 'Mama Adanna will know how to be appreciative.'

Mama Oji swiftly raised her blouse and tucked the soap into her threadbare bra. 'You know I am grateful.'

Raised voices came from the road, and they both went outside. A group of militia members holding machetes were pushing two women along. They cried as they staggered down the road; their wrappers were ripped and their eyes reddened. 'What did we do? We are not saboteurs! We are refugees from Ndoni! We have done nothing!'

Pastor Ambrose ran out to the road and began to pray. 'Father God, destroy the saboteurs that are showing the enemy the way! Holy-spirit fire!'

Some of the neighbours hurried out to spit and aim stones and jeer at the backs of the women. 'Sabo! God punish you! Sabo!'

'They should throw tyres round their necks and burn them,' Mama Oji said. 'They should burn every single saboteur.'

Olanna folded Mohammed's letter, thought of the slack, half-exposed bellies of the women, and said nothing.

'You should be careful with that Alice,' Mama Oji said.

'Leave Alice alone. She is not a saboteur.'

'She is the kind of woman who will steal somebody's husband.'

'What?'

'Every time you go to Orlu she will come out and sit with your husband.'

Olanna stared at Mama Oji, surprised, because it was the last thing she had expected to hear and because Odenigbo had never mentioned that Alice spent time with him when she was away. She had never even seen them speak to each other.

Mama Oji was watching her. 'I am only saying that you should be careful with her. Even if she is not a saboteur, she is not a good woman.'

Olanna could not think of what to say. She knew that Odenigbo would never touch another woman, had quietly convinced herself of this, and knew, too, that Mama Oji nursed a deep resentment of Alice. Yet the very unexpectedness of Mama Oji's words nagged her.

'I will be careful,' she said finally, with a smile.

Mama Oji looked as if she wanted to say something else but changed her mind and turned to shout at her son. 'Get away from that place! Are you stupid? *Ewu awusa!* Don't you know you will start coughing now?'

Later, Olanna took a bar of soap and knocked on Alice's door, three sharp raps in quick succession to let Alice know it was she. Alice's eyes looked sleepy, more shadowed than usual. 'You're back,' she said. 'How is your sister?'

'Very well.'

'Did you see the poor women they are harassing and calling saboteurs?' she asked, and before Olanna could respond, she continued, 'Yesterday it was a man from Ogoja. This is nonsense. We cannot keep beating people just because Nigeria is beating us. Somebody like me, I have not eaten proper food in two years. I have not tasted sugar. I have not drunk cold water. Where will I find the energy to aid the enemy?' Alice gestured with her tiny hands, and what Olanna had once thought to be an elegant fragility suddenly became a self-absorbed conceit, a luxurious selfishness; Alice spoke as if she alone suffered from the war.

Olanna gave her the soap. 'Somebody sent a few bars to me.'

'Oh! So I will join those using Lux in this Biafra. Thank you.' Alice's smile transformed her face, brightened her eyes, and Olanna wondered if Odenigbo found her pretty. She looked at Alice's yellow-skinned face and narrow waist and realized that what she had once admired now threatened her.

'*Ngwanu,* let me go and make Baby's lunch,' she said, and turned to leave.

That evening, she visited Mrs Muokelu with a bar of soap.

'Is this you? *Anya gi!* It has been long!' Mrs Muokelu said. A hole had split up His Excellency's face on the sleeve of her boubou.

'You look well,' Olanna lied. Mrs Muokelu was gaunt; her body was built for thickness and now, with so much weight loss, she drooped, as though she could no longer stand straight. Even the hair on her arms drooped.

'You, ever beautiful,' Mrs Muokelu said, and hugged Olanna again.

Olanna gave her the soap, and because she knew that Mrs Muokelu would not touch anything sent from Nigeria by a Nigerian, she said, 'My mother sent it from England.'

'God bless you,' Mrs Muokelu said. 'Your husband and Baby, *kwanu*?'

'They are well.'

'And Ugwu?'

'He was conscripted.'

'After that first time?'

'Yes.'

Mrs Muokelu paused and fingered the plastic half of a yellow sun around her neck. 'It will be well. He will come back. Somebody has to fight for our cause.'

They saw very little of each other now that Mrs Muokelu had started her trade. Olanna sat down and listened to her stories – about the vision that revealed that the saboteur responsible for the fall of Port Harcourt was a general of the Biafran Army; about another vision in which a *dibia* from Okija gave His Excellency some powerful medicine that would recapture all the fallen towns.

'They have started the rumour that Umuahia is threatened, *okwa ya?*' Mrs Muokelu asked, staring into Olanna's eyes.

'Yes.'

'But Umuahia will not fall. There is no need for people to panic and start packing.'

Olanna shrugged; she wondered why Mrs Muokelu was looking at her so intently.

'They say people with cars have started looking for petrol.' Mrs Muokelu's eyes were unwavering. 'They have to be careful, very careful, before somebody will ask them how they knew that Umuahia would fall if not that they are saboteurs.'

Olanna realized, then, that Mrs Muokelu was warning her, telling her to be prepared.

'Yes, they have to be careful,' she said.

Mrs Muokelu rubbed her hands together. Something had changed with her; she had allowed her faith to slip from her fingers. Biafra would win, Olanna knew, because Biafra had to win, but that Mrs Muokelu of all people believed that the fall of the capital was imminent dampened her. When she hugged Mrs Muokelu goodbye, it was with the hollow feeling that she would never see her again. She seriously contemplated, for the first time, the fall of Umuahia as she walked home. It would mean a delayed victory, a tighter squeezing of Biafra's territory, but it would also mean that they would go and live in Kainene's house in Orlu until the war ended.

She stopped by the petrol station near the hospital and was not surprised to see the sign scrawled in chalk: NO PETROL. They had stopped selling Biafran-made petrol since the talk of Umuahia's fall began, so that people would not panic. That night, Olanna told Odenigbo, 'We need to get some petrol on the black market; we don't have enough in case anything happens.' He nodded vaguely and mumbled something about Special Julius. He had just come back from Tanzania Bar and lay on the bed with the radio turned on low. Across the curtain, Baby was asleep on the mattress.

'What did you say?' she asked.

'We can't afford petrol right now. It's a pound a gallon.'

'They paid you last week. We have to be sure that the car will move.'

'I've asked Special Julius to do a cheque exchange. He has not brought the money.'

Olanna knew immediately that it was a lie. They did cheque exchanges with Special Julius all the time; it never took more than a day for Special Julius to give Odenigbo cash in exchange for a cheque.

'How are we going to buy petrol, then?' she asked.

He said nothing.

She walked past him and outside. The moon was behind a cloud and, sitting out in the blackness of the yard, she could still smell that cheap, vapour-heavy scent of local gin. It trailed him, it clouded the paths that he walked. His drinking in Nsukka – his auburn, finely refined brandy – had sharpened his mind, distilled his ideas and his confidence so that he sat in the living room and talked and talked and everybody listened. This drinking here silenced him. It made him retreat into himself and look out at the world with bleary, weary eyes. And it made her furious.

* * *

Olanna changed what was left of her British pounds and bought petrol from a man who led her into a dank outhouse with creamy-fat maggots crawling all over the floor. He poured carefully from his metal container into hers. She took the container home wrapped in a sack that had contained cornmeal and had just stored it in the boot of the Opel when a BIAFRAN ARMY open jeep drove in. Kainene climbed out, followed by a soldier wearing a helmet. And Olanna knew, with an immediate sinking wail of a feeling, that it was about Ugwu. It was about Ugwu. The sun burnt hotly and liquids began to spin in her head and she looked around for Baby but could not find her. Kainene came up and held her firmly by the shoulders and said, '*Ejima m*, hold your heart, be strong. Ugwu has died,' and it was not the news but the tight grip of Kainene's bony fingers that Olanna recognized.

'No,' she said calmly. The air was charged with unreality, as if she would certainly wake up in a minute. 'No,' she said again, shaking her head.

'Madu sent his batman with the message. Ugwu was with the field engineers, and they suffered massive casualties in an operation last week. Only a few came back and Ugwu was not one of them. They did not find his body, but they did not find many of the bodies.' Kainene paused. 'There was not much that was whole to find.'

Olanna kept shaking her head, waiting to wake up.

'Come with me. Bring Chiamaka. Come and stay in Orlu.' Kainene was holding her, Baby was saying something, and a haze shrouded everything until she looked up and saw the sky. Blue and clear. It made the present real, the sky, because she had never seen the sky in her dreams. She turned and marched down the road to Tanzania Bar. She walked past the dirty curtain at the door and pushed Odenigbo's cup off the table; a pale liquid spread on the cement floor.

'Have you drunk enough, eh?' she asked him quietly. '*Ugwu anwugo.* Did you hear me? Ugwu has died.'

Odenigbo stood up and looked at her. The rims of his eyes were puffy.

'Go on and drink,' Olanna said. 'Drink and drink and don't stop. Ugwu has died.'

The woman who owned the bar came across and said, 'Oh! Sorry, *ndo*,' and made to hug her but Olanna shrugged her off. 'Leave me alone,' she said. 'Leave me alone!' It was only then she realized that Kainene had come with her and was silently holding her as she shouted, 'Leave me alone! Leave me alone!' at the bar owner, who backed away.

In the following days, days filled with dark gaps of time, Odenigbo did not go to Tanzania Bar. He gave Baby a bath, made their *garri*, came home earlier from work. Once he tried to hold Olanna, to kiss her, but his touch made her skin crawl and she turned away from him and went outside to sleep on a mat on the veranda, where Ugwu had sometimes slept. She did not cry. The only time she cried was after she went to Eberechi's house to tell her that Ugwu had died and Eberechi screamed and called her a liar; at nights those screams rang in Olanna's head. Odenigbo sent word to Ugwu's people through three different women who went across enemy lines to trade. And he organized a service of songs in the yard. Some of the neighbours helped Alice bring out her piano and set it down near the banana trees. 'I will play as you sing,' Alice said to the gathered women. But whenever somebody started a song, Mama Oji would clap, insistently, loudly, in accompaniment, and soon all the other neighbours would join in the clapping and Alice could not play. She sat helplessly by her piano with Baby on her lap.

The first songs were vigorous and then Mama Adanna's voice broke out, husky and elegiac.

> *Naba na ndokwa,*
> *Ugwu, naba na ndokwa.*
> *O ga-adili gi mma,*
> *Naba na ndokwa.*

Odenigbo half-stumbled out of the yard before they finished singing, a livid incredulity in his eyes, as if he could not believe the words of the song: *Go in peace, it will be well with you.* Olanna watched him go. She did not entirely understand the resentment she felt. There was nothing he could have done to prevent Ugwu's death, but his drinking, his excessive drinking, had somehow made him complicit. She did not want to speak to him, to sleep beside him. She slept on the mat outside, and even the routine of the mosquito bites became a comfort. She said little to him. They spoke only of necessities, what Baby would eat, what they would do if Umuahia fell.

'We will stay in Kainene's house only until we find a place,' he said, as if they had many choices, as if he had forgotten that, before, he would have said that Umuahia would not fall; and she said nothing in response.

She told Baby that Ugwu had gone to heaven.

'But he's coming back soon, Mummy Ola?' Baby asked.

And Olanna said yes. It was not that she wanted to soothe Baby; it was that, day after day, she found herself rejecting the finality of Ugwu's death. She told herself that he was not dead; he might be close to dead but he was not dead. She willed a message to come to her about his whereabouts. She bathed outside now – the bathroom was slimy with mould and urine, so she woke up very early to take a bucket and go behind the building – and one morning she caught a movement at the corner and saw Pastor Ambrose watching her. 'Pastor Ambrose!' she called out, and he dashed off. 'You are not ashamed of yourself? If only you would spend your time praying for somebody to come and tell me what happened to Ugwu instead of spying on a married woman taking a bath.'

She visited Mrs Muokelu's home, hoping for a story of a vision that involved Ugwu's safety, but a neighbour told her that Mrs Muokelu's whole family was gone. They had left without telling anybody. She listened to the war reports on Radio Biafra more carefully, as if there might be clues about Ugwu in the ebullient voice reporting the pushback of the vandals, the successes of gallant Biafran soldiers. A man wearing a stained white kaftan walked into the yard on a Saturday afternoon, and Olanna hurried up to him, certain that he had come with news of Ugwu.

'Tell me,' she said. 'Tell me where Ugwu is.'

The man looked confused. '*Dalu*. I am looking for Alice Njokamma from Asaba.'

'Alice?' Olanna stared at the man, as though to give him a chance to take it back and ask for her instead. 'Alice?'

'Yes, Alice from Asaba. I am her kinsman. My family's compound is next to theirs.'

Olanna pointed at Alice's door. He went over and knocked and knocked.

'She is in?' he asked.

Olanna nodded, resentful that he had not brought news of Ugwu.

The man knocked again and called out, 'I am from the Isioma family in Asaba.'

Alice opened the door and he went in. Moments later, Alice rushed out and threw herself on the ground, rolling this way and that; in the evening sunlight, her sand-patched skin was tinted with gold.

'*O gini mere?* What happened?' the neighbours asked, gathering around Alice.

'I am from Asaba and I got word about our hometown this morning,' the man said. His accent was thicker than Alice's, and Olanna understood his Igbo a moment after he had spoken. 'The vandals took our town many weeks ago and they announced that all the indigenes should come out and say "One Nigeria" and they would give them rice. So people came out of hiding and said "One Nigeria" and the vandals shot them, men, women, and children. Everyone.' The man paused. 'There is nobody left in the Njokamma family. Nobody left.'

Alice was lying on her back, rubbing her head frantically against the ground, moaning. Clumps of sand were in her hair. She jumped up and ran towards the road but Pastor Ambrose ran after her and dragged her back. She jerked away and threw herself down again, her lips pulled back, her teeth bared. 'What am I doing still alive? They should come and kill me now! I said they should come and kill me!'

She was strengthened, emboldened, by the madness of grief and she fought off everyone who tried to hold her. She rolled on the ground with such force that the stones cut her skin in tiny red gashes. The neighbours said *oh* and shook their heads. Odenigbo came out of the room then and went over and picked Alice up and held her, and she stayed still and began to weep, her head resting on his shoulder. Olanna watched them. There was a familiar melding to the curve of Odenigbo's arms around Alice. He held her with the ease of someone who had held her before.

Finally, Alice sat down on a bench, blank and stricken. From time to time, she would scream '*Hei!*' and stand up and place her hands on her head. Odenigbo sat by her and urged her to drink some water. He and the man from Asaba talked in low voices as if they alone were responsible for her, and afterwards he came up to where Olanna was sitting on the veranda.

'Will you pack some of her things, *nkem?*' he asked. 'The man says he has some Asaba people in his compound and he will take her to stay with them for a while.'

Olanna looked up at him, her face blank. 'No,' she said.

'No?'

'No,' she said again, loudly now. 'No.' And she got up and went into the room. She would not pack anybody's clothes. She did not know who did pack Alice's things, perhaps Odenigbo did, but she heard the '*Ije oma*, go well,' from many neighbours as Alice and the man left late in the evening. Olanna slept outside and dreamed of Alice and Odenigbo on the bed in Nsukka, their sweat on her newly washed sheet; she woke up with a raging suspicion in her heart and the boom of shelling in her ears.

'The vandals are close!' Pastor Ambrose cried, and he was first to run out of the compound, a stuffed duffel bag in his hand.

The yard erupted in activity, shouting, packing, leaving. The shelling, like burst after burst of horribly loud, vile coughing, did not stop. And the car did not start. Odenigbo tried and tried and the road was already crowded with refugees and the crashing explosions of mortars sounded as close as St John's Road. Mama Oji was screaming at her husband. Mama Adanna was begging Olanna to let her get into the car with some of her children and Olanna said, 'No, take your children and go.'

Odenigbo started the engine and it whined and died. The compound was almost empty. A woman on the road was dragging a stubborn goat and finally left it behind and hurried ahead. Odenigbo turned the key and again the car stalled. Olanna could feel the ground underneath vibrating with each boom.

Odenigbo turned the key again and again. The car would not start.

'Start walking with Baby,' he said. Sweat clung to his brow.

'What?'

'I'll pick you both up when the car starts.'

'If we are walking, we will walk together.'

Odenigbo tried to start the car again. Olanna turned, surprised at how quiet Baby was, sitting in the back beside their rolled-up mattresses. Baby was watching Odenigbo carefully, as though urging both him and the car on with her eyes.

Odenigbo came out and opened the bonnet and Olanna climbed out, too, and let Baby out and then wondered what she would take from the boot and what she would leave behind. The compound was empty and only one or two people walked past the road now. There was the rattle of gunfire nearby. She was frightened. Her hands were shaking.

'Let's start walking,' Olanna said. 'Nobody is left in Umuahia!'

Odenigbo got in and took a deep breath and turned the key. The car started. He drove fast and, on the outskirts of Umuahia, Olanna asked, 'Did you do anything with Alice?'

Odenigbo did not answer, looking straight ahead.

'I asked you a question, Odenigbo.'

'*Mba*, I didn't do anything with Alice.' He glanced at her and then looked ahead at the road.

They said nothing else to each other until they arrived in Orlu, and Kainene and Harrison came out of the house. Harrison began to unpack the things in the car.

Kainene hugged Olanna, picked Baby up, and then turned to Odenigbo. 'What an interesting beard,' she said. 'Are we trying to copy His Excellency?'

'I never try to copy anyone.'

'Of course. I had forgotten how original you are.'

Kainene's voice was thick with the tension that surrounded them all. Olanna could feel it, moisture-heavy, hanging over the room when Richard came back and stiffly shook hands with Odenigbo and, later, when they sat at the table and ate the yam slices Harrison served on enamel plates.

'We're here until we can find a place to rent,' Odenigbo said, looking at Kainene.

Kainene stared back at him, raised her eyebrows, and said, 'Harrison! Bring some more palm oil for Chiamaka.'

Harrison came in and placed a bowl of oil before Baby. After he left, Kainene said, 'He roasted a fantastic bush rat for us last week. But you would have thought it was a rack of lamb the way he went on about it.'

Olanna laughed. Richard's laughter was tentative. Baby laughed too, as if she understood. And Odenigbo focused, unsmiling, on his plate. On the radio, there was a repeat broadcast of the Ahiara declaration, His Excellency's voice measured and determined.

> *Biafra will not betray the black man. No matter the odds, we will fight with all our might until black men everywhere can point with pride to this Republic, standing dignified and defiant, an example of African nationalism. . . .*

Richard excused himself and came back with a bottle of brandy and gestured towards Odenigbo. 'An American journalist gave it to me.'

Odenigbo stared at the bottle.

'It's brandy,' Richard said, holding it out, as if Odenigbo did not know. They had not spoken since Odenigbo drove to his house years ago to shout at him. They had not spoken even after they shook hands today.

Odenigbo did not reach out to take the bottle.

'You can have Biafran sherry instead,' Kainene said. 'Possibly more suitable for your tough revolutionary liver.'

Odenigbo looked at her and there was a small, sneering smile on his face, as though he was both amused and annoyed by her. He stood up. 'No brandy for me, thank you. I should get to bed. I have quite a walk ahead of me, now that Manpower has moved to the bush.'

Olanna watched him go inside. She did not look at Richard.

'Bedtime, Baby,' she said.

'No,' Baby said, and pretended to focus on her empty plate.

'Come right now,' Olanna said, and Baby got up.

In the room, Odenigbo was tying his wrapper around his waist. 'I was just coming to put Baby to bed,' he said. Olanna ignored him.

'Sleep well, Baby, *ka chi fo*,' he said.

'Good night, Daddy.'

Olanna placed Baby down on the mattress, covered her with a wrapper, kissed her forehead, and felt the sudden urge to cry at the thought of Ugwu. He would have slept on a mat in the living room.

Odenigbo came and stood close to her and she wanted to back away, unsure what he was trying to do. He touched her collarbone. 'Look how bony you are.'

She glanced down, irritated by his touch, surprised to see how it jutted out; she did not know she had lost so much weight. She said nothing and went back to the living room. Richard was no longer there.

Kainene was still at the table. 'So you and Odenigbo decided to look for a place?' she asked. 'My humble home is not good enough?'

'Are you listening to him? We didn't decide anything. If he wants to find a place he can go ahead and live there alone,' Olanna said.

Kainene looked at her. 'What is the matter?'

Olanna shook her head.

Kainene dipped a finger in palm oil and brought it to her mouth. '*Ejima m*, what is the matter?' she asked again.

'Nothing, really. There is nothing I can point at,' Olanna said, looking at the bottle of brandy on the table. 'I want this war to end so that he can come back. He has become somebody else.'

'We are all in this war, and it is up to us to decide to become somebody else or not,' Kainene said.

'He just drinks and drinks cheap *kai-kai*. The few times they pay him, the money goes quickly. I think he slept with Alice, that Asaba woman in our yard. I can't stand him. I can't stand him close to me.'

'Good,' Kainene said.

'Good?'

'Yes, good. There's something very lazy about the way you have loved him blindly for so long without ever criticizing him. You've never even accepted that the man is ugly,' Kainene said. There was a small smile on her face and then she was laughing, and Olanna could not help but laugh too, because it was not what she had wanted to hear and because hearing it had made her feel better.

In the morning, Kainene showed Olanna a small, pear-shaped vial of face cream. 'Look at this. Somebody went abroad and brought it for me. My face creams finished months ago and I've been using that horrible Biafran-made oil.'

Olanna examined the pink jar. They took turns dabbing the cream on their faces, slowly, sensually, and afterwards went down to the refugee camp. They went every morning. The new harmattan winds blew dust everywhere, and Baby joined the thin children who ran around with their naked bellies wreathed in brown. Many of the children collected pieces of shrapnel, played with them, traded them. When Baby came back with two bits of jagged metal, Olanna shouted at her and pulled her ear and took them away. She hated to think that Baby was playing with the cold leftovers of things that killed. But Kainene asked her to give them back to Baby. Kainene gave Baby a can to store the shrapnel. Kainene asked Baby to join the older children making lizard traps, to learn how to mat the palm fronds and place the cocoon full of *iddo* ants inside. Kainene let Baby hold the dagger of the emaciated man who paraded the compound, muttering, '*Ngwa*, let the vandals come, let them come now.' Kainene let Baby eat a lizard leg.

'Chiamaka should see life as it is, *ejima m*,' Kainene said, as they moisturized their faces. 'You protect her too much from life.'

'I just want to keep my child safe,' Olanna said. She took a small dash of cream and began to rub it into her face with the tips of her fingers.

'They protected us too much,' Kainene said.

'Daddy and Mum?' Olanna asked, although she knew.

'Yes.' Kainene spread the cream on her face with her palms. 'Good thing Mum left. Can you imagine her ever living without things like this? Or using palm-kernel oil?'

Olanna laughed. She wished, though, Kainene would not take so much of the cream, so that it would last as long as possible.

'Why were you always so keen to please Mum and Dad?' Kainene asked.

Olanna held her hands to her face, silent for a while. 'I don't know. I think I felt sorry for them.'

'You have always felt sorry for people who don't need you to feel sorry for them.'

Olanna said nothing because she did not know what to say. It was the kind of thing she would have discussed with Odenigbo, Kainene's voicing for the first time a resentment with their parents and with her, but she and Odenigbo hardly talked. He had found a bar close by; only last week, the bar owner had come to the house asking for him because he had not paid his balance. Olanna said nothing to him after the bar owner left. She was no longer sure when he went to the Manpower Directorate and when he simply went to the bar. She refused to worry about him.

She worried about other things: how her periods were sparse and no longer red but a muddy-brown, how Baby's hair was falling out, how hunger was stealing the memories of the children. She was determined that their minds be kept alert; they were Biafra's future, after all. So every day she taught them under the flame tree, away from the horrible smells towards the back of the buildings. She would have them memorize one line of a poem, and the next day they would have forgotten it. They chased after lizards. They ate *garri* and water once a day now instead of twice because Kainene's suppliers could no longer cross over to Mbosi to buy *garri*; all the roads were occupied. Kainene launched a Plant Our Own Food movement, and when she joined the men and women and children in making ridges, Olanna wondered where she had learned to hold a hoe. But the soil was parched. The harmattan cracked lips and feet.

Three children died in one day. Father Marcel said Mass without Holy Communion. A young girl named Urenwa's belly began to grow and Kainene was not sure if it was kwashiorkor or pregnancy until the girl's mother slapped her and asked, 'Who? Who did this to you? Where did you see the man that did this to you?' The doctor no longer visited because there was no petrol and there were too many dying soldiers to treat. The well dried up. Kainene went often to the Directorate at Ahiara to get a water tanker, but each time she came back with a vague promise from the director. The thick, ugly odours of unwashed bodies and rotting flesh from the shallow graves behind the buildings grew stronger. Flies flew over the sores on children's bodies. Bedbugs and *kwalikwata* crawled; women would untie their wrappers to reveal an ugly rash of reddened bites around their waists, like hives steeped in blood. Oranges were in season and Kainene asked them to eat oranges from the trees, although it gave them diarrhoea, and then to squeeze the peels against their skin because the smell of citrus masked the smell of dirt.

In the evenings, Olanna and Kainene walked home together. They talked about the people at the camp, about their school days at Heathgrove, about their parents, about Odenigbo.

'Have you asked him again about that Asaba woman?' Kainene said.

'Not yet.'

'Before you ask him, just walk up to him and slap his face. If he dares to slap you back, I will come at him with Harrison's kitchen knife. But the slap will shake the truth out of him.'

Olanna laughed and noticed that they were both walking at a leisurely pace and that their steps were in harmony, their slippers coated in brown dust.

'Grandpapa used to say that it gets worse and then it gets better. *O dikata njo, o dikwa mma,*' Kainene said.

'I remember.'

'The world will turn around soon, and Nigeria will stop this,' Kainene said quietly. 'We'll win.'

'Yes.' Olanna believed it more because Kainene said it.

There were evenings when Kainene was distant, immersed in herself. Once she said, 'I never really noticed Ikejide,' and Olanna placed an arm on her sister's shoulder and said nothing. Mostly, though, Kainene was in high spirits and they would sit outside and talk and listen to the radio and to the bats flying around the cashew trees. Sometimes, Richard joined them. Odenigbo never did.

Then, one evening, it rained, a flinty, blustery rain, a strange shower in the dry season, and perhaps it was why Odenigbo did not go to the bar. It was the evening that he finally accepted Richard's brandy, holding it to his nose and inhaling deeply before he drank, he and Richard still saying very little to each other. And it was the evening that Dr Nwala came to tell them that Okeoma had been killed. Lightning flashed across the sky and thunder rumbled and Kainene said, laughing, 'It sounds like shelling.'

'I'm worried that they have not bombed us in a while,' Olanna said. 'I wonder what they are planning.'

'Perhaps an atomic bomb,' Kainene said.

They heard the car drive in then and Kainene stood up. 'Who is visiting in this kind of weather at night?'

She opened the door and Dr Nwala came in, water dripping down his face. Olanna recalled how he had extended his hand to help her up after the air raid on her wedding day, how he had said that her dress would get dirty – as though it were not already dirty from lying on the ground. He was thinner and lankier than she remembered and looked as though he would break in two if he sat down abruptly. He did not sit down. He did not waste time with greetings. He had raised his loose shirt away from his body, was rapidly flipping it to get the water off when he said, 'Okeoma has gone, *o jebego*. They were on a mission to retake Umuahia when it happened. I saw him last month, and he told me he was writing some poems and Olanna was his muse, and if anything happened to him I should make sure the poems went to her. But I can't find them. The people who brought the message said that they never saw him writing anything. So I said I would come and tell you he has gone but I did not find the poems.'

Olanna was nodding without quite understanding because Dr Nwala was saying too many words too quickly. Then she stopped. He meant that Okeoma was dead. It was raining in harmattan and Okeoma was dead.

'Okeoma?' Odenigbo spoke in a cracked whisper. '*Onye?* Are you talking about Okeoma?'

Olanna reached out and grasped Odenigbo's arm and the screams came out of her, screeching, piercing screams, because something in her head was stretched taut. Because she felt attacked, relentlessly clobbered, by loss. She did not let go of his arm until Dr Nwala stumbled back into the rain, until they climbed silently onto their mattress on the floor. When he slid into her, she thought how different he felt, lighter and narrower, on top of her. He was still, so still she thrashed around and pulled at his hips. But he did not move. Then he began to thrust and her pleasure multiplied, sharpened on stone so that each tiny spark became a pleasure all its own. She heard herself crying, her sobbing louder and louder until Baby stirred and he placed his palm against her mouth. He was crying too; she felt the tears drop on her body before she saw them on his face.

Later, he propped himself on his elbow and watched her. 'You're so strong, *nkem*.'

Those were words she had never heard from him. He looked old; there was a wetness in his eyes, a crumpled defeat in his face, that made him look older. She wanted to ask him why he had said that, what he meant, but she didn't and she was not sure who fell asleep first. The next morning, she woke up too early, smelling her own bad breath and feeling a sad and unsettling peace.

32

Ugwu wanted to die, at first. It was not because of the hot tingle in his head or the stickiness of blood on his back or the pain in his buttocks or the way he gasped for air, but because of his thirst. His throat was scorched. The infantrymen carrying him were talking about how rescuing him had given them a reason to run away, how their bullets had finished and they had sent for reinforcements and nothing was forthcoming and the vandals were advancing. But Ugwu's thirst clogged his ears and muffled their words. He was on their shoulders, bandaged with their shirts, the pain shooting all over his body as they walked. He gulped for air, gasped, and sucked but somehow he could not get enough. His thirst nauseated him.

'Water, please,' he croaked. They would not give him any; if he had the energy, he would invoke all the curses he knew on them. If he had a gun he would have shot them all and then shot himself.

Now, in the hospital where they had left him, he no longer wanted to die, but he feared he would; there were so many bodies littered around him, on mats, on mattresses, on the bare floor. There was so much blood everywhere. He heard the sharp screams of men when the doctor examined them and knew that his was not the worst case, even as he felt his own blood seeping out, first warm and then clammy cold against his side. The blood took his will; he was too exhausted to do anything about it and when the nurses hurried past him and left his bandaging unchanged, he did not call out to them. He said nothing, either, when they came and pushed him to his side and gave him quick, unceremonious injections. In his delirious moments, he saw Eberechi wearing her tight skirt and making gestures to him that he could not understand. And in his lucid moments, death occupied him. He tried to visualize a heaven, a God seated on a throne, but could not. Yet the alternative vision, that death was nothing but an endless silence, seemed unlikely. There was a part of him that dreamed, and he was not sure if that part could ever retreat into an interminable silence. Death would be a complete knowingness, but what frightened him was this: not knowing beforehand what it was he would know.

In the evenings, in the dim half-light, the people from Caritas came, a priest and two helpers carrying kerosene lanterns, giving out milk and sugar to the soldiers, asking their names and where they had come from.

'Nsukka,' Ugwu said, when he was asked. He thought the priest's voice was vaguely familiar, but then everything was vaguely familiar here: The blood of the man next to him smelt like his, the nurse who placed a bowl of thin *akamu* next to him smiled like Eberechi.

'Nsukka? What is your name?' the priest asked.

Ugwu struggled to focus on the rounded face, the glasses, the browned collar. It was Father Damian. 'I am Ugwu. I used to come with my madam Olanna to St Vincent de Paul.'

'Ah!' Father Damian squeezed his hand and Ugwu winced. 'You fought for the cause? Where were you wounded? What have they done for you?'

Ugwu shook his head. One part of his buttocks was wrapped in fiery red pain; it consumed him. Father Damian spooned some powdered milk into his mouth and then placed a bag of sugar and milk next to him.

'I know Odenigbo is with Manpower. I will send word to them,' Father Damian said. Before he left, he slipped a wooden rosary onto Ugwu's wrist.

The rosary was there, a cold pressure against his skin, when Mr Richard came some days later.

'Ugwu, Ugwu.' The fair hair and the strange-coloured eyes swam above him, and Ugwu was not sure who it was.

'Can you hear me, Ugwu? I've come to take you.' It was the same voice that had asked Ugwu questions about his village festival years ago. Ugwu knew then who it was. Mr Richard tried to help him get up and the pain shot up from his side and buttock to his head and eyes. Ugwu cried out, then clenched his teeth and bit his lip and sucked his own blood.

'Easy now, easy now,' Mr Richard said.

The bumpy ride lying in the backseat of the Peugeot 404 and the fierce sun that sparkled the windscreen made Ugwu wonder if he had died and this was what happened at death: an unending journey in a car. Finally, they stopped at a hospital that smelt not of blood but of disinfectant. Only when Ugwu lay in a real bed did he think that perhaps he was not going to die after all.

'This place has been bombed quite a bit in the past week, and we will have to leave right after the doctor sees you. He's really not a doctor – he was in his fourth year in university when the war started – but he's done very well,' Mr Richard said. 'Olanna and Odenigbo and Baby have been with us in Orlu since Umuahia fell, and of course Harrison is there too. Kainene needs help at the refugee camp, so you better hurry up and be well.'

Ugwu sensed that Mr Richard was talking too much, for his benefit, perhaps to keep him awake until the doctor came. But he was grateful for Mr Richard's laughter, the normality of it, the way it came back with a force of memory and made him inhabit the time when Mr Richard wrote his answers in a leather-covered book.

'We all had a bit of a shock when we heard you were alive and at Emekuku Hospital – a good kind of shock, of course. Thank heavens there actually hadn't been a symbolic burial, although there was some sort of memorial service before Umuahia fell.'

Ugwu's eyelids throbbed. 'They said I was dead, sah?'

'Oh, yes, they did. It seems your battalion thought you had died during the operation.'

Ugwu's eyes were closing and would not stay open when he forced them. Finally he got them open and Mr Richard was looking down at him. 'Who is Eberechi?'

'Sah?'

'You kept saying Eberechi.'

'She is somebody I know, sah.'

'In Umuahia?'

'Yes, sah.'

Mr Richard's eyes softened. 'And you don't know where she is now?'

'No, sah.'

'Have you been wearing those clothes since you were wounded?'

'Yes, sah. The infantrymen gave me the trousers and shirt.'

'You need a wash.'

Ugwu smiled. 'Yes, sah.'

'Were you afraid?' Mr Richard asked, after a while.

He shifted; the pain was everywhere and there was no comfortable position. 'Afraid, sah?'

'Yes.'

'Sometimes, sah.' He paused. 'I found a book at our camp. I was so sad and angry for the writer.'

'What book was it?'

'The autobiography of a black American called Frederick Douglass.'

Mr Richard wrote something down. 'I shall use this anecdote in my book.'

'You are writing a book.'

'Yes.'

'What is it about, sah?'

'The war, and what happened before, and how much should not have happened. It will be called "The World Was Silent When We Died".'

Later, Ugwu murmured the title to himself: *The World Was Silent When We Died*. It haunted him, filled him with shame. It made him think about that girl in the bar, her pinched face and the hate in her eyes as she lay on her back on the dirty floor.

Master and Olanna wrapped their arms around Ugwu, but lightly, without pressure, so as not to cause him pain. He felt acutely uncomfortable; they had never hugged him before.

'Ugwu,' Master said, shaking his head. 'Ugwu.'

Baby clung to his hand and refused to let go and Ugwu's whole life suddenly gathered in a lump in his throat, and he was sobbing and the tears hurt his eyes. He was angry with himself for crying, and later, as he recounted the story of what had happened to him, he spoke in a detached voice. He lied about how he had been conscripted; he said Pastor Ambrose had pleaded with him to help carry his sick sister to the herbalist's and he was on his way back when the soldiers caught him. He used words like *enemy fire* and *Attack HQ* with a casual coldness, as if to make up for his crying.

'And they told us you were dead,' Olanna said, watching him. 'Maybe Okeoma is alive too.'

Ugwu stared at her.

'They said he was killed in action,' Olanna said. 'And I got word that kwashiorkor has finally taken Adanna. Baby doesn't know, of course.'

Ugwu looked away. Her news provoked him. He felt angry with her for telling him what he did not want to hear.

'Too many people are dying,' he said.

'It is what happens in war, too many people die,' Olanna said. 'But we will win this thing. Is your pillow in a good position?'

'Yes, mah.'

He could not sit on one part of his buttocks and so, during the first few weeks in Orlu, he lay on his side. Olanna was always beside him, forcing him to eat and willing him to live. His mind wandered often. He did not need the echo of pain on his side and in his buttocks and on his back to remember his *ogbunigwe* exploding, or High-Tech's laughter, or the dead hate in the eyes of the girl. He could not remember her features, but the look in her eyes stayed with him, as did the tense, dryness between her legs, the way he had done what he had not wanted to do. In that grey space between dreaming and daydreaming, where he controlled most of what he imagined, he saw the bar, smelt the alcohol, and heard the soldiers saying 'Target Destroyer', but it was not the bar girl that lay with her back on the floor, it was Eberechi. He woke up hating the image and hating himself. He would give himself time to atone for what he had done. Then he would go and look for Eberechi. Perhaps she and her family had gone to their village in Mbaise or perhaps they were here in Orlu somewhere. She would wait for him; she would know he would come for her. That Eberechi would wait for him, that her waiting for him was proof of his redemption, gave him comfort as he healed. It surprised him that it was possible for his body to return to what it had been and for his mind to function with permanent lucidity.

During the day he helped out at the refugee camp, and in the evenings he wrote. He sat under the flame tree and wrote in small, careful letters on the sides of old newspapers, on some paper Kainene had done supply calculations on, on the back of an old calendar. He wrote a poem about people getting a buttocks rash after defecating in imported buckets, but it did not sound as lyrical as Okeoma's and he tore it up; then he wrote about a young woman with a perfect backside who pinched the neck of a young man and tore that up too.

Finally, he started to write about Aunty Arize's anonymous death in Kano and about Olanna losing the use of her legs, about Okeoma's smart-fitting army uniform and Professor Ekwenugo's bandaged hands. He wrote about the children of the refugee camp, how diligently they chased after lizards, how four boys had chased a quick lizard up a mango tree and one of them climbed up after it and the lizard leapt off the tree and into the outstretched hand of one of the other three surrounding the tree.

'The lizards have become smarter. They run faster now and hide under blocks of cement,' the boy who had climbed told Ugwu. They roasted and shared the lizard, shooing other children away. Later, the boy offered Ugwu a tiny bit of his stringy share. Ugwu thanked him and shook his head and realized that he would never be able to capture that child on paper, never be able to describe well enough the fear that dulled the eyes of mothers in the refugee camp when the bomber planes charged out of the sky. He would never be able to depict the very bleakness of bombing hungry people. But he tried, and the more he wrote, the less he dreamed.

Olanna was teaching some children to recite the multiplication tables the morning that Kainene rushed up to the flame tree.

'Can you believe who is responsible for that small girl Urenwa's pregnancy?' Kainene asked, and Ugwu almost did not recognize her. Her eyes bulged out of her angular face, filled with rage and tears. 'Can you believe it is Father Marcel?'

Olanna stood up. '*Gini?* What are you saying?'

'Apparently I've been blind; she's not the only one,' Kainene said. 'He fucks most of them before he gives them the crayfish that I slave to get here!'

Later, Ugwu watched Kainene push at Father Marcel's chest with both hands, shouting into his face, shoving him so hard that Ugwu feared the man would fall. '*Amosu!* You devil!' Then she turned to Father Jude. 'How could you stay here and let him spread the legs of starving girls? How will you account for this to your God? You both are leaving now, right now. I will take this to Ojukwu myself if I have to!'

There were tears running down her face. There was something magnificent in her rage. Ugwu felt stained and unworthy as he went about his new duties after the priests left – distributing *garri*, breaking up fights, supervising the scorched and failing farms. He wondered what Kainene would say, what she would do to him, feel about him, if she ever knew about the girl in the bar. She would loathe him. So would Olanna. So would Eberechi.

He listened to the conversations in the evenings, writing in his mind what he would later transfer to paper. It was mostly Kainene and Olanna who talked, as though they created their own world that Master and Mr Richard could never quite enter. Sometimes, Harrison would come and sit with Ugwu but say very little, as though he was both puzzled by and respectful of him. Ugwu was no longer just Ugwu, he was now one of 'our boys'; he had fought for the cause. The moon was always a brilliant white, and once in a while the night wind brought the hooting of owls and the rise and fall of voices from the refugee camp. Baby slept on a mat with Olanna's wrapper over her to keep the mosquitoes away. Whenever they heard the far-off drone of the relief planes, nothing like the low-flying swiftness of the bombers, Kainene would say, 'I hope that one will manage to land.' And Olanna would respond with a light laugh. 'We have to cook our next soup with stockfish.'

When they listened to Radio Biafra, Ugwu would get up and walk away. The shabby theatrics of the war reports, the voice that forced morsels of invented hope down people's throats, did not interest him. One afternoon, Harrison came up to the flame tree carrying the radio turned on high to Radio Biafra.

'Please turn that thing off,' Ugwu said. He was watching some little boys playing on the nearby patch of grass. 'I want to hear the birds.'

'There are no birds singing,' Harrison said.

'Turn it off.'

'His Excellency is about to give a speech.'

'Turn it off or carry it away.'

'You don't want to hear His Excellency?'

'*Mba*, No.'

Harrison was watching him. 'It will be a great speech.'

'There is no such thing as greatness,' Ugwu said.

Harrison walked away looking wounded and Ugwu did not bother to call him; he went back to watching the children. They ran sluggishly on the parched grass, holding sticks as guns, making shooting sounds with their mouths, raising clouds of dust as they chased one another. Even the dust seemed listless. They were playing war. Four boys. Yesterday, they had been five. Ugwu did not remember the fifth child's name – was it Chidiebele or Chidiebube? – but he remembered how the child's belly had lately started to look as if he had swallowed a fat ball, how his hair had fallen out in tufts, how his skin had lightened, from the colour of mahogany to a sickly yellow. The other children had teased him often. *Afo mmili ukwa*, they called him: Breadfruit Belly. Once, Ugwu wanted to ask them to stop, so he could explain what kwashiorkor was – perhaps he could read out to them how he described kwashiorkor on his writing sheet. But he decided not to. There was no need to prepare them for what he was sure they would all get anyway. Ugwu did not remember the child's ever playing a Biafran officer, like His Excellency or Achuzie; he always played a Nigerian, either Gowon or Adekunle, which meant he was always defeated and had to fall down at the end and act dead. Sometimes, Ugwu wondered if the child had liked it because it gave him a chance to rest, lying down on the grass.

The child and his family had come from Oguta, one of those families who did not believe their town would fall, and so his mother looked defiant when they first arrived, as if she dared anybody to tell her she was not dreaming and would not be waking up soon. The evening they arrived, the sound of the anti-aircraft guns cut through the refugee camp just before dusk. The mother ran out and held him, her only child, in a confused hug. The other women shook her roughly, as the *wa-wa-wa* roar of the overhead planes came closer. *Come to the bunker! Are you mad? Come to the bunker!*

The woman refused and stood there holding her son, shaking. Ugwu still did not know why he had done what he did. Perhaps it was because Olanna had already grabbed Baby and run ahead of him and his hands were free. But he reached out and pulled the child from the woman's embrace and ran. The child was still heavy then, still weighed something; his mother had no choice but to follow. The planes were strafing and, just before Ugwu shoved the child down the bunker, a bullet flew closely past; he smelt rather than saw it, the acridness of hot metal.

It was in the bunker, while playing with the damp soil that crawled with crickets and ants, that the child had told Ugwu his name. Chidiebele or Chidiebube, he was not sure. But it was Chidi-something. Perhaps Chidiebele, the more common name. The name almost sounded like a joke now. Chidiebele: *God is merciful.*

Later, the four boys had stopped playing war and had gone inside when Ugwu heard the thin, strangled wail from the classroom at the end of the building. He knew that that child's aunty would come out soon and bravely tell the people nearby, that the mother would throw herself in the dirt and roll and shout until she lost her voice, and then she would take a razor and leave her scalp bare and bleeding.

He put on his singlet and went out to offer to help dig the small grave.

33

Richard sat next to Kainene and rubbed her shoulder as she laughed at something Olanna was saying. He loved the way her neck looked longer when she threw back her head and laughed. He loved the evenings spent with her and Olanna and Odenigbo; they reminded him of Odenigbo's dimly lit living room in Nsukka, of tasting beer on his pepper-drenched tongue. Kainene reached out for the enamel plate of roasted crickets, Harrison's new specialty; he seemed to know just where to dig for them in the dry earth and how to break them up into bits after roasting, so that they lasted a bit longer. Kainene placed a piece in her mouth. Richard took two pieces and crunched slowly. It was getting dark, and the cashew trees had become silent grey silhouettes. A dust haze hung above them all.

'What do you think accounts for the success of the white man's mission in Africa, Richard?' Odenigbo asked.

'The success?' Odenigbo unnerved him, the way he would brood for long moments and then abruptly ask or say something unexpected.

'Yes, the success. I think in English,' Odenigbo said.

'Perhaps you should first account for the failure of the black man to curb the white man's mission,' Kainene said.

'Who brought racism into the world?' Odenigbo asked.

'I don't see your point,' Kainene said.

'The white man brought racism into the world. He used it as a basis of conquest. It is always easier to conquer a more humane people.'

'So when we conquer the Nigerians we will be the less humane?' Kainene asked.

Odenigbo said nothing. Something rustled near the cashew trees, and Harrison leapt up and ran over to see if it was a bush rat he could catch.

'Inatimi has given me some Nigerian coins,' Kainene said finally. 'You know these Biafran Organization of Freedom Fighters people have quite a bit of Nigerian money. I want to go to Ninth Mile and see what I can buy, and if that goes well, I will sell some of the things our people at the camp have made.'

'That's trading with the enemy,' Odenigbo said.

'It's trading with illiterate Nigerian women who have what we need.'

'It's dangerous, Kainene,' Odenigbo said; the softness in his voice surprised Richard.

'That sector is free,' Olanna said. 'Our people are trading freely there.'

'Are you going too?' Surprise lifted Odenigbo's voice as he stared at Olanna.

'No. At least not tomorrow. Maybe the next time Kainene goes.'

'Tomorrow?' It was Richard's turn to be surprised. Kainene had mentioned it once, wanting to trade across enemy lines, but he did not know she had already decided when to go.

'Yes, Kainene is going tomorrow,' Olanna said.

'Yes,' Kainene said. 'But don't mind Olanna, she will never come with me. She's always been terribly frightened of honest free enterprise.' Kainene laughed and Olanna laughed and slapped her arm; Richard saw the similarity in the curve of their lips, in the shape of their slightly larger front teeth.

'Hasn't Ninth Mile Road been occupied on and off?' Odenigbo asked. 'I don't think you should go.'

'It's all decided. I leave with Inatimi early tomorrow morning, and we'll be back by evening,' Kainene said, with that finality to her tone that Richard knew well. He was not opposed to the trip, though; he knew many people who did what she wanted to do.

That night, he dreamed that she came back with a basket full of chicken boiled in herbs, spicy *jollof* rice, soup thick with fish, and he felt irritable when he was jerked awake by raised voices just outside their window. He was reluctant to leave the dream. Kainene had woken up too and they hurried outside, Kainene with a wrapper tied around her chest and he in his shorts. It was only just dawn. The light was weak. A small crowd from the refugee camp was beating and kicking a young man crouched on the ground, his hands placed on his head to shield some of the blows. His trousers were splattered with holes and his collar was almost ripped off but the half of a yellow sun still clung to his torn sleeve.

'What is it?' Kainene asked. 'What is it?'

Before anyone spoke, Richard knew. The soldier had been stealing from the farm. It happened everywhere now, farms raided at night, raided of corn so tender they had not yet formed kernels and yams so young they were barely the size of a cocoyam.

'Do you see why anything we plant will not bear fruit?' said a woman whose child had died the week before. Her wrapper was tied low, exposing the tops of drooping breasts. 'People like this thief come and harvest everything so that we will starve to death.'

'Stop it!' Kainene said. 'Stop it right now! Leave him alone!'

'You are telling us to leave a thief? If we leave him today, tomorrow ten of them will come.'

'He is not a thief,' Kainene said. 'Did you hear me? He is not a thief. He is a hungry soldier.'

The crowd stilled at the quiet authority in her voice. Slowly, they shuffled away, back to the classrooms. The soldier got up and dusted himself off.

'Have you come from the front?' Kainene asked.

He nodded. He looked about eighteen. There were two angry bumps on either side of his forehead and blood trailed from his nostrils.

'Are you running? *I na-agba oso?* Have you deserted?' Kainene asked.

He did not respond.

'Come. Come and take some *garri* before you go,' Kainene said.

Tears crawled down from his swollen left eye and he placed a palm on it as he followed her. He did not speak except to mumble '*Dalu* – thank you' before he left, clutching the small bag of *garri*. Kainene was silent as she got dressed to go down and meet Inatimi at the camp.

'You'll leave early won't you, Richard?' she asked. 'Those Big Men may be in the office for just thirty minutes today.'

'I'll leave in an hour.' He was going to Ahiara to try and get some provisions from relief headquarters.

'Tell them I'm dying and we desperately need milk and corned beef to keep me alive,' she said. There was a new bitter undertone in her voice.

'I will,' he said. 'And go well. *Ije oma*. Come back with lots of *garri* and salt.'

They kissed, a brief press of their lips before she left. He knew that seeing that pathetic young soldier had upset her, and he knew, too, that she was thinking that the young soldier was not the reason the crops failed. They failed because the land was poor and the harmattan was harsh and there was no manure and there was nothing to plant, and when she managed to get some seed yams, the people ate half before they planted them. He wished he could reach out and twist the sky and bring victory to Biafra right away. For her.

She was not back when he returned from Ahiara in the evening. The living room smelt of bleached palm oil that came from the kitchen and Baby was lying on a mat, looking through the pages of *Eze Goes to School*.

'Carry me on your shoulders, Uncle Richard,' Baby said, running to him. Richard pretended to try and pick her up and then collapsed on a chair.

'You're a big girl now, Baby. You're too heavy to be picked up.'

'No!'

Olanna was standing by the kitchen, watching them. 'You know, Baby has grown wiser but she hasn't grown taller since the war started.'

Richard smiled. 'Better wisdom than height,' he said, and she smiled too. He realized how little they said to each other, how carefully they avoided being alone together.

'No luck at Ahiara?' Olanna asked.

'No. I tried everywhere. The relief centres are empty. I saw a grown man sitting on the floor in front of one building and sucking his thumb,' he said.

'What about the people you know at the directorates?'

'They said they have nothing and that our emphasis now is self-sufficiency and farming.'

'Farming with what? And how are we going to feed millions of people on the tiny territory we hold now?'

Richard looked at her. Even the slightest hint of criticism of Biafra made him uncomfortable. Worries had lodged in the cracks in his mind since Umuahia fell, but he did not voice them.

'Is Kainene at the camp?' he asked.

Olanna wiped her brow. 'I think so. She and Inatimi should be back by now.'

Richard went outside to play with Baby. He placed her on his shoulders so that she could grasp at a cashew leaf above and then put her down, thinking how tiny, how light, she was for a six-year-old. He drew lines on the ground and asked her to pick up some stones and tried to teach her to play *nchokolo*. He watched her lay out and arrange the pieces of jagged metal from a tin: her shrapnel collection. Kainene was not back an hour later. Richard took Baby down the road to the camp. Kainene was not sitting on the steps in front of the Point of No Return, as she sometimes did. She was not in the sickroom. She was not in any of the classrooms. Richard saw Ugwu under the flame tree, writing on a piece of paper.

'Aunty Kainene is not back,' Ugwu said, before Richard asked.

'You're sure she didn't come back and then go off somewhere else?'

'I'm sure, sah. But I expect she will be back soon.'

Richard was amused by the formal precision in the way Ugwu said *expect*; he admired Ugwu's ambition and his recent scribbling on any paper he could find. Once he had tried to find where Ugwu left some of them so he could take a look, but he had found none. They were probably all tucked into his shorts.

'What are you writing now?' he asked.

'A small thing, sah,' Ugwu said.

'I'll stay with Ugwu,' Baby said.

'Okay, Baby.' Richard knew that she would hurry to the classrooms to find some of the children and begin hunting for lizards or crickets. Or she would look for the self-styled militiaman who wore a dagger round his waist and ask if she could hold it. He walked back to the house. Odenigbo had just returned from work and, in the bright evening sun, his shirt was worn so thin in front that Richard could see the curled hair on his chest.

'Is Kainene back?' Odenigbo asked.

'Not yet.'

Odenigbo gave him a long, accusing glance before he went inside to change. He came back out with a wrapper slung around his body and tied behind his neck and sat with Richard in the living room. On the radio, His Excellency announced that he was going abroad to search for peace.

*In accord with my own frequent affirmations that I would per-
sonally go anywhere to secure peace and security for my people, I
am now travelling out of Biafra to explore . . .*

The sun was falling when Ugwu and Baby came home.

'That small child, Nneka, just died and her mother has refused to
let them take the body and bury,' Ugwu said, after he greeted them.

'Is Kainene there?' Richard asked.

'No,' Ugwu said.

Odenigbo got up and Richard got up and they walked down to the
refugee camp together. They said nothing to each other. A woman
was wailing from one of the classrooms. They asked questions and
everyone said the same thing: Kainene had left with Inatimi early in
the morning. She told them she was going on *afia attack*, to trade
across enemy lines, and that she would be back by late afternoon.

A day passed, then a second day. Everything remained the same, the
dryness in the air, the dusty winds, the refugees tilling dried soil, but
Kainene was not back. Richard felt himself tumbling through a tun-
nel, felt the weight being sucked off him hour after hour. Odenigbo
told him Kainene was probably just held up on the other side, waiting
for the vandals to move before she came home. Olanna said this delay
happened all the time to women who did the attack trade. But there
was, in Olanna's eyes, a furtive fear. Even Odenigbo looked fearful
when he said he would not go with them to search for Kainene
because he knew she would come home; it was as if he was afraid
of what they would discover. Olanna sat beside Richard as he drove
to Ninth Mile. They were silent, but when he stopped to ask people
on the roadside if they had seen anybody who looked like Kainene,
she would say, '*O tolu ogo, di ezigbo oji*'; as if repeating what Richard
had already said, that Kainene was tall and very dark, would jog the
people's memory better. Richard showed them Kainene's picture.
Sometimes, in his rush, he pulled out the picture of the roped pot
instead. Nobody had seen her. Nobody had seen a car like Inatimi's.
They even asked the Biafran soldiers, the ones who told them they
could not go any farther because the roads were occupied. The soldiers
shook their heads and said they had not seen her. On the drive back,
Richard began to cry.

'Why are you crying?' Olanna snapped at him. 'Kainene is just stuck on the other side for a few days.'

Richard's tears blinded him. He veered off the road and the car screeched as it ran into the thick undergrowth of the bush.

'Stop! Stop!' Olanna said.

He stopped and she took the key from him and went around and opened his door. As she drove them home, she hummed steadily under her breath.

34

Olanna ran the wooden comb through Baby's hair as gently as she could, and yet there was a large tuft left on the teeth. Ugwu was sitting on a bench writing. A week had passed and Kainene was not back. The harmattan winds were calmer today, they did not make the cashew trees swirl, but they blew sand everywhere and the air was thick with grit and with rumours that His Excellency had not gone in search of peace but had run away. Olanna knew it could not be. She believed, as firmly and as quietly as she believed that Kainene would come home soon, that His Excellency's journey would be a success. He would come back with a signed document that would declare the war over, that would proclaim a free Biafra. He would come back with justice and with salt.

She combed Baby's hair, and again some of it fell out. Olanna held the thin wisps in her hand, a sun-bleached yellow-brown that was nothing like Baby's natural jet-black. It frightened her. Kainene had told her some weeks back that it was a sign of extreme wisdom, Baby's hair falling off at only six years old, and afterwards Kainene had gone out to look for more protein tablets for Baby.

Ugwu looked up from his writing. 'Maybe you should not plait her hair, mah.'

'Yes. Maybe that's why it's falling out, too much plaiting.'

'My hair is not falling out!' Baby said, and patted her head.

Olanna placed the comb down. 'I keep thinking about the hair on that child's head I saw on the train; it was very thick. It must have been work for her mother to plait it.'

'How was it plaited?' Ugwu asked.

Olanna was surprised, at first, by the question and then she realized that she clearly remembered how it was plaited and she began to describe the hairstyle, how some of the braids fell across the forehead.

Then she described the head itself, the open eyes, the greying skin. Ugwu was writing as she spoke, and his writing, the earnestness of his interest, suddenly made her story important, made it serve a larger purpose that even she was not sure of, and so she told him all she remembered about the train full of people who had cried and shouted and urinated on themselves.

She was still speaking when Odenigbo and Richard came back. They were walking; they had left in the Peugeot early in the morning to go and search for Kainene in the hospital in Ahiara.

Olanna sprang up. 'Did you?'

'No,' Richard said, and walked inside.

'Where is the car? Did the soldiers take it?'

'The fuel finished on the road. I will find fuel and go back and get it,' Odenigbo said. He hugged her. 'We saw Madu. He said he is certain she is still on the other side. The vandals must have blocked the way she had gone in and she is waiting for a new route to open. It happens all the time.'

'Yes, of course.' Olanna picked up the comb and began to untangle her own matted hair. Odenigbo was reminding her that she should be grateful that they had not found Kainene in hospital. It meant Kainene was well, only on the Nigerian side. And yet she did not want him to remind her. Days later, when she insisted on searching the mortuary, he told her the same thing, that Kainene had to be safely on the other side.

'I will go,' she said. Madu had sent them some *garri* and sugar and a little fuel. She would drive herself.

'There's no point,' Odenigbo said.

'No point? There is no point in looking for my sister's body?'

'Your sister is alive. There is no body.'

'Yes, God.'

She turned to leave.

'Even if they shot her, Olanna, they would not take her to a mortuary inside Biafra,' Odenigbo said, and she knew he was right but she hated him for saying it and for calling her Olanna instead of *nkem* and she went anyway, to the foul-smelling mortuary building, where bodies from a recent bombing were piled up outside, swelling in the sun. A crowd of people was begging to be let in to search.

'Please, my father is missing since the bombing.'

'Please, I cannot find my small girl.'

Olanna's note from Madu made the caretaker smile at her and let her in and she insisted on looking at the face of every female body, even those that the caretaker said were too old, and afterwards she stopped on the road to vomit. *If the sun refuses to rise, we will make it rise.* The title of Okeoma's poem came to her. She did not remember the rest of it, something about placing clay pot on top of clay pot to form a ladder to the sky. Back home, Odenigbo was talking to Baby. Richard sat staring at nothing. They did not ask her if she had found Kainene's body. Ugwu told her that there was a large, palm-oil-coloured stain on her dress, his voice low, as if he knew it to be the remnants of her own vomit. Harrison told her there was nothing to eat and she stared at him blankly because it was Kainene who had been in charge of things, who knew what to do.

'You should lie down, *nkem*,' Odenigbo said.

'Do you remember the words of Okeoma's poem about making the sun rise if it refused to rise?' she asked.

'"Clay pots fired in zeal, they will cool our feet as we climb,"' he said.

'Yes, yes.'

'It was my favourite line. I can't remember the rest.'

A woman from the refugee camp dashed into the yard, shouting, waving a green branch. Such a brilliant wet-looking green. Olanna wondered where she got it; the plants and trees around were scorched, blown bare by the dusty winds. The earth was sallow.

'It is over!' the woman shouted. 'It is over!'

Odenigbo quickly turned the radio on, as though he had been expecting the woman with this news. The male voice was unfamiliar.

> *Throughout history, injured people have had to resort to arms in their self-defence where peaceful negotiations fail. We are no exception. We took up arms because of the sense of insecurity generated in our people by the massacres. We have fought in defence of that cause.*

Olanna sat down; she liked the honesty, the firm vowels, and the quiet assuredness of the voice on the radio. Baby was asking Odenigbo why the woman from the camp was shouting like that. Richard got up and came closer to the radio. Odenigbo increased the volume. The woman from the refugee camp said, 'They said the vandals are coming with canes to flog the hell out of civilians. We are going into the bush,' and then turned and ran back to the camp.

I take this opportunity to congratulate officers and men of our armed forces for their gallantry and bravery, which have earned for them the admiration of the whole world. I thank the civil population for their steadfastness and courage in the face of overwhelming odds and starvation. I am convinced that the suffering of our people must be brought to an immediate end. I have, therefore, instructed an orderly disengagement of troops. I urge General Gowon, in the name of humanity, to order his troops to pause while an armistice is negotiated.

After the broadcast, Olanna felt dizzy with disbelief. She sat down.

'What now, mah?' Ugwu asked, expressionless.

She looked away, at the cashew trees covered in dust, at the sky that curved to the earth in a cloudless wall ahead.

'Now I can go and find my sister,' she said quietly.

A week passed. A Red Cross van arrived at the refugee camp and two women handed out cups of milk. Many families left the camp, to search for relatives or to hide in the bush from the Nigerian soldiers who were coming with whips. But the first time Olanna saw Nigerian soldiers, on the main road, they did not hold whips. They walked up and down and spoke loud Yoruba to one another and laughed and gestured to the village girls. 'Come marry me now, I go give you rice and beans.'

Olanna joined the crowd that watched them. Their pressed, smart-fitting uniforms, their polished black boots, their confident eyes filled her with that hollowness that came with having been robbed. They had blocked the road and turned cars back. No movement yet. No movement. Odenigbo wanted to go to Abba, to see where his mother lay, and each day he walked to the main road to find out whether the Nigerian soldiers were letting cars pass.

'We should pack,' he told Olanna. 'The roads will open in a day or two. We will leave early so we can stop in Abba and then get to Nsukka before dark.'

Olanna did not want to pack – there was little to pack anyway – and did not want to go anywhere. 'What if Kainene comes back?' she asked.

'*Nkem*, Kainene will find us easily.'

She watched him leave. It was easy enough for him to say that Kainene would find them. How did he know? How did he know she had not been wounded, for example, and unable to travel long distances? She would stagger back, thinking they would be here to care for her, and find an empty house.

A man walked into the compound. Olanna stared at him for a while before she recognized her cousin Odinchezo, and then she shouted and ran to him and hugged him and moved back to look at him. She had last seen him at her wedding, him and his brother, in their militia uniforms.

'What of Ekene?' she asked fearfully. 'Ekene *kwanu*?'

'He is in Umunnachi. I came immediately I heard where you were. I am on my way to Okija. They say that some of our mother's people are there.'

Olanna led the way inside and brought him a cup of water. 'How have you been, my brother?'

'We did not die,' he said.

Olanna sat down beside him and took his hand; there were bloated white calluses on his palms. 'How did you manage on the road with the Nigerian soldiers?'

'They did not give me trouble. I spoke Hausa to them. One of them brought out a picture of Ojukwu and asked me to piss on it and I did.' Odinchezo smiled, a tired, gentle smile and looked so much like Aunty Ifeka that tears filled Olanna's eyes.

'No, no, Olanna,' he said and held her. 'Kainene will come back. One woman from Umudioka went on *afia attack* and the vandals occupied that sector so she was cut off for four months. She came back to her family yesterday.'

Olanna shook her head but she did not tell him that it was not Kainene, not just Kainene, that she was crying about. She wiped her eyes. He held her for a moment longer and, before he got up, he pressed a five-pound note into her hand. 'Let me go,' he said. 'The road is long.'

Olanna stared at the money. The magical red crispness startled her. 'Odinchezo! This is too much!'

'Some of us in Biafra-Two had Nigerian money and we traded with them even though we were in the militia,' Odinchezo said, and shrugged. 'And you don't have Nigerian money, do you?'

She shook her head; she had never even seen the new Nigerian money.

'I hope it is not true what they are saying, that the government will take over all Biafran bank accounts.'

Olanna shrugged. She did not know. The news about everything was confusing and contradictory. They had first heard that all Biafran university staff was to report for military clearance at Enugu. Then they were to report at Lagos. Then only those involved in the Biafran military were to report.

Later, when she went to the market with Baby and Ugwu, she gaped at the rice and beans displayed in basins in the shape of mountains, the deliciously foul-smelling fish, the bloodied meat that drew flies. They seemed to have fallen from the sky, they seemed filled with a wonder that was almost perverse. She watched the women, Biafran women, haggling, giving out change in Nigerian pounds as if it was currency they had used all their lives. She bought a little rice and dried fish. She would not part with much of her money; she did not know what lay ahead.

Odenigbo came home to say the roads were open. 'We'll leave tomorrow.'

Olanna went into the bedroom and began to cry. Baby climbed onto the mattress beside her and hugged her.

'Mummy Ola, don't cry; *ebezi na*,' Baby said, and the warm smallness of Baby's arms around her made her sob louder. Baby stayed there, holding her, until she stopped crying and wiped her eyes.

Richard left that evening.

'I'm going to look for Kainene in the towns outside Ninth Mile,' he said.

'Wait until morning,' Olanna said.

Richard shook his head.

'Do you have fuel?' Odenigbo asked.

'Enough to get me to Ninth Mile if I roll down slopes.'

Olanna gave him some of her Nigerian money before he left with Harrison. And the next morning, with their things in the car, she wrote a hasty note and left it in the living room.

> Ejima m, *we are going to Abba and Nsukka. We will be back to check on the house in a week. O.*

She wanted to add *I've missed you* or *I hope you went well* but decided not to. Kainene would laugh and say something like, *I didn't go on holiday, for goodness' sake, I was cut off in enemy territory.*

She climbed into the car and stared at the cashew trees.

'Will Aunty Kainene come to Nsukka?' Baby asked.

Olanna turned and looked carefully at Baby's face, to search for clairvoyance, a sign that Baby knew Kainene was coming back. At first she thought she saw it, and then she was not sure she did.

'Yes, my baby,' she said. 'Aunty Kainene will come to Nsukka.'

'Is she still trading at *afia attack*?'

'Yes.'

Odenigbo started the car. He took off his glasses and wrapped them in a piece of cloth. Nigerian soldiers, they had heard, did not like people who looked like intellectuals.

'Can you see well enough to drive?' Olanna asked.

'Yes.' He glanced behind at Ugwu and Baby before easing the car out of the compound. They passed a few checkpoints manned by Nigerian soldiers, and Odenigbo muttered something under his breath each time they were waved past. At Abagana, they drove past the destroyed Nigerian fleet, a long, long column of burnt and blackened vehicles. Olanna stared. *We did this*. She reached out and held Odenigbo's hand.

'They won but we did this,' she said, and realized how odd it felt to say *they won*, to voice a defeat she did not believe. Hers was not a feeling of having been defeated; it was one of having been cheated. Odenigbo squeezed her hand. She sensed his nervousness in the tense set of his jaw as they approached Abba.

'I wonder if my house is still standing,' he said.

Bushes had sprung up everywhere; small huts were completely swallowed in browned grass. A shrub was growing at the gate of their compound and he parked near it, his chest rising and falling, his breathing loud. The house still stood. They waded through thick, drying grass to get to it and Olanna looked around, half-fearing she would see Mama's skeleton lying somewhere. But his cousin had buried her; near the guava tree there was a slight elevation of earth and a cross roughly made from two branches. Odenigbo knelt down there and pulled out a tuft of grass and held it in his hand.

They drove to Nsukka on roads pockmarked with bullets and bomb craters; Odenigbo swerved often. The buildings were blackened, roofs blown off, walls half-standing. Here and there were black carcasses of burnt cars. An eerie quiet reigned. Curved profiles of flying vultures filled the horizon. They came to a checkpoint. Some men were cutting the tall grass on the roadside, their cutlasses swinging up and down; others were carrying thick wood planks up to a house with walls that looked like Swiss cheese, riddled with bullet holes, some large, others small.

Odenigbo stopped beside the Nigerian officer. His belt buckle gleamed and he bent to peer into the car, a dark face with very white teeth.

'Why do you still have Biafran number plates? Are you supporters of the defeated rebels?' His voice was loud, contrived; it was as if he was acting and very aware of himself in the role of the bully. Behind him, one of his boys was shouting at the labouring men. A dead male body lay by the bush.

'We will change it when we get to Nsukka,' Odenigbo said.

'Nsukka?' The officer straightened up and laughed. 'Ah, Nsukka University. You are the ones who planned the rebellion with Ojukwu, you book people.'

Odenigbo said nothing, looking straight ahead. The officer yanked his door open with a sudden movement. '*Oya!* Come out and carry some wood for us. Let's see how you can help a united Nigeria.'

Odenigbo looked at him. 'What is this for?'

'You are asking me? I said you should come on come out!'

A soldier stood behind the officer and cocked his gun.

'This is a joke,' Odenigbo muttered. '*O na-egwu egwu.*'

'Come out!' the officer said.

Olanna opened her door. 'Come out, Odenigbo and Ugwu. Baby, sit in the car.'

When Odenigbo climbed out, the officer slapped his face, so violently, so unexpectedly, that Odenigbo fell against the car. Baby was crying.

'You are not grateful that we didn't kill all of you? Come on carry those wood planks quickly, two at a time!'

'Let my wife stay with our daughter, please,' Odenigbo said.

The sound of the second slap from the officer was not as loud as the first. Olanna did not look at Odenigbo; she carefully focused on one of the men carrying a pile of cement blocks, his thin, naked back coated in sweat. Then she walked to the pile of wood planks and picked two up. At first she staggered under the weight – she had not expected that they would be so heavy – then she steadied herself and began to walk up to the house. She was sweating when she came down. She noticed the hard eyes of a soldier following her, burning through her clothes. On her second trip up, he had come closer to stand by the pile.

Olanna looked at him and then called, 'Officer!'

The officer had just waved a car on. He turned. 'What is it?'

'You had better tell your boy here that it will be better for him not to even think about touching me,' Olanna said.

Ugwu was behind her, and she sensed his intake of breath, his panic at her boldness. But the officer was laughing; he looked both surprised and impressed. 'Nobody will touch you,' he said. 'My boys are well trained. We are not like those dirty rebels you people called an army.'

He stopped another car, a Peugeot 403. 'Come out right now!'

The smallish man came out and stood by his car. The officer reached out and pulled his glasses from his face and flung them into the bush. 'Ah, now you cannot see? But you could see enough to write propaganda for Ojukwu? Is that not what all of you civil servants did?'

The man squinted and rubbed his eyes.

'Lie down,' the officer said. The man lay down on the coal tar. The officer took a long cane and began to flog the man across his back and buttocks, *ta-wai*, *ta-wai*, *ta-wai*, and the man cried out something Olanna did not understand.

'Say *Thank you, sah!*' the officer said.

The man said, 'Thank you, sir!'

'Say it again!'

'Thank you, sir!'

The officer stopped and gestured to Odenigbo. '*Oya*, book people, go. Make sure you change those number plates.'

They hurried silently to the car. Olanna's palms ached. As they drove away, the officer was still flogging the man.

35

U **gwu stooped down** beside the wildly overgrown bush with the white flowers and stared at the pile of burnt books. They had been heaped together before being set on fire, so he dug through with his hands, to see if the flames had missed any underneath. He extricated two whole books and wiped the covers on his shirt. On the half-burnt ones, he still made out words and figures.

'Why did they have to burn them?' Olanna asked mildly. 'Just think of the effort.'

Master squatted beside him and began to search through the charred paper, muttering, 'My research papers are all here, *nekene nke*, this is the one on my rank tests for signal detection. . . .' After a while, he sat down on the bare earth, his legs stretched in front of him, and Ugwu wished he had not; there was something so undignified, so unmasterly about it. Olanna was holding Baby's hand and looking at the whistling pine and ixora and lilies, all shapeless and tangled. Odim Street itself was shapeless and tangled, with both sides knotted in thick bush. Even the Nigerian armoured car, left abandoned at the end of the street, had grass growing from its tyres.

Ugwu was first to go into the house. Olanna and Baby followed. Milky cobwebs hung in the living room. He looked up and saw a large black spider moving slowly in its web, as if uncaring of their presence and still secure that this was its home. The sofas and curtains and carpet and shelves were gone. The louvres, too, had been slipped off and the windows were gaping holes and the dry harmattan winds had blown in so much dust that the walls were now an even brown. Dust motes swam ghostlike in the empty room. In the kitchen, only the heavy wood mortar was left behind. In the corridor, Ugwu picked up a dust-coated bottle; when he raised it to his nose, it still smelt of coconuts. Olanna's perfume.

Baby began to cry when they got to the bathroom. The piles of faeces in the bathtub were dried, obscene, stonelike lumps. Pages had been ripped out of *Drum* magazine and used as toilet paper, crusty stains smearing the print. They lay strewn on the floor. Olanna hushed her and Ugwu thought of her playing with her yellow plastic duck in that tub. He turned the tap, and it squeaked but did not run. The grass in the backyard grazed his shoulders, too tall to walk across, so he found a stick to beat his way through. The beehive on the cashew tree was gone. The door to the Boys' Quarters hung half-open on crushed hinges and he pushed it back and remembered the shirt he had left hanging on a nail on the wall. He knew it would be gone, of course, and yet he looked at the wall for it. Anulika had admired that shirt. It thrilled and frightened him, the thought that he would see Anulika in a few hours, that he would finally go home. He would not allow himself to think of who was left and who was not. He picked up the things on the filthy floor, a rusting gun and a bloated, half-eaten copy of the *Socialist Review*. He threw them back down and, in the reverberating echo, something, perhaps a mouse, dashed across.

He wanted to clean. He wanted to scrub furiously. He feared, though, that it would change nothing. Perhaps the house was stained to its very foundation and that smell of something long dead and dried would always cling to the rooms and the rustle of rats would always come from the ceiling. Master found a broom and swept the study himself and left the pile of lizard droppings and dust just outside the door. Ugwu looked inside the study and saw him sitting on the only chair left, with a broken-off leg, so that he propped it against the wall for balance, hunched over half-burnt papers and files.

Ugwu poked at the faeces in the bathroom with a stick, muttering curses to the vandals and all their offspring, and he had cleared the tub when Olanna asked him to leave the cleaning until he came back from seeing his family.

Ugwu stood still as Chioke, his father's second wife, threw sand at him. 'Are you real, Ugwu?' she asked. 'Are you real?'

She bent and grabbed handfuls of sand, throwing in rapid movements, and the sand fell on his shoulder, arms, belly. Finally, she stopped and hugged him. He had not disappeared; he was not a ghost. Other people came out to hug him, to rub his body in disbelief as though the sand pouring had still not proved to them that he was not a ghost. Some of the women were crying. Ugwu examined the faces around him, all of them thinner, all with a deep exhaustion etched on their skin, even the children. But it was Anulika who looked most changed. Her face was covered in blackheads and pimples and she did not look him in the eyes as she said, in tears, 'You did not die, you did not die.' He was startled to discover that the sister he had remembered as beautiful was not at all. She was an ugly stranger who squinted with one eye.

'They told me my son had died,' his father said, gripping his shoulders.

'Where is Mama?' he asked.

Before his father spoke, Ugwu knew. He had known from the moment Chioke ran out. It should have been his mother; she would have sensed his presence and met him at the grove of *ube* trees.

'Your mother is no longer with us,' his father said.

Hot tears swarmed Ugwu's eyes. 'God will never forgive them.'

'Be careful what you say!' His father looked around fearfully, although he and Ugwu were alone. 'It was not the vandals. She died of the coughing. Let me show you where she is lying.'

The grave was unmarked. A vibrantly green cocoyam plant was growing on the spot.

'When?' Ugwu asked. 'When did she die?'

It felt surreal, asking *When did she die?* about his own mother. And it did not matter when she died. As his father spoke words that made no sense, Ugwu sank to his knees, placed his forehead on the ground, and wrapped his hands around his head, as if to shield himself from something that would fall from above, as if it were the only position he could adopt to absorb his mother's death. His father left him and walked back into the hut. Later, Ugwu sat with Anulika under the breadfruit tree.

'How did Mama die?'

'From coughing.'

She didn't answer any of his other questions in the way that he had expected, there were no energetic gestures, no sharp wit in her answers: yes, they had the wine-carrying just before the vandals occupied the village. Onyeka was well; he had gone to the farm. They did not have children yet. She looked away often, as if she felt uncomfortable sitting with him, and Ugwu wondered if he had imagined the easy bond they had shared. She looked relieved when Chioke called her, and she got up quickly and left.

Ugwu was watching the children running around the breadfruit tree, taunting and shouting, when Nnesinachi arrived with a baby on her hip and a sparkle in her eyes. She looked unchanged; unlike the others, she was not thinner than he remembered. Her breasts were a little larger, though, prodding the fabric of her blouse. She pressed herself against him in a hug. The baby yelped.

'I knew you did not die,' she said. 'I knew your *chi* was wide awake.'

Ugwu touched the baby's cheek. 'You married during the war?'

'I did not marrry.' She moved the baby to the other hip. 'I lived with a Hausa soldier.'

'A vandal?' It was almost inconceivable to him.

Nnesinachi nodded. 'They were living in our town and he was good to me, a very kind man. If I had been here at the time, what happened to Anulika would not have happened at all. But I had travelled to Enugu with him to buy some things.'

'What happened to Anulika?'

'You didn't know?'

'What?'

'They forced themselves on her. Five of them.' Nnesinachi sat down and placed the baby on her lap.

Ugwu stared at the distant sky. 'Where did it happen?'

'It has been more than a year.'

'I asked where?'

'Oh.' Nnesinachi's voice quavered. 'Near the stream.'

'Outside?'

'Yes.'

Ugwu bent down and picked up a stone.

'They said the first one that climbed on top of her, she bit him on the arm and drew blood. They nearly beat her to death. One of her eyes has refused to open well since.'

Later, Ugwu took a walk around the village, and when he got to the stream, he remembered the line of women going to fetch water in the mornings, and he sat down on a rock and sobbed.

Back in Nsukka, Ugwu did not tell Olanna about his sister's rape. She was often away. She was receiving message after message about where women who looked like Kainene had been seen, and so she went to Enugu, Onitsha, and Benin and came back humming under her breath. 'I will find my sister,' she would say when Ugwu asked her how it had gone.

'Yes, mah, you will,' Ugwu said, because he had to believe, for her sake, that she would.

He cleaned the house. He went to the market. He went to Freedom Square to see the mound of blackened books that the vandals had emptied out of the library and set on fire. He played with Baby. He sat outside on the steps that led to the backyard and wrote on scraps of paper. Chickens were squawking in the yard next door. He looked at the hedge and wondered about Chinyere, what she had thought of him, if she had survived. Dr Okeke and his family had not returned, and now a bow-legged man, a professor of chemistry who cooked on firewood and had a chicken coop, lived there. One day, in the failing light of dusk, Ugwu looked up and saw three soldiers barge into the compound and leave moments later, dragging the professor.

Ugwu had heard that the Nigerian soldiers had promised to kill five per cent of Nsukka academics, and nobody had heard of Professor Ezeka since he was arrested in Enugu, but it was suddenly real to him, seeing the professor next door dragged off. So, days later, when he heard the loud banging on the front door, he thought they had come for Master. He would tell them Master was not home; he would even tell them Master had died. He dashed first to the study, whispered, 'Hide under the table, sah!' and then ran to the front door and wore a dumb look on his face. Instead of the menacing green of army uniforms, the shine of boot and gun, he saw a brown kaftan and flat slippers and a familiar face that took him a moment to recognize: Miss Adebayo.

'Good evening,' Ugwu said. He felt something close to disappointment.

She was peering in, behind him, and on her face was a great and stark fear; it made her look stripped down to nothing, like a skull with gaping holes as eyes.

'Odenigbo?' she was whispering. 'Odenigbo?'

Ugwu understood right away that it was all she could say, that perhaps she had not even recognized him and could not get herself to ask the full question: *Is Odenigbo alive?*

'My master is well,' Ugwu said. 'He is inside.'

She was staring at him. 'Oh, Ugwu! Look how grown you are.' She came inside. 'Where is he? How is he?'

'I will call him, mah.'

Master was standing by his study door. 'What is going on, my good man?' he asked.

'It is Miss Adebayo, sah.'

'You asked me to hide under a table because of Miss Adebayo?'

'I thought it was the soldiers, sah.'

Miss Adebayo hugged Master and held on for too long. 'They told me that either you or Okeoma didn't make it back – '

'Okeoma didn't make it back.' Master repeated her expression as if he somehow disapproved of it.

Miss Adebayo sat down and began to sob. 'You know, we didn't really understand what was happening in Biafra. Life went on and women were wearing the latest lace in Lagos. It was not until I went to London for a conference and read a report about the starvation.' She paused. 'Once it ended, I joined the Mayflower volunteers and crossed the Niger with food. . . .'

Ugwu disliked her. He disliked her Nigerianness. Yet a part of him was prepared to forgive it if that would bring back those evenings of long ago, when she argued with Master in a living room that smelt of brandy and beer. Now, nobody visited, except for Mr Richard. There was a new familiarity to his presence. It was as if he was more like family, the way he would sit reading in the living room while Olanna went about her business and Master was in the study.

The banging on the door some evening later, when Mr Richard was visiting, annoyed Ugwu. He put his sheets of paper down in the kitchen. Couldn't Miss Adebayo understand that it was best to go back to Lagos and leave them alone? At the door, he moved a step back when he saw the two soldiers through the glass. They grabbed the handle and jerked at the locked door. Ugwu opened it. One of them was wearing a green beret and the other had a white mole on his chin like a fruit seed.

'Everybody in this house, come out and lie down flat!'

Master, Olanna, Ugwu, Baby, and Mr Richard all stretched out on the living room floor while the soldiers searched the house. Baby closed her eyes and lay perfectly still on her belly.

The one with the green beret had eyes that blazed red, and he shouted and shredded some papers on the table. It was he who pressed the sole of his boot on Mr Richard's backside and said, 'White man! *Oyinbo!* Don't shit hot shit here, oh!' It was he, too, who placed his gun to Master's head and said, 'Are you sure you are not hiding Biafran money here?'

The other one, with the mole on his chin, said, 'We are searching for any materials that will threaten the unity of Nigeria' and then went to the kitchen and came out with two plates heaped with Ugwu's *jollof* rice. After they ate, after they drank some water and belched loudly, they got into their station wagon and drove away. They had left the front door open. Olanna stood up first. She walked into the kitchen and poured the rest of the *jollof* rice into the dustbin. Master locked the door. Ugwu helped Baby up and took her inside. 'Bath time,' he said, although it was a little early.

'I can do it myself,' Baby said, and so he stood by and watched her bathe herself for the first time. She splashed some water on him, laughing, and he realized that she would not always need him.

Back in the kitchen, he found Mr Richard reading the sheets of paper he had left on the countertop.

'This is fantastic, Ugwu.' Mr Richard looked surprised. 'Olanna told you about the woman carrying her child's head on the train?'

'Yes, sah. It will be part of a big book. It will take me many more years to finish it and I will call it "Narrative of the Life of a Country".'

'Very ambitious,' Mr Richard said.

'I wish I had that Frederick Douglass book.'

'It must have been one of the books they burnt,' Mr Richard said and shook his head. 'Well, I'll look for it when I'm in Lagos next week. I'm going to see Kainene's parents. But I'll go first to Port Harcourt and Umuahia.'

'Umuahia, sah?'

'Yes.'

Mr Richard said nothing else; he never spoke about his search for Kainene.

'If you have time, sah, please find out about somebody for me.'

'Eberechi?'

A smile creased Ugwu's face before he hastily looked solemn again. 'Yes, sah.'

'Certainly.'

Ugwu gave him the family's name and address, and Mr Richard wrote it down, and afterwards they were both silent and Ugwu fumbled, awkwardly, for something to say. 'Are you still writing your book, sah?'

'No.'

'"The World Was Silent When We Died". It is a good title.'

'Yes, it is. It came from something Colonel Madu said once.' Richard paused. 'The war isn't my story to tell, really.'

Ugwu nodded. He had never thought that it was.

'Can I give you a letter, in case you see Eberechi, sah?'

'Of course.'

Ugwu took the sheets of paper from Mr Richard and, as he turned to make Baby's dinner, he sang under his breath.

36

Richard walked into the orchard and towards the spot where he had sat to watch the sea. His favourite orange tree was gone. Many of the trees had been cut, and the orchard now had stretches of cultivated grass. He stared at the point where Kainene had burnt his manuscript and remembered days ago in Nsukka, how he had felt nothing, absolutely nothing, watching Harrison dig and dig in the garden. 'Sorry, sah. Sorry, sah. I am burying the manscrit here, I know I am burying it here.'

Kainene's house was repainted a muted green; the bougainvillea that had wreathed it was cut down. Richard went around to the front door and rang the doorbell and imagined Kainene coming to the door and telling him she was fine, she had simply wanted to spend some time alone. The woman who came out had slender tribal marks on her face, two lines on each cheek. She opened the door a crack. 'Yes?'

'Good afternoon,' Richard said. 'My name is Richard Churchill. I'm Kainene Ozobia's fiancé.'

'Yes?'

'I used to live here. This is Kainene's house.'

The woman's face tightened. 'This was abandoned property. It is now my house.' She started to close the door.

'Please, wait,' Richard said. 'I'd like our photos, please. Can I have some of Kainene's photographs? The album on the shelf in the study?'

The woman whistled. 'I have a vicious dog, and if you don't go now I will turn it on you.'

'Please, just the photographs.'

The woman whistled again. From somewhere inside, Richard heard a dog growl. He slowly turned and left. As he drove, his windows down, the smell of the sea in his nose, he thought about the many times Kainene had driven him down the same lonely road. Inside the town, he slowed down as he passed a tall woman, but she was too light-skinned to be Kainene. He had delayed coming to Port Harcourt because he first wanted to find her so that they would visit the house together, look together at what they had lost. She would try to get it back, he was sure, she would write petitions and go to court and tell everyone that the federal government had stolen her house, in that fearless way of hers. The same way she had stopped the beating of the young soldier. It was his last full memory of her, and his mind edited it of its own accord – sometimes the sleep-tussled wrapper tied across her waist was flaked with gold, other times with red.

He would not have come to the house now if her mother had not asked him to.

'Go to the house, Richard, please just go and see.' Her voice was small on the phone. During his first conversations with her, when they first returned from London, she had sounded so different, so full of certitude.

'Kainene must have been wounded somewhere. We must get the word out. We have to do it quickly so we can move her to a better hospital. When she is well, I will ask her what we can do about that Yoruba sheep we thought was our friend. Imagine the man making us buy our own house. Imagine forging ownership papers and everything and saying we should be happy he was not asking for much; on top of that he took the furniture. Kainene's father is too afraid to say anything. He is grateful they let him keep a house that is his own. Kainene would never tolerate that.'

She was different now. It was as if the more time had passed, the more her faith had leaked away. Just go and see the house, she had said. Just go and see. She no longer spoke in specifics, in definites. Madu was staying with them in Lagos, now that he had been released from his long detention at Alagbon Close; now that he had been dismissed from the Nigerian Army; now that he had been given twenty pounds for all the money he had before and during the war. It was Madu who had received word that a thin, tall, educated woman had been found wandering in Onitsha. Richard went with Olanna to Onitsha and her mother met them there, but the woman was not Kainene. Richard had been so certain that it was Kainene – she had amnesia, she had forgotten herself, it all made sense – and when he looked into the stranger's eyes, he had felt for the first time a deep hate for a person he did not know.

He thought of it now as he drove to Umuahia, to the centre for displaced persons. The building was empty. Nearby, a bomb crater gaped unfilled. He drove around for a while before he found the address Ugwu had given him. The elderly woman he greeted looked completely indifferent, as though it was often that an Igbo-speaking white man came in to ask about her relative. It surprised Richard; he was used to his Igbo-speaking whiteness being noticed, being marvelled at. She brought him a seat. She told him she was the sister of Eberechi's father and, as soon as she told him what had happened to Eberechi, Richard decided that he would not tell Ugwu. He would never tell Ugwu. Eberechi's aunty had a white scarf tied around her head and a soiled wrapper around her chest and she spoke so quietly that Richard had to ask her to repeat herself. She looked at him for a moment before she told him, again, that Eberechi had been killed by shelling, that it had happened on the day that Umuahia fell, and that, only days later, Eberechi's brother in the army came back alive and well. Richard did not know why, but he sat down and told the woman about Kainene.

'My wife went on *afia attack* some days before the war ended, and we have not seen her since.'

The woman shrugged. 'One day you will know,' she said.

Richard thought about those words on his way to Lagos the next day and he became even more convinced that he would not tell Ugwu that Eberechi was dead. One day Ugwu would know. For now, he would not break Ugwu's dream.

It was raining when he arrived in Lagos. On the car radio, Gowon's speech was broadcast yet again: *No victor and no vanquished.* Newspaper vendors were running around in traffic with their papers wrapped in polythene bags. He no longer read newspapers because each one he opened seemed to have the advertisement that Kainene's parents had placed, with the photo of Kainene taken by the pool, under the heading MISSING. It was oppressive, as oppressive as Aunt Elizabeth telling him to 'be strong', her voice warbly over the phone, as if there were something she knew that he did not. He did not need to be strong for anything. And Kainene was not missing; she was just taking her time before she came home.

Her mother hugged him. 'Have you been eating, Richard?' she asked, in a fond, familiar way, the way a mother would speak to a son who had neglected to take care of himself. She held him tightly, leaning on him, when they walked into the sparse living room, and he had the glorious and uncomfortable feeling that she thought she was somehow holding on to Kainene by holding on to him.

Kainene's father was sitting with Madu and two other men from Umunnachi. Richard shook hands and joined them. They were drinking beer and talking about the indigenization decree, the civil servants being jobless. Their voices were low, as though being indoors was not secure enough. Richard got up and climbed the stairs to Kainene's old room, but nothing of hers was left. The walls were studded with nails; perhaps the Yoruba occupier had hung up many photos.

The stew that was served at lunch had too much crayfish; Kainene would not have liked it and she would have leaned towards him and said so. After lunch, Richard and Madu went out to sit on the veranda. The rain had stopped, and the leaves of the plants down below looked greener.

'The foreigners say that one million died,' Madu said. 'That can't be.'

Richard waited. He was not sure he wanted to have one of those conversations so many Biafrans had now, passing kernels of blame to others, oiling their own faces with a valour they had never had. He wanted to remember how he and Kainene had often stood here and looked down at the silver swimming pool.

'It can't be just one million.' Madu sipped his beer. 'Will you go back to England?'

The question annoyed him. 'No.'

'You'll stay in Nsukka?'

'Yes. I'm joining the new Institute for African Studies.'

'Are you writing anything?'

'No.'

Madu placed his glass of beer down; water droplets clustered on it like tiny see-through pebbles. 'I don't understand how we have found out nothing about Kainene, I don't understand it at all,' Madu said.

Richard did not like the sound of *we*, did not know who Madu included in it. He got up and walked across the balcony and looked down at the drained pool; the floor was made of polished, whitish stone, visible through the thin sheet of rainwater. He turned back to Madu. 'You love her, don't you?' he asked.

'Of course I love her.'

'Did you ever touch her?'

Madu's laugh was short and harsh.

'Did you ever touch her?' Richard asked again, and Madu was suddenly responsible for Kainene's disappearance. 'Did you ever touch her?'

Madu got up. Richard reached out and grasped his arm. Come back, he wanted to say, come back here and tell me if you ever laid your filthy black hand on her. Madu shrugged Richard's hand off. Richard hit him across the face and felt his hand begin to throb.

'You idiot,' Madu said, surprised, staggering slightly.

Richard saw Madu's arm raised, saw the swift, blurred movement of a coming punch. It landed on his nose, and the pain exploded all over his face and his body felt very light as it sank down to the floor. When he touched his nose, there was blood on his fingers.

'You idiot,' Madu said again.

Richard could not get up. He pulled out his handkerchief; his hands trembled and he got some of the blood on his shirt. Madu watched him for a moment and then bent down and held his face between wide palms and examined his nose closely. Richard could smell the crayfish on Madu's breath.

'I didn't break it,' Madu said, and straightened up.

Richard dabbed at his nose. Darkness descended on him, and when it lifted, he knew that he would never see Kainene again and that his life would always be like a candlelit room; he would see things only in shadow, only in half glimpses.

❊ 37 ❊

Olanna's moments of solid hope, when she was certain that Kainene would come back, were followed by stretches of raw pain, and then a surge of faith would make her hum under her breath, until the downward slide came and she would be crumpled on the floor, weeping and weeping. Miss Adebayo visited and said something about grief, something nice-sounding and facile: Grief was the celebration of love, those who could feel real grief were lucky to have loved. But it was not grief that Olanna felt, it was greater than grief. It was stranger than grief. She did not know where her sister was. She did not know. She raged at herself for not waking up early the day that Kainene left for *afia attack* and for not knowing what Kainene wore that morning and for not going with her and for trusting that Inatimi knew where he was leading her. She raged at the world when she boarded buses or climbed in beside Odenigbo or Richard to go to crowded hospitals and dusty buildings to search for Kainene and did not find her.

When she first saw her parents, her father called her '*Ola m*,' my gold, and she wished he wouldn't because she felt tarnished.

'I did not even see Kainene before she left. When I woke up, she was gone,' she said to them.

'*Anyi ga-achota ya*, we will find her,' her mother said.

'We will find her,' her father repeated.

'Yes, we will find her,' Olanna said too, and she felt as if they were all scratching desperate fingernails on a hard, scarred wall. They told one another stories of people who had been found, who had come back after months of being lost. They did not tell one another the other stories, of those still missing, of families burying empty caskets.

The two soldiers who had come and eaten her *jollof* rice filled her with rage. She lay on the living room floor and prayed that they would not find her Biafran pounds. After they left, she took the folded notes out from the envelope hidden in her shoe and went out and lit a match under the lemon tree. Odenigbo watched her. He disapproved, she knew, because he kept his flag folded inside the pocket of a pair of trousers.

'You're burning memory,' he told her.

'I am not.' She would not place her memory on things that strangers could barge in and take away. 'My memory is inside me.'

The weeks passed and the water started running again and the butterflies were back in the front yard and Baby's hair grew jet-black. Boxes of books came for Odenigbo from overseas. *For a war-robbed colleague*, the notes read, *from fellow admirers of David Blackwell in the brotherhood of mathematicians*. Odenigbo spent days poring over them. 'Look, I had the first edition of this one,' he said often.

Edna sent books and clothes and chocolate. Olanna looked at the enclosed pictures and Edna looked foreign, a woman who lived in Boston and had greasy-pressed hair. It seemed very long since Edna had lived next door to her flat on Elias Avenue, and it seemed even longer since this yard on Odim Street had formed the boundaries of her life. When she took long walks on campus, past the tennis courts and Freedom Square, she thought how quick leaving had been and how slow returning was.

Her bank account in Lagos was gone. It no longer existed. It was like being forcibly undressed; somebody had snatched at all her clothes and left her shivering naked in the cold. But she saw a good sign there. Since she had lost her savings, then she could not possibly lose her sister, too; the custodians of fate were not that wicked.

'Why is Aunty Kainene still at *afia attack*?' Baby asked often, with a steady, suspicious look.

'Stop asking me, this child!' Olanna said. But she saw a sign in Baby's questions too, although she could not yet decipher its meaning. Odenigbo told her that she had to stop seeing signs in everything. She was angry that he could disagree with her seeing signs of Kainene's return and then she was grateful that he did, because it meant he did not believe that anything had happened that would make his disagreeing inappropriate.

When some relatives came from Umunnachi and suggested that they consult a *dibia*, Olanna asked her Uncle Osita to go. She gave him a bottle of whisky and some money to buy a goat for the oracle. She drove to the River Niger to throw in a copy of Kainene's photo. She went to Kainene's house in Orlu and walked around it three times. And she waited for the week that the *dibia* had stipulated, but Kainene did not come home.

'Maybe I didn't do something right,' she told Odenigbo. They were in his study. The floor was littered with blackened paper crisps from the pages of his half-burnt books.

'The war has ended but hunger has not, *nkem*. That *dibia* was just hungry for goat meat. You can't believe in that.'

'I do believe in it. I believe in everything. I believe in anything that will bring my sister home.' She stood up and went to the window.

'We come back again,' she said.

'What?'

'Our people say that we all reincarnate, don't they?' she said. '*Uwa m, uwa ozo.* When I come back in my next life, Kainene will be my sister.'

She had started to cry softly. Odenigbo took her in his arms.

8. The Book: The World Was Silent When We Died

Ugwu writes his dedication last: *For Master, my good man.*

AUTHOR'S NOTE

This book is based on the Nigeria-Biafra War of 1967–70. While some of the characters are based on actual persons, their portrayals are fictitious as are the events surrounding them. I have listed below the books (most use the anglicized spelling *Ibo* for *Igbo*) that helped in my research. I owe much thanks to their authors. In particular, Chukwuemeka Ike's *Sunset at Dawn* and Flora Nwapa's *Never Again* were indispensable in creating the mood of middle-class Biafra; Christopher Okigbo's own life and *Labyrinths* inspired the character of Okeoma; while Alexander Madiebo's *The Nigerian Revolution and the Biafran War* was central to the character of Colonel Madu.

However, I could not have written this book without my parents. My wise and wonderful father, Professor Nwoye James Adichie, *Odelu Ora Abba*, ended his many stories with the words *agha ajoka*, which in my literal translation is 'war is very ugly.' He and my defending and devoted mother, Mrs Ifeoma Grace Adichie, have always wanted me to know, I think, that what matters is not what they went through but that they survived. I am grateful to them for their stories and for so much more.

I salute my Uncle Mai, Michael E. N. Adichie, who was wounded while fighting with the 21st Battalion of the Biafran Army, and who spoke to me of his experience with much grace and humour. I salute, also, the sparkling memories of my Uncle CY (Cyprian Odigwe, 1949–98), who fought with the Biafran Commandos, my cousin Pauly (Paulinus Ofili, 1955–2005), who shared his memories of life in Biafra as a thirteen-year-old, and my friend Okla (Okoloma Maduewesi, 1972–2005), who will now not clutch this under his arm as he did the last.

Thanks to my family: Toks Oremule and Arinze Maduka, Chisom and Amaka Sonny-Afoekelu, Chinedum and Kamsi Adichie, Ijeoma and Obinna Maduka, Uche and Sonny Afoekelu, Chukwunwike and Tinuke Adichie, Nneka Adichie Okeke, Okechukwu Adichie, and especially Kenechukwu Adichie; all the Odigwes of Umunnachi and the Adichies of Abba; my 'sisters' Urenna Egonu and Uju Egonu, and my 'baby bro', Oji Kanu, for believing I am better than I am.

Thanks to Ivara Esege; to Binyavanga Wainaina for his excellent complaints; to Amaechi Awurum for teaching me about faith; to Ike Anya, Muhtar Bakare, Maren Chumley, Laura Bramon Good, Martin Kenyon, and Ifeacho Nwokolo for being draft-reading friends; to Susan Buchan for those photographs taken in Biafra; to the Vermont Studio Center for the gift of space and time; and to Professor Michael J. C. Echeruo, whose erudite and generous comments made me search for the other half of the sun.

I am grateful to my inimitable agent Sarah Chalfant for making me feel safe; and to Mitzi Angel, and Anjali Singh, and Robin Desser, my brilliantly discerning editors.

May we always remember.

Chinua Achebe, *Girls at War and Other Stories*
Elechi Amadi, *Sunset in Biafra*
J. L. Brandler, *Out of Nigeria*
Robert Collis, *Nigeria in Conflict*
John De St. Jorre, *The Nigerian Civil War*
Herbert Ekwe-Ekwe, *The Biafran War: Nigeria and the Aftermath*
Cyprian Ekwensi, *Divided We Stand*
Buchi Emecheta, *Destination Biafra*
Ossie Enekwe, *Come Thunder*
Frederick Forsyth, *Biafra Story*
Herbert Gold, *Biafra Goodbye*
Chukwuemeka Ike, *Sunset at Dawn*
Eddie Iroh, *The Siren in the Night*
Dan Jacobs, *The Brutality of Nations*
Anthonia Kanu, *Broken Lives and Other Stories*
Alex Madiebo, *The Nigerian Revolution and the Biafran War*
Micheal Mok, *Biafra Journal*
Rex Niven, *The War of Nigerian Unity*
Hilary Njoku, *A Tragedy Without Heroes*
Arthur Agwuncha Nwankwo, *The Making of a Nation*
Flora Nwapa, *Never Again*
Flora Nwapa, *Wives at War*
Benard Odogwu, *No Place to Hide: Crises and Conflicts Inside Biafra*
Christopher Okigbo, *Labyrinths*
Ike Okonta and Oronta Douglas, *Where Vultures Feast*
Joseph Okpaku, *Nigeria: Dilemma of Nationhood*
Kalu Okpi, *Biafra Testament*
Wole Soyinka, *The Man Died*
John J. Stremlau, *The International Politics of the Nigerian Civil War*
Ralph Uwechue, *Reflections on the Nigerian Civil War*
Alfred Obiora Uzokwe, *Surviving in Biafra*

P.S.

Ideas,
interviews
& features...

About the author

About the book

Read on

The Stories of Africa: a Q & A with Chimamanda Ngozi Adichie

Q: What led you to write a book about the Nigeria–Biafra war?

I wrote this novel because I wanted to write about love and war, because I grew up in the shadow of Biafra, because I lost both grandfathers in the Nigeria–Biafra war, because I wanted to engage with my history in order to make sense of my present, because many of the issues that led to the war remain unresolved in Nigeria today, because my father has tears in his eyes when he speaks of losing his father, because my mother still cannot speak at length about losing her father in a refugee camp, because the brutal bequests of colonialism make me angry, because the thought of the egos and indifference of men leading to the unnecessary deaths of men and women and children enrages me, because I don't ever want to forget. I have always known that I would write a novel about Biafra. At 16, I wrote an awfully melodramatic play called *For Love of Biafra*. Years later, I wrote short stories, *That Harmattan Morning*, *Half of a Yellow Sun* and *Ghosts*, all dealing with the war. I felt that I had to approach the subject with little steps, paint on a smaller canvas first, before starting the novel.

Q: Given that at the time of the war you hadn't yet been born, what sort of research did you do to prepare for writing this book?

I read books. I looked at photos. I talked to people. In the four years that it took to finish the book, I would often ask older people I met, 'Where were you in 1967?' and then take it from there. It was from stories of that sort that I found out tiny details that are important for fiction. My parents' stories formed the backbone of my research. Still, I have a lot of research notes that I did not end up using because I did not want to be stifled by fact, did not want the political events to overwhelm the human story.

Q: Are memories of the Nigeria–Biafra war still alive in Nigeria, talked about on a regular basis, or do you feel that the conflict is being lost to history as time passes and that it has become less important to Igbo culture?
The war is still talked about, still a potent political issue. But I find that it is mostly talked about in uninformed and unimaginative ways. People repeat the same things they have been told without having a full grasp of the complex nature of the war, or they hold militant positions lacking in nuance. It also remains, to my surprise, very ethnically divisive: the (brave enough) Igbo talk about it and the non-Igbo think the Igbo should get over it. There is a new movement called MASSOB, the Movement for the Actualization of the Sovereign State of Biafra, which in the past few years has ▶

> 6 I would often ask older people I met, "Where were you in 1967?" and then take it from there. It was from stories of that sort that I found out tiny details that are important for fiction. 9

LIFE
at a Glance

BORN
15 September 1977 in
Nigeria. Adichie is from
Abba, in Anambra State,
but grew up in the
university town of
Nsukka where she briefly
studied medicine and
pharmacy.

EDUCATED
University Primary and
Secondary Schools,
Nsukka; Eastern
Connecticut State
University, Connecticut;
Johns Hopkins University,
Maryland; Yale University,
Connecticut

CAREER TO DATE
First novel *Purple Hibiscus*
published in 2003. It was
shortlisted for the Orange
Prize and the John
Llewellyn Rhys Prize, and
won the Commonwealth
Writers' Best First Book
Prize. Her short fiction
won the International
PEN/David Wong Award ▶

The Stories of Africa (*continued*)

◀ captured the imagination of many Igbo
people. MASSOB is controversial; it is
reported to engage in violence and its leaders
are routinely arrested and harassed by the
government. Still, despite its inchoate
objectives, MASSOB's grassroots support
continues to grow. I think this is because it
gives a voice to many issues that have been
officially swept aside by the country but which
continue to resonate for many Igbo people.

**Q: The book focuses on the experiences of
a small set of people who are experiencing
the conflict from very different points of
view. When we step into their individual
worlds, we don't know their every thought
– the narrator who follows them isn't
omniscient – but rather we seem to see and
understand them through a film. Can you
describe your narrative style and why you
framed these characters the way you did?**
I actually don't think of them as being seen
through a 'film'. I have always been suspicious
of the omniscient narrative. It has never
appealed to me, always seemed a little lazy
and a little too easy. In an introduction to
the brilliant Italian writer Giovanni Verga's
novel, it is said about his treatment of his
characters that he 'never lets them analyze
their impulses but simply lets them be driven
by them'. I wanted to write characters who
are driven by impulses that they may not
always be consciously aware of, which I think
is true for us human beings. Besides, I didn't
want to bore my reader – and myself – to
death, exploring the characters' every
thought.

Q: The character Richard is a British white expatriate who considers himself Biafran, drawing a certain amount of quiet – and some loud – criticism for his self-proclaimed identity. Another key narrator, Ugwu, is a 13-year-old houseboy who reacts rather than acts. Both are an interesting choice of character for the narrator to 'shadow'. Why did you pick them?

Ugwu was inspired in part by Mellitus, who was my parents' houseboy during the war; in part by Fide, who was our houseboy when I was growing up. And I have always been interested in the less obvious narrators. When my mum spoke about Mellitus, what a blessing he was, how much he helped her, how she did not know what she would have done without him, I remember being moved but also thinking that he could not possibly have been the saint my mother painted, that he must have been flawed and human. I think that Ugwu does come to act more and react less as we watch him come into his own. Richard was a more difficult choice. I very much wanted somebody to be the Biafran 'outsider' because I think that outsiders played a major role in the war but I wanted him, also, to be human and real – and needy!

Q: There is a conflict in this story between what is traditional and tribal versus that which is modern and bureaucratic. What is the mix today? How worrisome is it that some of the tribal ways have been lost?

Cultures evolve and things change, of course. What is worrisome is not that we have all ▶

LIFE *at a Glance*
(*continued*)

◀ in the same year. She has taught as a Creative Writing lecturer at Princeton University. Her third novel, *Americanah*, was published to critical acclaim in 2013.

LIVES
New Haven, Connecticut and Nsukka, Nigeria

FAMILY
Fantastic parents; two sisters; three brothers; three nephews; three nieces; two brothers-in-law; one sister-in-law

The Stories of Africa (*continued*)

◄ learned to think in English, but that our education devalues our culture, that we are not taught to write Igbo and that middle-class parents don't much care that their children do not speak their native languages or have a sense of their history.

Q: We see snippets of a book written by a character in *Half of a Yellow Sun* – it is an account of the conflict depicted in *Half of a Yellow Sun*, written after the fact. Its authorship may come as a surprise to some at the end of the story. What effect did you want this book within a book to have on *Half of a Yellow Sun*?

I wanted a device to anchor the reader who may not necessarily know the basics of Nigerian history. And I wanted to make a strongly-felt political point about who should be writing the stories of Africa.

Q: What is next for you in your career?

The next book. And I've just started graduate work in the African Studies program at Yale.

❝ I wanted to make a strongly-felt political point about who should be writing the stories of Africa. ❞

A Writing Life:

When do you write?
Whenever the story comes. I generally prefer night time because it is quieter.

Where do you write?
At my desk in my bedroom. At the dining table. In the bathroom.

Why do you write?
I write because I have to. I write because it is the only thing I truly care about doing. I write because it makes me happy when it's going well.

Pen or computer?
Computer.

Silence or music?
Silence.

Do you have any writing rituals or superstitions?
No. I do have a writing fear – that my computer and all my backup will be stolen and pages and pages of a completed manuscript would be left existing only in my head.

Which writer do you most admire?
Chinua Achebe.

Which book do you wish you had written?
One Hundred Years of Solitude.

What or who inspires you?
Everything. ▶

A Writing Life (continued)

◄ **If you weren't a writer what job would you do?**
A professor teaching whimsical, anecdote-filled, anti-establishment courses about which the university administration would have suspicions.

What's your guilty reading pleasure?
Essence magazine for the pages and pages of beautiful black women, the articles about makeup and clothes and hair...absolute bliss. ■

In the Shadow of Biafra

by Chimamanda Ngozi Adichie

I TAUGHT AN introductory creative writing class at Princeton last year and, in addition to the classic 'show don't tell', I often told my students that their fiction needed to have 'emotional truth'. I am not sure whether they knew exactly what 'emotional truth' meant. Sometimes I was not sure that I did either, or perhaps it was simply that I could never fully define it. I could, however, recognize it whenever I saw it: a quality different from honesty and more resilient than fact, a quality that existed not in the kind of fiction that explains but in the kind of fiction that shows. All the novels I love, the ones I remember, the ones I re-read, have this empathetic human quality. And because I write the kind of fiction I like to read, when I started *Half of a Yellow Sun*, set before and during the Nigeria–Biafra war of 1967–1970, I hoped that emotional truth would be its major recognizable trait.

I hoped, too, that it would be the kind of character-driven war novel brave enough to engage subtly with politics, as the Zimbabwean writer Shimmer Chinodya does in his remarkable *Harvest of Thorns*. What struck me most about *Harvest of Thorns* was that I emerged from it with a complex portrait of Zimbabwe's war of independence from – at last – the point of view of black Zimbabweans, without ever feeling as if I had been lectured. The wonderfully restrained sense of deep disappointment underlying Chinodya's narrative reminded me of how similar the histories of many ▶

9

In the Shadow of Biafra (*continued*)

◄ African countries are, how passionately people believed in ideas that would eventually disappoint them, in people that would betray them, in futures that would elude them. The Biafra stories in Chinua Achebe's *Girls at War and Other Stories* are also about what happens when the shiny things we once believed in begin to rust before our eyes. Achebe's trademark compassionate irony – he respects his characters but at the same time is amused by them and expects the reader to be also – is not very obvious in *Sugar Baby*, which is the best piece of fiction I have read about Biafra. It starts with the narrator watching his friend Cletus fling a handful of sugar out of the window. A symbolic act: Cletus is an unqualified sweet tooth (something he must have developed as a student living in Ladbroke Grove) and the unbearable sugar scarcity in Biafra led to humiliations, one involving the loss of his girlfriend, another the rage of an Irish priest. Now that the war is over, Cletus and his friends are eager to tell self-flagellating stories of hardship, they 'had become in those days like a bunch of old hypochondriac women vying to recount the most lurid details of their own special infirmities.' The narrator is reluctant to join in. For him, there is something still too painful, too sacred, about their recent history; he is not yet ready to laugh at the once-shiny rusted things.

Girls at War portrays a world inhabited by people who feel their metaphysical losses more strongly than their material ones. Their disillusion, their manic self-mockery, their

❝ The wonderfully restrained sense of deep disappointment reminded me of how similar the histories of many African countries are, how passionately people believed in ideas that would eventually disappoint them, in people that would betray them, in futures that would elude them. ❞

fixation on survival, are all corollaries of their deep faith in their cause. Achebe's war fiction then, humane and pragmatic as it is, becomes an oblique paean to the possibilities that Biafra held. The stories have an emotional power that accumulates in an unobtrusive way and stuns the reader at the end; there are sentences in them that will always move me to tears.

Successful fiction does not need to be validated by 'real life'; I cringe whenever a writer is asked how much of a novel is 'real'. Yet, I find myself thinking differently about these two war novels I admire. I have often wondered how much of the character Benjamin in *Harvest of Thorns* mirrors Shimmer Chinodya, how much of the muted defeat in *Girls at War* is in fact what Chinua Achebe himself felt about the loss of Biafra. Perhaps it is because to write realistic fiction about a war, especially one central to the history of one's country, is to be constantly aware of a responsibility to something larger than art. While writing *Half of a Yellow Sun*, I enjoyed playing with minor things: inventing a train station in a town that has none, placing towns closer to each other than they are, changing the chronology of conquered towns. Yet I did not play with the central events of that time. I could not let a character be changed by anything that had not actually happened. If fiction is indeed the soul of history, then I was equally committed to the fiction and the history, equally keen to be true to the spirit of the time as well as to my artistic vision of it.

The writing itself was a bruising ▶

6 Successful fiction does not need to be validated by "real life"; I cringe whenever a writer is asked how much of a novel is "real". 9

In the Shadow of Biafra (*continued*)

◄ experience. I struggled to maintain many fragile balances. I cried often, was frequently crippled with doubt and anxiety, often wondered whether to stop or to scale back. But there were also moments of extravagant joy when I recognized, in a character or moment or scene, that quality of emotional truth. ■

Images from Biafra

Photos given to the author in 2004 by Susan Buchan, who took them in Biafra in January 1970

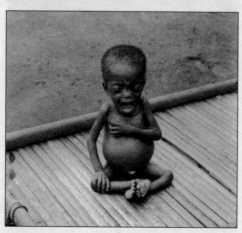

Images from Biafra (*continued*)

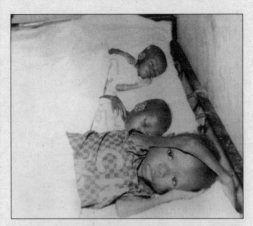

Have You Read?

Americanah

Americanah is a powerful new novel: a story of love and race centred around a young man and woman from Nigeria who face difficult choices and challenges in the countries they come to call home.

'Superb . . . a large, ambitious book . . . powerful, heartfelt and evocative'

Literary Review

....

Purple Hibiscus

Fifteen-year-old Kambili's world is circumscribed by the high walls of her family compound and the frangipani trees she can see from her bedroom window. Her wealthy Catholic father, although generous and well-respected in the community, is repressive and fanatically religious at home. Her life is lived under his shadow and regulated by schedules: prayer, sleep, study, and more prayer. She lives in fear of his violence and the words in her textbooks begin to turn to blood in front of her eyes.

When Nigeria begins to fall apart under a military coup, Kambili's father, involved in mysterious ways with the unfolding political crisis, sends Kambili and her brother away to their aunt's. The house is noisy and full of laughter. Here she discovers love and a life – dangerous and heathen – beyond the confines of her father's authority. The visit will lift the silence from her world and, in time, reveal a terrible, bruising secret at the heart of her family life.

'A sensitive and touching story of a child▶

Have You Read? *(continued)*

◄exposed too early to religious intolerance
and the uglier side of the Nigerian state'

J. M. COETZEE

The Thing Around Your Neck
The Thing Around Your Neck is a dazzling
collection of twelve short stories, in which
Chimamanda Ngozi Adichie turns her
penetrating eye on the ties that bind men
and women, parents and children, Nigeria
and the West. Searing and profound,
suffused with beauty, sorrow and longing,
this collection is a resounding confirmation
of her prodigious storytelling powers.

'She makes storytelling seem as easy as
birdsong'   JANE SHILLING, *Daily Telegraph*

The Web Detective

Some of Chimamanda's short stories are available on the web, and can be found on the links below:

You in America in *Zoetrope,* Winter 2001
http://www.zoetrope-stories.com/extra/issue38/adichie.html

Half a Yellow Sun in *Zoetrope,*
Summer 2003
http://www.all-story.com/issues.cgi?action=show_story&story_id=191

My Mother, the Crazy African in *In Posse Review*
http://www.webdelsol.com/InPosse/adichie_anthology.htm

The Grief of Strangers in *Granta* 88, 'Mothers', December 2004
http://www.granta.com/extracts/2217

Ghosts in *Zoetrope,* Winter 2004
http://www.all-story.com/issues.cgi?action=show_story&story_id=250

Tomorrow is Too Far in *Prospect,*
January 2006
http://www.prospect-magazine.co.uk/article_details.php?id=7208&AuthKey=037916efd3ab6cbaf4c7ed47aca230ad&issue=0

The Time Story in *Per Contra,* Spring 2006
http://www.percontra.net/2timestory.htm